HAZARDOUS LIES

A NOVEL

STEPHEN J. WALLACE

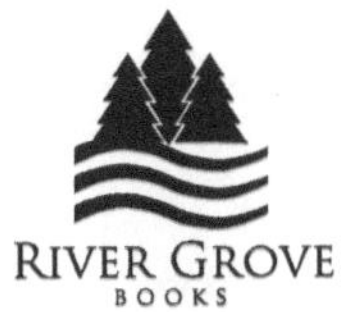

River Grove
BOOKS

Published by River Grove Books
Austin, TX
www.rivergrovebooks.com

Distributed by River Grove Books

Design and composition by Greenleaf Book Group
Cover design by Greenleaf Book Group

Publisher's Cataloging-in-Publication data is available.

Paperback ISBN: 978-1-63299-793-7

Hardcover ISBN: 978-1-63299-847-7

eBook ISBN: 978-1-63299-794-4

First Edition

PART I

HAZARDOUS START

1

Three inches to the left and it would have missed the man's heart. He might have lived.

Jon Barrett watched the pump split open as if it was happening in slow motion. He saw the shrapnel shoot out like a missile. He saw the man's eyes closing and his mouth opening into an O as the shard cut through his coveralls and into the center of his chest. He saw the blood splatter forward as the man fell back.

Jon had been lying with his eyes closed for hours, hoping sleep would come, but all that came was the flood of memories. He could still see the blood shooting out of the man's shirt from the accident in that chemical plant months ago. The shards of metal had not only taken that man's life but essentially destroyed Jon's as well.

Jon's new position meant that one day he would once again have to enter similar accident scenes. He had been hired by the United States Department of the Interior to do investigations and audits at chemical plants as part of a new office. Once again, he would have to see equipment slathered with blood and bits of flesh riding on water from fire hoses, slowly snaking their way toward the drains.

The events of that day were still fresh for him. He could see it clearly any time he closed his eyes. It was like someone had dipped a paintbrush in a slaughterhouse bucket and slung it around mindlessly.

Jon lay still on the gray air mattress, his eyes closed, while the images faded. He sensed it was still the middle of the night, and there was no reason to get up. Even in the daytime, this air mattress was the most exciting thing in his six-hundred-square-foot studio apartment in Springfield, Virginia.

Though this new position seemed to bring his nightmares back, at least it was a new beginning. His father had told him that. He also said he would visit Jon after he settled into his new job, and they would see the sights in Washington, DC, together. Jon just listened. Jon knew he never would come, but at least the thought would keep Dad hoping for something and not just waiting to die and join Jon's mom.

His father was right about one thing—Jon was lucky to be here, considering where he'd been just a few months ago after the accident. It was hard for a mechanical engineer in his mid-forties with few accomplishments and no network to find a job. Especially when the disgraced refinery he'd once worked for had successfully pinned its problems on him.

His eyes still closed, Jon reached under the blanket, where the sheets were tangled around his legs. Just as he'd nearly gotten them unwound, something vibrated on the makeshift table he'd crafted from his two softback suitcases.

Jon opened his eyes. A sliver of streetlight streamed in through a gap in the blinds, allowing him to make out some shapes in the still-unfamiliar room. There was another vibration from atop the suitcases, too far away to reach from where he lay. The only things there were his watch, a portable alarm clock, and the cell phone his new boss-to-be had given him a week before when he first got to DC. Probably just IT sending a message about network service, but he might as well check.

He slowly rolled off the air mattress onto the carpeted floor and crawled a few inches to the suitcases. The numbers on the clock read 3:32, and the face of the phone was lit up. Jon reached for the phone and clicked on the text icon. There was one message: URGENT—JON, CALL IMMEDIATELY.

He squinted at the screen. It was from Craig Higgins, his new boss.

Jon hesitated, still hunched over on his knees, holding the phone in one hand and supporting himself with the other. What could this be about? This would be his first official day. He didn't even have his Department of Interior badge.

The phone had gone dark again. He tapped the display to light it up and pushed the call-back icon with his knuckle. He moved the phone to his ear. The stream of light from outside faded.

Craig picked up on the first ring. "Jon?"

Jon jerked when he heard his name. "Uh, yes, Mr. Higgins, I—"

"I told you, call me Craig."

"Um . . . yes, Craig. I was going to wait to call, but—"

"Listen, Jon. There was an explosion at a chemical plant a little over an hour ago. I need you to go take a look and, you know, figure out what happened."

Jon looked at the clock again and scratched his temple. His boss's words started sinking in as the fog cleared in his mind—a little over an hour ago, just before 2:30 a.m., an explosion had happened, and he had to get up and go investigate it. The nightmares of the accident he had been involved in months ago were still there, but now a new nightmare was potentially awaiting him. He was the first—and so far only—employee. It would likely stay that way for some time,

Craig had said in his interview. Jon assumed, like everyone, that things move slowly in the federal government, and they could not start a big investigation with just one person, and a new one at that. It would give him time to ease into the job before stepping foot in any chemical plants again.

The earmark for the investigations office had come from Congress, after oil from a railcar spill ran into a ditch and ended up in some state park waterways. In the interview, Craig had said that he didn't foresee launching an investigation for months, so Jon didn't understand the rush now. He hadn't even officially started yet. But he would do as he was told.

"Craig, I'll be glad to go take a look," he said. "Where is it?"

Craig cleared his throat. "Charleston, West Virginia."

"Okay, I'll come in and get my credentials and find a flight. Who do I see to make travel plans?"

Craig was silent long enough that Jon wondered if he'd lost the connection. "Jon, you need to go now," he said finally. "I have a meeting this morning. Some people are trying to get money from other offices, and I want to let everyone know you've already deployed to an accident and we need to keep the funding."

So that was it. Jon needed to rush to "investigate" an accident, so his boss would have a reason to keep him—he hadn't even started yet, and his job was in jeopardy. So much for a secure government position.

"I'll forward the email from the National Response Center," Craig was saying. "It has the plant's address and phone number. They've called a shelter-in-place. Get going now. I want to tell them you're already in the plant. And"—Craig cleared his throat—"just take a look. Don't stir anything up. These plants give a lot of money to politicians here in DC. The last thing we want is some West Virginia congressman on the Appropriations Committee getting pissed at us."

"I understand," Jon said, trying not to sound sarcastic—he had to rush to an accident before he'd even officially started, but when he got there, he wasn't supposed to do anything. This must be the way Washington worked. But he had no choice. This job was all he had.

▲　▲　▲

On the south side of Charleston, the cat-shaped clock on the wall read 3:32. The Coleman family was in their kitchen, except for James. No light was on in the house, and the dim streetlight barely pushed through the window enough to illuminate three pictures on the wall: Black Jesus, Martin Luther King Jr., and Barack Obama. The picture of Obama had replaced a slightly larger one of John F. Kennedy, which had been there so long that the tan wallpaper was a different color where it once hung.

Kawana stood, rocking in her housecoat with a dress draped over one arm and holding a compact in the other hand. She looked at Emily, who was seated at the gray, worn Formica table. Darnell, her oldest, stood propped against the cabinet. It had only been a few minutes since Kawana had answered the phone, and her cry of "Oh God, no" had woken everyone. There was a fear in her children's big brown eyes that she'd seen only once before, when their old house burned down. That fire had taken everything they'd owned, but she knew this one would take more.

This time—her second oldest, James, had been burned, the woman at the chemical plant had told her in an almost mechanical voice. When Kawana asked if he was conscious, the woman only said that an ambulance transported him and some coworkers to a burn unit. She wasn't sure which one yet, but she would call back.

"What do you mean you'll call back? I want to see my son now," Kawana had demanded. "Where is he?"

"I'll have to call you back, ma'am," the woman said flatly, hanging up before Kawana could catch her breath.

"Kids, turn on the TV. See if there's any news about the fire. Get your phones. Do any of your friends live over there around the plant? If so, call 'em to see what's going on." None of the children moved. She sat down for a few seconds in a chair at the kitchen table and then flew up and pointed at the door. "Darnell, bring the car around—we need to go see James," she said, getting in his face.

"Mama, we don't know where he is," Darnell replied without looking up. "We have to wait till they call."

Kawana was proud of James. He'd had his rough spots, rougher than the other children. She'd had more fights with James than the rest of her kids combined. But lately, it seemed like he'd gotten his life on track. She'd thanked God that Darnell, her oldest, had stepped in to play the role of father.

James was never much for conversation, but she'd sensed his pride when he talked about his job at the plant. She could still see him on his first day of work, in his hard hat and blue coveralls with the name tag over his heart. He had even flashed a half-smile, which he never did, and pointed at his name tag. But she still rested uneasy with James, which is probably why she jumped to grab the phone mid-ring.

She backed away from Darnell's face. "Oh, dear Jesus, you gotta hear us, you gotta hear us right now." Kawana looked up, her arms bent at her sides, fists shaking, dress slipping to the floor with the compact falling next to it with a small shattering noise. The shock had been so sudden that her eyes had stayed dry, but now warm drops trickled down her face. "Please put your arms around him, Jesus, oh Jesus. Somebody call Aunt Chloe now. Wake her up—let's get a prayer chain going."

"Mama, maybe it wasn't James," said Emily, the baby, twelve. "Maybe they made a mistake," she offered as her eyes watered.

Kawana looked back at Darnell, barely seeing his outline through the blur of her tears. She remembered how he'd rocked James as a baby and how he had held him at his christening. She knew Darnell used to sneak out of the house at night to follow James, making sure he didn't get in trouble. James was as much a part of Darnell as Darnell's own bones. Now everyone except Darnell was wailing prayers. He was staring down at the anchor tattoo on his brown forearm, twisting his wrist back and forth. Through her own pain, Kawana's heart bled for Darnell. James was like the breath in Darnell's lungs, but now, in some cold room, James was breathing his last breath surrounded by strangers. The cruel lady on the phone didn't have to tell her that for her to know it.

2

As he pulled into the parking lot at Chemtrifuge Chemicals, all Sam Page could do was stare at the giant candle that shouldn't be there. He glanced at the clock on his dashboard: 2:47. This time of night, from the front parking lot, he'd normally see only faint constellations of light scattered throughout the back unit, like a small city in the distance. Instead, a massive fire lit up the rear of the plant, flares sending flames streaming hundreds of feet into the sky. The flames lit up the clouds from below, making an artificial dawn. It looked like a backyard full of propane tanks and out-of-control tiki torches.

Sam removed his glasses, sighed, and rubbed his face. As a plant manager, he'd dealt with fires and explosions before, but this one felt different. It would be a miracle if anybody within five hundred feet of the explosion had lived.

He looked around the parking lot. Employees in coveralls huddled in pods, the lights from their cigarettes like swarms of fireflies among blue trees. The torches from the flares had brought an early dawn light. Across the street, some neighbors had gathered, wearing nightgowns, T-shirts, and sweatpants. A few had crossed over to mingle in the employee huddles. Sam didn't like that. He needed to contain the flow of information. But first he had to find out what happened. Later, he would work in calls to alarmed customers and corporate. And, inevitably, the press would be here soon.

Sam stepped out of his car onto the wet pavement. The rain had almost stopped, though a few sprinkles dotted his glasses. There was an eerie silence, apart from the sound of the flames, like giant flags flapping in the wind. He was parked in his normal spot, directly in front of the administration building, where his office was. To its left, separated from it by a series of turnstiles that everyone had to pass through to go into the plant, was a small building that everyone simply called the guard shack. Sam turned left. He'd start there, with the security guards.

"Mr. Page!" Ruby greeted Sam nervously from behind the guard shack desk. "Big one, isn't it?"

"Doesn't look good," he muttered. "Any supervisors up here?"

"No, nobody here. There was another guard here earlier, but Mr. Collins came by and told him to go home."

Sam looked up. "Go home?" he barked. "When?"

"About ten minutes ago. When I stepped out to look at the fire, the guard was looking at the procedures. Then Mr. Collins came running in. When I came back inside the guard shack, the other guy was putting on his coat—said he'd been told to leave. I hope Marmont Security can find him another deal, but it don't look good to be sent home from a detail."

Sam grimaced. That idiot, Collins. The last thing that dipshit should have done was send the guy home. You collect witnesses, find out what they know, and then develop a company line. Collins knew that. He'd gone through the same media training as Sam.

Sam went out the side door of the guard shack and hovered his badge over the turnstile until it clicked. He passed through and headed toward the back door of the admin building.

Charlie, the short and scrawny HR manager, popped to attention almost spilling his coffee as Sam walked by his office. "One hell of a fireworks show, huh?"

Sam didn't bother to answer. "Get the supervisors on the radio," he barked. "Meeting in the conference room in five minutes."

Charlie's eyes shifted upward. "I think Turner and Plasco are leading the crew fighting the fire."

"I don't care. They can turn that over to the operators."

Charlie sniffed, a nervous habit he was prone to that drove Sam nuts. "But it might be good to—"

"Now!"

Sam bolted off to his office, slamming the door behind him. Once he was inside, he took a long, deep breath. He thought about calling corporate, but he didn't really know anything yet. He contemplated pulling out a glass and pouring himself a shot of bourbon. Drinking on company property was an offense he would have fired his men for, but rank had its privileges and one was hypocrisy.

Maybe later, he thought. After the press and the phone calls.

It was 3:02 a.m. when Sam bounded into the conference room. At the table with Charlie were six supervisors and two unit managers. Turner and Plasco sat across from each other, sweaty and reeking of smoke, their white hard hats on the table in front of them.

Sam looked from one somber face to another. "Alright. What happened, and what's the status now?"

They looked at each other. No one made eye contact with Sam.

"Come on!" Sam huffed, slapping his hand on the table.

Turner cleared his throat. "We had a process upset that led to a fire."

"No shit," Sam snapped. "I'm not the damned public. Talk to me. What the hell happened?"

Turner looked up, eyes peering over his safety glasses resting halfway down his nose like readers. "The fire's around the flash drum area. We had a high level in the E-101 vessel. You know how cold the liquid ethylene is there. We actually, uh, called Mr.—"

"We're not going there now," Sam cut Turner off. He knew what he was going to say. "We need another story for the media, one they'll accept and will make them go away. Thanks to what you idiots did, I assure you they'll be here soon."

"Bet they're on their way now," Charlie piped up.

Sam glared at him. "Thanks," he said, heavy on the sarcasm.

Johnson, the bald and rotund unit manager for the other side of the plant, exhaled through his nose, as if he was trying to hold back a laugh.

"It's not funny, dammit."

Johnson cleared his throat and wiped his head with his hand as if cleansing his shame. "Sorry."

Sam looked back at Turner. "What else can we say happened?"

Edwards, the other unit manager, rocked forward and rested his wrinkled cheek on his hand propped on the table—he always looked tired and this morning was no exception. "We could say a flange was loose around the vessel and released material. Could be due to bad maintenance. You know, some guys don't do leak tests like they're supposed to after working on the pipes. I've seen plugs left out, valves left open, gaskets not secured, shit like that."

Plasco shifted, his jowls rippling slightly under his bushy mustache. "Yeah. They forgot to put those seals back in that line back in March. We had that fire, damn near killed that guy when we started it back up."

"Maybe we could use that." Sam reflected. Chemtrifuge was having the same debate as other companies about the benefits of contractors versus full-time employees. The maintenance group was about half and half now, an arrangement that had been a source of conflict for years. The unionized employees saw contract workers as a threat. The contractors had incentives to work harder and take more hazardous jobs—if they refused, they were gone. If a contractor got hurt, Chemtrifuge was held harmless and the contract company covered medical expenses and lost wages. Recently, the company had started using contractors as plant operators as well. "Who did the maintenance on that line last time, our guys or the contractors?"

"I'm not sure who did it last time," Turner confessed.

Sam rocked back. This was a bad situation, but even a bad situation was better if he could blame someone else. "Okay, let's go with that. I'll say all indications point to shoddy maintenance by contractors. We need to round up the operators and 'suggest'"—Sam made air quotes—"that this is what happened. Otherwise, who knows what they'll come up with."

Heads nodded.

"Now," Sam continued, "what's the status of the fire?"

Plasco leaned in and propped his elbows on the table. "Mostly contained, but there's a lot of damage. We have water cannons positioned on the surrounding vessels and lines to keep them cool. We've closed the supply valves so we're not feeding the fire anymore. We're just letting it burn itself out. I figure there's enough residual fuel to go about another hour. A lot of stuff's going to the flare, so it may be less."

Sam leaned in, mirroring Plasco's position. "What about the material in the surrounding equipment? Should we drain it to avoid another explosion?"

Edwards slapped his portable radio on the table. "We looked at that, Sam. We think the water's keeping the vessels cool enough so the stuff inside won't heat up and explode. Eric—you know, the engineer—thinks it'll be okay. If we drain the surrounding tanks, it will take a lot longer to re-inventory and start the unit back up. Like Mr. Quinn always says, every second offline is a thousand bucks gone. I think it's fine."

"You think?" Sam snarled. "If everyone had been thinking right to begin with, we wouldn't be in this mess!"

Edwards dropped his head.

Sam leaned back and steepled his index fingers. "Okay. We know our cause." He moved his right index finger to his left middle finger. "Two, we know the fire status—or, we 'think' we know it." He moved to number three, his ring finger. "What about our head count?"

Charlie cleared his throat and started ruffling through the pages on his clipboard. "We've swept all the muster points. At this time, we've accounted for all but one man. We know three men were around the vessel." Charlie stopped and looked up. "We need to talk about one of those three before you call corporate."

Sam raised one eyebrow but said only, "And the guy that's still missing?"

Charlie sniffed. "It's the senator's son. We have no idea where he is. He didn't go to his group's muster point, and he doesn't show up on any of the head-count sheets."

"Did anybody look in the control rooms? Maybe he's hiding in the back of one of them," Johnson asked.

"We looked everywhere and didn't find him," said Turner.

"Look again. Okay, anything else?" Sam pushed his chair away from the table. He'd started to get up when he noticed Charlie raising his hand. "Okay, spit it out, Charlie."

"Do you want a status on the men who were hurt?"

"Oh, yes." Sam scooted his chair back to the table. "I'll be asked about that."

"Well, all three were contractors. They were all burned at the scene. I know one is, uh, gone. I think the other two were alive when the ambulance arrived, but they were badly burned and had been knocked several levels down."

Sam scratched his temple. "I didn't officially hear any of this. I'll just say they've been transported to the hospital, and we're closely monitoring the situation with great concern." He cleared his throat and looked at Collins. "You forgot one MIA."

The group looked at each other, puzzled. Sam had to resist rolling his eyes.

"The guard. Collins, what's this crap I hear about you sending him home? That was a stupid thing to do."

Collins exhaled. "Yeah, I thought about it after he left. I saw the light for the guard-shack line light up on the phone. I knew Ruby wouldn't be making a call—she'd know to call the ambulance and no one else. I didn't want talk over the radio, so I went to ask the guards who they had talked to. The new guy said he'd called the National Response Center, something about it being in the procedures or some bullshit like that, so I told him to get his ass out of here and never come back. I knew we had to keep this thing contained before going external—well, *if* we go external. I figured he'd do less damage away from here, especially if he's actually trying to follow procedures."

Sam softened. "I understand, but you shouldn't have sent him away. You've got to think—think and contain. That's key to controlling information."

"I know," Collins said contritely. "Won't happen again."

Just then the conference room phone rang. Sam jerked. "Who the hell? Turner, see who that is."

Turner glanced at the phone. "It's the guard gate." He hit the speaker-phone button. "Ruby?"

"Yes, sir, I got someone on the line for Mr. Page."

"Is the media here?" Sam asked.

"No, nobody here yet. Just the neighbors in the parking lot watching the fire."

Sam drummed his fingers on the table. "Well, I don't have time to talk to anybody now."

"I think you better take this one, Mr. Page. He said it was important."

"Where's it from?"

"Washington, DC."

3

nterstate 81 through central Virginia was a lonely road before sunrise. The farmlands, red barns, rolling hills, and small towns it rolled through were lost on Jon—though he wasn't sure, with this little sleep, that he'd be able to appreciate the scenery anyway. Jon yawned as he wound around its gentle curves, struggling to keep one eye open as his mouth widened each time. Craig's call for urgency meant driving was his only option.

After hopping from one staticky radio station to another, he finally gave up and settled on a best-of-the-eighties compilation CD. Tears for Fears's "Everybody Wants to Rule the World" came on just as he saw the first sign for Interstate 64 West. One line mentioned a lack of vision—he definitely identified with that. He'd come through a tough time, and he was still rethinking his decisions. Still feeling a little lost. He came from a family of farmers. His dad was the first to break the cycle when he went to college and became a teacher. He came back and taught at Kimball Middle School, but he'd warned Jon to steer clear of education because of all the local politics. He had been passed over for opportunities because of the 'who you know rather than what you know' syndrome that plagued local school boards.

When his cousin Dan chose engineering, Jon thought that might be the ticket. Jon entered as an agricultural engineer, but soon changed to mechanical, reckoning he could come back and design farm equipment if nothing else worked out. But now it seemed he was destined to fail. Jon, like his dad, never could play politics, and now he was in the federal government.

Tears for Fears gave way to James Ingram's "Just Once," and for a minute the doubt was replaced by memories of Tammy. Jon had first heard the song on a date with her. He thought of Tammy fondly. It didn't hurt anymore. Not much, anyway.

It had ended the day before Thanksgiving, almost eleven years before. They hadn't been able to go home to Nebraska for the holiday because Jon had to be at a project meeting on Friday. Wednesday morning, Tammy had said they needed to talk, and Jon had asked his boss if he could leave the refinery on time for a change, so that he could take his wife out.

They had finished their steaks without speaking. Finally, before dessert, Tammy told him she thought they should split up. Jon wasn't surprised or defensive. He'd calmly asked if there was anything he could do to change her mind. There wasn't.

They'd split what little they had accumulated, and stayed friendly afterward—not friends, but friendly. Occasionally, he saw her in town, when they were both there for holidays. She went back to school and became a nurse. She never remarried, but she adopted a child from China a couple of years after they split and settled in Lincoln, Nebraska.

Jon no longer felt sad when he thought about her, he realized now. Maybe because everything else felt even sadder.

The sun was rising now, but it wasn't helping him stay awake. He'd been on the road about three hours, and the yawns were coming more frequently. The lines on the lanes in the road were getting fuzzy. When he felt gravel crunch under his tires as he dipped briefly off the roadway, he knew it was time to pull over. Just beyond Lexington, Virginia, he pulled off at a service station. After filling up the car, he went inside and grabbed a French vanilla cappuccino out of the machine. Not much powder in the batch, he concluded, sipping the watery offering. Behind the counter was a skinny woman with tattoos covering both arms, wearing a brown polyester uniform. Her name tag read "Vicky."

"Kinda quiet out there," she said, taking his twenty-dollar bill.

"Yeah," Jon replied, sorting through his thoughts. "I listen to music to stay awake."

"We got NoDoz pills here if you need 'em," she offered, pointing under the register.

"I think I'll be okay," he said, holding out his hand for change. "How far to Charleston?"

"About three hours, maybe less, depending on how you drive."

Walking back to the car, he started thinking about his arrival at the plant. He had no badge or government ID. He couldn't just barge in—everyone from snoopy reporters to environmentalists was always trying to sneak into chemical plants. He'd have to tell Craig he couldn't get in, and Craig would have to share that at his morning meeting. A throbbing panic started to set in.

He'd keep going, he decided, and email Craig once he arrived. At least he could show effort.

The speakers blared when he turned the key, startling him. He must have cranked up the volume to drown out the road noise and the hopeless, chaotic doubts inside his head.

4

Sam Page leaned back, hands folded behind his head, staring at the trophy case in his office. It held the plant's awards: three years without a lost-time accident, exceeding production goals—and consequently profit targets—last year, and contributing more than any other business to the United Way for the past two years. There was a picture of Sam, too, from the groundbreaking on the new P-4 unit, standing beside Charleston's mayor. They were both wearing hard hats and together held a shovel with a little pile of dirt on it. Chemtrifuge's CEO had blathered on about all the jobs this safe, environmentally friendly unit would bring to the community.

Sam walked to the case and peered past the trophies at its mirrored back. His face was older and pudgier than when he started in this business. His hair was still mostly black, though there was less of it.

It was 6:05 a.m., and the first hints of daylight were breaking through the small window at the top of the wall. More than three hours since the meeting in the conference room, and the fire was still going strong. So much for Plasco's "about another hour." Dawn would bring more curious onlookers as people awoke and saw the flares. News of the explosion would spread through the community like liquid through pressurized pipes in the plant. It was newsworthy—this was a big one. And then some guys were "hurt"—okay, dead—but Sam hadn't heard that officially, so he didn't have to acknowledge it. Of course, they would demand details—the press was eager for a story. Things were quiet in Charleston, and human-interest stories only went so far. They'd be baying for fireworks, blood, guts, and a bad guy. And the kicker was the senator's missing son. Not just any senator, either. The son of A. C. Mounts, for God's sake.

With one exception, the others who'd died were just contractors. No one outside their families would be curious about them, and their families had no clout. The exception was an internal matter, and he'd deal with it later. But Mounts was different.

These thoughts made Sam uneasy, but even worse was the call from the guy in DC—Higgins—explaining that he was sending an investigator to the scene. Someone from OSHA or EPA, that was one thing. Those investigators came from the state offices, and Chemtrifuge had a good, almost chummy relationship with them. Even if those guys found something, he could negotiate. He could upgrade equipment he was going to upgrade anyway and write it off as environmental enhancements. Those investigators would rely on the company report, and the shoddy-maintenance theory would play well. He knew how to work that system. But this was a new office in Interior—an unknown. Sam didn't like unknowns.

Higgins had told Sam that the investigator would be in Charleston about midmorning, and had given him a link for information about this new office. Sam had instinctively pledged full cooperation. He'd cooperate in any way, he'd said; he was glad they were getting help from Washington. The managers in the room had rolled their eyes.

There was some potentially good news: Higgins said that his investigator just wanted to have a look. Maybe this was just a bureaucratic exercise. If he saw Sam as a good guy, doing all he could to figure out what happened, the investigator might just go away.

Still, Sam dreaded the call to corporate. He had no more news. The fire was still going strong and he didn't know when it would stop; the senator's son was still missing; the press would be on their way. He shut his office door. He'd have that glass of bourbon. But as soon as he'd pulled out the half-empty bottle and started pouring, the phone rang, causing him to jerk his arm.

"Damn," he barked, setting the bottle down next to the upended glass. A pool of liquor had spread over his desk, and now it dripped onto his pants. He picked up the phone, recognizing his home number.

"Hi, Sam. Is everything all right?" Glenda asked.

"Yeah, everything's fine," Sam said, looking around for something to mop up the bourbon.

"Are you going to be there all day?"

"Yes, the fire's still going, and we have one guy missing."

"Do you need me to bring you anything?"

Sam looked at the change of clothes on the back of the door. "No, I'm fine. Listen, I have to make a couple of calls. I'll call you back later."

Just as he hung up, there was a knock on the door. Before Sam could answer, it opened and Charlie came in.

"This place smells like a distillery. What happened?"

Sam ignored the comment. He popped the top on a box of Tic-Tacs and drained half the box into his mouth. "What is it?"

"Two things. I have a call in to the guys at CeMaC about this office at Interior, to see how much we can push back if they request anything. I'll let you know what they say."

Making that call was the one good idea Charlie'd had since the meeting in the conference room. CeMaC was the Chemical Manufacturer's

Council, a trade association dedicated to preserving the interest of chemical companies nationwide, with headquarters on M Street in the Dupont Circle area of Washington, DC. Sam wasn't sure what they did, besides put on a conference each year for dues-paying company members that was really more of a boondoggle. But for its annual dues of $500,000, Sam thought maybe someone there could get off their ass and research this new governmental office.

"Second thing," said Charlie, "I just got a call from someone with the news crew at WWCH."

After waiting a few seconds, Sam swallowed the mints. "And?" he said irritably.

"They heard about the explosion, and they're sending a crew over. I managed to hold them off some, telling them there wasn't much to see from the gate, but they said they'd be here in about an hour."

Sam scratched his neck. "I knew they'd come. At least we know. Forewarned is forearmed."

"I suspect others will follow. I'll delay them too, if I can."

"I better get back there and see the damage," Sam mumbled, reaching for his coveralls. He did in fact want to see what was happening, but it also wouldn't hurt if he had to be called from the fire at the back of the plant, sweating and reeking of smoke, when the press arrived. Fighting the fire shoulder-to-shoulder with his operators, that was the ticket.

Charlie had turned to leave when a blast of static on the radio channel announced someone keying the mic.

"Charlie, you there?"

"This is Charlie. Go ahead."

"Charlie, this is Edwards. Is Sam around?"

"He's right here."

"One of the emergency response guys found a hard hat on the ground, about a hundred feet from the structure. Singed pretty bad."

Charlie's face was grim. Sam knew what he was thinking. If that

hat was singed and blown away from the structure, then its owner would have been singed and blown apart too. They'd never find all the body parts.

Sam grabbed the mic attached to the radio by the curly cord. "Can you make out the name?"

Edwards kept the mic keyed as he spoke to someone in the background. "Let me see. . . . Oh, man, it's still hot. . . . Gimme a towel to hold it. . . . Uh, yeah, here it is, below this sticker. . . . Looks like, uh . . . Mounts."

Sam and Charlie looked at each other and then looked away.

5

Charlie was silent as they took the ten-minute golf cart ride to the back of the plant, where the fire was still blazing. Sam couldn't blame him—there was nothing to say. Senator Mounts's son's hat had been found blown a hundred feet away and charred. He was undoubtedly dead. The press was on the way, the sun was up, and some guy from DC was riding in to investigate.

Charlie pulled the golf cart up next to the back door of the control room, and Sam jumped out so fast his hard hat fell off. He picked it up and stormed toward the door, stopping short to look up at the fire. Water cannons on the ground were pushing a steady stream upward onto the steaming equipment. It was hard to see through the fog that had formed, but what he could see didn't look good. There were about twenty men on the ground, wearing bunker gear—long, heavy black coats with yellow reflecting stripes and Darth Vader–style helmets. The structure looked like a bookcase with no sides or back, a massive metal frame with eight platforms, each about twenty-five feet above the one below, holding horizontal and vertical tanks, most of them as big around as a person and three times as tall, though some were even bigger. Each platform was about two hundred feet long and a hundred feet wide, with a constellation of tanks, pipes, conduit lines, and various other equipment, in places packed tightly together. The equipment on the top levels looked mangled and black.

Sam put on his hard hat and pushed through the control room's outer and inner doors. Inside, Edwards and Turner, the manager and the supervisor, were sitting in front of the console next to some operators.

The control room was about fifty feet deep and seventy-five feet long, with a lot of open space. At the back, where Sam had entered, was a hallway leading to bathrooms and more offices. At the front of the room, to the left, was the supervisors' office, with two desks that supervisors shared and a large window facing the control room. Toward the front, a console ran about two-thirds the length of the room, holding a series of five monitors that looked like television screens. The operators could toggle back and forth to view different levels of the structure on each monitor. There were five chairs on wheels in front of the console, with plenty of chairs at the back of the room so others could crowd around the console during emergencies. In front of each monitor was about three feet of desktop space, where operators could put drawings and other documents, though it was usually littered with soda cans, Styrofoam cups, and hard hats. Some board operators put stuffed figures there, representing whichever field operator they were picking on that day. Sam noticed one of Beaker from *The Muppets*. The lead operator pushed it hastily out of the way when he saw Sam looking at it.

Sam glared at the monitors, which displayed schematic drawings of the different equipment and lines. "How's it look?" he asked no one in particular. On the monitor with the vessel that had exploded, he could see a computer-generated image—a cylinder representing the vessel, and lines of different colors for the material flowing in and out. The explosion had knocked out all the sensors, so the level and flow readings were all at zero, but the vessel on the screen looked beautiful—green, red, and white against a black background. If only the actual vessel looked that good.

Turner looked up from a stack of two-by-three-foot blueprints. "I was just looking at the P&ID, and I think I've found the fuel source we missed." He pointed to a small line on the lower left-hand side of the piping and instrumentation diagram, a detailed schematic drawing showing equipment, interlocks, and connected piping.

Sam peered at the diagram. "You sure?"

"Well, we've traced down every other line. Problem with this one is, there's no automatic valve to isolate it, just one manual valve. We'll have to send somebody up there to close it, and I'm not sure how close they can safely get. Janet's gone up to look from the platform below to see if it's open, and how close it is to the fire."

Sam nodded. If it was any other operator, he would have insisted on an extra set of eyes for something this critical. But Janet was sharp. Her promotion to lead field operator for the unit had been a big deal. The CEO flew in and bought lunch for the whole plant, and Chemtrifuge got a nice blurb in the local paper for promoting diversity. Image was important. Of course she was good, but they also wanted to celebrate her as a woman who'd made good in a man's plant. Sam was sure Janet knew why they'd done it—she was their token woman—but he doubted she cared. They'd been good to her, she'd been good for them, and she'd be happy to let it go on that way.

"She's on the second level, and thinks she sees the valve on the level above," said Turner. "She'll try to get close enough to see if the stem is sticking out or not."

Sam nodded again. If the stem was out, that meant the valve was open, and fuel was still flowing through it, feeding the fire. If they could close it, they'd cut off the fuel source, and the fire would burn itself out. Too bad there wasn't an automatic valve they could close from the control room, but manual valves had been much cheaper when the unit was built, and Chemtrifuge was always looking to keep capital costs low. Sam shook his head. Chemtrifuge could splash out on a celebratory lunch for Janet as long as it was good PR, but when it came to safety they pinched pennies with the force of lobster claws.

Turner's radio emitted a surge of static as someone keyed the mic.

"Tebo." It was Janet, using Turner's nickname. They could barely hear her through the roar of flames in the background.

"Yes?"

"I'm about twenty feet away. Can't see it great, but I think I can make out the stem position. It's—"

There was a tremendous *pop!* over the radio and a confusing roar.

"Janet!" Turner cried, but there was no reply. He dropped the mic and then looked around the control room. "God, that sounded like another explosion!"

Charlie looked at Sam, his face white.

▲　▲　▲

The day had started like any other for Lisa Rogers. She'd dragged herself out of bed at five a.m., started running water for the shower, and gone to flip on the coffee maker. It took a few minutes for warm water to travel up the old pipes in her two-level townhouse in downtown Charleston. Her cat, Katie, followed Lisa to the kitchen, rubbing against her leg while Lisa waited for the coffee to percolate. After a halfhearted attempt to brush Katie away, Lisa gave in and poured cream into her bowl.

After a shower, Lisa sat down at the dresser in her bedroom. Katie jumped onto the top, where Lisa put on her makeup. "Get down, Katie," Lisa said, as always. And as always, Katie stayed.

Lisa was pretty when she woke and progressed to stunning with a touch of makeup. Knowing how to present herself had helped lift her from her little hometown outside Huntington, just down the road from Charleston. Now her image graced every television set in West Virginia, southeast Ohio, and eastern Kentucky. Her silky black hair, piercing dark brown eyes, and olive skin went well with coffee, newspapers, and eggs.

She'd just started applying eyeliner when her phone vibrated. "Shit," she mumbled as a streak appeared that she'd need to correct. This interruption might determine where she spent the next three hours. Would she need to look smart at a new museum exhibit, or happily try a pie at a bakery? Those had been the potential options they'd discussed yesterday. She sighed.

She could do this scene a bit longer. Then she'd make the break to Atlanta and CNN, or maybe New York and one of the national networks.

She grabbed the phone and read the text. It was from Kenny, her combination cameraman and field producer.

Change of plans. Explosion at Chemtrifuge chem plant. Still burning. Pick you up in the van @5:45. Be ready!

She had ten minutes. They needed to get to the plant, set up, and arrange interviews. She quickly fixed her eyeliner and then ran to the closet and threw two outfits on the bed. She pondered these as she hopped on one foot and then the next, putting on her black pantyhose. Rethinking it, she grabbed a third, gray suit out of the closet. She stuffed her lipstick in her purse and dashed into the other bedroom, now her home office. Typing "Chemtrifuge Chemicals" into the browser, she scanned the home page and jotted down notes: where the company had facilities, what they did, how many employees they had. The link for safety brought up a general policy statement, a campaign called "Go to Zero" with a goal of no accidents. She knew it was fluff, but at least the company talked the talk. She had her opening statement. She clicked on the Charleston plant tab and wrote down two names and titles: Charles Branch, HR director. Samuel Page, plant manager.

She heard Kenny's van pull up just as she got to the *e* in "Page." Katie was making her way into the office. "Not now. Double cream at lunch—promise."

Kenny looked wide awake, as always. Shabby as always, too, but that didn't matter—he never had to be on camera, and he was good behind it.

"Sorry to do this, bright eyes, but we may be the lead at the seven twenty-five cutaway to local news."

"Okay," Lisa said, shutting the car door once she was inside. "Do you know anything about it?"

"No. Just that it's still burning. It's been going on a few hours. I bet that made a hell of a boom. That might be one of those plants that had problems with its neighbors—you remember, three or four years ago, that story about the environmentalists?"

"Uh-huh," said Lisa, fumbling with her phone. "When will we be there?"

"A little before seven. I can set up in about fifteen minutes. Should be some good spots—hopefully we can see the fire from the parking lot."

"Can't we go in and get a closer look?" Lisa asked, still fumbling.

Kenny braked for a red light. "We never go in a plant. I wouldn't if they paid me. Those places scare the shit out of me."

"I guess." Lisa shrugged. She didn't really care if they did or didn't, as long as Kenny found an angle that made her look good. "Anybody hurt?"

"Don't know." Kenny took out a cigarette and pushed in the lighter.

"What exploded?"

"Don't know."

Lisa finally looked up from her phone. "Any foul play?"

"I doubt it. Those guys just turn a wrong valve every few years, and something goes boom. Releases some kind of methyl-ethyl death, and everybody's excited for a couple of hours till the next story comes along."

"You're not much help."

Kenny smirked. "Guess not."

6

Neither jazz nor the rising sun had lifted Jon's spirits. He was headed for a chemical plant with no credentials or equipment. On a road to nowhere. This investigation already felt like his life.

A couple of hours outside Charleston, he pressed the radio scan button, wondering if he'd find any news about the explosion. On one station, the main host and his sidekick were bantering about a pill they should make to keep the host's dog from peeing on the carpet. Jon hit scan. Another station was giving a weather update. Apparently there had been a thunderstorm in Charleston earlier that morning, but it had passed quickly, heading east. He noticed small drops of water forming randomly on the windshield and twisted the knob for the wipers. On the next station, the host was wondering why people avoided parking in handicapped spaces but used handicapped stalls in the bathroom. More disabled people go to the bathroom, he opined, than drive. Jon hit scan again, settling finally on a station where the man and woman sounded more somber. They were doing an opinion piece about a labor contract with the United Mine Workers of America. In this part of the country, the mines were a lifeline. Mine owners were looking to immigrants to fill positions, the woman said, since fewer people wanted to do manual labor, which set up a tension within the labor union over immigrant rights.

Jon sipped his cold cappuccino as the man reflected that the negotiations had pitted two core constituencies of the Democratic Party against each other: organized labor and immigrants. Harsh words had been exchanged at local meetings, and Democratic leaders had failed to lower the volume.

The fog was lifting over the mountains. This was a lot like the area where he grew up, Jon thought. Replace mountains with flat land, coal mines with farms, and coal buggies with tractors, and you'd have southwest Nebraska. Values were strong, and independence stronger. Ahead, a faint ray of light was pushing through a mountain gap. He pushed scan again and found news, but nothing about the accident. Either it was no big deal or the media didn't know yet, or care.

7

"This looks like a good spot to set up," Kenny said as they pulled into the Chemtrifuge parking lot. The dashboard clock read seven exactly. They had time. He jumped out and started hauling klieg lights out of the back of the van. The fire was still going—if he got Lisa positioned just right, he could catch a nice angle of it over her left shoulder. He could put her in front of a pigpen and she'd look great, but he made her look even better. He shifted a little to catch the top of the "Welcome to Chemtrifuge" sign.

Lisa glanced back toward the fire, pulling a granola bar out of her pocket. "That's a big one."

"I've seen bigger," said Kenny, pulling his tripod's legs out.

"What is that, gasoline?"

"Don't know. Something from oil, I suppose."

Kenny knew a lot. His looks—gray hair collected in a ponytail, untrimmed goatee, and lined, leathery face—were deceptive. He had a thick Michigan accent, held unorthodox views on most everything, and had no formal education but retained a lot. It brought him some small pleasure knowing that Lisa relied on him to get her up to speed and answer questions her quick Internet searches could not. Despite their banter, he knew that deep down Lisa liked him, because she mostly ignored his smart-ass comments.

"Should I go see if we can talk to someone?" she asked.

"Let's get you set up first. I want to get a couple of shots here."

Lisa didn't argue, but she seemed antsy, tapping her shoe and looking at her watch. Kenny had her move a few inches one way and then the other. He put the points of his thumbs together and held his index fingers up, taking one final look through his goalpost. "Okay, hot stuff. Go find your prey." He pulled a pack of cigarettes out of his shirt pocket.

Another van was pulling up about thirty feet away, with four large black letters on the side. The competition. Rachael Jones stepped out, flashing Lisa a smile and quick wave.

Lisa smiled back and then turned to Kenny, holding her notepad up to block her face. "You're kidding—they sent her?"

Kenny lit his cigarette. "Sounds like a cat fight."

"You know I hate that expression," Lisa snapped. "Anyway, she always tries to find out what everybody else knows and report it. She never works herself."

"If she can take the easy way and get paid the same, more power to her." Kenny kept a straight face. He enjoyed pushing Lisa's buttons.

"Maybe you'd rather work for someone like that, all fluff?"

He smiled. "Different face, same pay."

"She goes through cameramen like you go through Marlboros." Lisa looked from the guard shack to the twelve-foot-high fence looped with razor wire at the top. "This place looks like a prison. I'm going to check in with the guard standing over there and try to find someone to talk to, or get a prepared statement from."

Behind Lisa, Kenny could see Rachael rummaging through her bag, occasionally glancing over in their direction. Finally, she seemed to make up her mind and headed toward Lisa and Kenny's van. Pretending not to see her, Lisa started toward the brick-and-stucco building in front of the plant.

"Hey," Rachael called out in Lisa's direction.

Kenny snickered as Lisa kept walking, momentarily deaf.

8

"Mr. Turner, you there?" the radio squawked. Sam jerked his head, anxious to hear Ruby's latest update.

Without looking away from the fire, Turner reached for the mic at the end of the curly cord draped around his shoulder. "Yeah, Ruby, go ahead."

"There are some reporters setting up in the parking lot. One's already been in here, wanting to speak with someone. She asked for Mr. Branch or Mr. Page."

Turner looked at Sam with raised brows. Sam held up an index finger and shook his head.

"Tell her to wait," said Turner. "We'll get back to her."

Sam turned to Charlie. "Guess it's showtime. Go stall them. I'll take the other cart back. Keep them calm till I get there, but watch what you say."

"Gotcha." Charlie nodded.

Sam stared back at the structure that looked like a giant bookcase with vessels and pipes crowned by a massive fire. "Any sign of her?"

Johnson exhaled strongly. "Not yet. A couple guys are going up to take a look. I told them to be careful. We don't want to lose another one."

Sam glared at him. He didn't like the implication that Janet was another casualty. "We don't know anything officially," he said loudly over the sound of the reinvigorated flames. "Let's shift to channel six. I don't want anyone overhearing us on Ruby's radio."

Edwards keyed his mic. "All down to six, now. Ruby, stay on one."

"Copy," said a ragged chorus of voices. Ruby's was the last.

▲ ▲ ▲

Sam was writing bullet points on a notepad in his office when Charlie came in.

"They're ready," Charlie said.

"How's it look?"

"Okay. There are three groups right now. I told them we'd do a press conference, so they can all hear the update at the same time."

"Sounds good."

"I also moved the staging area to the other side of the guard shack."

"Good idea." If there had to be a news conference, Sam thought, the far side of the guard shack was the best place. It didn't have a view of the fire, but it did have a view of the red, white, and blue "Safety First" banner spread across one of the warehouses just inside the gate. One negative image out, one positive image in.

"By the way," Charlie said, "got a message from the guy at CeMaC. Said he had news about that Washington, DC, thing. I'll call him after we finish outside."

"Okay." Sam ripped the top sheet from his notepad. "Let's go. If we wait too long, they might get antsy and go talk to neighbors."

From the door of the admin office, Sam could see three crews set up, as well as a woman with a notepad who he assumed was from local print media. He recognized two reporters, young things from the morning shows.

Charlie had brought out the podium that usually sat in the conference room corner. Sam walked to it and put his paper on top. He'd kept his smoky coveralls on, going for the arm-in-arm fighting-the-fire look. He glanced over at the three cameramen, who were adjusting the cameras on their tripods as he stepped into place. Once the last had gotten his angle and looked up at him, he cleared his throat.

"I just returned from the back of the plant, where I was fighting the fire with our brave men and women. I wanted to give a brief statement and then get back to my post. We may only have time for one question at the end. I'm sorry I can't give you more time, but I'm needed back there. I'll try to work in updates as things change."

He nodded and made eye contact with each reporter. "As most of you know, our company is committed to running the safest, most environmentally friendly chemical plant in the country. We've also worked with civic leaders over the years to improve the community, with projects such as our recent purchase of the swing set along the downtown Riverwalk."

He glanced over at Charlie, who nodded approvingly.

"Early this morning, we had an incident that resulted in a deflagration and subsequent fire. We're fairly certain we've located the source of the fuel and are isolating it now. The burning material is ethylene, but the fire should be out soon. We hope to be back up and running at full capacity to supply our customers and the public with important plastic materials that enrich their lives." He paused to allow note takers to catch up. "Our utmost concern is the welfare of our workers, customers, and of course, the public. We have an impeccable safety record." His eyes drifted toward the banner behind him. "This is an unfortunate incident, but it will not deter us from our mission." He looked at Charlie. "Now, we may have time for one question, right?" He intended to take more, but this way the media would think that he was doing them a favor.

Charlie held up one finger, exactly the way they'd rehearsed in media training. "Just one."

The stunning reporter with the black hair and olive skin jumped in first. "Do you know what caused the fire?"

Sam was ready. He would inject their theory of cause. Once repeated, it would become established and more difficult to refute. "It's still preliminary, but early indications point to a maintenance error that allowed a flange to come loose and release material. Much of our maintenance is provided by contractors. We trust everyone we work with to uphold our quality standards, and it's troubling to think anyone coming into our plant might not adhere to the same standards we do." He put his right hand over his heart, another media-training trick.

Charlie smiled.

"One more," Sam said confidently.

"Was anybody hurt in the fire?" asked the slender, short-haired print reporter.

Here, Sam fell back on uncertainty. "There were three men around the area at the time. They suffered some burns. We are making sure they get the treatment they need." He read the reporters' faces and nods with satisfaction.

"Mr. Page, anything else you want to tell us?" a woman he recognized from the local news as Rachael Jones blurted out.

"No, I think that covers what we know now. We'll keep you posted if anything changes."

Sam picked up his paper, waved, and started walking toward the admin building, hoping they'd get the hint and leave. He glanced over his shoulder briefly to see the three TV reporters stepping in front of their respective cameras to read from the notes they'd jotted down. He couldn't help but smile. They'd parrot words they didn't really understand, like *deflagration*, which Sam had intentionally used to avoid the word *explosion*. He was sure their papers looked like his, underlines and all: "There was a <u>deflagration</u> caused by <u>poor maintenance</u> by <u>contractors</u>. Three workers had received <u>some burns</u> but were being <u>treated</u>." He'd written their sound bites for them.

9

Sam was watching the TV in his office to see how they reported on the press conference when Charlie stepped in. He muted the sound as Charlie sat down but kept his eyes fixed on the screen.

"CeMaC got back to me," Charlie said. "The Washington thing is legit. It's a new office created by an earmark in a piece of legislation Congress passed a few months ago. That part got stuck in by a senator from a western state. No one from CeMaC knew or had a chance to review it."

"Why did we need it? Don't we already have OSHA, EPA, and that other little agency, forget what it's called?"

"I asked that. OSHA and EPA are apparently out of favor with Congress, and the other agency has so many management problems it may not survive. The senator had a bug up his ass about chemical safety, and apparently others agreed."

"Idiots!" Sam grumbled.

"Anyway, the good news is the bad news."

Sam's eyes drifted from the TV toward Charlie. "And that is?"

"There are no precedents, no challenges, no rulings. This new office has broad authority in theory, but nothing's been adjudicated in court."

Sam rocked back. "So they can kick us as far as they want, and we have to get our lawyers in a cage with their lawyers to fight to try and stop them."

Charlie sniffed. "If they really want to, yes. There's some potentially good news, though." He adjusted himself in the seat. "Apparently, they didn't get any superstar from the industry for this investigator position. I looked up Craig Higgins, the guy who called us. He's the office director. CeMaC knows all the chemical safety gurus, and none of them are moving to Washington." Charlie chuckled. "They must have found some low-level no-name to come in and play investigator."

"Glad our tax dollars find the finest," Sam snapped and then held up his hand. "Hold it—I like this part." He unmuted the sound. On the screen, Rachael Jones was saying, "Chemtrifuge is, quote, 'troubled,' the plant manager said, that their contractors have not adhered to the same standards that they do."

"That was brilliant," Charlie agreed, but then stopped smiling. A serious look took over his scrawny face. "Sam, there's something else."

Sam rocked back in his chair. "Okay. Is it about Janet, the Mounts kid, or the other, uh, internal matter with the victims?" He winced at this last comment.

"It's about the Mounts kid—no more news on the others. We've swept all control rooms, muster points, and smoke shacks. That hard hat's the only thing left of him."

Sam picked up the bourbon glass and let an ice cube slide into his mouth.

Charlie voiced what Sam was thinking. "It's better if he hears it from us."

Sam nodded.

"I'll call Senator Mounts," Charlie said. "Want me to call the corporate front office too?"

"No, I'll call corporate," Sam said mournfully, crunching on ice.

"What should I tell Mounts?"

Sam leaned back, crossed his arms, and looked up at the ceiling. "Leave it uncertain," he said, "but let him know there's a chance the kid was hurt badly."

"Should I tell him about the hat?"

Sam steepled his hands. "Play it by ear. If he wants to know more, tell him."

Charlie had gotten up to leave when Sam spoke again. "One more thing. Maybe you should touch base with the corporate legal department. They won't be much help, but they can alert that goon from the firm in DC that we have on retainer. I hate to bring him in, but if it gets worse, he can scare hungry dogs off a bone."

10

Craig Higgins rubbed his eyes and pushed away the spreadsheets. He'd never liked budgeting, but for a federal manager, it was a necessary evil. Craig needed an exceptional performance rating this year to bump up his salary, since federal employees' salaries had been frozen again. In that vein, this new investigation office had been a godsend—it meant a bigger budget and more staff. Well, at least one more staff member. If all went well, his boss could justify a salary bump for him.

Out of the corner of his eye, he saw a head poking in through his open door and then heard a knock on the frame. "Hi, Craig. How's it going?"

As he suspected, it was Sharon Hill. Sharon had an undefined role at Interior, though she seemed to be a carrier, ferrying messages between parties and taking credit if things went well. She was moderately attractive, with curly blond hair to her shoulders, a flat figure, blue eyes, and too much foundation on her face.

"All right," Craig mumbled.

Sharon got straight to the point. "The new deputy assistant secretary for social relations is looking for a few more dollars for his From the Park to the Stars campaign. We figured since you had that influx in your budget, you could help him out. Your office isn't really running yet, anyway."

Craig had expected paws to start clawing their way into his newfound booty, but it still made him nervous to hear someone already had plans for his budget. "But we *are* up and running," he said. "There was an explosion this morning, and my man is on site, collecting evidence." He knew the last part wasn't true, not yet. But it would be more difficult to stop something that was already operating than to prevent it from starting.

Sharon let out a barely audible "Hmm," her face expressionless. "Well, be prepared for tough questions at the ten a.m. meeting. He wants to expand this campaign to a national level." She backed out of the doorway to leave but put her hand on the frame. "Good luck—I hope you can keep it."

Craig knew that five minutes later she would be in the DAS's office, helping him scheme to get Craig's money. But he played along. "Thanks," he said, reaching for the spreadsheets.

11

Gloria's Grill was an old-fashioned place just off I-64. It was a favorite with locals like Kenny, who adored the worn red booths with cracks and exposed stuffing almost as much as the portions that were served as singles but more suitable for sharing. Kenny sometimes nursed coffee on his days off just to watch the phases of the patrons. The early-morning crowd was mostly silver-maned retirees and miners in coveralls that would be covered in coal dust soon, but by 8:30, when Kenny arrived with Lisa at his side, it was mostly just middle-aged workers in business casual dress finishing up and flagging down waitresses for the check. Lisa ordered toast, sliced melon, and decaf coffee. Kenny had a more substantial bounty of eggs, bacon, and hash browns.

"So, hot stuff, whatcha think?" Kenny asked, shoveling a forkful of eggs into his mouth.

She cut a slice of melon, ignoring his sexist humor. "About what?"

"Your first experience at a chemical plant."

"Okay. Looked like a bad fire, but I'm not sure what 'bad' is in a plant. Is it normal to have fires?"

"It happens. What about the plant manager?"

"He seemed like he cared. I'm sure it's a hard job. I wouldn't want it."

She bit into the melon. It always made him smile when she took her first bite of breakfast—she inverted the fork like his Aunt Martha used to.

"Me neither," he said, popping a slice of bacon into his mouth. "What about the chemical industry in general?"

Lisa daintily pressed her napkin to the corner of her mouth. "I don't know—I don't think much about it." She took a sip of coffee.

"Are you pro-industry or anti-industry?" he pressed further.

"Anti-industry, I guess," she said. "They seem to have a problem with pollution. I guess they employ a lot of people, but they should do better."

Despite the early hour, Kenny felt the combination philosopher-and-debater part of him kicking in. He pointed his fork at her. "What does it mean to you personally?"

She stopped chewing momentarily and then continued and swallowed. "Not much, I guess. I don't have anything to do with it."

"Oh, but you do. You're a major supporter and benefactor. Most everything you do every day is the result of the chemical industry. From your alarm clock to your sheets to your makeup. You flip on the light, electricity comes from utility plants." She started to speak, but he held up his hand. "Even if we go to alternative fuels, industry will still be involved. It takes iron, steel, and paint to make things like wind turbines. Crude oil's used in everything from pesticides to food coloring, to medicine, to that perfume you're wearing." He fanned in front of his nose at the last example.

"Okay, but I recycle. I try not to waste things, and my next car will be a hybrid."

But that just fired Kenny up more. "Recycled materials still have to be processed to be reused."

The waitress came back and refilled their glasses with water. Kenny pointed at her glass as the waitress walked away. "Are you going to drink all that?"

"Probably not," she responded innocently. "I prefer bottled."

"Why didn't you tell her to stop? I thought you tried not to waste things."

"Okay, I may benefit from their products. But I want them to produce things safely and protect the environment. Is that so bad?"

"Not at all. Just know you're aiding them all, even the bad actors, and of course there are bad actors in every industry—even ours."

The waitress walked back up and started to top up Lisa's coffee. Lisa held up her hand. "No, thanks. I'll just finish this one."

She looked at Kenny. "Happy?" she said sarcastically.

Kenny smiled. "I wouldn't call it a change of lifestyle, but it's a start."

Now that he had her rattled, he decided, he'd give her philosophical vertigo by flipping to the other side. "But there *are* the bad actors, and—"

"I think the guy at Chemtrifuge is one of the good ones," Lisa interrupted. "I sense it."

"Maybe, but—"

But before Kenny could commence his slaughter of the chemical industry, Lisa's phone chirped. She held up a finger and dug it out of her purse. "It says to call the office immediately," she said, frowning as she dialed the number.

Kenny watched her eyes widen and scarfed down his last strip of bacon—no telling how quickly they'd have to get out of here.

"He's coming here? Oh, yes, of course. Immediately!"

"What's up, gal?" Kenny asked between chews.

"A. C. Mounts is going to the plant."

Kenny's fork clattered to his plate. Everyone in media, even nationally, wanted to talk to the iconic Mounts. Although he was a public figure, he rarely granted media access. Rumor was, he'd had a bad experience early in his career and vowed to never let it happen again.

Lisa's phone chirped again, and she looked down. "His son was one of the ones who were hurt."

They both grabbed their coats and booked it—the waitress chased them into the parking lot to remind them to pay and Kenny dug in his faded brown wallet and pressed a ten and a five into her hand, telling her to forget the change.

12

Jon Barrett rolled into the avenue leading to the industrial park, muttering, "Get on-site by ten, Craig has his meeting then," a kind of mantra. He glanced at the dash clock: 9:39. It looked like he was going to make it.

In front of him, a line of cars was snaking through a series of Jersey barriers toward the Chemtrifuge plant. Gradually, the line slowed and then stopped. He advanced a little but realized that it was only because ahead of him cars were maneuvering out of the line, doing Y-turns, and heading back out. A dozen yards ahead or so, a policeman was stationed at the side of the road. As each vehicle reached him, he walked into the road, chatted for a few seconds to the driver, and then pointed back toward the interstate.

Great, Jon thought. Six hours on the road, and now they weren't letting anyone in. He could see the fire in the distance. It was worse than he'd thought, if it was still burning now.

The officer only let one vehicle in front of him pass into the industrial park, a van with big letters on the side. Jon watched the satellite dish on top of the van recede, snaking around the police cars and barricades. Why was the media here? Reporters didn't understand chemical plants, so they usually stayed away.

The policeman was just one car ahead now. He straightened his hat and slowly walked toward Jon, slapping the hood as he walked to the driver's side. Jon rolled his window down and was hit with the musty smell of the recent rain rising from the wet pavement. The officer leaned down toward the window. "Road's closed—there's a problem in one of the plants."

"I know," Jon said. "I'm from the Department of Interior in Washington, DC. I'm here to investigate it."

"From where? Let's see some ID, bud."

Jon leaned forward and fumbled through his back pocket for his wallet. He took his Wyoming driver's license out and handed it to the officer.

"Say you're from Washington, DC? Looks like you're from Wyoming to me."

"It's an old license." Jon glanced at the dash clock again. 9:44. It was getting close to ten. He didn't have time to discuss the ins and outs of his move to DC right now.

The policeman peered into the back of Jon's car, which was littered with fast food bags, papers, and CDs. "Well, let me see your credentials. What do you have, a badge or something?"

"I just started—I don't have credentials yet. To be honest, this is my first official day. I was supposed to pick them up this morning, but I had to come straight here instead."

The officer sighed and shook his head. Jon couldn't tell if he thought he was lying or telling the truth. "Son, I can't let just anybody in. We've got an emergency here. If you can't show me some credentials or an emergency pass from the company, I'm gonna have to ask you to leave."

"Wait, let me call Washington. I'll see what I can get."

The officer cleared his throat loudly, but Jon pretended not to hear. He pulled out his phone, thinking he'd type an email to his boss. But there was already an unopened message from Craig in his inbox.

"I've got something here," he said, clicking on the message.

"Listen, buddy, get out of line and get this all straightened out, and don't come back till you do."

Jon kept his eyes on the phone, trying to read Craig's email while the agitated officer talked, his volume riding a crescendo with every word.

Jon, already called plant, they're expecting you. Will cooperate.

He held the screen up so the officer could see it. "My boss in Washington already cleared it with the plant. He says they're expecting me."

The officer looked at the device for a second and then pointed to a bare spot beside the access road. "Move over there till I check this out."

As Jon was pulling over, he noticed a large black blob in his rearview mirror. As it got closer, he saw that it was a town car with tinted windows. The surly officer took the radio off his belt, listened for a few seconds, and then hurriedly started moving the cones and long portable blockade. Somebody important was entering the industrial park.

The town car slid past, and the officer gave whoever was in the back seat two thumbs up. His smile vanished as he turned his head, owl-like, to glance over at Jon. He started moving the barricades back into place but then stopped and held the radio horizontally in front of his face, still looking at Jon. After a few seconds, he put the radio back on his belt clip. To Jon's surprise, he pointed at Jon and then toward the plant and moved the barricades aside again.

Jon rolled down his window. He might as well play nice—the officer might be here the next day. "Thanks so much, officer. Is the plant on the right or the left?"

The policeman was looking at the car behind Jon's, stone-faced. "Just follow the fire, DC."

"Thank you." Jon rolled the window up, miffed but trying to focus.

He drove toward the flames and into the industrial park, passing guard gates, large white signs with company logos, and waiting tanker trucks along the way. Chemtrifuge was at the back, in line with the gate where Jon had entered the park. It was situated oddly, between a refinery on the left side and a row of houses just outside the fence on the right. He'd bet that had caused a lot of headaches.

He remembered a brief stint he'd had in Oklahoma, at a plant with residential neighbors. They were always arguing at community meetings about odd smells, the taste of their drinking water, and lights on all night in the parking lot. Once, the plant manager lost his temper. *The plant had been there first*, he'd yelled. *They knew what they were getting into when they got their houses dirt cheap.* He'd never attended another meeting.

A van that looked like an ambulance was going down the road in front of the houses as Jon reached the entrance to the Chemtrifuge parking lot. The lights weren't on, but it was moving fast. He followed it with his eyes for a moment before he pulled in and parked.

He switched off the ignition, pulled out his phone, and found Craig's last message. "I'm on-site," he wrote but then hesitated. Getting through the gates had been tough enough, but now he faced another challenge: getting inside the plant. He put the phone in his pocket without hitting Send.

13

Robin watched Tara's eyes widen on the other side of the glass, and she stood up and looked out the window. A. C. Mounts, state senator, had climbed out of his town car and was bounding up to the admin building, trailed by his two assistants. Today would be the most exciting day of being a receptionist at Chemtrifuge. She knew from watching TV that the world took on a supporting role whenever Mounts showed up.

At first glance, Mounts came across as caricaturish, with uncombed white hair on the sides and back of his round head, a reddened nose, and a barrel-shaped physique. His appearance was consistent with how she had seen him on television, though she hadn't expected him to be quite so short. He looked to be about five and a half feet tall, and he wore a colorful shirt and tie that wrapped tightly around his double chin. But she knew he could change the energy in any room instantly—he had that kind of charisma.

Robin watched as Tara darted out the door and Wanda quickly held

Lisa was fumbling with her heel, not looking up. "Well, from what Kathy told me, the HR manager at the plant called him, and then one of Mounts's personal assistants contacted her. They go back a long way, back to college I think—long before she became our station manager. Apparently she gives Kathy scoops from time to time."

They both looked up and spied Rachel Jones's van.

"Oh my God. I guess our station manager wasn't the only one Mounts's assistant called. So much for our scoop. I guess even the back-benchers heard about Mounts's son."

"Catfight!" Kenny replied, dangling a cigarette through clenched lips.

Lisa scratched her cheek with her middle finger. "See this? I'd hate for you to miss it."

Kenny chuckled.

Rachael opened her door before the van even stopped and ran to the guard shack.

"Maybe she forgot her pads," said Lisa, laughing.

▲ ▲ ▲

Jon rubbed his temples as he stepped out of his car. He didn't realize how hard he'd closed the door until he heard it slam. He looked around the parking lot. Several media crews were setting up. Each man setting up the klieg lights had a cigarette dangling from his mouth and long hair collected in a ponytail. In front of the lights were attractive young women holding microphones and notepads and fussing with their hair. The black town car that had passed Jon at the gate now sat in a plum spot in front of what he assumed was the administration building, blocking four handicapped parking spaces.

Jon breathed in and started toward the guard shack.

"Mister, we have a lot going on," the African American female guard said, looking at his chest. "No deliveries or job applications today."

"Actually, I'm here to investigate the fire. My name's Jon Barrett—management is expecting me."

"Let me call over to the admin building. Wait outside, if you don't mind."

"Okay, thank you," Jon said, glancing at her name tag. *Ruby.*

He walked out past a woman he had not noticed before, sitting by the door. She had long, flowing blond hair, and puckered her lips as she moved her head from side to side, checking herself in a compact mirror.

"They'll see you now," the guard said to the woman. "You need anything? Coffee?"

Jon exited the guard shack before he heard the answer. He felt like marching back to the quaint solace of his worn upholstery, gray steering-wheel cover, and eighties CDs. But out of sight really did mean out of mind, especially since they probably didn't want him on-site anyway; so instead he walked over to stand behind the gauntlet of reporters.

The stunning one with black hair and olive skin made eye contact but quickly looked away, apparently concluding he knew nothing. She was right about that, he thought, but maybe she did.

"It's a big one, isn't it?" he asked, nodding toward the fire.

The reporter glanced at him. "Yes," she replied mechanically.

"Do they know what caused it?"

The other reporters looked at him, appearing annoyed.

"Something about bad maintenance," the reporter said.

"Why's it still burning?" he asked.

"They're getting it under control." She sized him up. "Who are you? Do you work here?"

"No, I'm from Washington, DC. I'm here to investigate what happened." Jon hoped the DC reference would spark interest. It didn't.

"They already figured that out," another reporter with short, spiky hair, holding a notepad, said, not even looking at him. "Some contract company's fault."

Jon was puzzled. The reporters had a keen interest in something, but it wasn't the fire. "Is there something else going on?"

The olive-skinned reporter exhaled abruptly. "Mounts is here. We want to hear what he has to say."

"Who's Mounts?" Jon asked.

The reporter turned to face him. "He's a state senator, an institution here. His son may be hurt." Her expression changed and she glanced at the other reporters as if she had let a secret slip, but they didn't respond.

Jon nodded. "Anybody else hurt?"

"Just some workers," said the spiky-haired reporter. "They're being helped now."

Jon found the response callous, but there was no use in pressing further. The reporters were only interested in Mounts.

The guard opened the door and pointed in Jon's direction, motioning him in.

Jon pointed at himself, and the guard nodded.

Once Jon entered the guard shack, Ruby told him the HR manager was on the way, but he would have to watch a safety video first.

Jon glanced at his watch: 9:49. "Okay, how long does it last?"

"About five or ten minutes. It's mandatory."

Resigned, Jon sat down in the worn brown chair she'd gestured at. Discolored foam protruded through the cracks in its upholstery. Ruby grabbed the VHS tape sitting on top and stuck it in the side of the TV. Jon had not seen a VHS tape in years.

"Welcome to our plant," a voiceover intoned over the hiss and crackle of the old tape. "Your safety is our first priority. We want your visit to be as enjoyable as possible, but first we want to tell you about some safety rules. If there is a chemical release, look at the windsock to see which direction the wind is blowing. Never run in the direction of the wind when there is a release." The narrator droned on about assembly points, designated smoking areas, delivery points for truck drivers, and personal protective equipment requirements. Jon had no PPE, he realized. He'd have to ask for some. The negative thoughts came rushing back.

He wished he could have prepared better for this trip. "Designated smoking areas are in smoke shacks, not in any production unit. You must be escorted at all times." Even if he got on-site, would Craig keep his budget? He might be out of a job by the end of the day. He'd just signed a one-year lease on his Springfield apartment. "One blast means emergency in zone one, two blasts mean . . ." Could Craig be trusted? If they'd already figured out the cause, what the hell was he doing here? He had no team and no equipment.

A slender man with a white shirt and black, slicked back hair walked into the guard shack, interrupting Jon's anxiety tsunami.

"Mr. Charlie Branch is here, and the tape's finished. Go ahead and sign in," said the guard.

Jon wrote his name in the visitors' register sitting on the security desk, noticing that all the previous pages had been torn out. He turned to the guard. "Got any PPE for visitors?"

Ruby handed him a badge. "You'll have to ask Mr. Branch. Here's your visitor's badge—run that every time you go in or out of the turnstiles, here and at the admin building. Visitor's badges have codes, 9743 today. It changes."

As Jon passed through the turnstile, he looked at his watch: 9:56. He pulled out his phone and hit Send, praying that Craig would get the message before his meeting.

14

Rachael Jones pranced into Sam Page's office, sliding her compact into her purse with a big smile on her face as if fate had just dealt her a great hand.

Sam rose from his chair. Mounts and his assistants also rose. Rachael maneuvered her oversize purse onto her left shoulder as she bent awkwardly to shake their hands.

Before she could sit down, Mounts got to the point. "I understand you've got some news about my boy, young lady?"

"Yes, sir, Senator. You see, when we heard about your son, we were on our way back to the plant. My cameraman had to get gas, so we stopped at the station one exit up, and I went in for a soda. I was at the counter when I heard the guy in front of me talking about the fire."

Sam noticed that Mounts and both his assistants had started to fidget.

"I asked him if he worked at the plant, and he said he did, but that he took off when the explosion happened. When he took out his wallet to pay for a candy bar, I glanced at the name on his license—Mounts. I asked if he was related to you, and he said he was your son."

"Where the hell has he been? It happened early this morning."

"I asked him why he left, and he said—" Rachael stopped and looked around, as if someone had sneaked into Sam's office. She lowered her voice to nearly a whisper. "He said he'd been smoking pot behind the control room, and he thought he'd get in trouble."

"That stupid son of a bitch!" Mounts exploded. "We've been worried sick about him, and the idiot was off getting high?"

Sam looked confused. "But this happened hours ago."

Rachael looked at him. "He said he's been sitting in the field across the road, watching the fire. He had a few more joints with him. He also lost his hat earlier in the evening, when he was up on one of the—what did he call it? Platforms? He thought he'd get in trouble for that too."

"All this time he's been smoking weed?" Mounts shook his head. "You know he gets that shit from his mother. She always had a problem, since before we got married. I got her off the hard stuff, and now she's just on prescription drugs. It's from a doctor, so I think it must be okay. And the dumb shit blabbed about smoking pot to a reporter? I honestly wonder if that boy has any of me in him at all."

There was an awkward silence. One of Mounts's assistants cleared her throat and nodded toward Rachael.

Mounts apparently got the hint. "I'm glad it was you that found him, not another reporter," he said, turning on the charm. "Now, we really don't need to report all this stuff, do we? After all, there are more important things."

"Hmm. I guess not. But you know, Mr. Mounts, I really would love to do a one-on-one interview with you—at a time and place of your choosing, of course."

Mounts smiled. "Consider it done, sweetheart. Jane, give her a card and work out the details." One of his assistants nodded, opening her bag. "Sam, can I see you outside for a minute?"

▲ ▲ ▲

Out in the hallway, Mounts put his arm around Sam's shoulder. "Sam, my friend, you understand how embarrassing it could be if this little episode got around. I think we've taken care of missy in there with the interview. I know she took advantage of the situation, but this interview is a small price to pay for keeping this skeleton in the closet. But, along those lines, I'd really like you to do me a favor and keep this between us."

Sam nodded. "I understand, A.C. Our family members sure can embarrass us, can't they?"

Mounts laughed. "They sure can, buddy."

Sam paused a moment. "But there *is* something you can do for us, A.C."

"You name it."

Sam licked his lips. "We got this fellow from DC, came down here to sniff around. Says he's from Department of Interior and he's here to do an investigation. But see, we already got the cause figured out, and we're responding to the fire. We got our shit together. We really don't need some guy from Washington coming in here, telling us how to do things."

"Right you are. Hell, they can't get their own damn town straightened up."

"A.C., it'd really help us, since the press is already here, if you could go out and say a few words on behalf of our company. Let everybody know we're okay, and discourage this guy from sniffing around too long. My HR manager's taking him back to the scene right now. Hopefully that'll satisfy him, and he'll be on his way. But this is a headache I don't need."

"Sam, I'll be glad to do it. Hell, I may become a press darling again. You know, I hardly ever give interviews or make statements—less to have to apologize for later." Mounts gently elbowed Sam in the ribs. "But I'll do it for you. Give me twenty minutes or so. That work?"

Sam nodded. "Perfect—gives us time to set up. Our DC boy should be back from the fire by then, so he'll have a chance to hear you too."

Mount's countenance turned serious. "Okay, Sam, since I'm doing this conference for you—and I'll do you up right—you won't mention anything about my son and the drugs, right?"

Sam scrunched up his face in mock confusion. "What son?"

15

Charlie paused for a minute, feeling impatient while Jon fumbled with his phone. They had just cleared the turnstile and were inside the plant.

"Nice to meet you. I'm Jon Barrett from Interior."

Charlie took the visitor's hand reluctantly, sizing him up. He had light brown hair and a medium build. His had a boyish face, but he was starting to develop a slight middle-age spread—early forties, at a guess. Charlie couldn't place the accent, but believed it to be midwestern. Polite and probably timid. In other words, perfect.

"I'm Charlie," he said, a touch formally. "What do you need?"

"First, I'd like to see the scene."

"They're still fighting the fire, so we can't get too close—you'd be in the way. We can view it from a distance."

"A view from afar will be okay for now, just to give me a sense of the scene."

"Where's your gear?" Charlie asked curtly.

Jon looked sheepish. "Actually, I was wondering if you could help me out. Do you have PPE for visitors? I just started at Interior, and believe it or not, I don't have my equipment yet." He smiled. "You know how slow the government works."

If this guy thought a jab at the government would soften Charlie up, he'd have to think again. Charlie shook his head. "A professional investigator, and you don't even have gear? Come back to the guard shack, and I'll see what we have."

Charlie sensed he would win any battle of wills. The investigator's plan seemed to be to play nice and trust in Chemtrifuge's benevolence. Charlie's plan, developed during an earlier call with the DC attorney, was to handle the guy and insulate Sam, who might need to play bad cop later. Charlie would be businesslike. They'd use the old lawyer trick of shaking his confidence. Without being overtly antagonistic, they'd make him uncomfortable enough that he'd slink back to DC within a day or two.

The investigator was clearly authorized to come on-site, true. They couldn't do anything about that. But they'd control everywhere he went and everything he did. They'd give him the bare minimum of information—enough to say they'd complied, but no more. They were backed by the best lawyers in DC, and there were a number of politicians they could call on. If they had to fight, they would win.

On one level, Charlie felt sorry for this guy. But this was business. Let him go back to DC, push paper around for the next twenty years, and retire happy and ignorant.

▲ ▲ ▲

Jon struggled to fit into the very worn blue coveralls, as Charlie constantly looked at his watch and tapped his fingers on the counter in the guard shack. He was able to zip them about halfway up. Ruby handed him a hard hat with so many stickers with various company names that it looked like a piece of luggage sent around the world. He suspected it had been left behind by some contractor, and the company had snagged it for use by Very Unimportant Persons such as himself. He also dug around in the plastic bin to retrieve a pair of black safety glasses, yellow earplugs, and goggles to snug into the clip on his hard hat. Hat aside, he could have blended in with the rest of the contractors that entered the gate on any given morning.

Charlie swung his arm in a "come on" manner, and they both proceeded back through the turnstile to a row of golf carts at the back of the admin building.

"Jump in," Charlie barked, pointing to the golf cart closest to them.

Jon slid into the passenger's seat. He kept his hand on the side bar as the cart meandered down the dirt road, running through the middle of the plant between the units and then through paths between equipment.

For most people, a chemical plant was an alien environment, even a frightening one. But for Jon, who'd worked in plants like this for over twenty years, they were like a familiar sofa with unsightly pillows and worn upholstery. He felt at ease in the worn coveralls and ugly hard hat. In this massive patchwork of metal structures, among these vessels of every shape and size, these shells of steel, with the hiss of steam exhaust from condensate lines like music in his ears, he felt at home.

As the cart ran under horizontal conduits, which were about ten feet high, Jon thought about his days as a small child, in the car with his parents as they drove by a plant. He remembered his mother pointing at the clouds of steam rising from a large fat stack in the middle of the plant. She'd always worried about him, later, when he'd started working in plants. He'd reminded her of the statistics, told her that workers in plants are safer than people outside, but she didn't care. She knew her son had a good-paying job and had escaped farm life, but the plant was unknown to her, and the unknown was bad. And after all this caution, she'd died fairly young of ovarian cancer.

"You getting out?" Charlie snapped as the cart rolled up behind the control room, jarring Jon out of his thoughts.

"Yes, thanks."

Jon followed Charlie into the control room. He looked around, noticing the familiar long desk in the middle of the room with built-in monitors where the operators sat.

"Fred, me and this guy are going to look at the fire," Charlie said to the operator at the board. "We'll just stand in front of the control room and look."

Jon followed Charlie's lead and signed the unit log, sensing a chance to talk to someone other than Charlie. "Tough night, huh?" he said casually to Fred. "You guys know what happened?"

Fred glanced at Charlie. "Bad maintenance."

Charlie turned to Jon. "Come on!" he said impatiently, shepherding him toward the exit.

Outside, they gazed in the direction of the fire. The fog from the fire-water made it difficult to see clearly, but Jon counted eight men standing around water cannons, yelling at each other occasionally although he couldn't understand what they said over the loud hiss coming from the nozzles.

It looked like the flames had died down slightly since he first saw the fire from the parking lot. He wished he had binoculars or a camera with a zoom lens.

Beside him, Charlie jerked. He pulled the radio out of his pocket and walked away from Jon. Charlie's radio was smaller than the operators', and had no cord and mic attached. After a few seconds, he walked back to Jon.

"Well, seen enough?" Not waiting for an answer, Charlie walked back toward the control room.

Jon heard a voice as they walked into the control room.

"Did they get her out all right? Damn good thing she and the safety guy have that side gig with the ambulance crew."

"We're back," Charlie said loudly. All conversation ceased.

As Jon signed the register, he took one last shot. "Boy, Fred," he said, keeping his eyes on the register. "Bad maintenance can really hurt you, can't it? Do you know what specific piece of equipment failed, or what they did?"

Fred hesitated. Out of the corner of his eye, Jon saw him look at Charlie. "It was just bad maintenance," he said.

Charlie held the door open. "Let's go."

16

When Craig walked into the conference room for his ten o'clock meeting, the Office of Financial Management staff was already seated at one side of the large cherrywood table. Sharon was swiping through her phone. The director was also there between the two women, looking down at a paper filled with numbers. Craig took that as bad news. They were pulling in the big guns to go after his budget.

"Craig, I hope you remember me," said the director. "Ed Murphy. This is Julie, and I think you know Sharon." The two ladies smiled and nodded. Craig smiled back.

"How's everything going, Craig?"

"Okay."

"Good. You're pretty close to retiring, as I recall."

"I can go soon but haven't set a date," said Craig, playing along with the small talk.

"Well, you've done your time. I envy you." Then Ed shifted in his chair. "I've been reviewing your budget. That new appropriation went to your office. See, uh, I have a request from the new deputy assistant secretary that the money be reallocated to his office. It'd be a great favor to him."

"I heard that." Craig looked at Sharon, who was pretending to shuffle papers. "See, Ed, we plan to use the money as it was appropriated, to investigate chemical accidents."

Ed wrinkled his forehead. "I understand, and I mentioned that to the DAS. He's friends with the ranking minority member on the committee that wrote the bill. He said it wouldn't be a problem to get them to amend it and repurpose the money for him. You've only had it a few weeks—it's really just a matter of moving it around on paper, at this point."

Craig had been waiting for this. "But, Ed, we're already using it. I have a new investigator on staff, and he's on-site at a chemical plant right now. It was a terrible accident—multiple people hurt, maybe killed, possible damage to some of our lands," Craig embellished, though he doubted the plant was close to Interior-owned land.

Ed leaned back, eyeing Sharon curiously. Craig guessed she hadn't told him about their earlier meeting. "Your guy's already on board?"

"On board and on-site. He's surveying the damage and doing interviews as we speak. If we pull him back now, it would be a serious embarrassment for the department. The press is there and everything," Craig said, taking a gamble and hoping that they actually were.

Ed exhaled deeply. "Well, this thing's further along than I thought, him being on-site and all. And media attention."

"He tells me it's bad," Craig lied. "A big deal."

Ed started clicking his pen against the table. He leaned forward and then sat back in his chair. "I guess we can hold off a little longer and see how this unfolds," he said after a few seconds. "It could be embarrassing if this is a big deal and we pull back for no apparent reason." He tapped his fingers lightly on the table. "Any more discussion?"

Julie scratched her temple under her short-cropped, jet-black hair and then shook her head. Sharon pointed at the paper she had been pretending to shuffle and cleared her throat. "Well, the man who wants the money is a DAS." She glanced at Craig. "But I think we should proceed with the investigation," she said, winking.

Craig just nodded. He knew she would be in the DAS's office five minutes after this meeting, telling him how she'd fought for the money. But Ed seemed convinced, at least for now, so he had some cover.

"All right. Proceed." Ed lifted himself out of his chair, and the two ladies stood up on cue.

"Thanks." Craig jumped up.

"Craig, one more thing," Ed added, more seriously. "Don't let this get out of hand. It could embarrass us if we pull out now, but it could also embarrass us if we come across as jackbooted thugs. Don't ruffle the wrong feathers."

"Understood."

Craig walked back to his office, not wanting to dwell on the meeting he just had or the warning from Ed. He redirected his attention to the half-eaten granola bar on his desk and the stack of papers sitting next to it.

17

At the back of the admin building, the golf cart pulled into an open space. Through the opening where the turnstiles were, Jon could see a podium set up in the parking lot. Several people were standing around, most of them with mics, dictaphones, or lights in their hands.

"What's happening over there?" Jon asked.

"A. C. Mounts is going to make a statement about the accident," said Charlie, scrolling through the log on his cell phone.

"Oh, okay. By the way, is there an office I can use?"

"We're setting that up. But you have to be escorted everywhere, since this is an emergency situation. It's for your own safety."

Charlie walked back into the guard shack, Jon following. "We have to sign the visitor registry again," Charlie said.

Jon looked at his watch. It was 10:24. "Oh, are you leaving?" he asked, puzzled.

"I have to go outside the gate to attend the press conference. I'm your escort, which means you go, too. We have to sign every time we go in and out of the plant."

Jon had no desire to hear some blowhard local politician pontificate about what happened on the scene, but he had no choice. He followed Charlie out to the parking lot, where they stood at the left side of the podium. The eager press was standing directly in front of it.

"Here they come," a reporter said. Lights came on, and mics were raised toward the podium.

Jon turned around to see a parade of people coming toward him: some guy in front—the plant manager, he assumed—followed by Mounts (he couldn't miss Mounts), flanked on either side by his assistants. They all seemed to look at him, and then look away, expressionless.

Sam walked to the podium. "I'm Sam Page, plant manager. I gave you an update earlier, and there is really nothing new to report except that we believe we have a handle on the fire and it should be extinguished soon." The reporters scribbled notes. "We have the pleasure of a visit from Senator A. C. Mounts, who's offered to assist us in any way he can. We've asked him to say a few words. Unfortunately, he has to leave right afterward to go to the state capitol, so he won't be able to take questions."

Reporters flipped their note pages over as Mounts stepped to the podium. "How y'all doing?"

A wave of smiles crossed the small sea of reporters.

"It's good to come and talk with you this morning. You know, the chemical industry's been good to this area. We can thank industry for everything from the food on our plates to the shirts on our backs." He tugged at the shirt that covered his sizable body. "And some of us have more to be thankful for than others."

The reporters laughed politely.

"But seriously, this plant in particular has been a good friend. They've employed our people and contributed money to the community. This plant makes ingredients that go into a lot of things that make our lives better. Things like pipes that carry clean water, cups, fences, and even medicine. There are always risks, but they've done a good job managing those. And like you heard my good friend Sam say, this fire's under control."

Jon looked back at the fire. It was smaller than when he'd arrived, but nowhere near out. A plume of long and fluffy smoke clawed into the sky.

"Now, I know a lot of you may have come here to see how my boy's doing, and I appreciate that." Mounts put his hand over his heart. "This company was good enough to give my son a job, and I gladly sent him here to get experience at this fine organization. Turns out, he's fine—we just didn't look in the right place."

The sea of reporters mumbled various versions of "Glad to hear that."

"But I'll tell you one thing. This is a safe plant. I had no hesitations sending my dear son in here, and I still stand by that." Mounts's expression changed from jovial to serious, and he glanced at Jon. "And I guarantee you that management here is taking care of everything. The plant doesn't need help from any outsiders."

The reporters scribbled rapidly, looking at Jon, seeming to notice the body language.

Jon swallowed hard. It felt like he was the one on fire.

Mounts turned back to the reporters and smiled. "Now I got to get over to the State House and keep them folks straight. They start getting crazy when I'm gone too long."

He smiled as he waved, walking back to his car flanked by his assistants. He was trailed by Sam and Charlie, who each shook his hand as he got into his town car. They disappeared into the front entrance of the admin building.

Since Charlie had abandoned him, Jon was alone outside the fence again. He surveyed the pods of reporters scattered around the parking lot, breaking down their equipment. The reporters had been less than helpful so far, but Jon decided to find out what he could. His choices were that; go to the admin building and beg them to set him up with an office, which he wasn't sure they even had to do; or go back to his car. And what would he do then?

The pair closest to him had seemed like the most approachable earlier. He took a few steps and stood beside them. "So that was Mounts, huh?" he said to the ponytailed cameraman, who was squatting, adjusting the base of his lights. The pretty dark-haired reporter looked at Jon, her eyebrows rising. "Yes, that was the one and only Mounts. What did you think?"

"He sure can make a speech," Jon said. "I was surprised he didn't take any questions."

"We're happy he said anything. He almost never talks to the press alone."

"A politician with a press phobia? That's weird."

The reporter smiled. "I think it's part of his mystique. He doesn't need the press—he's one of a kind. I'm Lisa, by the way, and this is Kenny, my cameraman."

"Good to meet you. I'm Jon." Jon hesitated. This was going surprisingly well. He cleared his throat and started probing. "Any more word on what caused it?"

"Bad maintenance," said Lisa, picking at the heel of her shoe. "My mechanic did that once. It cost over a thousand dollars to straighten it out."

Did what? Jon wondered. "But what does that mean, exactly?" he persisted. "'Bad maintenance' is sort of vague. Did any employees talk to you?"

"No, I think they need some time to settle down before they're ready to talk."

Sure, Jon thought. That was a convenient line for the company to take. But the longer the delay in starting an investigation, the harder it is to figure out what had happened. Witness recollections are often the most important pieces of evidence, yet they're also the most fragile. Memories shift. People talk to each other, changing their stories to make sense of things they observed but didn't understand. "What about the guys that got hurt? Any word on them?"

"The plant manager said there's no change." Lisa looked down, adjusting her lapel mic. "I guess they're alright."

"I don't know," Jon said, pushing a little. "That fire was pretty big. Do you think anybody could have been close to it and not been hurt?"

Lisa glanced over at the fire. "Well, maybe not if they were *real* close. But apparently they're getting treated."

"Why aren't you following up on the other guys? There was a lot of concern for Mounts's son, but no one's asking about the others." Jon was surprised at his own tenacity.

Lisa exhaled and glared at him.

"I'm not telling you how to do your job," he said quickly, kicking himself. He'd overstepped. "I'm just trying to understand."

"Look. I know they're people too, and I hope they're alright. But the big story here, the one our station told us to cover, is Mounts's son. It doesn't sound fair, but the news business has to pick and choose. Everybody thinks their issue is the only one that's important, but news time is valuable, and only a few critical items make it into the broadcast. There's a lot going on now with the miners' strike. If we start chasing down the condition of everyone who might be hurt, our competitors have the jump on the next story."

Jon winced.

Lisa put her hand on his. Her tone softened. "Look, I didn't write the rules, but we have to follow them. Reporters look for conflict, and for bad things happening to important people—in this case, the son of an important person. I care about the others, but I don't have time or authority to go on a wild goose chase. Besides, I heard the guys who got hurt were contractors. It was bad maintenance by contractors that caused the accident, so maybe they had something to do with it. They still didn't deserve to get hurt, but it's not like they were innocent bystanders."

Her words hit Jon like an oil slick flowing over a paralyzed pelican. Those men's lives were not even part of the story. He thought about the conversations on the radio earlier that morning. Other issues were more important to the press, such as whether miners got 93 percent or 95 percent of their pay if they were laid off.

▲ ▲ ▲

As Lisa looked at the shocked and almost hurt look on the face of this guy from Washington, she was suddenly surprised at her own words. When had she become so callous? Was she now part of this media game too? Then another thought occurred to her: What was an investigator from Washington, DC, doing here in Charleston? She hadn't thought about this angle before. She recalled Mounts's words. What had he said? Something like, "They didn't need outsiders." He'd looked right at this guy when he had said it. Could this be the seeds of conflict between a federal agency and local politicians? Was she the first one with that scoop? Rachael Jones had been on the phone, talking and smiling, when she came back from the admin building. She'd gotten something out of the deal. But Lisa had this guy now. No one else was even talking to him.

"You seem to have a lot of passion for this work." She offered an alluring smile. "Why don't I interview you for the next segment, find out why you're here, and what the government thinks happened?"

Jon jerked slightly. "But I'm not sure what happened yet."

"Maybe you can just tell us why the government is investigating and what you'll be doing next."

Jon paused. Maybe an interview with this reporter could help his investigation. Charlie and the employees seemed less than eager to cooperate. If the fact that he was conducting a federal investigation was not enough to make them work with him, perhaps believing he had connections in media would. He glanced at the large safety banner on the building inside the plant. Image seemed important to Chemtrifuge.

18

The other reporters looked on curiously for a moment as Lisa switched back to her handheld mic, and then they went on with their own work. Kenny told Lisa to stand on the left and told Jon to stand on the right. As Jon looked backward, he saw the still-burning fire between them, understanding how that would look on camera. Nice move, he thought.

"Okay," Lisa said, "so I'm going to ask you what you are doing here and what you will do now."

What *would* he do now? Jon ran his fingers through his hair. "Okay, I got it."

Lisa turned toward the camera and held her arms at her sides. "Have you been on television before?"

"Yes," Jon said, without elaborating. The fact that the local press in Kimball, Nebraska, had interviewed him after his uncle won the prize for the largest pig at the fair didn't really make him appear TV-worthy.

"Good, you know the drill."

"I think so."

"Ready in two minutes," said Kenny, a cigarette dangling from his lips.

"This won't be live," said Lisa. "We're going to replay it next time they cut to us from the studio, so don't be nervous. We can reshoot if we need to."

"Good," Jon said, though he preferred to get it right the first time. He was not sure what had changed Lisa's mind from dismissing him earlier to interviewing him now, but it showed how quickly things could change. He started rehearsing bullet points in his mind. *I'm here to find the cause. We care about the people. We want to help the company, make sure it doesn't happen again.* He wasn't sure about the policy at Interior regarding talking to the press, but the benefits seemed to outweigh the risks. He could always claim ignorance, since he was new.

Kenny held up a thumb. "Okay, ready when you are."

"Now," Lisa said, turning to the camera. "I'm here today with Jon Barrett, an investigator from Washington, DC. He is on the scene with us at Chemtrifuge Chemicals, where a fire that started early this morning is still raging. Jon, want to tell us a little bit about who you are and why you're here?"

Jon glanced at the camera and then at Lisa. He cleared his throat. "I'm from a new office at the Department of the Interior, in DC," he said awkwardly. "Our office investigates accidents to help companies figure out what happened, and keep it from happening again."

"So how many accidents has your office investigated?"

Jon didn't like the question, but he couldn't escape. "We're actually a new office. This is our first investigation." He scratched his cheek nervously and then stopped. "However, I've investigated accidents in the private sector before coming to the government."

"I see. So why did your office choose this company for its first investigation? I mean, is there a particular problem with Chemtrifuge? Do you—I mean your office—not trust them to find the accident's cause?"

She was looking for red meat, Jon thought. "That's a good question," he said, hedging for time. Maybe best to take the high road and stay vague. "We have no reason not to trust the company, but you have to understand how complex an investigation like this can be. The more resources, the better."

"Does that mean you don't think they have the resources, or that they don't know how to use them?" Lisa was not giving up. Jon saw the cameraman smile.

"Well, it's difficult to know exactly what you need, this early in an investigation like this." Jon hesitated, realizing he was off his talking points. "But I'd like to add that our goal is to prevent these accidents in the future."

Lisa was expressionless. "Can your office send people to jail if you find wrongdoing?"

That one threw him. He didn't know the answer, and didn't want to guess. "We're not thinking about anything like that," he said, settling on a non-answer. "We just want to help find the cause."

Behind Lisa, Jon could see the two other cameramen hurriedly packing equipment into their respective vans. One reporter had her cell phone wedged between her ear and shoulders, and the other was scribbling notes on her pad.

Lisa switched hands for the mic and looked at Kenny and then back at Jon. "What about the burning material? Could it cause a problem with local residents?"

Jon was not sure what was burning. "That's one of the issues my office will be investigating," he hedged, but Lisa was no longer listening. She'd turned away from the camera and was holding her finger up to her earpiece.

"Hold on. Bert, what is it? Who? Each other? And they were caught where?" Lisa's voice rose higher with each question. "They what? In *print*? Yes, right away." She closed her notepad and reached down to pick up her purse.

"But about the community being affected—" Jon began, trying to get back on track.

Lisa didn't even look at him. "We're going to have to cancel this interview. There's a breaking story at the state capitol."

Kenny rose up from behind the camera. "What's happening, sweet stuff?"

"Seems our new Speaker of the House, Inez Shoemaker, got caught in the sack with the lead transportation lobbyist. Her husband, Richard, aka Richie Rich, is the richest man in the state. He owns half the coal mines and car lots."

Kenny flicked his cigarette into the gravel. "I know who he is. I remember it was a controversy when she got elected because of all his business shenanigans. She had to take the oath she'd recuse herself from any mining legislation. I heard Mounts pulled strings for her."

Lisa exhaled. "Yeah, but that's not the half of it. You remember when that vote came out about two months ago, lowering penalties for railcars with the wrong placards? Hers was the deciding vote, which was strange, since she'd repeatedly said during her campaign that everybody had to follow the law, especially big companies. Remember, she singled out the railroad company that didn't conduct the right training when that child got killed at a crossing about a year ago?"

"I remember," Kenny said. "We must have done twenty stories on it that week."

"Turns out this lobbyist sent a message to her email—her state government email—the morning before the vote, that read, 'Tonight we'll celebrate after the vote. I know where I'll put my placard . . . ha, ha.' And she replied, 'LOL . . . Absolutely, you'll drive every car in my train tonight. See you at the spot.' Someone in the district attorney's office leaked it to the media. There's a press conference in half hour. They may get her on conflict of interest and using state email accounts for personal use. They may even go after her husband too."

Kenny shook his head. "The DA is running for governor next year. If he brings her and Richie Rich down, he'll say he ended corruption." He put the camera and tripod in the back of the van and then walked around to the driver's side. "Even Mounts isn't powerful enough to protect people from rampant stupidity."

Jon was perplexed. "When do you want to talk again?"

Lisa looked at him and smiled. "I don't know. I mean, this is a big story. We have to cover it."

"I know, but what about the men who got hurt here? Isn't that important too?"

"I'm sorry. We don't make the rules. Good luck with your investigation." She turned and headed for the van.

"Wait," Jon said. "Do you know anything that could help me?"

Lisa shook her head as she climbed in, but Kenny took his hand off the gear shift and rested his forearm on the top of the steering wheel. "I recall their neighbor over there in the green house had problems with the plant," he said, pointing west. "She's involved with some environmental group, and rumor has it they collected a bunch of info on the plant—safety violations, shit like that. She sent some stuff to the station, but we had other stories going on so we never did anything with it. She never did anything either, as far as I know. No lawsuit, nothing—I don't know why."

He shifted the van into reverse. "Good luck."

Jon watched as the van drove out the gate. It was quiet now. Lisa and Kenny had been the last to go. There were no more reporters, no more commotion, no more attention. He was alone in the parking lot. The roar of the fire had died down some. Management was in the building. They wanted him to go away. They had the most powerful politician in the state on their side, and Jon didn't even have his credentials.

He looked across the parking lot at the guard shack. He could see the guard through the window. She was flipping through a magazine, oblivious to him. He looked at the admin building. Inside were managers who made many times his salary. He had worked for them his whole career. They had offices to work in, families to go home to, community meetings to schedule, lives to lead. Their chemical suppliers took them to the best restaurants, sponsored their golf tournaments, and took them to strip clubs. Jon had none of that. They were better than him. He had nothing. Should he go to the admin building and beg them for an office? Should he ask them for supplies? Charlie had belittled him for asking for protective equipment. His chance to go to the media was gone, wiped away by a sex scandal at the state capitol that obviously meant more to the press than this tragedy.

He looked at the fire, low but still burning, where he was sure that lives were lost. Then his eyes dropped to the ground. This time, he walked back to his car.

PART II

One Equation, Two Unknowns

19

The week following the accident yielded little in the way of evidence. Jon checked in to a Hampton Inn about fifteen minutes from the plant. He left Craig a couple of messages, saying he was on-site, but things were moving slowly. The only change was that Chemtrifuge put out a three-sentence press release confirming that three contract workers at the plant had passed away from an accident caused by bad maintenance by a contract company. Chemtrifuge had revoked the company's contract. No victim names, no evidence, no discussion of any investigation. As far as the company was concerned, the matter seemed to be closed. Jon looked in the local papers and watched the news, but everyone was consumed with the scandal involving the Speaker of the House. No mention of the earlier accident.

Chemtrifuge had given him a vacant office that felt more like a large closet, furnished with an old surplus desk and a folding chair. The beige walls and drab carpet were only interrupted by small windows about a foot tall at the top of the wall, too high to peer out. When Jon asked Sam after a chance meeting in the hallway if there was a spare computer he could use, Sam just smirked and said, "Washington has more money than we do, son." Jon went and bought a notepad, pens, and sticky pads at the local office supply store.

There seemed to be a lot more concern for Jon's safety than for his working conditions. When he arrived on the morning of his second day, he was escorted to his office. If he needed to leave for any reason, he had to call Charlie, who'd show up ten minutes later. If he called a second time, Charlie scolded him for his impatience.

"Why do I need an escort to go to the bathroom?" Jon asked Charlie, one day as he was leaving the plant.

"We have to take care of visitors," Charlie said, not meeting Jon's eyes. "There was an accident here, and there is an ongoing emergency response."

Jon knew that this escort protocol had nothing to do with safety—the explosion had happened at the back of the plant, several thousand feet from the admin building. It was meant to intimidate and control him. He decided to raise the issue with Craig when he returned to DC. Honestly, he wasn't sure his agency would back him up. As demeaning as it was to be escorted to the bathroom, that was nothing compared to the shame he would feel if he confronted the plant management and his department didn't support him.

He'd pick no battles now, Jon decided. It was Friday. He'd go back to DC, hopefully meet with Craig on Monday, and return to Charleston better prepared. He was upset at Chemtrifuge, but he was also upset at Interior. They'd sent him here without a badge and given him no support. While Craig was sitting in his plush chair, looking out over the National Mall, Jon sat on a folding chair in a glorified broom closet.

The longer Jon stared at the blank pages of his notepad, the more anxious he felt. He wanted to do a good job, but circumstances were against him. "At least I've tried," he said out loud and then reached for the phone. Ten seconds after he called, Charlie stood at his door.

At the exit, Jon turned to Charlie. "I'll probably come back late next week."

Charlie nodded.

"I'd like to do some interviews with the operators."

"We'll see."

Jon turned to go but then swung back around. "Oh, if you guys want to do anything with the damaged equipment, let me know. I want to be here when you do." He handed Charlie a piece of paper with the main number to DOI and his email address scribbled on it.

Charlie's eyebrow rose. "Okay," he said, hurriedly grabbing the paper. He sniffed as he walked back through the turnstile.

20

"**M**ust be someone special," the busty blond woman at the tattoo parlor said. "Is it your girlfriend?"

Darnell's arm was stinging from the first two numbers. "He was my brother," Darnell replied solemnly, looking straight ahead at the artistic photos on the wall of eagles, dragons, and crosses on various body parts.

She pulled the tattooing gun away and looked up from his arm. "Oh, I don't get many men requesting their brother's birthday. You two must be close."

"We were, very close. But he's dead now."

"I'm sorry," she replied, stopping momentarily. Then she looked back at his arm, and the stinging feeling resumed. "I got two brothers somewhere. I don't speak to either one of them, and I don't think they talk to each other. I talk to my sister occasionally. I think it's easier for sisters to be close than brothers. They kinda have that macho thing going. All my brothers ever did was fight—I mean fist fight, not just argue."

Darnell exhaled, sure he had sounded annoyed if she could hear him over the whirring sound of the tattooing gun. His mind wandered to that day around ten years ago, and the house fire. James had been fighting with his mother all day, and Darnell had locked himself away in his room, sick of the yelling. But that night, he'd awakened to Kawana running through the house, screaming. Darnell had jumped out of bed and followed her outside in his boxers and white T-shirt.

Emily was standing beside her mother rubbing her eyes. "They're burning, Mama," she said through tears.

Kawana had pulled her close and started yelling, "James! James!" her voice rising with each repetition. All three had looked around but didn't see him anywhere. "Oh, no, my baby's still inside!"

Without thinking, Darnell had charged back into the house, hearing his mother yelling, "Darnell, no!" from behind.

Half the house was consumed with flames, and they were getting close to the stairwell. Darnell could feel the hot banister as he ran up to James's room. He was stunned to see James sitting calmly on his bed, crying. "Come on!" he had yelled, but James didn't move.

"She don't love me. It's better if I just die."

Darnell had grabbed him in both arms and carried him down the stairs in a run. They had just cleared the bottom of the stairs when the top part started crackling loudly, and Darnell could hear the crash behind them. Both collapsed beside their mother and sister on the ground outside. Kawana and Emily had gotten on their knees and hugged them, and they were all one connected mass.

"I love you, baby," Kawana said to James as she'd kissed the top of his head and held him close rocking back and forth. "We'll never fight again."

They'd all looked at the house as a window burst in James's room. Tongues of flames came through the broken glass and started licking the outside of the house. Darnell could see fire through the windows. The entire inside was consumed.

"We've lost it all—we've lost everything," Darnell had said, still looking at the fire.

He'd felt his mother's fingers on his chin gently turning his face toward her. "Not everything. We still have each other." Even at this time, the rock of the family was solid.

James had pulled away from his mother and wiped his face with the back of his sleeve. Then he'd reached over and hugged Darnell, which he had never done before, and Darnell held him close and rocked him just like his mother had. It was the same way James would initiate a hug a couple of years later, after Darnell had taken a beating trying to save James from a gang that was recruiting him, but that time James had cradled Darnell and held his jacket to Darnell's bleeding face, calmly saying, "It's okay, we'll get them back, together."

Now Darnell sniffled and turned his head away from his arm as the strong memories and pungent smell invaded his nostrils, bringing him back to the present. "Sorry about the smell," the blond woman said. "It's this new ink, hard to get used to. Kind of smells a little like oil burning."

"Yes, it does," Darnell replied. He knew that smell, and James knew that smell the last night he was alive.

Later at home, his mother, who was no fan of tattoos, held his forearm in her hand. To Darnell's surprise, she said nothing critical about him getting a new one.

"I remember that day, like it was yesterday. You came in the room shortly after he was born. It was just you and me and the nurse, and I said, 'What am I going to do? How can I take care of another one?' You remember what you said? You said, 'I'll help you take care of him,' and you started patting his arm, very gentle. And you did, you always took care of him."

Darnell looked away and nodded, touching his own arm where James's birthday was memorialized, gently, like he had touched James's arm the day he was born.

21

In Sam's office, smoke snaked up toward the ceiling from two freshly lit cigars—his own and Alphonse Scott's. Sam was leaning back, one foot on the edge of his desk, holding a glass of bourbon. Alphonse sat in the guest chair, resting his elbow on the padded arm to support the hand that held his cigar. He was wearing classic coveralls, faded and full of holes.

Alphonse had been the union steward at the plant for as long as Sam could remember. He hadn't touched a wrench in over five years, but he still liked to dress like he worked on the line. He'd just returned from a two-month trip around the country, visiting other unions and attending a conference. His black convertible had rolled into the industrial park Friday afternoon, just seconds after the DC investigator's car pulled out.

The first Black union leader in the Charleston area, Alphonse had a compelling life story. He'd grown up dirt-poor in the worst house in the poorest area of West Virginia. He'd known a series of fathers, but none for long. His mother cared about her family, but her own troubled childhood had driven her to turn to drugs at an early age. Alphonse had learned early to make it on his own.

When Alphonse ended up at Chemtrifuge, he was already entrenched in the local union hierarchy. Much as Janet exemplified the company's commitment to women, Alphonse illustrated its commitment to African Americans, or Blacks, the term he preferred. He was respected by both the rank and file and plant management.

Sam blew on the end of his cigar and gazed at the glowing tip. "How was the conference?"

Alphonse leaned back and put his boot against the table, mirroring Sam. "Good. Saw old friends. They talked about some payback legislation to unions that may come out of the new Congress, but I doubt we'll see any of it. Meet the new boss, same as the old boss, right?"

Sam laughed nervously. He hated any talk of pro-labor legislation. He had a good relationship with the union, but he liked to make concessions because he wanted to, not because he was legally required to. "Where was it this year?" he asked, changing the subject.

"Oh, Vegas again. I lost some money, but at least I saved some for the Crazy Girls revue. That's worth the trip!"

Sam cleared his throat. "We had some excitement here—I'm sure you heard."

Alphonse put his cigar in the ashtray and straightened in his chair. "Yeah, Fred called me that morning. Pretty bad. I stopped by to see Janet on the way in."

"How is she?"

"Feisty as ever, and damned lucky. It was bad breaking her leg and all, but if she had fell three feet over to the left, she would have had that relief valve rammed up her ass."

Sam shook his head, trying to clear his mind before the visual took hold. "Good thing our safety man works on the ambulance crew at night. He was able to get them in and out of here quietly, no sirens."

"Yes it is."

Sam took his foot off the desk and leaned forward. "Alphonse, there are a couple of things you could help me with."

"What do you need?"

"Well, I think this thing's died down. We were lucky—the Speaker at the State House had that affair, and the story broke the same day. You should've seen the press, jumping out of here like they were running from another explosion. They're camped outside her house now."

Alphonse smiled. "I heard about that. Emails with something about her wanting him in her caboose?"

"Her story now is something like 'Mistakes were made'—you know, the usual. But I think any day she'll step down"—Sam made air quotes—"to 'spend more time with family.'"

Alphonse snickered. "Or maybe her conductor."

Sam smiled. "Anyway, the press is off our backs for now—sex is more interesting than death." He paused. "We talked to the operators early that morning. But if anybody asks, I need them to keep saying it was bad maintenance that caused it."

"You got it," Alphonse said. "Have you taken the line out yet to get a look?"

Sam exhaled. "No. DEQ gave us a variance to send material to the flare, and we are running at reduced rates. We don't want to shut the unit down totally because it takes so long to start back up. After that spike we had earlier, demand for ethylene's dropped off the last couple weeks, so we were planning to reduce rates anyway. This came at a good time, if there's a good time for this sort of thing."

"Makes sense. Okay, shoddy maintenance it was. I assume we're still blaming this on contractors. That'll make my guys happy."

"Absolutely." Sam hesitated again. "And, uh, one more thing. Some guy came down from DC to investigate. Our lawyers say his office is legit. I think we can roll him, but it's complicated. He wants to be here when we take the line out. Our lawyers say that since he made a verbal request and Charlie acknowledged it, we could be in some serious shit if we take it out and he's not here. That's another reason we're in no hurry to get it out and take a look. It won't support our story."

"Got it," Alphonse said. "If he comes back around, my folks will know what to say."

"I knew I could count on you." Sam tipped his glass to Alphonse. "Also, it'd be great if you'd suppress any talk about the dead guys. I've got a big enough problem, especially with one of them. I don't need any more discussion around the plant."

"No problem. And Sam, there's one thing you can do for me. We'll go with you on this story, but my guys want the contractors out. We can blame this on the contractors working in the maintenance department, but we want the ones in operations out of here too. I mean, I'm glad it was none of our guys who died, but we still want the contractors out. That's been about the biggest problem between you and me for years."

Sam curled his lips and nodded. "You know they cost us less in the long run. Corporate puts a lot of faith in cost-benefit analysis."

Alphonse smiled. "I'll give you a benefit. We got your back on this one."

Sam looked at his trophy case and then smiled and held out his hand. "You got it. Give me a couple of months, and we'll get rid of them. No more contractors."

Alphonse shook his hand and then stood up and smashed the end of his cigar into the ashtray. "Okay, we got our story straight."

As soon as Alphonse was gone, Sam poured another glass of bourbon. With the union on board, the final piece was in place. He tipped his glass to an invisible partner in his guest chair. Glenda would be at the therapist's, but he'd get home early for a change.

22

Jon hesitated outside Craig's open office door. Inside, he could see his boss sitting at his desk, white shirt and thin, red-striped tie just like at his interview, poring over spreadsheets. Craig's short salt-and-pepper hair looked more salty than he'd recalled. Jon took a deep breath and knocked gently.

"Yes?" Craig spoke without raising his head.

Jon cleared his throat. "I just wanted to let you know I'm back."

Finally, Craig looked up. "Come in. How is everything?"

Jon eased into one of the guest chairs. "Well, I got a few things done at the plant, but they're still trying to get back to normal."

Craig tapped his pen against his chin and nodded slowly. "I guess these things are pretty complicated."

Jon nodded. He'd stress the positives before he got to the problems. "I visited the scene, talked to some reporters, and got a workspace."

"Sounds like you've been busy. Figured out the cause yet?"

"They still think it was shoddy maintenance."

"Well, they should know."

"I guess," Jon said dubiously. "Trouble is, we really don't know. They don't seem to have any plans to test the equipment. I heard them say they got approval from the West Virginia Department of Environmental Quality to bypass the damaged equipment and send gas to the flare, so they can still run the unit."

Craig nodded, though Jon wasn't sure he understood.

Jon shifted in his chair. "If they remove the equipment, we can inspect the welds and gaskets to see if there were problems."

Craig tilted his head back and looked upward. "Hmm. What do the guys there say they saw?"

"That's another thing. I haven't been able to talk to anybody. They keep saying the operators are too traumatized, and the ones who know for sure are dead."

Craig nodded. "I can see where that's a problem."

Jon swallowed hard. "I'm trying to do a good job on this investigation, but it's hard. They control everything I do. I can't talk to people. They even escort me to the bathroom. They seem to monitor me every second I'm there."

"Sounds tough." Craig frowned. "Did you do anything to upset them?"

"Just showing up, I guess."

Craig rocked back in his wine-red leather chair. "So what do you propose?"

Jon leaned forward. "I want to interview people, I want to request records, and I want to inspect the damaged equipment. I'll put an interview list together this week. I don't have names, but I can start with positions. I also want to read the digital outputs, anything from their DCS—"

"Their what?" Craig interrupted.

"Digital control system. It should tell us what was going on in the unit that night." Jon sat back. "I want to know whether we can ask for these things, and whether they have to produce them. Will our lawyers support us if they refuse?"

Craig gazed out his window. "I'll speak to them and let you know. Meanwhile, let's get you settled in. See Rita—she'll get you fixed up with a computer, keys, supplies, essentials."

Jon stood up. "Can I get a laptop to take with me when I return to the site?"

"Ask Rita," Craig replied.

▲ ▲ ▲

As soon as Jon left, Craig swallowed hard and swiveled his chair around to look out the window. He knew Jon was just trying to do his job, and he felt sorry for him. It must be humiliating being escorted to the bathroom and monitored. He had no idea if his office could ask the company for documents and interviews. He didn't know if the lawyers would go to bat for Jon if the company refused. Right now what mattered was protecting his budget, and Jon's position, from this greedy new deputy assistant secretary. If he lost the money for the office, Jon's requests wouldn't matter anyway.

23

Jon spent the next week settling into the DC office. He was issued a badge, a key, and a credit card for travel. The building was rectangular, with windows overlooking an interior courtyard below. His cubicle was one of four workspaces in the office, with an L-shaped desk in a corner, facing away from the windows. Only one other space was occupied, diagonally across from him, one of the two workstations facing windows. His office mate was an older guy, and no fan of small talk. When Jon asked for the other space at the window, he was told another department was reserving it for additional employees.

He soon learned where the vending machines, breakroom, and bathrooms were, and developed a routine of walking two laps around the floor once every morning and afternoon. He got a cup of coffee in the morning, and a snack in the afternoon. His favorite table in the ground-floor cafeteria had indigo-blue chairs covered with Native American designs. From here, he could look at the stucco walls inside the dining room, or out the sliding glass doors to the courtyard. The culture of Interior was to eat alone. Only the college interns ate together and talked at lunch.

The courtyard was pleasant. Jon guessed that it was about 150 feet long by 80 feet wide, bookended by two statues: at one end, a Black woman with a child holding onto her skirt, at the other, a young Abraham Lincoln holding an ax.

His routine did not make things easier. He wasn't sure what the next steps for the investigation should be. His home life was almost nonexistent: he arrived, he stared at a portable TV, he drank an occasional beer, and he slept on his air mattress. He would eventually have to confront Craig again if he was to move forward, but he was delaying that for as long as possible. As long as he didn't hear a no, he could assume that the answer might be yes.

▲　▲　▲

Craig rocked back in his chair and locked his fingers together behind his head, propping his foot against the credenza. A smidgen of the mid-morning autumn DC fog lingered over the reflecting pool he could see from his office. He had a dilemma. He knew he'd have to deal with Jon eventually, but a well-connected political appointee was eyeing his budget. The implied threat was clear: if anything went wrong, the money would be yanked. If that happened, his ambition to expand his department would not be the only thing affected. Jon was on a two-year probationary period, and none of the protections for seasoned federal employees were available to him. Craig would simply have to let him go. That argued for a cautious, don't-rock-the-boat approach to the investigation.

On the other hand, his office would eventually have to show some progress on this investigation. They could just take the company's word for the cause and write up a report, but what value would his office be adding then? The appropriation was for conducting investigations, after all. Taking a company press release and fluffing it into a report was not investigating.

And Craig knew he was leaving Jon hanging. It wasn't fair to put him in a position where he couldn't succeed and then penalize him for not succeeding. Jon had made a reasonable request and was now responsible for his own destiny. If he did too little, or too much, he was out. Hell, he might still be out if he did just the right amount.

Craig watched ducks flying into and out of the pool across Constitution Avenue. He tapped his pen against his chin and decided to chat with a confidant in the Office of the General Counsel.

▲   ▲   ▲

It had been a week and a half since the explosion, and the Coleman house had been turned upside down. The family still ate dinner together, but no one spoke. The chair where James used to sit now sat empty. Kawana had always kept a clean house, but now dishes piled up in the sink, dirt collected on the tile floor, and mounds of mail lay unopened on the couch. They'd had two visits from their pastor, both ending in wailing sessions.

The papers had completely dropped the story. Only a day after the incident, the headlines were all about some White woman in the State House caught up in a sex scandal. A sex scandal. Men had lost their lives, including her baby, and the papers only talked about dirty emails!

One night, Darnell walked into James's bedroom and found Kawana on her knees on the floor cradling a blanket, tears rolling down her face. When she looked up and saw Darnell, she cried out, "They took my baby!" Darnell got down on one knee and held her head to his chest.

That night, Kawana opened the Bible to a random spot, hoping to find some comfort there. She started reading the story of Abraham taking his son Isaac up the mountain, and God telling Abraham to sacrifice Isaac. She remembered how it ended: the angel held Abraham's hand, so he could not bring the knife down to Isaac's throat. Abraham was rewarded for his faith, for his willingness to sacrifice his child, the one promised to him and his barren wife.

Kawana closed the Bible and held it to her cheek. Of all the passages, she had to open it to this one. Abraham's child was saved. Hers was not. Clutching the Bible in both hands, she bowed her head.

24

Craig always had mixed feelings walking into the Office of the General Counsel wing at Interior. The attorneys' doors were always closed. On the bookcases, volumes bound in matching black, gold, and beige leaned against each other beside carefully placed golf and maritime statues and memorabilia. Mahogany panels lined the walls. The administrative assistants dressed up every day, even casual Fridays, and they always sounded like they were in a job interview. And they always said the lawyers were in a meeting.

Once Craig had finally convinced the gatekeeper assistant that he was expected, he walked through the wing and tapped lightly on a door with a brass nameplate that read "Chris Kollar." He knew he could not put off this conversation any longer.

A few minutes passed before Chris opened the door. Craig liked Chris and overlooked the lawyerly bullshit, such as making him wait even when he had an appointment. To Craig, Chris came across more like an aged, stuffy frat boy with his perfect black mane, navy suit that stayed buttoned, and condescending "you should be glad I'm even talking to you" tone when they were around others. At least Chris always dropped it when they were alone.

"How's it going?" Chris asked.

"Going well. How's everything with you?"

"Fine, always busy. Got a couple of strange cases with a park out west. Seems this Indian tribe is claiming that a hundred acres of our land is their land, and has an ancient burial ground. We have no record of that, and the guys at EPA don't want us to dig up the place to find out. We're in a bind. Piss off the Indians or piss off the enviros, what are you gonna do?"

Craig nodded politely. "What *are* you going to do?"

"Nobody knows. We want friends on both sides. The Bureau of Indian Affairs is adamant that we have to give it to the Indians, while the Bureau of Land Management says it's a national park that has been protected from . . . uh, how do they say it . . ." He leaned over and looked at a paper on his desk. "Oh yes, 'any molestation which could lead to or reasonably lead to development that could impact the natural habitat of the area.' Doesn't that make it easy?"

"Well, if they want to honor their dead . . ."

"That's the damnedest part. They want to put a casino there, call it Sacred Hearts Casino, make the burial ground into a courtyard. Can you believe it? And if we give it to them, they can do anything they want with it, by law."

"Wow, that's tough," Craig said, trying to sound sympathetic.

Chris rocked back in his navy-blue executive chair. "Well, there's an old judge hearing the case. My guess is he'll sit on it and shit around until he retires and leaves it for his replacement, maybe in a year or so. What about you? How's that new office working out? Congrats on that, by the way. It's tough in this budget climate to get new staff."

Craig drew in a long breath. His eye floated to the displays behind

Chris. On his credenza were photos of Chris with Tiger Woods, and large bronze golf and sailing trophies. On the wall were photos with the last three presidents, and handwritten thank-you cards in frames.

"We're doing our first investigation, a chemical plant in West Virginia. Actually, that's what I wanted to talk to you about." Craig clutched the arms of the guest chair gently while Chris leaned forward and rested his elbows on the desk. "The company's not playing nice. My investigator says the office they gave him is more like a closet. He has to ask them every time he goes out, even to the bathroom. They won't let him do any interviews, and apparently they're in no hurry to take the damaged equipment out so it can be examined. We're stuck taking their word for what happened."

"Sounds like they're getting legal advice. Stalling us until the situation goes away. Either that, or they're just assholes. How do they justify holding him hostage in the office?"

"They say it's an ongoing emergency and they have to protect visitors. But the explosion happened at the back of the plant—Jon's office is in the front, in the admin building."

Chris nodded. "So what do you want to do?"

Craig's eyes drifted toward the bookcase and then back to Chris. "I want my guy to be able to do interviews and see the equipment. We need to know how far our authority goes. I thought about having my guy make the written request, but we don't want to huff and puff if we can't blow their house down."

"Well, huffing and puffing can be a good strategy, but if they call it and we have to back down, it puts us in worse shape than when we started. We need to get that sorted out. If they're getting good legal advice, they'll keep stalling. But even if we have the authority to do something, it can still get sticky enforcing it. We may have to go to a local judge. Where is it?"

"Charleston, West Virginia."

Chris raised his eyebrows. "Well, that's not great, but it's not the worst. In my experience, there's more corruption in New England." He pursed his lips and then continued. "Getting off the legal stuff for a minute, what else is going on? Any political dynamics that might work against us?"

Craig exhaled. "Yes, unfortunately—on two fronts."

Chris cocked his head slightly.

"Jon said they had a big press conference, and there was some bigwig from the state senate, Mills . . . Mouse . . . no, Mounts—that's it. This Mounts showed up for the press and had a love-in with the company. Really deflated my guy."

"I bet it would. Hmm, Mounts from West Virginia. Think I've heard that name before."

Craig picked up a pen from the desk and started tapping it against his leg. "I looked him up. Apparently, he's the most important guy in the state. Even the governor listens to him."

"Well, that doesn't make it easier." Chris smiled faintly. "But then we'll just have to make sure we're airtight on our authority. What's the other front?"

"That one is internal to us. Seems like the new DAS has his eyes on the budget for my new office. Wants to take it for some PR campaign, so he may be looking for an excuse to shut down the office if things don't go smoothly."

"The new DAS?" Chris's smile vanished. "That guy's a piece of work. My boss says we'll have to hire another lawyer just for him. He has all these plans, and he's very connected. Goes sailing down the Chesapeake Bay with the chairman of the Ways and Means Committee."

Craig dropped his head. "You see where I'm at. Talk about your rock and a hard place. If we do too little, he can say we're not needed. If we do too much, we could cause a storm and the politicos could come down on us. No good option—kinda like your Indian burial ground."

Chris nodded. He opened a folder on his desk and started making notes on a yellow pad inside. "I tell you what, Craig. We still need to answer the question about the extent of our authority. You may decide not to push, but if you do, you need to know how far you can really go. You want to know, first, can we make them give us interviews, right?"

"Yes. My guy didn't make any formal requests when he was there, but sounds like all his interactions with employees were tightly controlled. Not even the operators would talk to him."

"How long after the accident did he get there?" Chris asked, scribbling.

"A few hours."

"Then they're definitely getting legal advice or following a playbook. The guys may have been in some shock, but most people like to talk after something like that happens. Let's see . . . you also want to know if we can examine the equipment. Take it down, test it, something like that?"

"Yes, that would be best. To be honest, I'm puzzled why they don't want to do it themselves. They think it was their contract maintenance group that screwed up. Seems like they'd want to prove it and charge that company for damages."

"Okay, I'll see if we can make them take it out so we can test it. Anything else?"

"We want some documents."

"Documents—got it. But we need to make sure there's a specific need for the investigation. We don't want to be seen as arbitrary and capricious. We may not be able to defend ourselves in court if we go too broad and they challenge it. I got tangled up in a document request case early in my career. Never want to do that again."

"I understand," Craig said.

"All right—interviews, testing equipment, docs. Anything else?"

"I would like for Jon to be able to go to the bathroom by himself."

Chris put his pencil down. "Ah, the human equation. That may be even thornier than the rest. I'm sure I won't find that specifically mentioned in the office's authority. I mean, it is their plant, and we'd have to make the case that it's impeding our investigation. But I'll see if I can find some precedent in statutes or the law about unnecessarily restricting mobility."

"Thank you."

"No problem. Give me a few days—I'll work it between the tasks on this casino burial ground thing."

Craig got up to leave, but Chris held up a hand to stop him, clearing his throat. "Craig, as a friend—besides the legal stuff, be careful. These companies that have political connections. . . . It can get messy. I know you want to support your guy, but you have to think of yourself. And the new DAS sounds dangerous. Rumor is, at his last job, he took no prisoners. If you tell him no, it's a risk, and a big one. Make sure it's worth taking. At some point, you might have to ask yourself the hard questions—is it worth it, or is it better to sacrifice your guy?"

"I understand," Craig said. Walking down the OGC wing corridor, he heard himself say aloud what he said to Chris seconds ago—"no good option."

25

Jon slipped a potato chip into his mouth. He'd just returned from his afternoon walk through the corridors to the vending machine and the courtyard downstairs and back. He checked the Charleston newspapers online and surfed the local television stations, but there was no mention of Chemtrifuge or the accident.

It had been a couple of days since he'd given Craig the list of the things he wanted for the investigation, but he decided not to pester his boss yet again. Craig had said to come to him about any concerns, but Jon was hesitant. He'd had problems early in his career in telling whether managers really meant it when they said that.

A crusty old engineer named Ermine had given Jon the best advice he'd ever received on dealing with managers. One day, when they were riding through a refinery's units in a golf cart, Jon told Ermine about a meeting that morning that hadn't gone well. Ermine had turned off the key, depressed the brake, and told Jon how things really worked.

"Understand the difference between what management tells you and what they mean. Throw out that crap about them wanting you to voice your opinions. They don't. They only want you to speak up when you agree with them."

Jon had tried to follow this advice, but it didn't seem to work for him. He still had problems understanding the difference between what managers said and what they meant. Maybe some people were just meant to fail.

Finally, he decided to take an indirect approach. He wasn't sure how to get information from the company, but maybe he could get information from others. Two groups came to mind. First was the union. They normally wanted to get to the truth after an accident, yet Jon hadn't sensed any interest from the operators he'd encountered. Hopefully, he could interview them later.

The other possibility was the environmentalists. Being part of industry, he'd had mixed experiences with these groups. They sometimes seemed inconsistent, like the protestors outside paper mills holding up paper signs or continuing to use all the convenient products from chemical companies they denounced. However, he knew they kept needed pressure on chemical manufacturers. He recalled the TV cameraman mentioning an environmentalist next door to the plant.

He couldn't remember the cameraman and reporter's names or even the station call letters, so he logged on. It wouldn't be hard to recognize the dazzling reporter with olive skin and dark hair—she'd stand out in the sea of blond pasties at the press conference. But he had to watch snippets of thirty or so clips from various stations before he found her. The clip was about buying puppies versus adopting older dogs from shelters, which made him wonder why she'd been tapped for the explosion. The station must not have felt it was important enough to warrant a serious investigative reporter. In the clip, she discussed which dogs shed most and how to treat one from an abusive household. Jon couldn't help reflecting on how much time she was able to give the dog story, when she'd so quickly dropped an accident where men had died to cover a state-level political scandal. Finally, her name popped up: Lisa Rogers. He decided to find out if the station had any more information about the environmentalist the cameraman had mentioned.

After wading through six screens, he found a telephone number and staff email addresses for the station. He decided to call rather than send an email.

The woman who answered sounded friendly. "Hello, may I help you?"

"Could I speak with Lisa, please?" He hoped that using her first name would imply a personal relationship.

"Lisa who?"

"Lisa Rogers, the reporter."

"May I ask what this is about?"

Jon cleared his throat. "I'm working with her on a story, and I'm following up." This was partially true.

A few seconds passed. Finally the woman said, "Hold, please."

After four rings, a recorded voice came on the line. "This is Lisa Rogers. I'm sorry I can't take—"

Jon hung up, not sure what to say. Then he remembered the cameraman.

"Hello, may I help you?" Same woman, same tone.

"Yes, this is . . . uh, I called for Lisa, but I was wondering if you could put me through to her cameraman."

"I believe she usually works with Kenny. Hold on."

Jon scratched the name Kenny on his notepad, and the word *camera* beside it as he waited. He immediately recognized the voice that came on the answering machine. This time he left a message. "Hello, Kenny, this is Jon, the investigator on the Chemtrifuge explosion. Had a quick question, just need a minute of your time. Please call me when you get the chance." Jon left his number and thanked Kenny for his time.

He was trying. If this didn't work out, and the lawyers shut him down, it was over. He shoved away that thought, and made an unscheduled second trip to the vending machines.

26

Charlie looked around the waiting room lobby at the CAMC Cancer Center. The old blue padded chairs with wooden arms were as uncomfortable as they looked. Magazines with corners flipped over were strewn across the tables. One of the men on the cover of the golf magazine lying on the chair next to him reminded him a little of Jon, the investigator. Like Jon, the golfer looked to be in his mid-forties, had a pleasant face that you had to look at closely to see wrinkles forming, and brown hair, though he had caught a couple of gray hairs peeking through on Jon's temples. But there was one big difference. This golfer was confident, raising his fist in victory, apparently following a putt. Jon had an uncertain, almost lost look on his face, especially when Charlie had pushed back and belittled him. Charlie wondered what Jon's life was like at home. Maybe he had a wife that he loved, like Charlie did.

Charlie started thinking about how rude he'd been to Jon. He was playing along with the company's plan, but being the bad cop was starting to make him feel uncomfortable. He wasn't even sure why he, as the HR manager, was wrapped up in this investigation at all.

The receptionist behind the open window glanced at him, expressionless, and then looked back at her screen as a heavyset nurse walked up to his seat. "Sir, her tests are completed. We have the results. Please come with me."

Charlie Branch put down the magazine he was pretending to read. He had not absorbed a single word.

His wife was already sitting on a plastic chair in the small side room. She had changed out of her gown, but still had a hairnet on.

"Do you have to keep that on?" Charlie asked, hoping his smile looked natural.

"What?" she said distantly. There was a look on her face he'd only seen one other time, at her mother's funeral in Ohio eight years ago.

He reached out and pulled the hairnet off.

"Oh," she said finally, smiling. "Guess my mind was somewhere else."

The tall, curly dark-haired doctor walked in with his lab coat unbuttoned and a thermometer in his pocket. The nurse took a seat in the corner behind them. The doctor glanced at them both, exhaled, and wrinkled his forehead.

"I have the confirmatory results from your previous visit. I'm afraid they're consistent with what we found earlier. You have ovarian cancer at an advanced stage."

Charlie moved to the examination table and sat beside his wife, and she put her head on his shoulder and gently took his hand. His other hand went across her shoulder, pulling her closer. The diagnosis wasn't a surprise, but he'd somehow convinced himself he would hear something else.

"What—uh, what are our options?" he asked.

"Well, we have to start chemo right away. I have to be honest—there are no guarantees at this stage, but it's a chance." The doctor exhaled again, and licked his lips. "You might want to get your affairs in order. The good news—" The doctor seemed to catch himself, as if he knew there was no good news. "The thing is, at least you have great insurance, the best in town. It will pay for everything that needs to be done. You'll be able to keep that throughout the treatments, right?"

A distant roar filled Charlie's ears. He looked at the wall behind the doctor, at the degree from Johns Hopkins University, the framed certifications, and a photo of him in a blue-and-black-striped shirt, standing on a sailboat.

The doctor cleared his throat. "You'll be able to keep that insurance for the foreseeable future, right? We should get that figured out before we start treatment."

Charlie looked at the top of his wife's head. She had not moved since getting the news. He glanced back at the nurse behind him, who forced a nervous smile. He looked at the fake fern in the corner, and up at the ceiling with stained tiles. It was true: Chemtrifuge had one of the best insurance plans in town. Charlie knew it. He'd had a hand in negotiating for the package. The plant pinched pennies elsewhere, but not with insurance. However, there was a price. They expected extreme loyalty.

"I know what to do to keep it," he said finally. "Yes, we'll keep it."

"Good. We'll start treatment next week. Here, call this number to get everything set up." The doctor scribbled a number on his notepad.

"Thank you," Charlie's wife said, not raising her head from Charlie's shoulder.

Charlie walked silently to his car with his wife of thirty-six years, the words running through his head like a mantra.

I know what to do to keep it. We will keep it.

27

Every morning, Jon searched the Charleston newspapers online, but he could find nothing about the accident. He trawled through online databases for previous accidents in similar chemical plants, but too little information was given to help draw meaningful comparisons to the Chemtrifuge accident.

Outside the office, he learned the patterns of life in the nation's capital. Once a week, a Peruvian flute band played outside the Metro station close to the Interior building, wearing coarse ponchos. They sold CDs and collected tips in an upside-down derby that sat on a folding chair. Protesters held up signs at various street corners, denigrating the administration of the day.

Jon learned that most people in DC were intelligent and insightful. They had interesting-sounding titles, though few could really explain what they did. Most were not from DC, and most had come to DC to change the world. If you didn't fit into their plans, they had no time for you. Every meeting was a screening, and people were always in job-interview mode. Jon wasn't a mover, shaker, leader, follower, or interested party, so new acquaintances quickly moved on.

One afternoon, he'd returned from his vending-machine run and saw that his message light was on. He took a bite of a chip as he listened. Craig was asking to see him. Jon looked at his office mate, hunched over at his desk with his back to him.

"I have a meeting," Jon said, more out of surprise than to get any sort of reaction. His office mate just grunted.

28

Just as he was about to step out for lunch, Craig received a call from Chris Kollar, the agency lawyer.

"Yo, Craig—how's it going?" Chris asked.

"Fine. How are things in your world?"

"Crazy, crazy. One of the members of an Indian tribe came up to the secretary and asked for his autograph. And guess what, the secretary signed it. He's not the brightest we've had. Oops, you didn't hear me say that."

Craig understood. Chris liked to leave the impression that he was in such high esteem that he could insult the secretary of the interior.

"Anyway," Chris was saying, "guess what was on that paper. It was a deed to land adjacent to the reservation, drawn up by a lawyer and everything. I guess he folded it when he showed it to the secretary. Now we got this legal document that gives the tribe millions of acres of land. This is a real mess."

"That sounds bad," Craig said. "What happens now?"

"Oh, we're going to fight it, on the basis that he signed it not knowing what it was." Chris lowered his voice for effect. "I might even argue that even if the idiot read it, he still wouldn't know what it was." He paused. "Oops, you didn't hear me say that either."

"Do you think it will work?"

"Eventually. But it's going to tie up all kinds of time to make that case, and we still have to argue that the standing is in federal court, not on tribal lands. That could get sticky." Chris cleared his throat. "Anyway, that's not what I'm calling about. I looked over that legislation for the investigative powers that you asked me about. To be honest, it's a little vague, which is kind of both good news and bad news. Good news is, I think we can ask for the documents you wanted and for interviews with employees."

"And the bad news?"

"Well, it's kind of in a gray area, how we would enforce it. If they push back, we'd have to go to the Department of Justice, and that takes time. We don't have our own enforcement group here at Interior."

Craig's chair squeaked as he leaned toward the window. "So how do we make them play ball with us?"

"Well, an old trick in the legal world is to act like you have the authority until someone tells you that you don't. It depends on how aggressive your investigator is."

"Let me get this straight," Craig said. "We probably have the authority, but we have to act like we know we do. But if they call our bluff, then we have to go to Justice, and that could take years."

Chris hesitated. "It could take a long time. They might have the plant torn down and moved to India by then."

Craig rocked back in his chair to another squeak. Either Jon pushed the company and bluffed them or the investigation was over. He started massaging his temples with his free hand. "Chris, if push comes to shove, do you guys have our back? I mean, if the company refuses to give us the documents and interviews, will GC back us up?"

"Craig, we can only go as far as we know that we'll succeed," Chris said, his voice somber now. "We got burned badly a few years ago when we defended a decision by the Office of International Affairs. I won't bore you with the details, but our GC at the time was good friends with the chairman of the House Budget Committee, and he still bit the dust. We can ask for the documents, and we can ask for the interviews. I found a case at the Department of Labor where people were compelled to testify in an investigation back in the eighties. That was sort of an ad hoc office created out of an earmark, like yours. But that may be all we have to hang our hat on."

"Okay, thanks, Chris. One more thing. Who signs the request? Can GC at least do that?"

"I asked that question, and I got a no. The request will have to come from your investigator." Chris paused. "Have your investigator push them. What does he have to lose?"

After he hung up with the lawyer, Craig left Jon a message to come to his office. He licked a cracker to get a salty taste and then slipped it into his mouth. Chewing slowly, he reflected on the conversation he'd just had with Chris and the earlier one in which Chris had suggested he might have to sacrifice Jon to save his own hide and give the money to the DAS. This agency was hanging Jon out to dry. They'd set him up to fail and then blame him for failing. That's the way the game was played in DC. Craig didn't like it, but he couldn't deny that he was part of it.

He thought about Chris's last question.

What does he have to lose?

"Everything," Craig said out loud.

▲ ▲ ▲

Jon entered Craig's office and saw his balding crown over the back of his chair.

"Pretty view, isn't it?" Craig said, without turning around.

Jon cleared his throat. "Very nice."

"When I started my career, I never thought I'd end it with a view like this. You never know where the twists and turns will lead you."

Jon wasn't sure how to react. Was he getting fired? "Yes, careers go like that sometimes," he said cautiously.

Craig spun his chair around slowly and motioned to his guest chair.

Jon sat down and looked around the office. Ten bottles of wine from Northern Virginia sat on the credenza, all neatly arranged. The bottle with a unicorn on the label caught his eye. Craig had told Jon during his interview that he had been a lifelong beer drinker, but about ten years ago he'd gotten into wines. Wines, he explained, engage all the senses, from the pop of the cork to the feel of the glass to the bouquet in the nose, and finally the swirl and taste on the tongue. He told Jon that exploring northern Virginia wines was his way of becoming a wine drinker without becoming a wine snob. Elites in DC prided themselves on ignoring Virginia wines, but Craig enjoyed hitting three or four NoVA vineyards on a Saturday afternoon.

"Jon, this case is kind of sticky," Craig said, breaking into Jon's thoughts. "These chemical operators are tough customers."

Jon started shaking his leg nervously up and down, anchored by the toe. "Yes, I've been in that field all my career," he said and then wondered if he sounded condescending.

Craig looked at his wine collection. "Yes, you know that better than anyone."

After a few seconds, he continued. "I know you need to get some info to figure out what happened. The lawyers think we can ask for it. There's no case history for us. Even OSHA and others still have their requests adjudicated in court sometimes, but at least our lawyers support us asking for it."

Jon felt a tinge of optimism in his boss's words. "Thanks, Craig, I appreciate that." He scratched his lip. "What do they mean by 'supporting us asking'? Will they back us up if the company doesn't deliver?"

Craig nodded slightly without changing his expression. "Good question. They really didn't elaborate. The land management stuff, they know all that, but not this chemical plant stuff. It's something we're going to have to figure out."

Jon looked at the bottle of wine with the unicorn. "You mentioned OSHA. Are they or any other agency investigating this? Maybe they can make the request, and we can piggyback on theirs?"

Craig half smiled. "I looked into that. Apparently everyone else is passing on this one. It's just you—I mean . . . us."

Jon nodded. "I'll type up the request. What is the full name of the general counsel?"

Craig rocked forward in his chair and folded his arms. "Jon, we need to be careful. This is all new for us. We need to be politically astute."

Jon was confused, but he didn't push the matter. "Okay, I'll work on the draft." He got up to leave.

"Uh, one more thing. The lawyers want the request to go out under someone else's signature. They don't want the GC to get involved at this point."

"Understood. I'll make that note. Who'll be signing it? A different attorney?"

Craig looked back at his wine collection. "No. You."

The phone rang, and Craig glanced at the number. "I need to take this."

Jon nodded a goodbye and left.

The exchange haunted him all the way back to his office. This strategy was a statement. The general counsel didn't want to get involved, and even Craig wouldn't sign the letter. Were they just letting him hang himself? He had thought that if they let him send the request, he'd be content. Now, he wondered if he should have even asked.

29

"What the hell is this?" Sam yelled as Charlie walked into his office. Sam held up the letter that had just come in and then slapped it down on his desk. "A request for documents, interviews, and a damn proposed testing protocol for the equipment?"

Charlie sniffed. "I had a message this morning. He said to expect it."

Sam, fighting his urge to choke Charlie, flung the letter across the desk. "I thought you were taking care of this. I told you to make it go away. This request is on government letterhead, for Chrissakes."

Charlie took off his glasses and wiped his forehead with the back of his hand. "I called the trade association to see if he can do this. Their initial take is that he probably can. There's vague language in the earmark about 'necessary measures to obtain information.'"

Sam exhaled. "I told you to take care of it," he said, enunciating each word.

Charlie looked at his feet. A short silence fell, broken by a loud *clunk* in the hallway.

"What the hell?" Sam barked.

Charlie got up and grabbed the office door frame and swung his head outside. He pivoted his head back into the office and lowered his voice. "It's just the janitor. Looks like his mop fell against the bucket."

"Sorry, sir," they both heard a voice in the hallway say.

Charlie kept his hand on the door frame. "The guy's mopping up something. You want him to go away?"

Sam took off his glasses and rubbed his eyes. "No, that dumbshit Plasco spilled coffee in the hallway."

Riiiiiiing!

"Shit!" Sam jumped and then hit the speakerphone button. "What?" he snapped, seeing his assistant's number.

"Sam, what's this I hear about a letter?"

Sam sat up. The voice was Wheelan Drew's, and the Chemtrifuge CEO sounded unhappy.

"Just got a call from the executive director of the association. Seems you boys are losing control down there. Do I need to call in the DC guns? They cost a pretty penny, but at least I can count on them."

"I'm sorry, sir—I just saw the letter myself." Sam shot Charlie a look as if to say, *Your call to the trade association just brought me more headaches.* "Charlie called the association to see if they have authority to make this request. We're waiting to hear back."

"You're waiting? So now you're a bunch of damn waiters down there? It was a little accident, and now we have this stupid request. What are you doing in the meantime?"

Sam offered a white lie. "Charlie's looking at the legislation now, and we're figuring out how to answer."

Drew exhaled on the other end. "Well, don't figure too long. You're supposed to anticipate things like this. If you can't take care of little problems and I have to get involved, I don't need you." He emphasized the last phrase.

"I understand, sir. We'll take care of it."

"I pay good money to keep politicians and the media on our side. Can't you figure out how to use them?"

Sam shook his head. Charlie looked away.

"Yes, sir. We had a good press conference the day it happened. We controlled the information, everything went our way."

"Well, it doesn't seem to be going your way now. Take care of this! I don't want to call down there again."

"Yes, sir, we'll take care of it."

"Hold on a second," said Drew, and there was a chime on the line.

"Sir, I have both Mr. Quinn and Mr. Leska on the line," Drew's personal assistant said.

"Great. You guys on?"

"I'm here," said two gruff voices simultaneously.

"Did Betty brief you on what we know so far?"

"Yes," one of the voices said.

Sam Page rolled his eyes and mouthed "Oh, God." Now he was on the phone with the CEO; Andrew Leska, the high-dollar lawyer from DC; and Cain Quinn, the most powerful person in the company—even more than Wheelan Drew.

Drew spoke. "Welcome, gentlemen. I was just telling Sam they need to do better."

"I'll keep on top of this, Wheelan," said Leska.

"Cain, did Betty brief you on everything?"

Quinn cleared his throat and in a deep voice replied, "I've been briefed."

"Like I said on the night it happened, we're really sorry for all this," Sam tried to sound as sympathetic as he could. "We are really sorry that—"

"What's done is done," Quinn cut him off. "The most important thing now is to get this under control and protect the company, no matter what it takes. You hear me? Make this go away—fast."

"Well put," said Drew.

"Got it, sir." Sam hung up.

Charlie tapped the desk nervously with his fingers. "Do you think Mr. Quinn is pissed?"

"Wouldn't you be?" Sam answered without thinking.

Charlie kept tapping. "What should we do?"

"Check with CeMaC again about that scope of authority. Then figure out how to make this government puke go away. We don't want to play ball, but this damn letter kicks it up a notch. Drew is talking about bringing in the DC lawyers they have on retainer. If they come in, we've lost all control."

30

Jackie had known a lot of grief in his life. He learned you never forget someone's last words. Hearing them calmly spoken from a bed brings sadness but also a sense of peace. But when those last words are screams, they seep deeper into your memory.

Every hour since he was kicked out of the plant the night of the accident, Jackie had relived the sound of those screams over the plant radio. He sat at his kitchen table, but he could hardly eat a bite. He only slept in segments, until once more the sound of burning men washed into his bedroom, like a deluge of blood spilling out a slaughterhouse door. He didn't know what else to do, but he couldn't live like this. He'd tried to do the right thing, and he'd been punished. They had no more work for him, the security agency had told him. He could pick up his check for the portion of the evening he had worked. He needed the money, but he couldn't bring himself to go back to the agency for the check.

Jackie had not died like the men on the platform. But he had stopped living, just the same.

31

Jon had to talk to someone. He loved his father, but recently it seemed like every time Jon tried to discuss problems, his dad just said the problems would get better. He lived in a small world.

Jon had acquaintances. He'd met many engineers at the refineries, but most were only passing through. Eventually they all moved and fell out of touch. He still talked occasionally to one friend from the refinery in Cheyenne, an older engineer full of wisdom but empty of political savvy. But that man had moved to the Philippines years before to chase young women, and now they rarely spoke. Everyone had fallen out of touch, including his ex-wife, Tammy.

Jon dug through his backpack: a copy of the first check he'd ever received, a picture of his mother, tickets to a rodeo, and other papers that meant nothing to anyone except himself. Then he found it, the last letter from Tammy. She'd seen Jon's dad at the grocery store when she was home, and she'd written. She'd heard Jon was going through a tough time and hoped he was okay. Tammy was a caring person. Jon felt that way even through their divorce. But he knew the letter was not an attempt to get back together. She'd closed by saying that if he ever needed to talk, he should call. He'd thought about replying, but as time passed, that seemed more awkward, so he didn't. Until now.

He nervously dialed the numbers on the letter, afraid a man might answer. After the fourth ring, he started moving the phone from his ear. Then he heard that voice.

"Hello."

"Hello, Tammy?"

"Yes. Jon?"

"Yeah, I'm surprised you remember." He forced a small laugh.

She forced a laugh too. "It's been a while, but I remember. Uh, how are you?"

He cleared his throat. "Doing okay. I live just outside Washington, DC, now. People call it DC here. How are you?"

"Fine. I still live outside Lincoln. My daughter's almost nine. She's a handful."

"Yes, I got your letter. I'm so happy that worked out. Sorry I never wrote back—I was going through a lot at the time."

"It's okay. I just wanted to let you know how I was doing, and let you know about Kim. I didn't really expect you to write back."

They made small talk about mutual acquaintances. She had run into the wife of one of his engineering colleagues last year at a mall. They'd traded emails and promised to stay in touch.

"Jon, you sound preoccupied," she said after a few minutes. "Is everything all right?"

"I've got a job with the government now. I'm doing an investigation at a chemical plant in West Virginia. I've been through a rough patch, but I thought this might get me back on track. But Tammy, I feel like I'm alone.

Nobody in the agency supports me. I don't even know if it's worth it anymore. I mean, who really cares about what happened? It's not going to bring anybody back. I think I'm the only one who cares about this, and I don't even know if I do any more. The local press has zero interest. My boss speaks in code at work. If I had somewhere else to go, I would."

There, he'd said it. He'd been trying so hard not to allow himself to believe it until now. Everything had gone wrong since he moved to DC, from his cold, damp, lifeless apartment in Springfield to his nice but unconcerned boss to his rude office mate. Everything screamed at him that he'd made a mistake. He was all alone in an unstable job, working for people who didn't care.

Tammy waited a few seconds. "How bad was the accident?"

"Yeah." Jon sighed. "It was bad. Some guys got killed."

"Well, maybe they care—or I mean their families, friends, somebody. Maybe there's someone out there who wants to know what happened. You could investigate for them."

Jon raised his head. That was true. He could not bring the men back, but he could try to let their families know what had happened. There was a truth out there about what happened, and it was more likely to come from someone outside the company, at least with a company like this one.

"You know, Jon," Tammy said, "sometimes you just have to do what you think is right, even when nobody else seems to care. I remember you telling me about that time your grandfather walked out of a meeting with the local farmers' association because he thought they were fixing prices and not looking out for the local farmers. Nobody else walked out with him, but he was always proud he did it."

Jon remembered that well. He had heard the story many times while sitting on his grandfather's lap on his tractor, holding the steering wheel. His grandfather had never regretted walking out of that meeting, even though he had offended powerful men on the association board. Jon overheard people in the grocery store talking about his grandfather being a hothead, but he'd just act like he didn't hear them.

"Jon, I think he'd be proud of you for carrying on."

Jon wiped a tear from the corner of his eye. "Thanks, Tammy, you always knew what to say. I feel better."

"Good. Take care of those people in Washington—or, uh, should I say, DC. They're not like the rest of us."

Jon laughed, for real. "No, they're not. It seems to be all about power here. I'll hang in there." He hesitated. "Tammy . . . can I call again if I need to?"

She was silent for a moment, and during that silence, Jon considered telling her more. There were things about the refinery accident that still hung like a dark cloud over him.

"You can call if you need to," Tammy told him. "I don't mind being an occasional therapist, as long as it doesn't become full-time."

"Point taken." Jon forced another laugh. "I won't abuse it."

"Take care of yourself."

"You too, and congrats on the kid. She has a great mom."

"Thanks, goodbye."

That was it. His problems were still there, but he could keep going for the victims, for the truth. And to make his grandfather proud. Also, he had no other option, besides despair.

32

As Jon drove down I-81, he passed beautiful red barns and signs for wineries throughout northern Virginia. The highway threaded between rolling hills, past exits to small towns that sprinkled the landscape—towns where people just like the ones in Jon's hometown lived. The scenery was so different from the chaos playing out in Jon's mind.

It had been three weeks since the explosion. He'd heard nothing since sending his letter, but his boss had said to keep working with the site. Jon knew a call wouldn't get him anywhere, and besides, a trip to the plant removed the potential excuse that he was not on-site to receive the requested documents.

He was headed back to Charleston, on his own, to a place where they hated him. He was disrupting their world. Three guys lay in graves, and all the local press could do was obsess about some illicit romance and racy emails between politicians. It was as if the accident had never happened. Three men gone, and Jon seemed to be the only one who cared.

33

"So that government guy's showing up this week?" Sam grumbled. "Great, that's all we need." Charlie watched as Sam poured two more fingers of bourbon into his glass. "I'll have corporate jumping down my ass again."

Charlie rocked uneasily, watching Sam set the bottle down. "The guys at CeMaC got back to me. They advise that we get him out of here as soon as possible. Best case, he'll accept our version and move on."

"Well, hopefully we can do that. Alphonse is on board, and he'll keep his union guys in line. I want this finished, Charlie."

"I'm doing what I can," Charlie snapped—he was finding it difficult to keep his cool, and his tone was sharper than usual. Sam didn't seem to notice. "I'll keep him contained."

Sam took another sip and swirled his glass, clinking ice. "Just keep me away from it. Right now I'm trying to calm corporate and Wheelan down. I don't like this talk about sending in the DC lawyers."

"Me neither."

Sam started tapping his glass on the desk. "Alphonse has his story straight, so I don't think this investigator will get anything from interviews. We also need to make sure he doesn't do any equipment testing or get anything out of the documents. There are things we really don't want him to see. Why don't you collect the original process documents, maybe lock them up in your office?"

"Good idea—I'll do that today."

There was a light tap on the doorframe. "Need me to collect your trash today, sir?"

Sam reached under his desk without replying, and the janitor stepped in and took his trash can. "Any recycle today, sir?"

Sam shook his head. "It's all in there." He turned to Charlie. "Stupid corporate initiative. Takes me longer to sort trash than just throw it away."

As the janitor walked out, Sam rocked forward and put his hands on his desk. "Charlie, I'm serious—make this thing go away. I want this guy to talk to a couple of people, get our story, go back and print that up, and then get the hell out of our hair."

Charlie stood up. "Got it, Sam, and I'll take care of those documents."

"Charlie, one more thing. I told Alphonse we'd use this as an excuse to get rid of the contractors."

"But, Sam, that's against the new cost-benefit policy. It's cheaper to hire contractors."

"I know, but I had to make sure Alphonse plays ball. Let's get through this government thing, get rid of a few contractors, and then slowly sneak them back in when Alphonse is busy with other stuff. In the meantime, if he asks you about it, tell him we're getting rid of them all."

"Consider it done," Charlie said as he left. He felt less comfortable than his words implied. He now had to take on company policy about hiring contractors, as if he didn't have enough to deal with already.

▲　▲　▲

A light rain nipped at Jon's windshield all the way to Charleston. He arrived at the Hampton Inn and checked in.

"Good afternoon, sir. Will you be staying all week?" the young, tattooed man with dirty blond hair at the front desk said, scratching his goatee.

Jon hesitated. That depended on how much the company cooperated. "I plan to stay till Friday, but will it be a problem if I check out early?"

"No, we're not busy. Just let us know before noon if you're checking out that day."

Jon grabbed a chocolate chip cookie from under the small glass dome on the counter. It was hard as he bit into it. He went to his room and lay on the bed.

That evening, he walked to the diner across the street for a burger and fries. He asked for a wakeup call at 6:30, though he knew he'd wake up long before then. Tonight would be tough, and tomorrow tougher. After that, he had no idea. Back in his room, he listened to cars passing by on the interstate until he fell into a restless sleep.

34

“Yes, we got your letter. Here’s our response.” Charlie shoved a sheet of paper into Jon’s hand.

Jon studied it for a moment and then read it out loud. “The request for drawings for ‘equipment related to the accident’ is too vague. The equipment in this facility is all interrelated. To some degree, every piece of equipment in the facility was involved or affected in some way. This request is arbitrary and capricious.” The last three words were underlined. Charlie had thought that was a good touch.

Jon frowned slightly. “There are no drawings here, none of the information we requested,” he said, emphasizing *we*.

“Well, *we* think it’s too broad,” Charlie snapped. “Thus *our* response.”

“You think requesting the drawing for the specific equipment involved is too broad?”

Charlie sniffed. Chemtrifuge’s strategy—developed earlier on a call with corporate and CeMaC—was to wear Jon down with delays, hoping the political machinery they had invested in would apply pressure and make all this go away. The last minute of the teleconference with CeMaC and corporate was still resonating in his mind.

"What if we just ignore this request?" he'd asked.

There'd been a few seconds of silence on the line. "You would be impeding a federal investigation," the CeMaC representative had told him. "That could have serious consequences for individuals and the company."

"He was the one who signed the request, nobody above him," Charlie persisted. "We don't know how much support he really has in DC."

"Correct, we don't know. That's the wild card. Is he a rogue investigator who we can intimidate, or does he have support? But regardless of who signed it, it's on government letterhead. You have to take it seriously."

Charlie had tried to convince Sam to give this liaison duty to someone else. He was tired of playing bad cop with this investigator. But Sam had insisted Charlie was the best one to do it. "We just need to keep the game up a little longer," he'd said.

Charlie shook his head slightly, returning to his real-time discussion with Jon. "Excuse me?" he said, stalling.

"Do you really think the request for the specific piece of equipment involved in the fire is too broad?" Jon sounded incredulous.

Charlie scratched nervously behind his ear. "Well, you didn't say *specific* piece of equipment."

"Okay, let's start with that one."

"What specific piece do you mean?" Charlie asked, pretending to be confused.

"We seem to be going in circles. I assume you know which piece of equipment caught fire. You know, maybe I need to call DC to see how to word this so we can get something done." Jon looked at his cell phone and started to punch in a number.

"All right, we can show you that one," Charlie said hastily. "I'll be back in a few minutes to take you to the library."

▲   ▲   ▲

"Sam, I don't like it," Charlie said as he came into Sam's office. The lawyerly worded pushback had not worked, and he was nervous. "He was calling DC. I think we need the lawyers now. I can't handle this anymore."

"Just stick to the plan we discussed," Sam said calmly.

On the earlier call, CeMaC and corporate staff had assured Charlie that everything was fine. The CeMaC rep had reviewed the request and seen a loophole. It asked for a drawing, but it didn't ask specifically for the drawing that existed at the time of the accident. They had a plan. Jon would get a drawing, but he wouldn't find anything.

"Take him to the company library and let him look," Sam said now, "but keep an eye on him."

Charlie couldn't help but think they had overlooked something. As he rounded the corner toward Jon's office, he realized that he and Jon might have the same question. How much support did Jon really have in DC? Charlie guessed that neither of them knew.

35

Charlie led Jon to the company library, a nicer room than Jon was used to seeing in chemical plants. It had dark wood paneling, with a circular desk at the front. Wooden shelves lined the walls, filled with matching books, like those Jon had seen in law offices. There were five tables, with four chairs neatly aligned around each one. The one area that was not opulent was a wall of what appeared to be World War II surplus bookcases.

Behind the desk sat a woman. Jon guessed she was in her late fifties, with dark but graying hair gathered into a bun. She wore odd glasses, with arms that connected at the bottom of the lenses. A chain was attached on each side behind the lenses to hold the glasses against her chest when she took them off, which she did often while talking to Jon.

"Kathy, this is Jon Barrett from DC," said Charlie. "He's here to investigate the accident. Please show him whatever he asks for."

Jon realized that this could either be cooperation or a trick.

Kathy stoically lowered her glasses and then took them off. "We have proprietary information here, business confidential. I need to see evidence that you have a need to know." Jon suspected she had been coached to ask for that.

She raised her glasses again and looked at his identification and then at his face. "Uh-huh. What specifically do you need to see?"

"I need to see the P&ID for the specific piece of equipment involved in the fire."

Kathy walked toward the file cabinets, Jon following. He noticed that she shot a glance at Charlie, who was standing by one of the bookcases, holding an open book.

Kathy opened the middle drawer of one of the cabinets. It was only about half full on one end, and the divider was marked "Ethylene Process."

"Are these all the P&IDs from the process?" he asked.

Kathy glanced over at Charlie, but he was still focused on the book. "It is what it says it is."

Jon started leafing through the expandable green folders in the file cabinet. Most of them were empty, but he finally came to a folder with a drawing inside. He pulled the folder from the cabinet and took it to one of the tables.

"Be careful," said Kathy curtly. "I have to keep everything filed in order."

"I understand," Jon said, but he couldn't resist adding, "It should be easy to find the place for this one. Seems like it's the only folder with anything in it."

Kathy turned abruptly and walked back to her desk.

Jon unfolded the piping and instrumentation diagram and laid it out on the circular desk closest to the cabinets. He checked the bottom right-hand corner for the specifics about the drawing and saw the following:

| Piping and Instrumentation Diagram |
| Equip: Ethylene Overhead Vessel E-101 |
| Rev and date: 00-XXXX |

It was interesting that the revision was 00, and there was no date. In Jon's experience, these drawings went through several iterations, and the date should have been on the drawing. Another thing that struck him was that this drawing looked new, but his online research showed this wasn't a new plant. It was odd that this drawing was the only one in the file.

His eyes drifted to the vessel on the drawing. It was dominated by a graphical representation of a horizontal vessel, much as he'd expected. A line came in on the left side, showing where the material flowed into the vessel. Two more lines, one going out the bottom and the other coming out the top, showed where the material was separated inside the vessel. A level indicator on the right side represented an interlock, which ensured that a valve on the bottom would automatically open to let material flow out if the level got too high. This would prevent liquid from rising so high in the vessel that it flowed into the overhead line, which was usually only meant for vapor. A high alarm, a high-high alarm, and a high-high-high alarm were shown on the drawing. Overfilling this vessel was something the designers obviously wanted to avoid, although Jon was not sure why. He was not familiar with this process. It might just be a production concern, not a safety one. He started jotting down a note.

"Don't write on the drawing," Kathy barked from behind her desk. Jon held up his notepad, and she looked back down.

Just then, Jon heard a ring. He turned to see Charlie putting his cell phone up to his ear. "He's right here," Charlie said in a hushed tone, glancing up and making eye contact with Jon. "Wait a minute." He walked out the door.

Jon realized this might be his only chance to see what else was in the file drawers away from Charlie's watchful eye. He slowly scooted his chair back, got up, and walked to the cabinet. He opened the drawer and gently put the file back, mindful that Kathy was watching. Then he turned his back toward Kathy and tried to open the drawer above that one, but it wouldn't budge. Remembering that many of these cabinets were designed to have only one drawer open at a time, he pushed the first drawer closed and then tugged at the drawer above. This time it opened. Kathy's chair squeaked, and he heard her footsteps coming in his direction. She must have heard the movement of the drawer.

"May I help you?"

Jon turned around, looking for Charlie, but he hadn't returned. "He said it was okay," Jon said.

Kathy stopped and looked toward the door for Charlie and then busied herself by picking up books on the various tables and restocking them. Jon waited a moment and then turned back to the file cabinet.

The drawer above the one with the "Ethylene Process" file was completely empty. Jon closed it, leaned down, and opened the bottom drawer. It was completely empty too. There had to be more than one drawing of equipment in this plant. There had to be hundreds, but where were they? He'd have to speak to Charlie about this, but for now, he thought the best strategy was to play nice.

"Thank you," he said, turning back to Kathy. "Do you need any help restocking books?"

Kathy looked surprised. She quickly glanced toward the door.

"Uh, no, thank you."

Just then Charlie walked in. "Are you finished?"

Jon looked at him. "For now. Doesn't seem to be much here."

"Well, we don't like clutter." Charlie glanced at his watch impatiently. "Ready to go?"

At the door to Jon's makeshift office, Charlie paused. "Anything else?"

"A couple of things. I'll need a copy of that drawing, and drawings of the equipment connected to it. That is relevant. I also want to tour the area and do interviews. I'll come up with a list of positions I want to talk to, and it would really help if you could give me names."

"We'll see what we can do," Charlie said, and left.

Jon had started making an interview list on his notepad when he heard a creak somewhere down the hallway. It sounded as if a door had just closed.

36

"I told you I don't like it," Charlie said, barging into Sam's office. "I think we missed something, or he'll find something. He wants names. He wants to start doing interviews!"

Sam tapped on the desk with his fingers. "Stop worrying, Charlie. We have this all figured out. All the guys know what to say—we've been over this. Alphonse will keep the union folks in line. Look, if he has this bug up his ass, he's not going to stop until he does interviews. CeMaC said we have to give him the names, remember? All we have to do is make sure they stick to the story. Then he goes back to DC, files some report saying we were right all along."

"I guess, but you and CeMaC aren't the ones dealing with this guy. I am. What if I say something wrong, and he catches us?"

Sam sighed. "You're starting to sound like my wife. Just stick to the plan, and we'll be fine. Besides, this guy's some two-bit bureaucrat, probably couldn't make it in the chemical industry. That's the kind of people that end up in government. We can outplay them every time."

Charlie nodded. Jon was asking questions now, but they had a plan. They had covered their tracks, right down to the drawings. The employees were going to toe the company line—nobody wanted to make waves. And if all else failed, Charlie knew Chemtrifuge could call in political favors, maybe even get this bureaucrat fired. He felt relieved as he walked back to his office to collect the newly created organizational chart, the list of eyewitnesses, and a copy of the recently revised drawing that Jon had already seen.

▲　▲　▲

Jon was not in his chair when Charlie brought the documents to his temporary office. Charlie froze and then saw Jon coming down the hallway.

"Where were you? You know you need an escort at all times," Charlie snapped.

"I was in the restroom."

"You need an escort."

"Here in the admin building? Is there something hazardous in the bathroom I should know about?" Jon sounded almost lighthearted.

Charlie decided to drop it. It was a pain to escort Jon to the restroom every time he wanted to go. Also, if Jon couldn't reach him on the phone, he might be tempted to walk to his office. Going that way would take Jon past occupied offices and the conference room in the corner. He could strike up impromptu discussions with admin staff, who might let the wrong thing slip. At least between Jon's temporary office and the bathroom, there were only two empty offices that held no secrets.

"Okay, to the bathroom and back, but nowhere else," Charlie conceded. "Here are the documents you requested. Let me know what positions you want to talk to, and we'll see what we can do."

"Thanks." Jon opened the slim binder. "Uh, Charlie?"

Charlie turned around slowly.

"There's only one drawing here. I want drawings for all equipment connected to the vessel that exploded."

"We're still locating the others. And by the way, it's too soon to call it an explosion. We're still determining what happened."

"From the damage I saw, it looked like an explosion. What should we call it?"

"You're the big investigator," Charlie snapped. "You tell us."

▲   ▲   ▲

Jon looked over the documents for a few minutes and then glanced at his watch and realized that it was after six. He decided to go back and work at the Hampton Inn. As he walked to Charlie's office, he paused at an open door marked "Accounting." Inside, two attractive young women were working in an open space, the computer screen of the nearest one partly visible. Jon shifted a little to get a better view, but she noticed him and immediately grabbed her mouse and minimized the image. Jon gave what he hoped looked like a casual wave and kept walking.

Charlie jumped when he looked up and saw Jon in the doorway. "Escort," he said curtly.

"I didn't find one between my office and here," Jon said, more calmly than he felt.

Charlie put down his pack of orange peanut butter crackers. "What do you need?"

"I'm going to the hotel to work." Without looking back, Jon started walking toward the back door of the admin building. He could hear Charlie's footsteps behind him as he hurried to catch up.

"I'll have a list of positions I want to interview tomorrow," Jon said as he passed through the turnstile.

"We'll see what we can do," said Charlie.

It was a phrase Jon was getting to know well.

37

"Darnell, won't you come to prayer meeting with me tonight?" Kawana asked. "It's helping me—they're a good support group."

"I don't feel like it, Mama," Darnell said hazily, looking at the anchor tattoo on his forearm.

"Now, son, you moping around here ain't gonna bring James back. He wouldn't want you to stop living just because he did. Come with me. You've been working so much overtime lately. Besides, there are a couple of girls about your age at Bible study."

"Maybe next time," said Darnell, still staring at his arm.

"Sweet Jesus, what I am gonna do with this family?" Kawana asked no one, picking up her keys and heading for the door.

That night there was a new young man at Bible study. His name was Jackie. He didn't say anything at first, but eventually he told everyone that he had been through a trauma and couldn't eat or sleep. He had tried everything else, so his grandmother had talked him into coming and trying Jesus, he said.

Kawana walked up to him after the group had dispersed and hugged him. "I'm Kawana. Do you want to talk about it?"

"Well, ma'am, I was a guard at this chemical plant, and they had an explosion. I was there, monitoring the radio. I could hear the screams of the people on the platform when the fire started."

Kawana felt the blood drain from her face, and a warm wetness flow down her cheeks.

Jackie tilted his head toward her. "You remember when that happened?"

Kawana buried her face in her hands. "Oh my God, do I ever."

They hugged and spent the next twenty minutes talking. Kawana told Jackie about James and how proud she had been of him. Jackie told her how he'd been fired for doing the right thing, and how that made it even harder to move on.

"I remember one of the last things I heard," he reflected. "After the screaming stopped, the guys in the control room were talking. One of them—I think it was the manager—said something like, 'I know it was that overhead pipe. That engineer said it could be—' But then this other guy cut him off." Jackie paused, frowning in concentration as he thought back. "He said something like, 'Is your mic keyed on the radio?' When the first guy said yes, he said, 'Turn it off.'

"I called the NRC—the National Response . . . uh, Center, I think. That's what the procedures manual said to do. I tried to tell my company what I heard, but they didn't care. They just wanted me out of there."

He wiped a hand over his eyes and looked away silently for a moment. "It didn't seem right, how they acted," he said finally. "I was only trying to help."

▲   ▲   ▴

The house was dark and silent when Kawana got back that night. She found Darnell sitting in the same chair where she'd left him, still staring at his forearm. When she told him about Jackie, he finally looked up.

"You really should go with me next week," she said. "It might do you some good."

Darnell gave a slight nod. "I think I will," he answered.

▲   ▲   ▴

In the back room of the TV studio, surrounded by rusty tripods missing screws and klieg lights missing cords, Lisa Rogers curled her lips as she brushed blush onto her cheeks, her eyes glued to the looking glass. Her makeup table, mirror, and cushioned chair with the white metal back in the shape of a heart sat incongruously between a couple of old brown desks strewn with crumpled papers.

Lisa wasn't in the office much, usually preferring to leave straight from home for assignments. Today she'd supposedly come in to deal with some administrative issues with her last paycheck, but she really just wanted to be seen around the office and subtly let a few people know she would like to work on something different. There'd been that explosion a few weeks before, but since then she'd had nothing more exciting than flower shows and stories on school bullying. When she left Chemtrifuge, she'd hoped to be covering the breaking story about the affair involving the state's Speaker of the House. But a more senior reporter—Sarah, a woman in her late thirties whose voice was so sweet that it burned Lisa's ears every time she spoke—had snagged that plum.

Kenny barged in, carrying a box. "Hey, sweetcakes, didn't know you were here."

Lisa put down her brush and turned to Kenny with a we-need-to-talk look.

"Oh no, what's wrong?" he asked.

"Kenny, don't you get sick of these stories they put us on? I mean, flower shows? Come on. We should be out there doing investigative journalism. Get to the bottom of something. Expose something for the public good. Don't you feel like we are just, I don't know, wasting time?"

Kenny chuckled. "A lot of old women and dirt huggers love these flower shows."

"Come on, Kenny! We need to be players. This can't be the pinnacle of my career."

Kenny came over and put his arm around her. "Sometimes, as a journalist, you have to make your own excitement."

Lisa sighed. "Whatever happened to journalists reporting the news, not creating it?"

Kenny's laugh had an annoying revving sound, like an almost dead car engine trying to start. "That's not been the case since Watergate. What rock you been living under?"

Lisa pursed her lips. "Maybe you're right."

"Make your own story, or take a story and find a new angle," Kenny said, putting down the box.

Lisa nodded slowly. "I will. I don't know what, yet, but I will."

38

Craig straightened up and stretched and then grimaced. After hours of hunching over his desk, reviewing hard copies of spreadsheets, his back was sore. He had just approved Jon's travel voucher for his latest trip to Charleston, but he didn't know how much longer this investigation could fly under the radar. He had ignored two voice messages and an email from Sharon Hill indicating that they needed to talk about the money again.

"There you are," Sharon Hill said from the doorway in a singsongy voice, simultaneously knocking. "You sure are a hard one to reach. What's taking up all your time?"

Craig spun his chair toward the door. "Oh, you know, this and that. Everything takes longer than it should in this bureaucracy."

"Don't I know it? Hey, listen, busy man, I needed to catch up with you about that funding again. The DAS still wants it."

"But I thought we settled that at the last budget meeting. We're using the funds for our investigation."

"I know, but he still has big plans for the money, and we need to get it de-obligated from your budget and re-obligated into his. When do you think you might be able to take care of that on your end?"

"We're still wrapping up loose ends. My guy's there right now. I'm not sure how much expense we've incurred with his travel and testing equipment."

"Well, do what you need to do. You don't want to piss some people off, and he's one of them." Sharon gave him a quick fake smile and then left.

"Bitch," Craig mumbled under his breath. He'd dealt with people like Sharon all his life, people who'd back you into a corner and manipulate you into doing what they wanted and then try to convince you they were doing you a favor. He reached around and started massaging the painful point on his back with one hand.

39

Jon was sitting in the corner conference room, close to Charlie's office. He felt he had memorized the room by now. One large table in the middle, about fifteen feet long by five feet wide, with curved corners. Black chairs with webbed backs scattered around, a few lined up against the wall. A bookshelf at one end, a podium in one corner, and video screen on the wall at the other end.

Jon still had not received any additional drawings, but at least he'd managed to secure some interviews. Charlie had given him a list in the morning of four witnesses he could interview that day. Charlie kept saying that Chemtrifuge wanted to cooperate, but Jon suspected Chemtrifuge would not have agreed to the interviews if they could have avoided it. Apparently, they'd explored how much authority he had and found that he actually had some.

From the organizational charts and job descriptions Charlie had given him, Jon was able to piece together some information about

Chemtrifuge's structure, and where its employees fit in. Some of the job descriptions were matched with names. Earlier that morning, he'd sat at his uncomfortable folding chair in his makeshift office at the plant with his yellow pad of paper and pencil and stitched together what he knew about the organization:

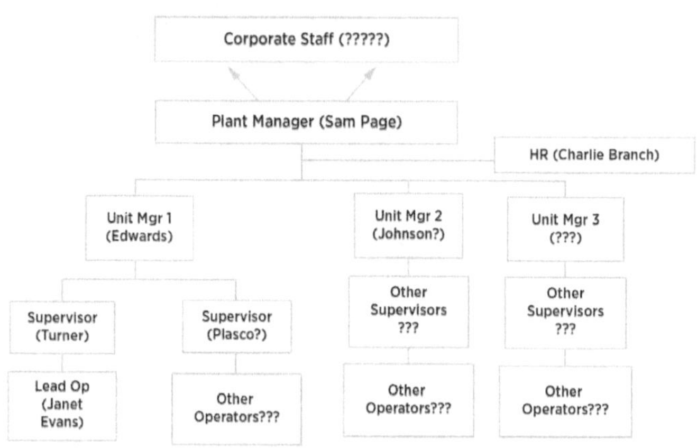

He had asked to start by interviewing people from the ethylene unit who'd been on shift the night of the accident. Today he was supposed to interview Edwards, Turner, Plasco, and Evans. He wasn't sure where Plasco fit in, but he knew he was a supervisor, so he put him under Edwards on the org chart. Assuming the other units were similarly organized, he added placeholders for positions there.

The door to the conference room flew open so hard it hit the wall, snapping Jon back to the present.

"Your first one's here," Charlie said gruffly, ushering in a stocky middle-aged man in a pair of blue Nomex coveralls, wearing a hard hat and stylish wraparound sunglasses. These new glasses were generations removed from the thick, clear safety glasses Jon used to wear, with detachable side shields that looked like tiny transparent hang gliders on each side of his face.

"Oh, thanks." Jon looked at his makeshift org chart. "And you are, uh—"

"This is Edwards," Charlie cut in.

Jon got up to shake hands with Edwards, but the man just plopped down in a chair and exhaled hard through his nose.

Jon walked back to his chair. "Thanks, Charlie," he said, glancing down at his notepad. But when he looked up again, Charlie hadn't left. In fact, he'd taken a seat at the head of the table, unzipped his planner, and laid it down.

Jon looked at the planner and then back at Charlie. "Do you plan to stay?"

"Yes, go ahead," Charlie barked.

"We never agreed that you'd be sitting in on these interviews," Jon said, confused.

Charlie leaned forward. "We're agreeing now. The deal is, you want him, or any of the managers, you get me too."

Jon thought about stopping the interview and calling DC for legal advice but then reflected on how little support he had received to date. It was probably better to go ahead with the interview and contact DC later. If necessary, he could press for a second interview.

"Okay. We didn't discuss that, but in the spirit of working together, let's proceed, understanding that I'd like to speak with interviewees uninterrupted."

Charlie rolled his eyes. "What if you get something wrong that I can correct?"

Jon paused a few seconds. "Good question. Tell you what, at the end of the interview, I'll give you a chance to correct anything I may have wrong."

"We can't have you making wrong conclusions or veering into areas outside the scope of the investigation."

"I understand. I just want to make sure no one gets blamed for try-ing to interfere with a federal investigation," Jon said, using a term he remembered from some movie.

Charlie looked at the door nervously and then got up and gently closed it. "Okay, we'll see how it goes."

Jon turned back to Edwards, who was slouched in his chair, both legs stretched out, staring blankly at the hard hat he'd set on the table. Jon started reading the script he had written based on an online legal form he'd found the night before. "This interview is part of the investigation into the fire and explosion that recently occurred."

Charlie mumbled what sounded like "explosion," and shook his head.

Jon decided to ignore him. "Your participation here is voluntary, but I ask that you answer all questions fully and accurately to the best of your ability." He paused and then, without looking up, went off-script to remind Charlie of the deal they'd just struck. "Anyone else present must not interfere with the questioning in any way and must be here by your and my consent."

Jon set down the paper. "Charlie has requested to be present during your interview. Do you agree that he can be present?"

Edwards looked at Charlie, expressionless, and then at Jon. "That's fine."

"Thanks," Jon said, looking back at his paper. "I'm Jon Barrett, inves-tigating this accident on behalf of the United States federal government. Your responses will help us determine what happened and hopefully prevent future similar accidents. Do you understand everything I have read, and do you agree to be interviewed?"

"Uh, yes," Edwards said, eyes fixed on his hard hat.

"Go ahead," Charlie said impatiently, making a circular get-moving motion with his hand.

Jon grabbed his mechanical pencil and clicked the end a couple of times until lead came out. "Please tell me about your position here at

Chemtrifuge, and what you do." He remembered being told in an accident investigation class that it was good to start with questions that put the interviewee at ease.

Edwards sat up a bit. "I'm the ethylene unit manager. I oversee production. Supervisors report to me. I also, uh . . ." He looked at Charlie, who gave him a stern look. "Uh, I guess that's about it."

Jon noticed the interaction. He'd also been coached in a past life on how to respond during interviews: Answer the question and stop. Say nothing more that might open a new line of questioning. "I'm sorry, I missed one part," he said, pretending to look at his notepad in confusion. "You were getting ready to say you also . . ."

Edwards sat back. "No, I, uh, didn't mean to say anything else."

"Sounds like a lot of responsibility," Jon said. Maybe flattery would work.

"I guess."

Jon ripped the makeshift org chart out of his notepad. "I'm trying to understand the organization. I drew this up based on information given to me by Chemtrifuge, but I'm not sure it's correct. I have you here as the unit manager." John pointed to the Edwards block. "Who are the supervisors that report to you?"

"Turner, Sharp, and Gilbert. You got Plasco there, but he's in another unit. He's over here." Edwards pointed to the Unit 2 branch, under Johnson.

Jon nodded. "Thanks. That helps a lot. I'll fix that. By the way, have you seen a drawing like this that might be more accurate than mine?" Jon asked, pulling out the P&ID.

Edwards looked at Charlie, who silently nodded. "Uh-huh, there's one. I've seen it."

"Great." Glancing over at Charlie, who was taking notes, Jon added, "I'll request that, so I don't waste time referring to wrong information. Okay, let's talk about the night of the fire and explosion."

Charlie inhaled loudly.

"Sorry—the fire and rapid release of energy." Jon paused. "Were you at the unit the night of the fire?"

"Yes," Edwards responded.

"Tell me about the minutes that led up to the fire, everything you remember."

"Everything *specifically* related to the fire," Charlie clarified.

"Everything related to the fire," Jon added calmly, "and everything you think will help the government understand what happened and why."

Edwards leaned forward and folded his arms in front of him on the table. He'd obviously been waiting for this question. "The evening of the fire, I was in my office, going over time cards. Someone came to my door and said there was an upset in the unit. I went to the console in the control room and saw what they were talking about. There was a release and a fire in the line from the overhead drum." Edwards stopped talking and leaned back again.

Jon sighed inwardly. This would be a series of well-rehearsed short answers to questions requiring long ones. "That overhead drum would be E-101—this one?" He pointed at the P&ID.

"Yes, that's it."

"So, what was happening just before the fire?"

"Like I said, I was in my office doing time cards."

Jon smiled. "Yes, you said that. But do you know what was going on in the unit?"

"Well, we were doing a production run, like, you know, like we do." Edwards seemed to twitch.

This was going to be painful. Jon decided to switch strategies. The next series of questions would be more of a rapid-fire between Jon and Edwards.

"So was there anything different about the run that evening?"

"Well, like I said, I was in my office doing time sheets, so I was not on the board."

"But were you aware of what was happening?"

"Well, we were doing a production run."

"Was there anything different or unique about that run?" Experience had taught Jon that when there was an accident, something was different. A plant could chug along for years, with nothing happening, if everything stayed the same. But even a deceptively small change could cause everything to go wrong. Some safety practitioners referred to this phenomenon as the "Swiss cheese model." There were layers of safeguards in a chemical plant, warning systems and the like. You could view the safety layers as a series of Swiss cheese slices in parallel, like dominos. Changes in the process caused the slices of cheese to rotate, and sometimes that caused the holes in the slices to line up. That was when accidents happened.

"Well, I guess, you know, every day here is a little different. Like everywhere."

"Yes, I guess that's true." Jon pretended to laugh as he thought about his next question. There were three possible changes to consider. The first possibility was in throughput—pumping more or less through the system than normal. Status was another type of change to consider, as in whether the vessel was being maintained rather than operating. Lastly, there was the functioning—or malfunctioning—of some safeguard. Sometimes safeguards were taken out of service, or they were rendered inoperable. But before he probed those three possibilities, he might as well get the company talking point out of the way. It was clear that Edwards had been coached.

"What do you think could have caused the fire?"

Edwards cocked his head as if he was trying hard to think about his answer. "I'll tell you exactly what happened. The people who did the maintenance . . . they were contractors. They screwed something up during maintenance. That's your cause. If I were you, that's where I would focus." He sat back and smiled.

"Hmmm. Thank you, that's helpful. I'll have to look at that. Is there normally maintenance on the equipment while it's in operation, with material in it?"

Edwards wrinkled his brow.

"Uh, well, there can be, depending on what the problem is. But it's kind of unusual to actually do cutting or welding on equipment with material in it. I mean, that's more of what we call a hot tap. We usually take equipment out of service to do maintenance."

Charlie's phone vibrated audibly. "Shit," he said, pulling it out and squinting at the screen. Jon took the opportunity to probe Edwards further on the unit status.

"So were any parts of the ethylene unit out of service that night?"

Edwards looked nervously at Charlie, who was still reading the text on his phone. Jon repeated the question.

"No, nothing was out of service that night," Edwards conceded.

"So help me understand this. If there was no maintenance going on, how could bad maintenance cause the problem?"

Edwards grabbed his hard hat on the table and snuggled it to him. Again he glanced over at Charlie, who was now frantically typing on his screen. "Uh, well, bad maintenance can mess things up down the road."

Jon nodded. "Oh, I see. They messed something up before, and it caught up with you that night."

"Yes, you can have an accident waiting to happen." Edwards looked at Charlie and recomposed himself. "Bad maintenance, that's what happened."

Jon made a note on his pad. "When was the last time maintenance had been performed on that overhead drum?"

"Uh . . ." Edwards frowned. "I don't remember."

"But it would be in the maintenance logs, correct?"

"Uh, I guess it should be, but it's been a while."

"I'll have to ask for that." Jon turned to Charlie, who'd just put his phone down. "Can you get that to me?"

"What's that?" Charlie looked up, confused.

"A copy of the maintenance logs for that vessel and surrounding equipment," Jon said briskly. "I need to see the last time work was done on it, and what that work was."

"We'll see what we can do," Charlie said, making a note. "Edwards needs to get back to the unit. Any last questions?"

"Just one."

Charlie picked up his pen and looked at his planner.

Jon turned back to Edwards. "I see you have a UWV sticker on your helmet. How do you think they'll do this year?"

Charlie looked confused, but Edwards smiled as he started thinking about the upcoming football season at the University of West Virginia. "You know, I think they might go all the way. They got that kid from Huntington, best recruit in the country. Alabama wanted him as their quarterback, but he came to us. Always wanted to play for us."

"That's what I heard," Jon lied, trying to make a connection.

"This has nothing to do with the investigation," Charlie snapped. "Anything else?"

"Well, it's not all about the investigation. Football matters too." Jon winked at Edwards, who cleared his throat.

"But seriously, one last thing." Jon pretended to look at his notepad. "Why that night? I mean, if they screwed up the maintenance, maybe left a gasket out of place or something, why didn't you have a fire as soon as you started the unit back up?"

"That sounds speculative," Charlie butted in boldly.

"Well, he knows this unit better than anybody," Jon said. "I'd be interested in his opinion."

Charlie sighed. "Go ahead."

"Well, you know, things change daily during production," Edwards offered. "Throughputs vary, things like that, so it's hard to say. We just hit on the wrong cylinders that night."

"Thank you so much." Jon stood up and reached his hand out to Edwards. "And good luck. I hope that quarterback comes through for you."

This time, Edwards took his hand and shook it.

40

Jon stretched and looked at his watch. About twenty minutes had passed since Charlie stormed out.

Jon was pleased with the Edwards interview, though he realized Charlie might not be. After the interview, Charlie had rushed out the conference room door so fast that he bumped into the janitor, who was passing by with his trash bin. Jon could see another employee in blue coveralls standing outside the open door. "Come with me!" Charlie had said, grabbing the guy by the arm before he could knock and marching him off toward his office. He was probably re-coaching the next interviewee now, based on Jon's questions.

Early in his career, Jon had learned that that was the way interviews worked. The company had the advantage of knowing the questions that have come before—especially if a mole like Charlie was present, taking notes. But the interviewer has the advantage of being able to ask different questions.

Jon had actually learned a lot from Edwards. He'd confirmed that the unit was in normal production mode, not being maintained. Jon could also tell from Edwards's hesitation that the equipment that exploded had not been maintained for some time. Edwards would have remembered if it had been. Edwards was not going to volunteer any information, but though he had been evasive, Jon also got the sense that he did not want to lie. When Jon tried to pin him down on what was different that night, he'd waffled, but he hadn't said the unit was being maintained. Jon knew other interviewees might be evasive, too, but at least they might not flat-out lie.

The other thing he'd learned was that there had been some change that night. Edwards had evasively said that every day was different, instead of saying that everything was the same that night. That was important. And it was important what Edwards said while Charlie was preoccupied with his phone. *You can have an accident waiting to happen.* Jon had drawn a bracket around his notes during the period when Charlie was not paying attention. That might have been the only time Edwards was unfiltered.

Jon had also learned he could thaw the relationship with interviewees at least some by talking about something like sports. Charlie would warn the others, but it might still work.

Jon needed to use the restroom, but he decided to wait. Finally he couldn't wait any longer. He opened the door and found himself face-to-face with Charlie, who looked taken aback.

"Where are you going?" Charlie asked.

"To find you," Jon said impatiently. "I need to go to the restroom."

Charlie shrugged. "Your next interview's here."

"Can he wait a few minutes?"

"They need him back in the unit. Get him now, or you don't get him for a while."

Behind Charlie was a short, stocky man, dressed in the ubiquitous blue coveralls. Curly black hair flowed out from under his scratched and filthy hard hat, which might have been white years ago. He looked like a figure on a pizza box.

"Okay, let's talk now," Jon conceded.

"This is Plasco," Charlie said after the three settled into place in the conference room.

"Nice to meet you, Mr. Plasco," Jon said politely. Plasco nodded.

Jon read the introductory statement, pausing to ask Plasco if he objected to Charlie's presence.

"That's fine," Plasco said matter-of-factly.

"Okay, tell me what you do here."

Plasco leaned back, held a Styrofoam cup up to his mouth, and spat out some tobacco juice. "I'm a supervisor in the P-4 unit."

"Is that close to the unit that exploded—" Charlie looked up. "Uh, I mean, caught fire?"

"Pretty close." Plasco spat again as his tongue dug behind his lower lip.

"And what does the P-4 unit do?"

"Well, processes chemicals and stuff."

Plasco was even more guarded than Edwards. Jon decided to take a different approach. He looked up from his notepad. "What is your role in ensuring safety in the plant?"

Plasco stopped lifting the cup midway to his mouth and, without turning his head, turned his eyes toward Charlie.

Charlie stopped writing and looked up. "Uh, you're not supposed to ask questions outside the scope of the accident."

Jon grabbed his pencil. "You don't believe a question about a supervisor's role in safety has anything to do with the accident?"

Charlie squirmed, and Jon decided to press the point. "Is that the company's position?"

Charlie dropped his pencil and rubbed his forehead. The next few seconds hung in the air as Jon waited. Jon had learned two cardinal rules for interviews in training years ago: Be nice—and be quiet. Do not fill the air gap. People will often talk even when they don't mean to if there is silence, the instructor had said.

Charlie finally looked up. "Go ahead and answer."

"I guess my responsibility is the same as everyone's. I come in, work safe, and try not to get hurt." Plasco sat back and spat again.

"That makes sense, but that's your personal responsibility. What is your safety responsibility for your crew?"

"Well, here, safety is a line responsibility. That means that as a member of line management—you know, a supervisor—I take responsibility for assuring safety for me and my crew. But what I said is still true. Everyone has responsibility for their own safety." Plasco said this smoothly, as if he were quoting a company motto. He put his cup back on the table.

Jon smiled. "I assume that helping your men would include helping us figure out what happened that night to help prevent fires in the future, right?"

Plasco looked at Charlie, who was writing.

"Uh, yes," Plasco said uncertainly. It sounded more like a question than an answer.

Jon leaned in. "So tell me what happened that night, so we can keep it from happening again."

Plasco looked at Charlie, who gave a slight nod. "Well, I was over in P-4, and I heard commotion on the radio. It sounded bad, and they started calling for the fire brigade. As the supervisor on the adjacent unit at the time, I take command of the fire brigade when there's a problem in the ethylene unit. I heard some crosstalk on the radio, and about that time we heard the boom."

Charlie interrupted. "Don't say 'boom'—he'll get the wrong idea. You mean you heard a loud noise, right?"

"Yes, that's what I meant," Plasco said obediently.

Jon nodded. "Okay, you heard a loud noise. Who was closest to the blast?"

"I'm not sure. I heard on the radio that some guys were around there."

"Who was there?" Jon pressed. He needed to identify anyone who could answer firsthand what had happened, assuming they were still alive.

"Oh, I don't know. It wasn't our guys, it was those others—"

Charlie slammed his hand down on the table so loud it sounded like someone had fallen through the ceiling.

Plasco stopped talking, startled. "Uh, I mean, I'm not sure," he said finally. "I was in a different unit."

"Do you remember any of the names of people who were there?"

"I was in a different unit," Plasco said doggedly.

Jon knew he would get nothing more from this interview. Plasco was now on guard. Charlie had made it clear, nonverbally, that he'd gone too far.

"Is there anything else we haven't talked about that might help me figure out what happened?"

"We've covered the things I know," Plasco said evasively.

"Hey, one last thing," Jon said, as all three started to rise. "What do you think about that new Mountaineer quarterback?"

"I'm from Pittsburgh. I really don't give a shit unless he comes to play for the Steelers," Plasco said, smiling. "But he seems good, plays a good short game—"

Charlie cleared his throat, and Plasco reluctantly shook Jon's hand.

"Good luck to those Steelers," Jon said.

"Thanks." Plasco's voice was cold. He turned right as he walked out the door.

Jon watched as Charlie marched straight ahead toward Sam Page's office, almost tripping over a vacuum cleaner. A door slammed down the hallway.

41

Craig Higgins was adjusting the height on the new chair in his office. He had requested an ergonomic assessment, hoping it would fix the subtly increasing pain in his back. The ping on his screen jarred him. He had not slept well and had felt on edge all morning. The Outlook meeting invite was from Sharon Hill. He could feel his face flush. It was an invite for next Thursday, and the location was the DAS's office. There was no call-in number. He would have to attend in person.

Craig leaned back. The invitees included the DAS and Ed Murphy. Ed had acted as a heat shield in the earlier meeting with Sharon, letting the investigation move forward once he learned that Craig already had someone actively working on it. But with the DAS there, Craig bet Ed would be reluctant to provide any more cover for keeping the money in his budget.

His eyes drifted to the cryptic subject line: "Discuss funding issues." Craig knew there was only one issue: the DAS wanted his money.

That would mean no more investigation office, and no more Jon. Craig wouldn't even be able to find him a different position, given the secretary's recently implemented hiring and reassignment freeze.

Craig couldn't blame the secretary. He'd attended the congressional hearing where representatives from both parties grilled the secretary about the bloated bureaucracy at Interior. Even the often government-friendly *Washington Post* ran a series of editorials calling for a drastic shrinkage of the federal workforce, using Interior as an example. The only good news, if he could call it that, was that the meeting was over a week away. At least Jon would have a little more time, and a couple more weeks of pay.

But Craig was even more worried about Jon's emotional state. During his interview, Jon had confided that he hadn't worked for a while and didn't have a great track record. Craig sensed that he was not a problem employee. Sometimes bad luck befalls good people. That was part of the reason he'd taken a chance on Jon. Also, he'd hired Jon under a special hiring authority to get him onboard quickly, even though he did not have previous government experience. The downside was that Jon was on probation for two years, and so could not get status credit for being a federal employee. He would have to compete with everyone else for a new position.

Craig rocked back. He felt sorry for Jon, and this meeting meant his days were numbered. Reluctantly, he clicked "Accept" on the invitation and stood up. He'd go for a walk on the National Mall.

42

"Dammit to hell, Charlie, what's wrong with you?" Sam asked between coughs, spewing out coffee. He looked down to check if his shirt had been spared. It had. "You scared the shit out of me."

"It's bad," Charlie huffed, small beads of sweat forming on his forehead under his receding black hair. "Sam, it's bad. Plasco let it slip about the guys around the vessel when it exploded. If that guy puts it together, he'll know the contractors were the ones working around there."

Sam motioned for Charlie to sit down—he needed him to relax. "Calm down. Even if he figures that out, they're all dead, so they can't tell him anything. The only one who was around there that's still alive is Janet, and she knows what to say."

Charlie sat, breathing hard. Sam rocked forward. "Look, we're following the plan. Remember the strategy call with Chemtrifuge and the corporate attorneys early this morning, before you rounded up the interviews? They recommended that we provide access to operators and supervisors, but coach them on what to say. We've done that."

"That's easy for them to say—they're not here." Charlie's voice was rising with every word. "They also said there could be problems, you remember that? Like the documentation. They said it was better not to give any than to falsify it, that falsifying documents given to a federal investigator was 'problematic'"—he air-quoted—"and we should steer clear of that. And about the interviews—that guy's asking questions that go off our script. We need to get the lawyers in. I can't handle it anymore."

Charlie had a point, Sam thought. Problem was, once they called in the corporate guns, it would be viewed as a failure on Sam's part. It'd look like he couldn't hold his plant together.

"Charlie, I know it's tough," he said, "but if we get those assholes in here, we've lost control. We'll never get that genie back in the bottle."

Charlie leaned up and put his elbows on Sam's desk. "Sam, I'd love for this to go away. I've been a loyal soldier. I've played hardball with this guy. But stuff is leaking out. Just in the two interviews this morning, stuff's already leaked out. If he's paying attention, he knows that there wasn't any maintenance being done, and that the contract guys were there. What if he figures out what really happened? That we sent out inexperienced contractors to deal with it? What if he finds out about Mr. Quinn? Sam, this could get bad—it could get real bad!" Charlie's voice, which had been getting higher and higher, reached a crescendo.

"Okay, Charlie, I give. Let's do this. Cancel the other interviews for today, and we'll get you some backup. I'll get the high-powered attorney out of DC in here. He's the most ruthless one. I didn't want to, but maybe bringing him in now is best. Have you taken care of the documents?"

Charlie leaned back, his face relaxing. "Yes. All tucked away in folders in the bottom of my credenza. I made another pass through the library with Kathy, and there's nothing else he can find. One of the old drawings was there, but it'd fallen behind a drawer. He didn't see it."

There was a bump outside Sam's door, and they could hear voices. "Can you vacuum the lobby?" someone said.

Sam motioned for Charlie to close the door. Then he stood up and walked around his desk. He leaned on the edge in front of Charlie. "Look, we'll get you backup. We probably need to kill this now before it gets any worse. But I still want you involved. You've handled it up to now, and I need you to keep your eye on the government guy, and this lawyer. Can I count on you?"

"Absolutely," said Charlie, half smiling.

Sam went back around his desk and grabbed a bourbon bottle, setting it in front of Charlie. He motioned for Charlie to lock the door. "By the way, how's your wife?" he asked, bringing out two small glasses.

Charlie's smile faded. "Not good."

Sam tried to look sympathetic, but his mind kept racing. He didn't want to bring in the lawyer, but Charlie was right. Information was leaking out.

He poured another full glass for himself and pretended to listen, his mind in a fog. He nodded occasionally, catching a few words: words like *terminal*, *better off dead*, and *suicide*.

43

Jon stared at the empty page on his notepad for a few seconds. Charlie had just told him that the rest of the interviews for the day had been canceled, and he did not have any additional documents yet. Then he looked up.

"Can we at least take another tour of the site?" Jon asked.

Charlie scratched his elbow. "We'd need to plan. We'll see."

The interviews had been beneficial, but they were not nearly enough. The longer things like this dragged on, the more memories faded and equipment was changed out. Jon knew that.

He called Craig to give an update, but got voicemail. "Hi, Craig, this is Jon. I wanted to let you know that I had two good interviews this morning. I'm still waiting on more documents, but I'm working with what I have. Talk to you later."

Another hour passed. More staring at the ceiling and rereading interview notes. Jon rubbed his temples and dialed Charlie's number.

"Charlie, I'm going out to lunch. Do you think maybe I can get some documents to review when I get back?"

Charlie hesitated. "I said I'm working on it. We'll see." Then he added, "Have a good lunch. Take your time," almost sounding cheerful.

Jon decided to heed his advice about the time but not the lunch. He went to the hotel business center and Googled the incident to see if there was any recent information, trying every bastardization of "Chemtrifuge explosion." Nothing. It was as if everyone had forgotten the explosion but him—him and those he was annoying at the plant.

All he was able to find were reports from the day of the accident. All the newspapers were consumed with the scandal at the state level related to the Speaker of the House, it seemed. Having read enough to realize that it was in some way related to sex, emails, and transportation, Jon made a mental note to go back and read it sometime for pleasure.

Finally, he found footage from the day of the accident. And that caused him to remember the earlier message he'd left at the television station.

▲　▲　▲

Sam stuck his head in Charlie's door. "Where is he?"

Charlie looked up from the personnel action report he'd been reviewing the last half hour or so. "At lunch. I told him to take his time. I think he got the hint there's nothing for him to do here this afternoon."

"Good. Hey, I called corporate. They're supposed to call me back about the lawyer."

Charlie smiled. "Glad to hear it."

Sam scratched the back of his neck. "They suggested we just string this guy along until the lawyer gets down here. Could you round up a couple of interviews for him, either later today or tomorrow? These would be guys who know nothing about the accident, maybe in other units or not even on-shift that night. He won't get anything out of them, but it'll look like we're cooperating."

Charlie nodded. "I'll set up a couple for tomorrow."

"Sounds good," Sam said. "Just keep him chasing his tail so he stays away from ours."

Charlie chuckled. As Sam left, he picked up the phone.

▲　▲　▲

"Aren't you going to drink that beer? I brought it for you," Janet said to Kirby, her longtime drinking buddy and fellow EMT. Janet had stopped by the firehouse on her way home after her shift.

"I'm on duty," Kirby said. "I may get a call."

She tilted her beer top in his direction. "Oh, come on, wuss. When has that ever stopped you?" She took out a wrapped red-and-white-swirled peppermint out of the pocket of her coveralls and flipped it at him.

Kirby fumbled to catch it. "You think of everything, you conniving bitch." He reached for the beer, laughing, tipped it up to his mouth, and took a long drink. "Hey, whatever happened with that investigation of the explosion?"

Janet shrugged. "It's pretty much died down. There's still some guy from the government hanging around. I see him sometimes in the parking lot. I think they pretty much shut him down—I bet he'll be leaving soon."

"I see you still limping around. When you gonna get better?"

Janet shrugged again. "Could be months. It was a pretty bad fall. I'm starting physical therapy next week. They say a lesser man wouldn't even be walking now." They both laughed.

Kirby finished his beer and reached for another. "What about those other guys that were hurt? Whatever happened to them?"

Janet wrinkled her mouth. "Oh, they're dead. They were basically burned up that night."

Kirby shook his head. "I don't understand why we didn't hear more about that. I would have thought the TV people here would have been on that like stink on shit."

Janet took a swig. "I don't know. I think the company kind of kept it hush-hush. They were contractors. Then all that news broke about the politician and that sex stuff."

Kirby nodded. "I remember that. I guess it blew every other story off the front pages."

Janet set down her empty bottle and wiped her mouth with her sleeve. "Yeah, I think everybody's pretty much moved on. They told us operators to ignore the government guy if he tries to contact us. They said something about breaking attorney-client privilege or some bullshit like that. I don't plan to talk to the guy anyway. The company's taking care of us, and our union's on board."

Kirby's beeper went off, and he spilled his beer. "Shit," he said, fumbling with the buttons. "I guess it's better to just move on, if they're taking care of you," he added as he popped the mint into his mouth.

44

That evening, Jon stayed in the hotel. They had fajitas and beer for happy hour. The tortillas were stale, the meat was cold, and the lettuce was wilted, but it was edible—and free.

He thought about doing more Google searches in the business center but decided to just go back to his room. Maybe he'd call his father or Tammy. But instead, he just lay on the bed, staring at the ceiling.

He'd hoped the DC job would give him a second chance, but that hadn't happened. The people at the plant hated him, and he seemed to have no support from his agency. The afternoon had been a total bust.

He was in his mid-forties, divorced, and had no friends. He thought about going back downstairs for another beer, but the thought of getting up suddenly seemed too hard. His body was like a sack full of sand. He remembered his mother had not felt like getting out of bed for two years before she died. That was when she started taking those pills that the family never talked about. When Jon had asked his father what was wrong, he'd just said, "She's just tired, she'll be fine."

Then he saw the light flashing on his phone. It was a message from Charlie. *You have two interviews tomorrow morning.*

Life crept back in. True, the afternoon had been a bust, but on the whole, the day was pretty good. The interviews had been painful, but he got some good information. And he would have two more tomorrow. Maybe things were turning around. Optimism resurfaced for the first time in weeks. Maybe he could find the cause of the accident and help keep it from happening again. Maybe he did have a purpose. Maybe he could save a life. Springs started to replace the sand. He suddenly felt like getting dressed and going downstairs. But first, he was going to call his father and tell him things were going well.

▲　▲　▲

The next morning, Jon went to the diner close to the hotel. He had slept through most of the night, and he felt better. The diner was shaped like a large cable car. It had booths by the windows with red-and-white-checkered tablecloths.

He scanned the seats at the counter. One scruffy patron with salt-and-pepper stubble was sitting in front of the grill, sipping coffee and watching a cook. The cook was wearing a greasy white T-shirt and hair-net, and was sprinkling salt onto something beneath the counter.

"Booth or bar, honey?" bellowed a plump older woman with a scratchy voice.

"Booth, please." The hostess walked in front of him and put the menu down on the side of the booth facing the wall. Jon wanted to look out the window, so he sat down on the other side and pulled the menu and silverware toward him.

"Suit yourself," the hostess said under her breath, walking away.

A couple of minutes later, a slightly younger waitress walked over to his table. She had blond hair, except for the black roots, and wore the same brown uniform as the hostess. Her name tag read "Flo." Jon remembered that name from a waitress on the old TV show *Alice*, which he'd watched on reruns as a kid. On that show, Flo was a promiscuous redheaded Texan who always smarted off to her boss. This Flo put her pen to the order pad she was holding and cleared her throat, snapping him back to the present.

"I'll take the special with scrambled eggs," he said, folding his menu.

"I don't think I've seen you in here before," Flo observed. "You live around here?"

Jon smiled. "No, just here on business. I haven't felt like a big breakfast lately, but thought I'd treat myself today."

"If you want a treat, add a side of scrapple. It's a specialty, best stuff outside Pennsylvania."

"Then go ahead and add some scrapple," Jon said, smiling. Flo smiled back as she wrote the order.

"Today is going to be a good day," he mumbled to himself. He looked at his watch: 6:42. Charlie would not even be there to let him in until after eight. The waitress came by with the morning paper and put it on the table. He thought about picking it up or checking messages on his phone. Instead he looked out the window. He was going to stare, reflect, and eat for the next hour.

"Today's going to be a good day," he said, a little louder. The scruffy patron with the salt-and-pepper stubble stopped drinking his coffee mid-sip and glanced over.

45

"How are you today?" Jon asked Charlie when he showed up twenty minutes after Jon arrived at the guard shack.

"Fine." Charlie used an I-hate-small-talk tone.

Jon ignored it, keeping his own voice friendly. "I see I'll have two more interviews today. What time?"

Charlie looked down as they walked briskly down the hallway. "We're still confirming that, but it'll be this morning."

Jon smiled. "Good. Any more documents?"

"Working on that too," Charlie replied curtly.

Jon plopped down in the steel fold-up seat in his makeshift office. Charlie grabbed the door to close it. "I'll come and get you when they're ready."

"Thanks," Jon said, adding, "Just leave the door open."

Charlie stopped closing the door midway. Jon always sat in the room with the door closed, like he was at a doctor's office. But today, the door would be open. One crack at freedom.

Charlie wrinkled his face, but he released the doorknob and walked away.

▲   ▲   ▲

Twenty minutes later, Jon heard footsteps. Charlie stopped at Jon's door.

"Okay, they're ready."

Jon grabbed his notepad and makeshift org chart.

"Great." As they walked down the hallway, Jon asked, "What are their positions? Did they witness the fire?"

"You can ask them that," Charlie snapped.

When they got to the conference room, three people were sitting on the same side of the table. Jon took a seat on the other side.

Jon looked at the men for a minute before reading his introductory statement. All three were wearing blue Nomex coveralls with various stains and tears. The hard hat for the one in the middle sat on the table. He was wearing glasses with brown frames and clear side shields. He looked to be in his upper fifties or maybe early sixties.

To that man's right was a younger man with a pouched bottom lip, holding a white Styrofoam cup. He had a stream of ambeer on his chin. His safety glasses were in his coverall pocket, wedged beside what Jon assumed was a container of dipping tobacco. As soon as Jon sat down, the younger operator put the cup to his mouth and spit into it, adding fresh tobacco juice to the stream on his chin.

To Jon's right was a third man. He was African American, probably in his late forties, chubby, and graying around his temples.

"I thought there were only two of you today," Jon said.

The Black operator leaned forward in his chair and stuck out his hand. "I'm Alphonse Scott, local union steward. I represent the hourly workers here."

Jon stood up and reached across the table to shake Scott's hand.

"Nice to meet you." He turned to the two other operators. "Is it okay with you if he sits in on the interview?"

Alphonse smiled. "It's fine with them. I represent them, so I need to be here. I won't get in the way."

Jon wanted to hear from the men directly—but he didn't want to have a confrontation with the union steward before the interview even started. Besides, this was better than having Charlie there. Charlie said he would only sit in on interviews with managers. Hopefully, Alphonse could be an ally in the investigation.

"Okay. Will you be in on the other interviews with the hourly guys, too? Assuming there will be more interviews with other operators?"

Alphonse nodded. "Probably so."

Jon looked at the two operators. "I'm going to read an introductory statement where I ask you directly if it's okay for Alphonse to be here. It's just a procedural thing."

When Jon reached the part where he asked if they consented to have someone else there, he paused. The older man in the middle just nodded. The younger man spat into his makeshift spittoon and said, "No problem."

"Okay," Jon started, "tell me about your job here at the plant."

The operators looked at each other, and then the older one looked back at Jon. "We're outside operators. We go around, take samples, check readings on equipment, make sure everything is running right. If the board man needs something outside, he calls us on the radio and we take care of it."

Jon sensed the older operator would be talking for both of them.

"We do things inside the control room too," the man continued, "like update procedures, coordinate when maintenance is done—you know, whatever needs to be done with the equipment, we usually have a hand in it."

The younger operator nodded between spits.

"Oh, I see. You have a critical job here," Jon said politely.

"We think so." The operators looked at each other and chuckled. Alphonse sat silently.

"Are you in the unit that had the explosion?" Jon asked. He was curious about whether they'd correct him when he said "explosion." They didn't.

"No, we're both over in the polymers unit, at the other end of the plant."

Jon was confused. He wondered if maybe they had some role in fighting the fire. "So are you both on the emergency response brigade?" he asked.

"Used to be. Was a requirement until a couple of years ago. Now it's voluntary." The older operator hesitated, and then continued. "I think it's better this way. I didn't like going to the training anyway. They'd send us to Morgantown to the fire school. One time they put me in an SCBA, and I—you know what an SCBA is—self-contained breathing, uh, appendage, I think?"

"Apparatus," the younger operator corrected.

"Yeah, that's right—apparatus. Anyway, one time I put it on and, well, the instructor wasn't looking. The air line was closed, and I thought I was going to smother. I ripped off the helmet. That was scary. I never want to do that again. You don't know what it's like, feeling like you can't breathe."

Jon nodded. "That does sound scary," he said. "Can you tell me what you were doing the night of the explosion?"

The older man squirmed a bit in his seat. "I was home. I didn't hear about it until the next day."

Jon looked at the younger operator. "And you?"

"I was over at my cousin's, playing pool and having a couple drinks. That was during my three days off."

"So neither of you work in the unit or were here that night?"

They both nodded.

"Do you know anything about that unit?"

"I subbed over there for a couple of days a year or so ago. I tell you, I like my unit better. I could have bid on one of those operator jobs when they came open, but I didn't want to do it."

Jon nodded. "Why not—what's wrong with that unit?"

"Well, I tell you, some of those catwalks they got over there are cluttered and close together. When I was walking around taking readings, I could barely squeeze through. In my unit, things are spaced out. But over there, I tell you, it looked like a royal clusterfuck in some areas."

Jon laughed before he could help it. He had heard that word many times in plants. It was reserved for really terrible situations. "So you may not know firsthand, but what do you think happened?"

At this, Alphonse sat up. "I tell you what happened. They had contract operators over there. Not like these guys. They weren't experienced. I think they did something."

Jon scribbled a note on his notepad.

"That's interesting. Some people think it was bad maintenance—maybe equipment didn't get put back together well before start-up."

Alphonse nodded. "Well, it could have been both. Mistakes by contractors who did the maintenance and those who did operations. Contractors—that's your problem right there."

"Anything else you know about the explosion that might help me figure out what happened?"

The three of them shook their heads. The older one spoke. "No, I don't know anything else. It was a bad thing that happened."

Jon stood and shook hands with all three. The older operator chimed in. "I remember that time I thought I was smothering. Scary."

He was still talking about it as all three walked down the hallway.

46

The operators were courteous, but they didn't offer any insights. They hadn't been there the night of the accident and didn't even work in that unit. Alphonse was a surprise. Union stewards usually didn't buy the company line so quickly. Maybe he really felt that way, but most union stewards were very suspicious of their employer's explanations. Some opposed it even before it was offered.

Jon went back to his office alone, a privilege he'd recently acquired. He suspected Charlie had gotten tired of escorting him everywhere. Now Jon could go to and from the conference room and the restroom and straight out the turnstile for lunch when Charlie called ahead to the guard. Everywhere else was still off limits without an escort.

It was 11:30 already, and Jon had not seen or heard from Charlie since the interview, so he decided to go to lunch. Charlie picked up on the first ring.

"Charlie, I'm going to lunch, unless you have more interviews lined up."

"Uh, no, nothing right now."

"Do you think maybe you can get me some interviews this afternoon?"

"We'll see."

Jon ignored the brush-off. "That would be good, thanks. And if it could be actual eyewitnesses to the event or someone who works in the area, that would be most helpful."

"We'll see."

At the diner, Flo brought Jon a chicken club sandwich held together with a long, thick toothpick with a small American flag on the end.

He looked across the diner. A couple of people were hunched over plates at the counter. Two men walked in, their faces and overalls covered in coal dust. One of them was wearing a hard hat that looked like the ones operators wore in the chemical plant.

Jon's mind drifted back to his childhood in Nebraska. He remembered sitting in diners and truck stops. It was a similar scene, except that there, the overalls were stained with dirt and grass from the farm. Is this any different from where I grew up? he wondered. The only difference Jon could see was that these people were stained with coal dust instead of corn husks. Their coal mines are basically our farms, he mused.

Flo interrupted Jon's pondering. "Is that okay, honey?"

"Yes, everything is great. Thanks."

"You haven't even touched it," she pressed. "Are you sure it's okay?"

"I know it'll be good." Jon decided to strike up a conversation. "So how long have you been a waitress?"

"Oh my God, honey, probably before you were born."

Jon smiled. "Is that what you always wanted to do?"

"I don't think anybody wants to be a waitress—it just happens. I didn't want to work with the mines. Didn't want my husband or kids to, either. My daddy got killed in them when I was a child. I thought they were creepy. This big black hole you go into every day. He got killed by a miner."

"Another miner killed him?"

Flo laughed. "No, honey, a miner is a machine. Some call it a continuous miner. It cuts coal out of the seam. He got pinned between the blade and the seam. They say it chewed him up like ground beef."

Jon looked down, ashamed he had asked. "I'm sorry."

"Don't be. Happened so long ago, I don't think much about it anymore."

"So what *did* you want to do?"

"When I was a little girl, I wanted to be in the movies. I used to dream I was on the screen. But life takes over. You just make the best of it where you are. Bloom where you're planted, as they say."

Jon nodded. "I understand. But what if you can't bloom where you're planted?"

Flo looked out the window. "Then I guess you either move somewhere else or just accept it and hope the next generation does better than you."

"What if you are the last generation?"

Flo started to speak, but one of the miners cleared his throat loudly and waved at her. "Excuse me," she said, and walked away.

Jon sat mindlessly eating his sandwich and fries. Maybe he was obsessing too much about the useless morning interviewees. He just wanted to keep the investigation moving forward.

"Looks like you finished. Anything else, honey?" Flo asked.

"No, just the check."

Flo pulled a black bifold out of her apron, opened it, and handed the receipt to Jon. "You know, honey, I learned a long time ago to just accept some things. The world ain't always as we like it, but we can still try to do our best."

Jon thanked her and paid the bill. As he walked to his car, he reflected on what Flo had said. From dreams of becoming an actress to being a waitress. But Flo had a plan B—staying in this community where she had grown up and living a simple life. Jon had no other plan but this one—redeem himself with this investigation and maybe get some stability. Bloom where you are planted. That was what he was going to do. But he needed help. "I need to move this along," he said aloud, opening his car door. The two coal miners were coming out of the diner and looked at him curiously.

He started his car, waving as he exited the parking lot. They replied with awkward waves and curious stares.

47

Jon did a double take, glancing at the patio with picnic tables and umbrellas. He had been on this road going from his hotel to the plant a few times, but had never noticed the cedarwood custard stand shack before. Maybe he would stop by some evening. He wanted to talk to Craig before he got to the plant. He slowed down and punched the button on the phone screen, but got Craig's answering machine.

"Hi, Craig. Hope all is well. I wanted to give you an update. I did a couple of interviews this morning. The guys didn't know much about the explosion, but I'm going to ask the HR director to give me eye-witnesses or people from the unit. I'll let you know how it goes. I'm thinking of staying here over the weekend and getting started early on Monday. Let me know if that's a problem—I'll be glad to adjust. Talk to you soon."

One down, one to go. Jon thought about the next call he would have to make when he got to the plant. He dreaded that one even more. He passed the parking lot for a grocery store, and thought about turning the car around and going back to the custard stand and sitting under one of the umbrellas for the rest of the afternoon.

▲ ▲ ▲

Charlie picked up the phone reluctantly, seeing Jon's extension show up. This was the last thing he needed this afternoon. Over lunch, he'd gone to the doctor with his wife. News about her cancer was worse every visit. Months had changed to weeks, and Charlie feared that, by the next visit, weeks would change to days.

"Hi, Charlie," said Jon, "can we talk about the interviews and the pace of the investigation?"

Charlie had wanted to avoid this discussion, but he figured it would happen sooner or later. "I'll be right there." He walked to Jon's office and stepped inside, resting his hand on the doorknob.

"I'd offer you a seat, but . . ." Jon waved his hand across the tiny room.

"That's all right. I won't be staying long. What's up?"

Jon furrowed his brow. "Charlie, I want to do meaningful interviews. The guys this morning were nice, but they didn't know anything about the accident or the unit."

Charlie bristled. "You wanted people to interview, and we gave you people. I can't help it if you're not able to get the information you want. You should ask better questions."

Jon shook his head. "I believe you can help by giving me people who know about the explosion—either eyewitnesses to what happened or people who know the unit. We need to move this along. I still don't have access to the equipment, I haven't talked to critical eyewitnesses, and I don't have documents. When am I going to get the information I need to move forward?"

Charlie was already upset about the doctor visit, and smart talk from this government employee was the last straw. "You have what you're going to get," he snapped, emboldened by Sam's promise that he would be getting legal backup. "We're busy, and we've been generous with our employees' time. I've given you the drawings you asked for. I can't help it if you don't know what to do with them." Charlie raised his voice and started shaking. "Maybe you just don't know what you're doing."

He thought he saw moisture well up in the corner of Jon's eye.

"Maybe we can talk about this later," Jon said softly, his voice shaking.

"Or maybe we won't," Charlie said.

"Excuse me, sir, you need your trash picked up today?"

Jon and Charlie both looked at the figure in the doorway, Jon with relief and Charlie with annoyance.

"No, I don't have any trash today," Jon said. "Thanks, though."

"Excuse me." Charlie turned sideways to get past the guy, bumping into him before charging down the hall.

The cleaning guy watched Charlie walk away. "He seems mad about something," he said, without turning back to Jon.

"Yes, he's very mad. I'm trying to do my job and figure out what caused the explosion, and he gets pissed at me for that," Jon said without thinking. He put his head in his hands.

"Sorry," the cleaning guy said and then walked away.

Jon closed the door and laid his head on his desk. He didn't want to leave; he didn't want to stay. He didn't know what to do. Charlie's last comment struck him like an arc flash from an electrical circuit. The gloves were off. Charlie had turned the conversation from the issue of the company's cooperation to Jon's competence. This personal attack cut him deep, and he hoped Charlie had not seen him tearing up. He sat up and checked the messages on his phone. No call back from Craig. Nothing.

That evening, Jon skipped happy hour at the hotel. He watched television for a while and then turned it off and reached over to turn out the light. It was only 6:47, but he decided to try to sleep anyway. There was nothing else to do.

Jon stacked a second pillow on the first, which had flattened out. His stare had oscillated between the black-speckled ceiling vent with patches of paint missing and the dull beige wall still visible from the fading light outside. He lay still for what seemed like hours, thinking about the events of the day. Charlie had challenged him, and he had made no response. He thought about the interview and the older operator talking about wearing the SCBA. *It felt like I couldn't breathe.*

Tonight, Jon knew how that felt.

48

Around four a.m., Jon finally got up. He'd been lying in bed with his eyes closed for hours, hoping he could go back to sleep, but it was no use. His encounter with Charlie, coupled with his fear and doubt, had left him feeling small. There was no one he could call. His father and Tammy would each probably take his call, but he couldn't keep bothering them. Besides, there was nothing they could do. Tammy had long ago moved on with her life, and conversations with his father had devolved into Jon complaining and his father continually repeating some variation of, "It will be fine." Jon was alone.

He put on sweatpants and a baseball cap to cover his morning hair and walked down the hallway. In the lobby, he grabbed a cup of coffee, waving to the front desk attendant, who was hiding behind a newspaper, slurping her own.

Jon quickly inserted then removed his plastic room key into the slot and opened the door to the cramped hotel "business center," a room that was more like a closet that happened to hold two monitors. He sat down at one of these and hesitated, his fingers hovering above the keyboard. He decided to broaden the keywords for his search to include anything about Chemtrifuge, not just the explosion. Some history on the company might help the investigation.

A general search showed hundreds of pages, so he tried adding "noncompliance," "deviations," and "exceedance" to his search string. He'd waded through five Google results pages and was ready to give up when his eyes locked on the words *allegations, environmental,* and *Chemtrifuge,* bolded in a two-line article summary. He took a sip of coffee and clicked on the article. It was three years old, and discussed a meeting between a group of environmentalists and Chemtrifuge management in the company parking lot.

The article discussed the environmental group SHEAN and their so-called bucket brigade. Jon started chasing threads in the article. First he visited SHEAN's website, which wasn't very helpful. Then he tried searching on the words "SHEAN," "bucket brigade," "Chemtrifuge," "environment," and "safety" in various combinations. He grabbed a piece of paper out of the printer and started making notes.

After several more searches, Jon stretched and looked up from the computer screen. The clock on the wall read 6:07 a.m. His stomach growled as he heard clanking sounds from the lobby, announcing that they were setting up breakfast. The more he dug into the articles, the more he learned about a potential ally. The conversation with the cameraman in the parking lot the day of the fire starting coming back to him. Apparently Chemtrifuge had a thorn in its side, and that thorn was named Wanda Ripwhile. Two articles shed a lot of light on Wanda, and fortunately one was a lengthy puff piece (complete with photos) that made him feel like he already knew her.

For years, Wanda Ripwhile had lived in a small house just feet from the Chemtrifuge fence line. Even her name was catchy, and one of the articles Jon ran across claimed that "nobody who ever met her forgot her." She was in her upper fifties but looked older. She had dirty-blond hair streaked with white, and she was medium-sized with a stern expression. One photo showed her with a furrowed brow that looked like she had just heard something she didn't like.

The article summarized interviews with other community activists. Everyone in the community knew Wanda for her environmental work, but otherwise she was a mystery, even to those who claimed they knew her well. She apparently had a degree in public health and nursing, though no one remembered her ever working. She had two kids, both adults. A few years ago she'd started SHEAN, which stood for Save our Health through Environmental Action Now. They had a one-page website that looked like it was done in 1990.

Another article was less flattering but still descriptive. Wanda was critical of all industrial companies in the area, but her main goal seemed to be making Chemtrifuge management miserable. When they had a town hall meeting, as required by the Environmental Protection Agency, to discuss their theoretical worse-case scenario accident, she attended with her entourage. Jon studied the picture for a few minutes. She had six colleagues in tow, three sixty-plus-year-old rejects from the 1960s adorned with tie-dye shirts and sandals, and three youngsters who looked college age and sported dreadlocks and T-shirts with anti-corporate logos. One of the youngsters had a video camera, and the article noted that he went around taping Wanda every time she questioned company representatives at their booths. SHEAN's only real possession, besides the camera, seemed to be a really old van wallpapered with various bumper stickers about how good the earth was and how bad industry was. Its license plate read SHEAN.

Twice a year, this entourage would show up at the Chemtrifuge parking lot and demand to speak with management to discuss the results of their latest bucket brigade. The bucket brigade was made up of people loosely associated with SHEAN who used makeshift air monitors consisting of a plastic bucket with a hose and a small tarp to capture samples from the air. This contraption was designed by a sympathetic professor at West Virginia University, a member of the Union of Concerned Scientists who occasionally donated to SHEAN. Supposedly, samples showed that Chemtrifuge and other nearby companies were spewing toxins into the air, putting neighborhood residents at risk.

▲ ▲ ▲

"Just a minute," came a gruff woman's voice, apparently far from the front door. A yellow tabby curled around Jon's leg. He looked down. "Hi," he said awkwardly, not knowing if he was being watched. It was bad to start a conversation with someone discussing how rude you were to their pet. This cat was on her porch, so he assumed it was hers.

It was a one-level wooden house, the kind Jon had seen built near a lot of chemical plants. Oftentimes, plants could get permits to build in less affluent parts of town. Or it might have been that this house was nice fifty years ago, but was now overcome by time and neglect. The green siding was stained with soot and grass, the grass was high, and weeds grew through the cracks in the walkway to the front porch.

Raaaaoouu, cried the tabby, looking up at Jon. He could hear it purring. Hopefully its owner would be just as friendly.

The inner door opened, and Jon could see a woman standing behind the screen door.

"I see you've met Frisky."

Raaaaoouuu, accompanied by purring.

"She seems friendly," Jon said, reaching down to scratch her head.

"Too friendly," barked the woman. "What do you want?"

"Uh, my name is Jon Barrett. I'm investigating the explosion that happened at the plant next door. I assume you know about it."

"I know all about that place," she said sternly. "Why do you want to talk to me?"

"Well, I found your organization through an internet search. It gave this address for SHEAN. I understand you have some history with the company, and I thought you might have some insights that might help with the investigation. Are you Wanda?"

"Yes, I'm Wanda. Don't know much about that explosion, but I guess I can talk to you."

She opened the door, and Frisky ran in. Jon reached down to grab her but missed.

"Oh, that's all right. She does what she pleases." As Jon was walking into her living room, Wanda added, "Like that company over there does."

"I know what you mean," Jon said, seeing a chance to bond.

Wanda waved at the sofa. "Have a seat. Place is a mess—I wasn't expecting company."

"It looks fine," Jon said, though she was right. Unfolded laundry was draped over an easy chair, papers were spread out in one corner, and the carpet was yellowish and stained. "Sorry to barge in like this. I just thought I'd see if you had time to chat about Chemtrifuge. Anything that might help me understand what happened."

"You want some coffee?"

"Sure." Jon had already had three cups, but coffee would give him a reason to stay longer.

Wanda walked into the room a minute later with a cup on a cracked saucer, along with a small spoon and packets of powdered creamer and sugar. She put them down on a weathered brown coffee table that Jon might have seen at any Nebraska yard sale.

"Thanks," he said, adding creamer as he looked around the room.

"It's not much to look at, but it's home," Wanda said defensively.

"It's nice. I grew up in a home like this in Nebraska."

"Where did you say you were from again?"

"Actually, I'm from the government, Department of Interior."

"The government," Wanda said with disdain. "Now there's a good one. Probably the only institution more corrupt and inept than these chemical companies."

Jon chuckled. "Can't really argue with you. The government does a lot of things badly, but I'm trying to get this investigation right."

"Well," she reflected, looking out the window, "I guess they're trying, but they sure need to try harder when it comes to the environment."

"Good point." Jon took a sip.

"Like I told you at the door, I don't know much about the explosion, but we heard it. My boy was home—he comes sometimes—and it really rattled him. It was at night. Just a big boom, and then a fire. The fire was so hot, it felt warm in the front yard."

Jon cleared his throat. "Do you mind if I take notes?"

"No, if you think it'll help."

"Thanks. Did you notice anything different that day, or just before the explosion?"

"I noticed they had a lot of flaring earlier. I was on the porch that evening. You know those big stacks are called flares. They usually just have smoke, but that evening they had a big flame coming out—a flame as long as the stack. It looked like a roman candle."

"And that was the evening before the explosion?"

"Yes. I remember looking out my window just before I went to bed, and it was still going on. I go to bed around 11:30, so it must have been about then. As I recall, the explosion happened around two the next morning."

"That's helpful, thanks," Jon said. "And the flame was unusual?"

"Yes, that was unusual. They have flaring like that sometimes when they're starting up, you know, after the plant has been down for maintenance or something. They send us notices, like a flyer in the mailbox, to let us know they're starting up and to expect more fire from the flare stack. I bet they're required to do that by law—they wouldn't let us know anything if they didn't have to. We had to take them to court to get the most current SDSs about the chemicals they use." She looked at Jon writing. "Sorry, an SDS is a safety data sheet."

Jon nodded. "Yes, I know what they are. I worked in chemical plants in a past life, so I know some things about them." Seeing her forehead wrinkle, he added, "But I also know how secretive they can be, even with their own employees."

Wanda seemed satisfied. "This time, it was like they were starting up, but I didn't get a notice, so I thought something was wrong. I didn't call the police or the plant or anybody. I've done that so much, they just ignore me. I think their management has most of the movers and shakers in town in their back pockets."

"This is very helpful. Can you tell me anything else, like your work with the bucket brigade? I read about that online."

"Well, a bunch of us in the neighborhood have these makeshift devices to collect air samples. We do that regularly and have the samples analyzed. Here, I'll show you a bucket." She walked into a back room and came out with a blue bucket like ones Jon had seen by the front door at George's Hardware Store in Kimball. "I have an apparatus that I hook to it."

"What have you found?"

"That they're polluting our air. They say our methods of sampling are flawed and the lab we send the samples to is biased, but we offered to let them test them with us, and they refused."

Jon nodded, making notes.

"Anyway, they're a secretive bunch over there. I can't believe they're cooperating with the government."

Jon put down his mechanical pencil. "Well, I wouldn't exactly say they're cooperating. I'm still trying to get information."

"Figures. What do you think caused that explosion?"

"I'm still working on that." Jon took a sip. "The company's saying it was bad maintenance by contractors—that they left a gasket out or something, and somehow a leak started because of that and caused the explosion. But I'm not totally buying it. I think something else contributed."

"I'm not surprised that bunch would blame somebody else. I think I heard that a couple of guys died when that happened, but I never heard much else about that. Strange. I guess the company wanted to keep it hush-hush. I think they own the media here too."

"They sure do seem to have friends in high places." Jon put his cup down. "But I've taken enough of your time. Anything else you can remember that might help me figure this out? I think the day of the explosion, a reporter told me that your organization might have some logs or something."

"Not really," Wanda said, rising. But as they walked out to the front porch, she added, "The only other thing I remember was seeing an ambulance leave by the south entrance, down that way." She pointed. "It didn't have any lights on. I just happened to see it going out. Maybe it was carrying one of the dead guys, and there was no need to rush."

"Maybe. I'll check it out," Jon said. He wrote himself a note before he got into his car.

49

"Damn them!" Lisa slammed her mic on the desk, almost smashing it.

"Calm down, sweetheart," said Kenny. "What's wrong?"

"Another damn dog show, then an exposé on a kid who can't stop belching. They're killing my career!"

Kenny snickered. "People want to see you do those—they like it."

"I want to work on a real story," Lisa said, ignoring him. "On some actual news. Look at Rachael Jones. She's out there covering real stories. And don't get me started on Sarah, what she's been able to do with that stupid story about the Speaker of the House and that email. There's nothing new, and she's still doing a story every other day. They'll be in DC or New York on a major network in no time."

"Boy, somebody pissed in your Cheerios."

"It's not funny, Kenny. They're not giving me *anything*. I asked the station manager to give me something besides these stupid dog and flower shows, but he said the other stories are covered."

"Like I told you—make your *own* opportunity."

"Easier said than done."

"Maybe not." Kenny pulled out his phone and punched in a code. "Listen."

Lisa put the phone to her ear and listened for a moment. She lowered it and looked at Kenny. "Is this for real?"

"I think so. Just got it in the station voicemail today. They forwarded it to me. But let's see if it's for real—call him back. Unless you'd rather prep for the flower show."

"You idiot," Lisa said abruptly and then laughed. She raised the phone up to her ear again and hit the number to repeat.

"Hi, I'm trying to reach the reporter who covered the story about the explosion at Chemtrifuge. She started to do an interview with me that day, but we had to cancel. I'm still investigating the explosion, and I had an idea for a story. I'd like to talk to her and maybe meet to discuss . . ."

Lisa reached for a pen and wrote down the numbers Jon had given for his cell and the hotel where he was staying. When she'd finished listening the second time, she handed Kenny the phone. "What if he doesn't have anything new?"

Kenny put down the headphones he had been rewiring. "You were just griping about how the other divas put something together even when there's no story. Make a story." He picked up the headphones again. "Unless they're better than you."

"You bastard," she said. He chuckled.

She closed her notepad and tapped her pen on the cover. Kenny was right. She had to make a story. She wasn't sure about the angle, but one thing she knew: the next story she submitted was not going to be about flowers or dogs or belching boys. It was going to be—in some way—about the explosion. Either in print with the station's affiliate paper or, she hoped, on air, she was going to do a story.

"Hand me the phone," she said, opening the notebook again.

He smiled. "That's my girl."

50

Jon had entered a new phase in the investigation, and he was taking a big chance. By going outside the company to the environmental group and the reporter, he risked blowing up any relationship he'd developed with Chemtrifuge. But he felt time was running out.

He still hadn't heard from his boss. Either Craig didn't care, or he was playing a waiting game, avoiding giving Jon bad news.

Even if his options were not good, he had to try something. He had an ominous feeling that if he didn't make a breakthrough soon, everything would have been for naught. The company was slow-walking the investigation. They'd given him two operators who didn't know anything and then cut off all interviews. He was getting nothing from DC, no pressure to finish, no support. This was his investigation. He could let it drop and let the company get away with dragging its feet, or he could go outside the company and see if that would push them to cooperate. It was risky, but he had little to lose.

Jon decided to go to the plant. His presence wouldn't make the company cooperate, but if he didn't show up, they would have an excuse to delay more. They could say they'd tried to schedule interviews but couldn't find him.

As he drove to the plant, the way they controlled him started playing on his mind—he'd only recently been given the "privilege" of going to the restroom by himself. He was working for the US government. People had died. He should be able to go where he wanted and talk to whoever he wanted to talk to. But the reality was, it was the company's property, and they seemed to have enough political support to keep lawmakers, media, and most of the public at bay. He was just one person, even if he did work for the government. Still, how they were acting bothered him, and more so today, because he knew going in was a waste of time.

The security guard was on the phone. He did not recognize her.

"I'm sitting here with it now," she was saying. "He must have dropped it at the badge reader on the way out."

"Excuse me, ma'am," Jon interrupted.

She held up a finger and turned away. "Oh, so he's from the Baltimore plant. I see." She listened a few seconds. "Okay, I'll put it in the bin. If he comes back in the next couple weeks, we'll have it for him. But sounds like he's got another one already and doesn't need it?"

She hung up and turned toward Jon. "What can I help you with?"

Jon smiled. "I'm here investigating the accident that happened a while back. I come here every day and have an escort from HR."

The guard tossed the lost badge into a blue plastic bin, talking as she placed the bin at the end of the long counter. "I don't know anything about that—I just got here. Let me go in the back and ask Jerome if he knows about you. What's your name?"

"Jon Barrett."

"Jon Barrett," she repeated. "Okay, wait a minute, I'll be right back."

She walked to the back of the guard shack, to the room where Jon had watched the safety tape when he had first arrived on-site. He could hear her talking to someone. As he stood at the counter, he looked at the bin that she'd just set down. He thought about her phone call. Apparently this badge belonged to someone from the company's Baltimore plant. If it was programmed, it could allow someone to get into the Baltimore plant, and maybe even the plant here in Charleston too. That could be valuable if he ever needed to get in for any reason without an escort. The more he thought about it, the more valuable this piece of plastic seemed, and apparently the person who lost it already had another one. But even so, if they knew he'd taken it, they could accuse him of stealing.

He could hear movement in the back, and then the guard's voice, getting louder, as if she was approaching. In one swift motion, he turned his back to the camera in the corner to block the view, picked the badge out of the bin, and put in in his pocket. Then he began rummaging around in the lost-and-found bin to see if there were any other items of interest.

The guard came around the corner and saw him looking in the bin. "Something wrong?"

He shook his head, thinking fast. "I lost an umbrella a couple of weeks ago. I just wanted to see if it was here."

"Nope, don't remember ever seeing an umbrella in here." She grabbed the bin and shoved it under the counter. "Your story checks out with Jerome, but we need to call HR. Nobody told us to expect you today."

Jon smiled. "They probably just forgot."

Charlie showed up fifteen minutes later, breathing hard. "I didn't know you were coming today."

"Investigation's still going on," Jon said calmly.

Charlie exhaled forcefully. "Come on."

Jon followed him, afraid they might have added a new security measure. Maybe they'd make him walk through a metal detector, or have some other way of finding out that he stole the badge. But nothing happened.

"If you have any documents or interviews, you know where to find me," Jon said in the hall leading to his office.

Charlie snorted. "Yes, I know."

When Jon got to his office, he closed the door, sat in his folding chair, and exhaled. He had made it to his office with his badge. All he needed now was to get out with it.

▲　▲　▲

Clink.

The three wineglasses all touched at the same time, followed by laughter. Wheelan Drew, CEO of Chemtrifuge, looked out the window of his Manhattan office at the Statue of Liberty, a small figurine from this distance.

"Gentlemen, what you're drinking is a grand cru from one of my favorite villages in Burgundy. I don't share this with just anybody."

Leska was a scotch man, and he knew Quinn to be a beer drinker, but Drew had enticed them to indulge with him today.

"Well, guys, this is cause for celebration. The price of ethylene just spiked unexpectedly while two of our competitors were down for turnarounds. Life couldn't be better."

The other two guys tipped their glasses toward him and drank.

Leska winked at Drew as he sipped. He had flown up from his DC law office that morning to provide care and feeding for his main client. Earlier that morning, he'd been looking at the US Capitol out his window, and this afternoon he was looking at the Statue of Liberty. Life was good, money was flowing like liquid pumped through a pipe, and he'd just celebrated his tenth year as partner. As long as Chemtrifuge stayed healthy financially, he would too. He would do what he could to ensure Chemtrifuge's health and, more importantly, his own.

▲ ▲ ▲

Cain Quinn scratched his day-old stubble. This was not his scene. He'd rather be trolling around in one of the plants and having a Rolling Rock at a local bar afterward. He indulged Drew occasionally by letting him show off his New York digs, but they didn't impress Quinn. Though his title—senior advisor—was somewhat nondescript, Quinn was the real power in the company. Everyone else knew it too, including Drew. Quinn bled Chemtrifuge blue and would do anything to keep the company on top. He already had. Whether it was pressuring the accounting group behind the scenes to hide expenses so the profitability would look better, or pushing a hesitant plant manager to ramp up production and work through a scheduled maintenance outage, Quinn made the company run, and win. To Quinn, that was key. The company had to win. It was not about the money, he had plenty of that. And it was not just about winning—it was about destroying. He did not want Chemtrifuge to simply exist alongside other competitors. It wasn't even enough for it to make more money than they did. He wanted to destroy all the company's competitors, and everyone who had anything to do with them.

Drew drained the last of his grand cru and topped off everyone's glass. "Hey, guys, one more bit of business before we break and go to the 21 Club. How's that investigation going at the Charleston plant? I hear happy talk from Page, but I'm never sure if he has his folks in line."

Leska swirled his glass. "I think it's okay, but Sam called me last week. I think he wants me to come there and kill this thing once and for all. I know how to handle these government types. Bark at them, and they back down."

"Good," Drew said. "I feel better knowing you're on top of it. So you're going there next week?"

Leska swallowed. "I didn't commit, but I told him I could be there in a few hours. I might go over next week, not sure. He said he doesn't even know if the investigator's coming back. Why waste a first-class plane ticket to Charleston if I don't need to?"

Leska and Drew laughed. Quinn didn't. He saw the value Andrew Leska brought, and even admitted he was a hell of a lawyer. But he'd never liked smug East Coast attorneys.

Leska took another drink and swallowed, adding an *ahhh* obviously for Drew's benefit. "In the meantime, I got my assistant finding out all we can about that office, the scope of their authority, and the investigator. There's not much on him—he's apparently made no mark in industry—but we'll find something. We'll play hardball if we have to."

"Good," Drew said. "I don't need any uncertainty in the midst of all this good news. Let me know if you need a favor with the politicians there. This guy Mounts carries sway, and he'd lick my floor if I asked him."

Quinn said nothing. He held his head still, shifting his eyes from one to the other.

Drew continued. "Don't make me call in my ultimate reinforcement here." He tipped his glass toward Quinn. "Things get ugly when we have to get him involved."

Quinn put his glass down on the rim of the four-foot globe bar in the middle of the office. "But they get fixed fast, and with no loose ends," he said.

Drew and Leska both laughed nervously. Quinn didn't laugh or smile.

51

Thursday started and ended like the days before it. Jon went to the plant and sat in his office. He walked around the room when the hard folding chair wore on his backside. He knew this week had been a bust, but things could get better after the news report. He was both hopeful that it would help Chemtrifuge's cooperation and concerned that it would not. He didn't have much leverage left—the media and Wanda from the environmental group were his last remaining bullets. He'd given up on his agency. He hadn't heard from his boss, and the lawyers wouldn't even sign the document requests.

He sat with his arms behind his head, head tilted back, looking at the grid of tiles in the ceiling. He noticed mold forming on some and started thinking about their shapes. The brownish patterns on the porous speckled tiles looked like distorted faces or odd-shaped balloons. Then he started thinking positively. He had gone to the media and the concerned neighbor on his own. And now he had a badge to the plant—which might or might not work—back in his hotel room in his duffel bag.

When he walked by the previously vacant office on his way to the restroom, he noticed that there were two people there now. They were talking, but when they saw him pass by, they stopped. He went to lunch around noon—same place, same waitress, same club sandwich. Even the same booth. Someone had left a local paper in the booth. There was an update on the state Speaker of the House and her email chain with the railroad guy. Apparently, there was more evidence that she had steered additional contracts to his company. There were emails where she said something about "exploring her tunnels." Jon decided to keep the paper. He made a mental note to go back and read old articles about the story and emails later.

Back at the plant, Charlie met Jon at the gate. They didn't talk on the way to the admin building. That afternoon Jon sat at his desk, scrolled through his phone, read the news, and paced around his office. There was a small window at the top of one wall, just under the ceiling. It was only a foot tall, and positioned too high for him to look out. He stood on his chair, but still could not see out. He thought if he could find some books and stack them on the chair, he could get higher. But then he thought how embarrassing it would be if a government employee, there to investigate an accident, fell off a chair and had an accident himself. He abandoned the idea.

Finally Jon decided there was no point in staying past five. He called Charlie to escort him back to the guard shack. "I'll probably come in at the same time tomorrow," he said when Charlie arrived, "but I may leave early. I'm thinking about going back to DC."

"Fine," Charlie muttered.

"Do you think you'll have any interviews or documents ready tomorrow?" Jon asked at the guard gate.

"Probably not," Charlie said flatly.

Jon knew there was no reason to push it. The trip in tomorrow would be a waste, too, but if he didn't come in, the company could say they tried to find him but couldn't.

It was chimichanga night at the hotel. He had two, and one cheap beer in a plastic cup. He retired to his room and watched television. An old episode of *Cheers* was on, the one where Cliff went on *Jeopardy*. Jon turned off the TV and rolled over in bed. He started thinking about the investigation. What if his recent moves amounted to nothing? What if the media, the neighbors, the environmental group, and the government could not get the company to cooperate? He did not want to think about it. He reached over and turned out the light, trying to think about the *Cheers* episode to quiet his mind.

52

Sam slept restlessly. He and Glenda had fought the night before, when she asked again if he would go to therapy with her. He didn't need one more thing on his plate.

▲ ▲ ▲

During the night, Charlie's wife had coughing spells that continually woke him up. He finally got out of bed and went to the living room and started reading a book he had been reading for months, but his eyes only scanned the words as he wondered how much further his wife's cancer had progressed.

▲ ▲ ▲

Cain Quinn had a dream about an incident in grade school. In the dream, he pushed a girl in his class out the door and down the steps of the red building after she called him rude. She fell on the gravel and skinned up her face. She started crying, and he told the teacher it was an accident. That had really happened. In his dream, though, he jumped on the little girl and started beating her. She'd called him rude. He wanted to show her what "rude" looked like. When he woke, he reflected on the missed opportunity. She had insulted him. She should have been taught a lesson. Instead of crying for five minutes, she should have cried for five days. He was older now. He woke up thinking about that girl who he'd never heard of after high school, hoping she was living a hard life or perhaps had died young.

▲ ▲ ▲

Jon lay awake until close to seven. He made a mental note to grab a newspaper from the hotel lobby so he would have something to do. He didn't feel like going to the diner. He knew the biscuits in the lobby would be hard, the gravy would be cold and sticky in clumps, and the eggs would be microwaved patties. But it was edible, and he could watch TV while he mindlessly lifted the fork to his mouth.

It was the same routine at the plant. Jon waited at the guard shack for almost a half-hour. When Charlie finally showed up, he looked more disheveled than usual.

"Everything okay?" Jon asked on the way to the admin building.

"Everything's fine," Charlie snarled.

"Good." Then Jon asked the obligatory question. "Will I get interviews or documents today?"

"We'll see," Charlie mumbled.

Once inside, Jon stepped into his office, and Charlie kept walking.

"I'm leaving early this afternoon," Jon reiterated.

"Okay!" Charlie bellowed, with an I-don't-care tone.

Jon sat down in the uncomfortable chair in his makeshift office.

He opened the paper he had snagged that morning on the way out of his hotel. The story on the front page was about the Speaker of the House. The investigation seemed to be pulling in other politicians, including A. C. Mounts. It seemed that Mounts's name had surfaced on some documents related to one of the contracts the Speaker had allegedly steered toward her lover's company. Also, the company had made a "sizable contribution" to Mount's reelection fund within hours of his announced support for a change to the state procurement process, which he'd previously opposed. That change allowed the Speaker to unilaterally sole-source contracts to companies without going through open competition. Polls showed that while the Speaker's favorability rating had tanked, Mounts's rating among his constituents was holding steady, though the number who were "somewhat or very concerned about his role in the alleged scheme" was growing.

Jon took a longer than usual lunch that day, and afterward he drove along the back roads to the plant to see something, anything, new. When he got back to the plant, Charlie met him at the gate and walked him to the admin building without saying a word. Jon stopped at his office, and Charlie walked on.

Jon opened the door and gasped. Piles of folders stuffed with papers were heaped on top of the desk in his office. Even his chair had folders on it. Were they moving someone else into his office? Why hadn't Charlie said something to him? Or maybe that's why Charlie hadn't said anything. They didn't even respect him enough to let him have his own space, just slightly bigger than a closet with a folding chair.

He was mad that even this small convenience was being taken away. There was no other chair. Was he supposed to share his chair with another person?

He grabbed one of the folders. Maybe it would contain a clue to who was moving in. He opened the folder, and then stared at it in shock.

▲ ▲ ▲

Craig Higgins cringed when the email from Sharon Hill popped up.

> *From: Sharon Hill <Interior>*
> *To: Craig Higgins <Interior>*
> *Subject: Courtesy Reminder: Meeting next **Thursday** to*
> *discuss budget.*

He was pissed off even before he opened it. He hated the way Sharon had bolded and underlined the day, as if he wouldn't see it otherwise. She wanted to make sure that anyone else who saw the message knew she had idiot-proofed—*Craig*-proofed—this email. He wanted to delete it without reading, but she might have sneaked some text bomb in that he needed to try to either diffuse or dodge. When he opened it, he was glad to see there was no action or response required, no lines or sentences that ended with a question mark, and nobody else was copied, though he was sure she had blind-copied others. He didn't reply.

She sent this stink-bomb message on a Friday. He hated her. He also knew that as of next Thursday, it was the end of his new office, the end of the investigation, and the end of Jon. He thought about calling Jon and telling him to update his résumé but decided to wait. Let the guy have one more good weekend. He might not feel supported now, but at least he had a job. In four business days, that would end.

▲ ▲ ▲

The first folder Jon opened was marked "HAZOP"—hazard and operability analysis, a method that chemical plants and refineries used to identify hazards. All three folders in that stack contained copies of the HAZOP. The top folder on another stack contained folded drawings of the ethylene process. The first he unfolded was a large CAD drawing of the flare system, the system which was connected to the drum that had exploded. In another stack, there were procedures for operating the unit.

Jon's eyes started watering, but for the first time in months it was because of hope, not despair. His persistence had paid off. The company was playing ball. There were nine files of information, even more than he had asked for. He didn't know what had changed the company's mind. Maybe it was the press, or the environmental group, or perhaps the union had finally come to its senses. Right now he didn't care. All he knew was that his investigation had new life. He would spend the weekend poring over the information.

Jon sat back in his chair and smiled. He wouldn't go back to DC this weekend. The drive would take precious time from this revived investigation.

He'd walk to Charlie's office and thank him, Jon decided. This treasure trove of documents meant the company was cooperating, so Charlie shouldn't mind him walking unescorted.

With a renewed sense of confidence, he strode past the conference room in the corner and made the right turn. He'd never walked this far by himself before. Charlie's office was on the left, just before another corner office marked with a placard that read "Sam Page, Plant Manager."

Jon rapped softly on Charlie's open door. Charlie was hunched over a paper on his desk that looked like something from a doctor's office. He looked up, startled.

"I wanted to thank you for the documents," Jon said calmly. "I really appreciate it."

Charlie cocked his head. "What are you talking about?"

Now Jon was confused. He had to think fast. Maybe he was wrong about the company giving him the information, or maybe the company hadn't told Charlie yet. Perhaps the union had something to do with it. Whatever the source, Jon had the documents, and Charlie didn't know about it. Now Jon had to get those documents to his car without raising suspicions.

"Sorry, I was thinking about another conversation I just had. Government benefits stuff. But, uh, I probably will still be leaving early this afternoon. I didn't know if I told you or not." Then Jon added, as Charlie opened his mouth, "I'm going straight back to my office. Sorry if I bothered you."

"Yes, go straight back now. Leave whenever you want to—I have something to take care of." Charlie looked down and appeared to be preoccupied with the paper on his desk.

"Yes, sir," Jon said meekly.

In an ideal world, Jon would have asked the company for boxes. But this was not an ideal world, so he decided to carry all the folders out himself. He had one chance, he thought. Charlie had said to leave whenever he wanted to, and the time was now.

He first tucked five folders under one arm and the rest under the other, but they kept slipping out. In the end he decided to carry all nine in front of him. Remembering seeing a cardboard box broken down and lying flat in the empty office next to his, he peered out his door then walked into the other office and grabbed the box. He didn't have any tape, but he hoped that refolding the box with the flaps inserted correctly would hold the folders, at least until he got to his car.

As he walked out the back door of the admin building, balancing the box in front of him with one hand on the bottom and one on the top, he passed a woman coming into the building. She looked at him, surprised. He nodded. "Leaving," he said, making it sound like it was for good. The woman lowered her eyes and walked on.

When he went through the turnstile and passed beside the guard shack, Ruby stepped out the side door with a clipboard in hand, blocking his way to the parking lot.

"I'm sorry, where are you going with that box?"

"I'm leaving for the day." He tilted his head toward the admin building. "They know."

Ruby grabbed the microphone of her radio. "I think I need to clear this with HR."

Jon looked serious. "Charlie knows—he told me to go. He's in an important meeting and told me he didn't want to be bothered the rest of the day. But I guess you can go ahead and take a chance. I just hope he doesn't get upset." Jon paused. "They seem to go through guards a lot here."

Ruby slowly lowered her mic. "I guess it's okay. What's in the box?"

In Jon's experience, being exaggeratedly compliant with guards sometimes deterred further questions.

"Want to see? Charlie said it was proprietary information, not to be shared with anyone, but I'll tell him you wanted to go through it. By the way, have you signed a nondisclosure agreement with Chemtrifuge?"

Ruby paused, looked toward the admin building and then back at Jon. She stepped out of the way. "Okay. Go on."

"Thanks," Jon said, walking toward the parking lot. He had never been good at gambling, but this bluff had paid off. He put the box in the back seat and got into his car, his heart pounding so hard it scared him.

▲　▲　▲

Ruby watched Jon drive away and wondered for a second if she made a mistake not calling Charlie. But this guy from the government always complied with Charlie's requests. He waited in the guard shack for almost an hour sometimes. She saw the way Charlie disdained him, but this guy never snapped at her or Charlie. She actually felt sorry for him. It was obvious the company didn't want him there, but he seemed to do whatever they said. He wouldn't be so bold now as to steal property. Besides, he was right about Chemtrifuge going through guards. If she bothered Charlie at the wrong time, there was a chance she would be gone.

53

After he stopped by the hotel to leave the box, Jon decided to take a walk along the river. He drove to downtown Charleston and parked in a garage. He felt content. This was a day to celebrate.

As Jon walked on the red bricks along the Riverwalk, he stopped to watch a white dog with black spots chase a tennis ball. "Bring it back, Sandy!" someone shouted. Jon turned and saw a trim, thirtysomething woman in athletic clothes, bending over and clapping her hands.

Jon looked at the Kanawha River, lazily flowing through the middle of the city. He walked along at the same pace as the river flowed. He looked to his left and saw a mixture of buildings. Some looked like black mirrors, with bank names prominently displayed, and some were old brown buildings like the ones in Nebraska, only taller. Others were red brick or off-white, with symmetrical rows of windows and arches at the top.

Jon thought about his father and wondered what he was doing this afternoon. He made a mental note to call him. He thought of Tammy. He remembered a time in Wyoming when he and Tammy had talked about moving somewhere bigger. That day they'd agreed that as long as they were together, they could make it anywhere. The memory made him sad. Then he thought about the investigation and felt content again. He didn't know what he would find in the documents, but at least they held hope. Someone wanted him to have them, which meant there must be something worth finding.

He sat down on a bench and started worrying again. It was odd that he'd had no documents that morning, and now he had piles of them. What if this was all a company trick? The spotted dog now had friends fighting over the tennis ball. The trim woman was standing with arms folded, talking to a group of other women who looked like her. Jon could see the top of the state capitol in the distance, a miniature version of the one in DC. Then his mind drifted back to the documents. What if they had fed him false documents that would show nothing, or confuse him?

No one was within hearing distance, so he started talking out loud to himself. "There are three possibilities. First, the company wanted me to have the documents, but just didn't tell Charlie. Second, it's a trick to throw me off the trail. And third, somebody else wants me to have the documents. Okay, let's take these one at a time. What are the chances that management made a decision to give me the documents, but didn't tell Charlie? He's been my contact the whole time. The only thing that may support that possibility is that he seemed preoccupied when I went to his office. Maybe he was tied up with something else."

Jon looked at the water. Two kids in inner tubes were kicking water at each other, screaming and floating down the river.

"A decision like that wouldn't be quick, not after resisting so long. Even if Charlie was busy today, I think he'd know about it. I don't think they came from the company."

Jon stood up and started walking toward the dogs, continuing to think through why he now had the documents.

The company might be shrewd enough to produce false documents to throw him off, but it would take work to go in and doctor them. And why would they have done so many? Wouldn't it be easier to just keep holding out? Especially since they seemed to be getting away with it. Maybe they got wind the media was going to run the story. It would have been a quick decision, leaving little time to doctor all those documents, but he couldn't rule it out.

Jon passed the spot where he'd started his walk. The dogs were standing by the edge of the river, barking. Apparently the ball had rolled in and no one was willing to get wet.

Jon resumed his line of self-questioning, out loud again.

"It might be the company, but if it isn't, who could it be? I think the docs are legitimate, but where did they come from?"

He stopped and looked at the water again.

"Other than the company, there are two possibilities. They either came from the environmental group or the union. The environmental group wouldn't have gone to the plant—they would have given the documents to me at the hotel. Wanda knows how to get in touch with me. So that leaves the union."

Jon passed a couple on a bench. By now he didn't care if people saw him talking to himself.

"I thought the union steward had bought the company line, but maybe not. Now that I think about it, the conference room walls may not be soundproof. Maybe he was pretending, and knew he'd feed me information later."

After concluding that the documents were legitimate and either from the company, which had been shamed into giving them to him, or from the union, which wanted him to investigate, Jon felt better. The investigation lived!

On the way to his car, he saw a small, quaint-looking coffee shop and bistro. He decided to make an afternoon of it with a flavored coffee and a pastry. He took a seat by the window next to an old cappuccino maker that looked like a miniature time machine. A canopy of trees provided spotty shading on the street outside. A large clock on a tall stand was just a few feet from the shop door. A green mural on the side of the building sported an ad for "The Oldest Restaurant in Town." People walked by slowly. Across the street under an awning, he saw "Woolworth," and wondered if those stores were still around. He ordered a second cup to-go, with a chocolate-filled bear claw. For the first time in a long time, he felt happy. He mindfully ate the bear claw, taking small bites and chewing slowly, savoring the potpourri of chocolate, cream, and sweet bread flavors.

54

The next morning, Saturday, after devouring two eggs with salsa and biscuits with gravy, Jon asked if he could use an open room just off the hotel lobby.

The young, tattooed front desk guy scratched his goatee. "Sure. You can use it till somebody else needs it. If you reserve it, we'll have to charge."

"Is anybody scheduled to use it today?"

The attendant opened a binder. "Not today. You're probably okay. I just can't guarantee that—somebody else might be willing to pay."

Jon decided to take his chances. "I understand. I'll move if somebody pays."

He put his coffee cup and half-empty plate on one of the tables and brought the box with all nine folders to the room. He put two tables together in an L shape and started lifting the folders out one by one.

Setting his mechanical pencils and highlighters down in a neat stack beside the yellow notepad, Jon started taking documents out of folders.

On the document marked "HAZOP," he noticed the heading on the first page: "Pre-Construction." This was the hazard analysis that was done before the equipment was put in place. In the folder were all the procedures he could have asked for, including filling vessels in the ethylene unit—with a specific section for each one—and "venting material to the flare system during unit upsets." There was a procedure on emergency response. He unfolded the twelve piping and instrumentation diagrams, or P&IDs. By tracing the line number that fed the vessel through the other drawings, he found the drawings for the vessel that had exploded and the equipment directly upstream.

Once all the documents were laid out in stacks, he went to the HAZOP and leafed through it until he found the vessel that had exploded, Ethylene Overhead Vessel E-101. HAZOP, Jon knew, was a structured brainstorming method that used guide-words to determine the consequences of equipment upsets, or deviations, documented in columns on a page. The deviations were combinations of equipment characteristics like level or temperature, and some change, like too much or too little.

Jon remembered the first time he took a HAZOP class. The instructor, a white-haired Santa Claus type, used a cooking analogy. "Okay, folks, what if I'm making a soup and I scoop in too much salt?"

"It would taste like my wife's soup," one class clown blurted out.

"I suppose that's a bad thing, seeing how you look like you're starving," the instructor said. The entire class broke into laughter, except for the portly class clown.

"So let's walk through that. Let's say the deviation would be too much salt, or maybe we could say 'high flow of salt.' The cause would be pouring in too much from our scoop. We still have to list safeguards, and any recommendations to keep it from happening. What are the safeguards?"

"Well, the recipe could have the right amount noted," someone in the back yelled.

"Very good," the instructor said. "And a recommendation might be that we review the recipe before we start to make the soup. Or if we don't need much salt, maybe we add it with a tablespoon rather than a scoop. Always easier to put more in than take it out."

Everyone nodded.

"And the consequence is, the soup tastes like our shy friend's wife's soup, and he starves, or eats it and gets high blood pressure." Everyone, including the class clown, burst out laughing.

Jon laughed at this memory as his mind slowly returned to the real document on the table. He was not sure what had caused the explosion, so he decided to look through the deviations. He traced the row that documented a high level of process material in the vessel with his finger, moving from column to column to understand the scenario.

Cause(s)	Consequence	Safeguard(s)	Recommendation
• Blocked outlet on the discharge line • Manually overfilling the vessel	Potential to send ethylene overhead and damage equipment downstream, leading to loss of containment and potential fire/explosion	• High-level alarm and high-level shutdown • Material of construction in overhead line compatible with hazard of ethylene	

Jon stared at this entry. The potential consequences were serious, but there seemed to be good safeguards. He wondered what "Manually over-filling the vessel" meant. In his experience, once they started a process like this, it just ran automatically until they shut it down or interfered.

Then he looked through the rest of the deviations for the vessel. He noticed—as he'd expected—that high pressure could cause a rupture, but was guarded against by a pressure safety relief valve. If the pressure got too high, the relief valve would open—that is, assuming the relief valve was functioning properly. Jon didn't think a bad relief valve had caused the explosion, but he made a note to request maintenance records for the valve.

Jon noticed that low pressure could also cause the vessel to rupture. The cause was listed as "Heating up the vessel (such as for steam cleaning) and letting it cool while it is blocked in." Jon remembered the time this was demonstrated by his high school chemistry teacher. The teacher had taken a full, unopened can of Coca-Cola, heated it over a Bunsen burner, and put it in a small refrigerator. A few minutes later, he opened the door and removed the can. It was crumpled, as if someone had squeezed an empty can in their hand.

"I know how long to do this because I cleaned a lot of refrigerators in my early days," the teacher had said, to laughter.

Jon didn't think low pressure had caused the explosion. The vessel was actually operating, not shut down. Also, the company could have immediately blamed contract maintenance staff for this scenario, but they didn't. Jon looked through other deviations, making notes along the way.

He decided to look through the procedures, starting with the one to commission the unit. That contained the usual steps: pressure testing to make sure process pipes were not left open, filling vessels with material, and then slowly bringing the temperatures and pressures up to operating set points. If there had been poor maintenance while the unit was down, it would have caused an accident during this phase. Jon knew from his interviews that there had not been maintenance on this part of the unit recently. This point nagged him. Why would a critical mistake—like leaving a gasket out of place—go unnoticed for so long?

Keeping an open mind was crucial at this point. Jon didn't dismiss the possibility that prior maintenance could have been a factor. There might have been a small leak that became bigger over time, but that cause just didn't feel right. He thought the cause was probably something else, something less convenient for the company. Something the company had done, or failed to do.

He turned his attention to the procedures for normal operations. They were a combination of numbered steps and callout boxes with cautions. He scanned each page, occasionally highlighting sentences. One of the cautions that he noted related to high level in the vessel. It was in a different font than the rest of the text, and italicized.

> *Caution: Never allow the liquid level to go above the set point. If the level goes above the set point, **immediately <u>shut down</u> the unit and the feed into the vessel!***

Jon scanned the rest of the procedures to see if any other caution boxes looked like this one. None did—this one was unique. High level in this vessel was something the company cared much more about than other problems. Jon looked up at the clock on the wall: already 12:38. His stomach growled like a rattle. He decided to get lunch, but did not want to leave all the documents open in the room. He walked out to the front desk where a new attendant had taken the goatee guy's place.

"Would it be possible to lock the room?" Jon asked the new attendant. "I have some things I don't want to pack up."

Without changing expression, she looked at the clock. "I guess nobody's gonna rent it today." She opened a drawer and pulled out a ring with several keys. She came out from behind the front desk through the side door and walked toward the room. On the way, she scrolled through the keys and then pinched one between her thumb and index finger, put it into the lock, and turned it.

"I should be back in an hour or so," Jon said.

The attendant walked back to the desk. "No problem," she replied, not looking up from her phone.

Jon's mind was racing as he pulled out of the parking lot. He thought of going to the diner but decided to go back to the coffee house downtown. He kept thinking about the explosion and the possible scenarios. He grabbed the same seat as the day before and slowly ate a chicken sandwich with cranberry mayonnaise. He smiled at people passing by the window. For the first time, he felt like he would find the cause of the explosion.

▲   ▲   ▲

Craig was sipping a new wine at a northern Virginia winery. The grapes were from California and the winemaker, from France; but the wine was made in Virginia. As he lifted the glass of zinfandel, he reflected on how Virginia's wine industry had changed. It had evolved since the days of concentrating on grapes that grew well in Virginia. Things changed— sometimes for the better, sometimes for the worse. For a minute, his mind drifted back to the procedure he reviewed earlier on dismissing employees, since he was going to have to let Jon go. Then he took another sip and watched the legs of wine flow back down into the glass.

▲   ▲   ▲

After lunch, Jon went back to the hotel. As he approached the front desk, the attendant, still expressionless, retrieved the ring of keys. Jon exhaled in relief as the door opened. Everything seemed to be as he had left it.

Jon grabbed his pad and reviewed his notes from the morning. High pressure, or even low pressure, could have caused a rupture. But the problem of getting too much material into the vessel resulting in a high level kept showing up in his notes. He laid the drawing of the vessel that the company had previously provided beside his newly acquired drawing, and studied them. He'd hoped the new one would provide more information. It definitely did.

The new drawing showed gauges not shown on the other one, and there were notes. Lots of notes. One bolded note at the bottom read, "Do not overfill." With his finger, Jon traced the line into the vessel, the vessel itself, and the lines out its bottom and top. He started marking up the drawing with highlighters. He outlined the vessel in blue, and then traced the line into the vessel in orange, the line out the bottom in green, and the overhead line out the top in yellow. It would be easier to find these lines quickly on other drawings if he color-coded them this way. He decided to color lines on the two drawings both upstream and downstream of the vessel to get a better sense of what was going on in vessel E-101. He wanted to know what should be coming in, what should be going out, and what could go wrong.

Jon decided his time was best spent probing the potential issue of high level in the vessel. If he could understand what safeguards had been in place to prevent this problem, he might understand why they'd failed that night.

55

Jon was still hunched over the folders on the table in the room off the hotel lobby when he felt a crick in his neck. He looked up at the clock. 6:17. The day had flown by. The investigation was a puzzle, but it seemed some of the pieces were coming together.

Jon needed to know more about the ethylene process, though, and since he couldn't rely on Chemtrifuge to cooperate, he'd need to learn it on his own. He walked out of the room to the front desk, where the female attendant was typing on her phone.

"How are you?" he said with a smile.

She looked up slowly from the text she was writing. "Have to do a double shift today. Adam called in sick."

"Sorry. I know what long days are like."

She half grinned. "Ah, it's okay. More money, and we're not busy anyway."

"Would you mind locking the room again?"

She lazily opened the drawer and pulled out the ring of endless keys. As she walked over to the door and began locking it, Jon decided to do her a favor. He hadn't planned on going out, but she might be a good friend to have, as long as he had notes spread out in the room.

"Do you want me to bring you back anything?" he asked.

"No, that's okay."

"No, really, you've been a big help to me. I'll be glad to pick you up something. You want a burger or a piece of pizza?"

The clerk's eyes went skyward. "That'd be great. You know that custard stand about a half mile down on the right?"

Jon nodded.

"They make the best peanut butter milkshake. If you pass by there, can you bring me one? I'll pay you back."

Jon held up his hands. "This one's on me. I'll be glad to bring you one. Might even try one myself."

▲　▲　▲

When Jon got back to the business center, a guy was on the other computer, throwing a tantrum because he couldn't print his boarding pass. The clerk was trying to help, but they weren't having any luck. Jon sympathized, but that was not his problem today. He had a puzzle to solve.

He raised the striped straw to his lips and slurped his peanut butter milkshake as he searched, trying not to think about the calories.

One website noted that ethylene was the most-produced organic chemical in the world, often converted into polyethylene to make plastic products like cups, containers, and even raincoats. Jon had not worked with ethylene much, but he knew that it could cause an explosion. He thought he remembered that it was cold when it was liquid, but now he learned that liquid ethylene was not only cold; it was *very* cold. The temperature varied, but different websites noted that ethylene liquefied *below* minus fifty degrees Fahrenheit.

On the CeMaC website, he found engineering specifications. CeMaC noted that the type of steel used to construct equipment in liquid ethylene processing was important. Stainless steel was best. At temperatures as low as that of liquid ethylene, other materials, like carbon steel, could become brittle and lose strength.

A clump of peanut butter clogged the bottom of the straw. Scrolling down the page, Jon pulled out the straw, inverted it, and chewed off the peanut butter. He made additional notes and then backspaced on the browser and went to another site, where he read that embrittlement could happen in different ways, one way being cryogenic embrittlement, in which equipment got so cold that an impact can cause a "brittle fracture" and rupture. Equipment in this state was like glass—when some metals got really cold, even the flick of a fingernail could crack them.

Jon rocked back in his chair. He tried to picture this. He visualized something like a tin can in a huge, super-cold freezer with ice hanging off it. If it fell, it could shatter. If it wasn't cold, it would fall on the floor and there would be no problem. He knew how fragile his own skin felt when it got cold, how it cracked. He was starting to understand.

Jon looked away from the screen and reflected. Even though Chemtrifuge was a hard company to deal with, they were sophisticated. They would know that equipment made of the wrong material was a big problem, and they would have designed their equipment appropriately. He saw their name on the list of CeMaC supporters, so they obviously cared about safety.

Jon started flicking his pen against his chin. In this scenario, the company had to have used the wrong steel in the vessel or piping design and gotten liquid ethylene there. There also had to have been some impact that caused the rupture. Jon shook his head and read more.

Even something like a heavy rain could cause a rupture if equipment was embrittled. Jon remembered listening to the weather report while he drove toward Charleston that first night. A thunderstorm had passed through. He remembered the drops of rain on his windshield.

Still, the big question remained—How could a company like Chemtrifuge have made such a fundamental design error as using the wrong steel in a dangerous process? Jon slurped the last of his milkshake and finished off the clumps of peanut butter clogging the straw. The scenario was credible, but at the same time it didn't make sense. Not even a metallurgical engineer fresh out of school with access to the internet would make a rookie mistake like that. It would be like using a wooden poker to stir logs in a fireplace. To process liquid ethylene, you needed stainless steel—*period*. If Jon knew that after less than twenty minutes online, there was no way that Chemtrifuge could *not* know it.

He walked up to the clerk's desk. "Can I get back in the room? This will be the last time I bother you."

As he walked back into the room, he had a sinking feeling. The more he thought about the scenario he had dreamed up, the more far-fetched it seemed. He'd spent the whole day chasing down this ridiculous notion that the engineers at Chemtrifuge could have overlooked a fundamental design flaw. Besides, didn't the HAZOP say something about having the right material of construction in the overhead line? Yes, it did. Now he really felt stupid. Maybe Charlie was right. Maybe he wasn't cut out for this work after all.

He started putting the documents back into folders. But as he began folding up the drawing of the vessel that had exploded, he glanced at it again, and stopped. There were small notes and symbols on the drawing, so small he hadn't noticed them before. He spread the drawing out on the table again and bent down for a closer look. He could see what looked like letters, but he couldn't make them out. He was curious, especially about one shape just above the vessel, on the pipe going out the top. It looked like a flower someone had drawn by hand. Why would somebody draw a flower on a P&ID drawing? Sometimes old CAD drawings had notes like this about instruments, but this symbol was different from others he had seen.

He walked out of the room and crossed to the front desk. "Excuse me, this sounds weird, but do you have a magnifying glass?"

The clerk was still working on her milkshake. "I think there's one in the back room that the girl who does the bookkeeping uses. Lemme check."

Jon heard drawers opening and closing and papers ruffling and then the clerk's voice from the back. "You're in luck," she said, emerging with a black-handled magnifying glass about eight inches in diameter.

"I'll just need it for a minute," said Jon, reaching out.

The clerk tipped her milkshake to him. "Keep it as long as you need." The $2.34 spent on the milkshake was paying dividends.

Back in the room, Jon held the magnifying glass over the fine print next to the flower symbol. "SS → CS," it read. He made a note on his notepad. Then he held the magnifying glass over the flower symbol and moved it back and forth until it came into focus.

There was handwriting inside the flower: "Per ACQ." Jon wasn't sure what ACQ was, but he guessed it was some engineering society, perhaps the American Council of Quality or Association of Chemical Quality. Using good engineering standards from reputable organizations was a good practice in the chemical industry. Jon had used standards from a few of these, but he'd never come across a group called ACQ. He made a note to look it up online the next day. He could check to see what the group said about the material of construction for lines or pipes—people in the chemical industry generally used these terms synonymously.

Then he noticed something else. Marked on the line into the vessel were the letters SS. Jon guessed this stood for stainless steel. However, the line coming out the top of the vessel was labeled CS. Carbon steel? He hadn't expected that. Looking through the magnifying glass, he confirmed that the letters were definitely CS, not SS. He unfolded the next drawing, which showed the continuation of the overhead line. It, too, was labeled CS. Why would the overhead line have been changed to carbon steel, especially since the company seemed concerned with high level in the vessel?

Jon wanted to capture this thought before stopping for the day. He took out his notepad and wrote: *Pipe coming out of the top of the vessel changes to CS—assuming this is carbon steel. Pipe in this unit should be stainless steel, but it seems to change "Per ACQ."*

The next thought he set off in asterisks. *Need to find out what ACQ is, and what it says about stainless steel versus carbon steel.*

Maybe ACQ had done new research that showed that carbon steel was fine in this application. Or maybe the CS on the line number did not mean carbon steel at all. There were plenty of questions, but Jon knew one thing. His earlier potential scenario—that use of the wrong steel might have ultimately led to a rupture—was back on the table.

He folded all the drawings and dutifully put all the documents back into their folders. He put the stack of folders back in the box and lugged it to his room, half waving at the clerk as he passed by.

▲ ▲ ▲

That night, Jon awoke from a dream, damp with sweat. He was trapped in rushing water, his head barely bobbing above the surface. Pieces of pipe were floating by. He tried to grab them, but they sped up when he reached for them.

56

Sam sat in his office, slowly sipping his coffee. All he wanted was a few moments of peace and quiet. He'd had a shouting match with Glenda the night before, and he'd only slept about three hours, if that.

The calm he craved didn't last long. The door flew open and Charlie burst wide-eyed into Sam's office. "Shit, shit, shit!"

Sam dropped his cup, hot coffee splashing onto his white shirt and tie. "Jesus Christ, Charlie! What the hell's wrong with you?"

Charlie shook his fists in the air. "They're gone! They're gone!"

Sam grabbed a handful of tissues out of the box on his desk and started wiping his shirt. "What are you talking about, dumbass?"

"The drawings, the procedures, everything about the unit I was hiding in my office. They're all gone!"

Sam dabbed the tissue ball with his tongue and began to rub at spots on his tie. "Are you sure you didn't move them? You've misplaced shit before."

"No, I didn't move them. I took everything out of the library and put it in the bottom drawer of the credenza behind my desk, like we discussed."

"Maybe the librarian took them back. Did she know they were there?"

"I don't think so. You told me to take care of them the night of the explosion. Some of the guys in the meeting may have guessed they were in my office, but I never told anybody where they were."

Sam nodded. "Check with the librarian. I need to run down to the unit anyway. I think Plasco is on today—I'll see if he knows anything about this."

Charlie sniffed. "You think the union double-crossed us, Sam?"

"I don't think so, but I'll pull Alphonse off to the side and check it out."

Charlie cleared his throat. "Sam, I don't need to tell you how bad it'd be if that government puke ever gets his hands on those documents and figures out what really happened."

Sam nodded. "I agree, but let's make sure there's a problem before we panic. Check with the librarian. Even if she didn't do it, maybe someone else found them and turned them in to her. We'll deal with that 'someone else' later."

Charlie shook his head vigorously. "I've said for years we need to get surveillance in this building. I want to know everybody who comes and goes. I've said it a thousand times. I swear, I—"

"We'll think about it," Sam said, cutting him off. "Right now, let's find those documents."

Sam's secretary stepped into his office behind Charlie. "I'm sorry, sir—I have a call for you."

"I'm headed to the unit," Sam snapped. "Take a damn message."

"I think you'll want to take this call, sir."

Sam and Charlie both looked at her, surprised.

"Who is it?" Sam asked.

"A reporter. She said it's about the explosion."

57

Jon's phone buzzed Monday morning.

"Hi, Jon. This is Lisa, the reporter you spoke to last Thursday. Listen, I wanted to let you know I plan to call the company this morning to follow up and get their side."

Jon thought back to their chat on Thursday—the conversation had lasted only a few minutes.

"We're hopeful that we'll be getting relevant interviews soon," he'd told her, "but we haven't been given access to people who know the most about what happened that night. People like the operators in the unit, or the engineer. We need to talk to people like that, and we need the documents we've requested."

"Do you think the company's stonewalling because they have something to hide?"

Jon hadn't been ready for that one. "Maybe," he blurted out without thinking. "It's odd that they haven't worked with me." He cleared his throat. "I think that, together, we can figure out what happened and take steps to make sure it doesn't happen again and hurt any-one else."

He'd asked Lisa if she could let him know before she talked to the company. He thought that if they started to cooperate, he could brag on them and hopefully keep the cooperation going rather than pro-voke them and put it in jeopardy. Lisa had agreed, but now Jon had a dilemma. He had the documents he wanted—except he was pretty sure they'd come from someone in the union, not management. He'd spent the weekend reviewing them. When Lisa called to say she was getting ready to call the company, he said he still hadn't been able to interview the right people. That was still true. He didn't mention the documents, and fortunately, she didn't either.

"I hope this can be a turning point in their cooperation," he said and then added, almost without thinking, "But, Lisa, I don't want this to make it worse."

"Well, let's see what they have to say. Maybe things will change, and your investigation can move forward."

Jon really wanted to believe that.

"Before I go," Lisa said, "do you think you know what happened?"

Jon paused. He had a theory now: high level in the vessel had caused an overhead line made of the wrong material to get too cold, become brittle, and rupture. However, he didn't feel comfortable discussing it yet, espe-cially with a reporter. He needed more time to research the plausibility of this odd theory. How could a sophisticated company like Chemtrifuge have totally blown the design of a unit that they had designed many times in other plants, and for which they were considered an industry leader?

"I have some thoughts on what *could* have happened, but nothing definite yet."

Lisa sighed softly, as if disappointed. "Hm. Okay, maybe we can talk about that on a future call?"

"Sounds good," Jon said.

▲ ▲ ▲

"Any trash?" A voice from the doorway startled Sam. He was in his office with Charlie and his secretary.

Charlie glanced at the custodian in the brown shirt and pants and shook his head.

"Leave me and Charlie, and close the door," Sam told his secretary as he picked up the phone. "Sam Page here."

Charlie rocked back in Sam's guest chair. He looked nervous.

"Uh-huh. Yes, miss, I remember you. That was a tough day for all of us, but I recall you were very nice and professional." Sam rolled his eyes at Charlie. He had no idea who this reporter was.

"Hmm." Sam pretended to be surprised. "There must be a mis-understanding. We let him go through our whole library. We pulled operators away from their work to talk with him. He doesn't think they were the right people. . . . Okay. . . . I see. . . ."

Sam fell silent as the reporter told him what Jon Barrett, federal investigator, had said. "My goodness, miss," he said finally, feigning surprise again. "I wasn't aware of any of this. My people have strict instructions to work with him and give him what he needs. This after-noon, for instance, he has an interview scheduled with the operator who was out there the night of the accident. You can't get a better eye-witness than that." Sam listened for a minute. "Yes, yes, he's going to talk to the unit engineer too. Not sure of the schedule for that one, but we're going to make it happen this week. We need our people to stay on the job to maintain safety, but we've done our best to make them available. We all want to find the cause of this tragedy."

Sam propped the phone on his shoulder and held his head against it as he reached into his desk for the flask of bourbon and a glass. He didn't care if the guys in the unit smelled alcohol on his breath. This day had started bad and was only getting worse. He took a gulp and set the glass down.

"Oh, I hope we get this straightened out. I think when he spoke to you last week, some of these interviews hadn't been scheduled, but we're on top of it now."

Sam paused for a minute, listening, and then shook his head.

"I don't think there's much of a story here, young lady. We're cooperating. This guy must not realize what it takes to keep a plant running safely and conduct an accident investigation at the same time. Like I told you, the day after the explo—" Sam caught himself "—the *incident*, we know the cause was shoddy maintenance by contractors, and everything we've found since then has only confirmed that. . . . Uh-huh. . . . Don't hesitate to call me if you need anything."

Sam ended the call and took a swig of bourbon. He looked over at Charlie, who was holding his head in his hands.

"Well, Charlie, seems our federal friend is not very happy with our lack of cooperation. He went to the media and told them he thought we have something to hide."

Charlie stood up and paced. "Sam, I told you this thing was getting out of control. I've tried to string him along, hoping he'll just go away, but he keeps hanging around."

"I don't need any bad press out of this—that's the last thing I want Wheelan to see. Look, I promised her that he would talk to the operator who was there and the unit engineer. Get him an interview with Janet this afternoon. She's been coached. I'll double-check with Eric when I'm in the unit—make sure he knows what to say too."

Charlie looked toward the ceiling. "I think Janet's at the fire station today. It's her day off."

Sam rose. "Well, make it her day on. Pay double time if you have to. I want this little puke to talk to her and Eric and then get the hell out of my plant!"

"Will do," Charlie said meekly and then hesitated. "I hate to bring this up again, but I think we need the lawyer from DC."

Sam exhaled. Charlie was right. "I'll call Leska."

Charlie smiled. "I think that's the right thing to do."

"Jesus, Charlie," Sam said. "It's only Monday. I thought this whole stupid mess would have blown over by now."

"Take a deep breath—I'm sure Andrew Leska, our DC buddy, will drive this government guy off," said Charlie, suddenly almost cheerful. "That DC punk doesn't know what a shitstorm he's created."

Sam nodded. "I need to get down to the unit. I'll let you know any scuttlebutt I hear from Alphonse about the union. I think he's keeping his guys in line, but we need to clear up the mystery of the missing documents."

Charlie slapped his head with his hand. "Damn, I forgot about those. I'll go see Kathy and see if anybody turned them in to her, or if she took them. If she did, she's in a world of hurt!"

Sam drained the last of the bourbon and put the glass back in his desk. "See you in a couple of hours. We need to get this all sorted out before lunch. I'll call Leska before I head to the unit. If he leaves now, he can be here this afternoon."

58

Charlie rounded the corner toward Jon's office, walking slowly. His head was swimming. He'd just finished his second meeting with Sam that morning. The investigation was not going the way he and Sam wanted. He'd thought that stonewalling Jon with a heavily redacted drawing and granting him useless interviews would frustrate him, and he would just go away, but that wasn't working.

The longer the investigation continued, the more likely the real cause would be discovered. Chemtrifuge didn't want the real cause of the explosion, or the reason behind it, to ever see the light of day. Charlie was missing documents, and no one seemed to know anything about it. Both Kathy and Alphonse denied taking them, and he believed them. By now, Charlie was even questioning himself. Did he know for sure he hadn't moved them? He'd been going through a lot lately, with his wife and the medical reports. But he'd been so careful with those documents. He didn't even risk carrying them to his car, lest the investigator see him do it and ask questions.

Sam had struck out with A. C. Mounts—Charlie had heard everything on the speakerphone. Sam asked Mounts to call in favors from his friends in Washington and get the investigator to back down. For the first time, Charlie heard Mounts in a different light. He no longer spoke like the smooth politician; he had an I'm-protecting-myself tone.

"Well, now, Sam," he'd said, "I'd love to help you boys, but you may've heard I'm in a bit of a mess myself. This thing with the Speaker, and my supposed ties to the contracts, has put my office in damage-control mode. I'm not in much of a position to call in any favors right now. If I call them DC boys, they're gonna wanna talk about my little problem here. That's not a conversation I want to have right now. I hope you understand."

Mounts had been an insurance policy. If the investigation went bad, as it was going now, they had thought they could rely on him. He'd only have to make a call to DC, and the problem would go away. But for the first time in his political career, Mounts was in trouble. The man who'd consistently enjoyed a 90 percent favorability rating among his constituents was now hovering around 40. The opposition was speaking openly about challenging him for the seat. Local press was running a new story every day. There was less about salacious emails, and more about an illegal pay-to-play scheme involving kickbacks from a railroad company. The insurance policy Chemtrifuge thought they had was now expired.

On the other hand, Charlie was pleased with some of the new developments. The lawyer was coming in from DC—the company had a new "bad cop." Charlie had never liked that role. He didn't dislike the investigator—deep down, he almost sympathized with him. He knew Jon was trying to do his job. He was annoyed that Jon had gone to the media, but he understood why. But if Jon succeeded, he would discover something that would destroy the company's reputation and put market shares in jeopardy. And Charlie didn't even want to think about the liability some individuals might have for decisions made that night. And then, of course, there was his wife. He took a deep breath when he finally reached Jon's door. He looked at his watch. Only 9:12. What a way to start a Monday.

Jon was on the phone when Charlie opened the door. He held up a finger. "Just give me a call when you can. Bye."

Charlie exhaled. "Jon, you have an interview today. It's with the operator who was in the unit the night of the incident. She's off today, but we're bringing her in to talk to you. It'll probably be late afternoon—I'll let you know."

Jon smiled. "Great! Should I stay around for lunch, in case she comes in earlier?"

Charlie hesitated. Even if Janet came in earlier, he wanted to give the DC lawyer—already on his way—time to get to Charleston so he could sit in on the interview. Janet had agreed to come in for double pay—which Charlie had readily agreed to, as long as she stuck to the script.

"No, take your lunch. The interview won't be until late afternoon."

Jon couldn't believe it. He was getting a key interview, and Charlie was—almost—nice. That was the first time the man had called him Jon. Maybe going to the media had worked, and Chemtrifuge would cooperate now. This was a new day for the investigation.

▲   ▲   ▲

Craig put down the phone and then looked at the fillable form for employee termination on his screen. He'd just finished listening to a voice message Jon had left minutes before. "Give me a call," Jon had said. "I might have news."

Craig stared at his screen again, his fingers poised over the keyboard. He'd already filled in Jon's name and the reason for termination. All he had left to do was hit the submit button. This was one of the hardest things he'd ever done, but he had no choice. The DAS had outmaneuvered him. That was the way things rolled in Washington.

He'd leave it for later, Craig decided. He'd talk to Jon in the afternoon and tell him to come into the office on Friday for outboarding. He put a note on his electronic calendar for 3 p.m.: "Call Jon, termination discussion."

This place sucked. He was ashamed of it, and he was ashamed of himself.

59

Jon looked around the conference room, even though he had essentially memorized everything in it. He looked at the Sony icon at the bottom of the video screen. It would be nice to have a TV this big in his apartment back in Springfield.

He'd been in the conference room for almost half an hour and was beginning to worry. This had been an odd day. Around 8:30 that morning, he'd received the call from Lisa, telling him that she was going to call the company. He'd feared that might make matters worse, but then he got good news. He could interview the only living operator who'd been out in the unit—as opposed to sitting in the control room—the night of the explosion. He'd lunched at the coffee shop, with his favorite sandwich slathered in cranberry mayonnaise. Everything seemed good. But then he got a cryptic message from his boss: "Thanks for the voice message. We need to talk." It sounded like a breakup text. Jon had sent a text back about the interview he had set up late that afternoon, and Craig had replied, "Okay, call me afterwards on my cell."

Jon wasn't sure what was going on in DC. Still, the investigation finally seemed to be going in the right direction. He even considered bringing the drawing of the vessel with all the information to the interview, since the company seemed to be cooperating, but he concluded it was safer to only bring the sanitized version the company had provided earlier.

Jon looked at his watch. It was 4:08. He'd been in the room with the door closed since 3:30, waiting for the interview.

Just then Charlie opened the door suddenly. "Your interviewee is here. She's getting paid double for her time today, so don't keep this going longer than you have to." The tone in his voice was stern, with none of the friendliness of the morning.

Jon stood. Behind Charlie was a tall, athletic woman with short, punky bleached hair, a square, almost masculine face, and piercing light-gray eyes. She was wearing street clothes and had muscular, rounded shoulders. Her red T-shirt bore an image of a single hand holding a fire-hose nozzle above the words "Volunteer Firefighter." One sleeve was rolled up, and he could make out the shape of a pack of cigarettes underneath. Jon guessed she was in her early thirties, though her face had a tough, almost leathery quality that made her look older. She didn't acknowledge Jon's extended hand but pulled out the closest chair and flopped down.

Before Jon could start his introduction, someone else bounded into the room past Charlie.

"This is—" Charlie started, but before he could finish, the new entrant extended his hand and grabbed Jon's.

"Andrew P. Leska the Third. Some people add Esquire, but I don't require it. Nice to meet you, Jonny boy." He had a distinct New England accent, and his grip hurt Jon's hand.

"He's going to be sitting in on the interviews from now on," Charlie said, inching toward the door.

Jon cleared his throat. "I thought it was only the union rep who sits in with operators. Isn't that what we agreed to?"

Charlie opened his mouth, but Leska held up his index finger. "Charlie, if I may."

Charlie nodded.

"Jonny boy, I help the company with legal matters, and this is certainly a legal matter. The nature of the agreement, as I understand it, is that the individual being interviewed can choose whoever they want to sit in for the interview. Janet here chose me, and the union steward's fine with that. Now, if you want to get wrapped up in protocols, you can do that. However, we'll have to put a hold on interviews until we get this straightened out."

Jon sat silent. It seemed this new lawyer was playing hardball. He had to make a decision fast. He remembered the breakup text message from Craig. Good news rarely follows the phrase "We need to talk." His only good option was to proceed with the interview and get as much information as he could.

Charlie raised his eyebrows. "Well?"

"Let's go ahead with the interview. Mr. Leska is aware of the other provision of not interrupting the interview, correct?"

"You won't even know I'm here, Jonny boy," Leska said with a smile. Charlie backed out, closing the conference room door behind him.

Jon was silent for a moment, studying both Janet and Leska. Janet had grabbed a coaster from the pile on the table and was rolling it from one hand to the other. Leska pulled a small laptop from a leather case, and the Rolex on his arm jingled as he opened it. He was wearing a light gray suit that looked like it had a metallic sheen. Jon guessed it probably cost more than his own monthly salary. He was clean shaven except for a mustache, and he wore rust-colored glasses that Jon had seen on fashion shows when he was flipping channels. He was around fifty, and had obviously accomplished much more during his years than Jon could have imagined.

"Well, are we ready?" Leska asked condescendingly.

"Yes," Jon replied, snapping out of his musings, and started his scripted statement. "This interview is part of the investigation into the fire and explosion that recently occurred at the plant—"

"Uh, sorry," Leska interrupted. "I couldn't help noticing you used the word *explosion*. We're still assessing that."

"Okay, *incident*." Jon looked at Janet. "Is there any confusion about why I'm here?"

He thought he saw a half-smile from Janet, though she didn't look up from the coaster. "No," she said.

"Your participation here is voluntary," Jon continued, "but I ask that you answer all questions fully and accurately to the best of your ability. If you need me to clarify any question, please ask. Anyone else present during the interview must not interfere with the questioning in any way and must be here by your, and my, consent."

Jon put down the paper. "Mr. Leska, company attorney, has requested to be present. Do you agree?"

Janet finally looked up. "I guess so."

"I need something more affirmative. Are you comfortable with him being present?"

Janet looked at Leska and then back at Jon. "Yes, it's okay."

"Of course it is," Leska said, as if he was talking to himself.

"Thank you." Jon looked at Leska. "Anyone else present in the interview must not interfere with the questioning in any way."

Leska was looking down at his laptop, shaking his head. Jon was annoyed but merely asked, "Are you ready?"

Janet shrugged and dropped the coaster. Jon cleared his throat and flipped to an open page in his notepad. "Tell me about your job here at the plant."

Janet looked at Leska, who was typing, and then at Jon.

"Not much to tell. I'm an outside operator in the ethylene unit."

"So, what do you do on a daily basis?"

Janet shifted in her chair and slouched, draping one arm over the back. "I make rounds and take readings and make sure the unit's running well. Sometimes I, you know, take samples and stuff. Whatever needs to be done."

Jon nodded. "How long have you been with the company?"

At this, Leska breathed in very deeply and then exhaled loudly through his nose. It seemed he was bored, or couldn't believe that question had been asked.

"I've been here a few years," Janet mumbled. "I don't know the exact date."

Leska breathed out through his nose in short burst, the way some people do to substitute for a laugh. Janet had obviously been coached. She was not going to volunteer any information, and Jon wasn't going to loosen her up by making small talk about her job. He would probably have to switch from open-ended questions to specific ones, but he tried one more time.

"Tell me what happened the night of the incident."

Leska exhaled loudly.

"What do you mean?" Janet said. "The whole night? In the whole plant? I didn't write down every second."

Leska laughed through his nose again.

Jon put down his mechanical pencil. This was his one shot at talking to Janet, and she was a critical witness. She was not going to be able to just wait him out.

"Janet, I'm here on behalf of the United States government to find out what happened the night of the accident. Three men died. If something like this happens again, either here or at another plant, more people could die. Next time, it might be another operator here, maybe even you." He paused as Janet's eyes widened. "I apologize if my question is too general, but I want to know what you were doing out in the unit the night of the explosion, or sudden release of energy, or whatever the company wants to call it. You are apparently the only one alive who saw what happened. I want you to tell me what you were doing out there in the moments before the explosion. Is there anything about what I want to know that is not clear?"

Leska looked at Jon. This time, he did not make a sound.

Janet glanced at Leska and then at Jon. She leaned forward in her chair. "I heard commotion on the radio. I couldn't understand it because people were talking over each other, almost shouting. When that quietened down, I heard my name. I got a call from the console operator. He told me to go where I could see the vessel from the ground and make sure the guys were looking in the right place to check the level and open the valve. I moved to where I could see them from the ground. They seemed to be looking in the right place. I told him that, and he said to keep an eye on 'em."

Jon didn't want to break her verbal stride, but he had a couple of pressing questions. "Who were the guys checking the level?"

Janet looked at Leska, who'd resumed his cadence of a bored exhalation. Then she turned back to Jon. "The contract operators who were there. The guys who di—" She caught herself. "The guys who were helping out in the unit that caught fire."

"The three guys who perished in the fire, correct?" Jon clarified.

Janet looked down and nodded.

Jon probed further. "What exactly were they trying to do?"

"I heard Tebo say that they needed to make sure the valve out the bottom was open all the way, and they couldn't open it any more from the control room. I think they were also going to open the manual valve on the bypass line. They were checking to see how fast the level was rising, to see if it would go into the overhead line."

"Who is Tebo?" Jon asked, writing the name down and putting a star beside it.

"Oh, that's Turner, the supervisor. We call him Tebo."

It was sounding like Jon's theory was not so far-fetched after all.

"What was the problem with getting liquid ethylene into the overhead line?"

Janet rapidly launched into an obviously rehearsed answer. "You'll have to discuss that with the engineer. I am not the appropriate person to respond to that inquiry." Jon noted the formal wording of this response.

"Okay, then what happened?"

"I heard someone yell something like, 'She's full,' and another one said, 'Valve won't budge.' The equipment was shaking. It looked like the whole structure was shaking, like in an earthquake. Right after that, I heard the first explosion."

Jon stopped writing. She'd used the word *explosion*, so he would as well. "So there was more than one explosion?"

"Yeah, later, after the vessel had blown up. I was up there trying to close a manual valve to stop the flow into the vessel so the fire would stop, and that's when it happened."

"You're lucky you didn't get hurt."

"The hell I didn't!" she snapped. "Shit, it knocked me a whole level down on the platform. I damn near got killed!"

Leska cleared his throat. "You know, I don't want to interfere, but Janet's here on her day off. She's had to relive some traumatic moments. We need to move this along, for her sake."

Jon ignored him. "So, Janet, you've been around this unit a lot. What do you think happened?"

"I'm sure it was substandard work by contract maintenance workers," she said without hesitation. "They put my life and the life of other operators in danger."

Another rehearsed response. Jon glanced at Leska, who was smiling. He decided to recap her story and fill in blanks if he could.

"Well, Janet, I appreciate you coming in on your day off. Let me recap. You were out in the unit the night of the incident. The three contract operators were up on the platform, checking the level in vessel E-101, trying to open the valve on the line out the bottom, I assume to lower the level in the vessel. There is a problem with getting liquid up into the overhead line, but you're not sure why." He paused and looked at Janet, who remained expressionless. "The equipment began to shake, and then there was an explosion and fire, which you believe was because of bad maintenance by contractors. That's when the men died. The fire continued, and you went up to try to close a manual valve to stop the feed to the vessel so the fire would stop, but there was another explosion and you were knocked down a level. Is that about right?"

Janet nodded slowly, playing with the coaster again. "Sounds about right."

"Okay, thank you. Just one last question. Why did the inside operator send the other guys up to check the level, and not you?"

Janet and Leska both looked at Jon, puzzled. "What do you mean?" Janet said.

"Well, you were the outside operator most familiar with the equipment. The console operator relied on you to make sure they were looking in the right place. Why didn't they just send you?"

With an almost indignant smirk, she burst out, "I'm an FTE. They were just contractors. At the time we didn't know—"

Leska subtly put his hand on Janet's arm, and she stopped midsentence. Jon wanted to follow up on why the company found contractor's lives more expendable, but he had what he needed. It had been a good interview. She'd confirmed that it was a problem with the level that had led to the explosion. He had not wasted his time during the weekend.

"Anything else I haven't asked that might help me understand the accident?"

"I don't think so," Janet said, rising out of her seat.

"Thanks, Janet." Leska opened the door behind her. "I'll walk you down to your office, Jonny boy."

"I think she got it right, about the bad maintenance and all," Leska said as they walked down the hallway. "You know, I let you go on today, but some of those questions weren't really related to the investigation."

"Like what?" Jon asked.

"Well, let's just say I was nice about it today. You could just say that this was a poor maintenance job by some contractors, like we say it is, and we could all get on with our lives, including you."

Jon didn't respond.

After Leska left, he reflected on the interview. Leska had been a pain with his annoying exhalations, but it had turned out pretty well. Jon now knew what had happened; he just didn't know why. He would try to understand that from the engineer.

It was time to call Craig. He looked at his watch: 5:38. He had two pieces of—dare he say—good news. The media was reengaged, which had caused the company to reengage, and he was pretty sure he knew the cause of the explosion. But he wasn't sure what Craig had to say.

60

Sam sat behind his desk, fingers steepled in front of him. Charlie and Janet were seated at the small table in his office, and Leska was leaning against the trophy case. Leska generally stood up in Sam's office, or half sat on his credenza. Sam assumed it was some kind of I'm-higher-than-you power thing. He ignored it. It had been a long day for everyone.

"How'd it go?" Sam asked.

Leska smiled at Janet. "She did great."

"Did he ask anything, uh, uncomfortable?" Sam tilted his head on the last word.

"Well, he did go into the whole thing about the men dying and what they were doing out there. But little Janet here pivoted nicely back to our position—bad maintenance by contractors."

For years, Sam had noticed Leska's constant use of patronizing variations of people's names. It reminded him of Jay Gatsby in *The Great Gatsby*, always calling people "old sport." Sam hated that character. But

Janet seemed to ignore the "little Janet" comment. Sam assumed that, as a female operator in a chemical plant, she'd learned to ignore men a lot.

Sam rocked back in his chair. "I knew she would. Maybe once he talks to Eric, he'll have his fill and get the hell out of here."

Leska folded his arms. "We ought to let little Janet get back to her day off."

Sam rocked up in his chair. "By all means." He nodded to Janet. "Thanks for coming in."

Janet nodded back, pushed herself up out of the chair using the arms, and walked out, not bothering to close the door behind her.

After she left, Leska pushed some of the awards on Sam's credenza aside and sat down where they had been. Sam was annoyed, but bit his tongue.

"You know, gents," Leska said, "I don't like him asking about the level. She said the lines just like we rehearsed, about getting liquid in that overhead line, but I want to stop this now. If he tries to hang his hat on this interview, we can say she's an outside operator and doesn't know about the equipment metallurgy. But if he asks the engineer, that's a different story. I'm going to be more aggressive in the next one. I know what his statement says about not interfering, but I have to jump in." Leska chuckled. "Besides, what can he do?"

"We might as well call Wheelan Drew and Cain Quinn. They wanted to know how this one went." Sam hit the number 1 and then the speaker button on his phone.

"Wheelan Drew's office," said Drew's executive assistant.

"Hi, it's Sam Page. Wheelan's expecting me."

"One moment."

"Sam," Drew said, coming on, "how's it going down there in Mountaineer country?"

"Just fine. How's New York City?"

"'Bout the same. I just heard a click. Is that you on the line, Mr. Quinn?"

"I'm here," Cain Quinn's gruff voice replied.

"I'm on the line with Charlie and Andrew Leska," Sam said. "He just got out of the interview with Janet. Andrew, tell us how it went." Sam moved the phone closer to Leska and motioned to him to speak.

"Well, gentlemen, it went fairly well. Janet delivered the points we rehearsed, and she toed the company line—bad maintenance by a contractor." Leska paused for a response.

No one spoke for a moment. Finally Drew cleared his throat. "That's good to hear. Anything else?"

Leska moved closer to the phone. "It got a little uncomfortable at one point. He started asking about what the guys were doing up there when they got burned up, and then he started asking about the level in the vessel—"

At the mention of the level, the previously subdued Quinn came to life.

"What did he want to know about the level?"

"Well, sir, when he asked what the problem was, Janet went back to her talking point about not knowing, and said he would have to talk to the engineer."

"He's talking to Eric?" Cain Quinn raised his voice.

Sam jumped in. "We told the reporter that we'd already arranged for him to interview the outside operator who was there that night, and the engineer. We think he'll leave after that, and the press will be off our back."

"What the hell are you doing down there, Leska? I thought we sent you down there to fix this. I knew those idiots at the plant couldn't handle it, but I thought you could. Why are we paying your hourly rate to screw this up? We were doing that ourselves."

Leska cleared his throat. "The question about what the guys were doing was bound to come up eventually. Janet stuck to the script and got back on message about bad maintenance."

"This damn thing has dragged on for weeks," Quinn went on, his voice rising. Drew seemed to have gone silent. "You guys assured me this little piece of shit from the government was going to give up and go away, but he hasn't. He's still there, and now he's digging into questions about the level. Why don't you little girls down there just lift up your dresses and show him your panties? Since nobody's man enough to take care of this, I'm coming down there this week. I'll take care of him myself."

Sam and Leska said in unison, "That won't be necessary."

"I didn't ask you three foreskins if I *could* come down. I *informed* you that I *am* coming down. I'm going to the Baltimore plant on Thursday, but I'll swing by there on Wednesday. Do you think you morons can keep this puke from wiping his ass with you too much until then?"

No one dared answer. In the silence, they could hear a bump in the hallway. Sam motioned for Charlie to look out the office door. Charlie glanced out and then closed the door. "Nothing," he silently mouthed to Sam.

On the speakerphone, Cain Quinn was still yelling. "Hello? Are you three shitholes still there? What are you doing, exchanging tampons?"

Sam rolled his eyes and leaned forward. He had not come this far in his career to be verbally abused, but he knew that arguing was futile. "We're here, sir. Just listening."

Leska's phone started vibrating. He held up his finger, opened the office door, and stepped out into the hall.

"We look forward to seeing you, Mr. Quinn," Sam said politely. "You can use my office if you need to."

Leska burst back into the room. "Cain, Wheelan, we found something."

"What do you mean, you found something?" Wheelan asked.

"We found out how to make this little government guy go away."

"And what are you going to do, shoot him?" Quinn said sarcastically.

"Worse," Leska replied. "We're going to destroy him."

61

After returning from a solo trip to the bathroom, Jon listened to the message the reporter had left while he was in the interview. Her station planned to do a print story on the investigation update on Wednesday, she was saying, adding that they might do a TV slot over the weekend.

Afterwards, he punched in Craig's number. Craig picked up on the first ring.

"Hi, Craig. This is Jon. Long time no hear."

"Yes, it's been a while. How are you?"

"Doing fine. I've got some news about the investigation, but you said you need to talk to me first?"

Jon heard Craig sigh. "You go first, Jon. My news can wait."

"I know what caused the explosion. I just interviewed the only operator who's alive, and I know what happened. I expect that after talking to the engineer, I'll know *why* it happened. I have the documents. The company is cooperating now." The last part was a stretch, but Jon liked how it sounded.

"That's good, Jon. Sounds like you have done good work."

"The other thing is that the press is doing a story on it. I have a reporter who helped me put pressure on the company, and she's running a story with an update on the investigation."

Jon could hear the shuffle of papers. There was a pause. "Really? When does it come out?"

"Supposed to be Wednesday."

There was silence. Finally Jon spoke. "Did you have something you needed to talk about?"

Craig exhaled. "What you just told me might change what I wanted to tell you. Can I call you in about fifteen minutes?"

"Sure," Jon said.

▲ ▲ ▲

As soon as he hung up with Jon, Craig called his boss, Dan Samot. Dan would still be in the office. He always stayed late.

Dan had been in the Senior Executive Service in the government for several years. He was a career SESer, which meant he had less power than political appointees but stayed in place even when administrations changed. It also meant he had to walk the tightrope of helping short-time appointees with their goals while looking out for the agency's long-term interest. The way Dan had been acting lately, making snide comments about the appointees, Craig assumed that tightrope was getting wobbly.

"There's something I'd like to talk to you about," Craig said when Dan picked up. "Can I come up?"

"Yeah, come on, just reviewing directives. I can't believe what they're trying to do."

Craig took the stairs up two flights. Dan's door was open, but he knocked anyway. Dan motioned him in with a hand wave.

"Can I close the door?" Craig asked, just above a whisper.

"Of course." Dan shut the laptop beside his monitor. "Sit down. What's up?"

"Dan, a few months ago, we started this new investigation branch. I hired one guy, and he's in the field right now."

"Yes, I remember. I approved it. I thought it was a good idea."

"Long story short, almost from the beginning, Sharon Hill has been nagging me, wanting to take the money earmarked for the investigation branch. It seems that the DAS for social relations, the one appointed a few months ago, wants it for some new initiative, From Parks to the Stars or something like that—he wants to sweep the money from my budget and put it in his. He thought we hadn't tapped it yet, so it'd be easy to just move it around on paper. I put her off by letting her know we have an ongoing investigation. I didn't bother you before because I was trying to handle it, but they want to have a meeting on Thursday and discuss moving the money over. They think it's a done deal, and I don't think I can hold them off anymore."

"I see," said Dan.

"But I just got some news today—it looks like my investigator's made good progress on the investigation. The company's cooperating, and the press is doing a story this week. It'd be embarrassing if the agency were to pull the funding right now. I hate to bother you, but I'd really like your support to keep the money in our office. Can you back me up on this?"

Dan started swirling a pen in his hand. "Sharon Hill, Sharon Hill. Where do I know that name from?"

"She's been here a while. Curly blond hair."

"Too much war paint?" Dan cut him off. "Heavy on makeup, light in the chest?"

Craig chuckled uncomfortably. "That's her."

Dan opened his laptop and moved in front of his monitor.

"What's the title of the DAS?"

"Social Relations, I think."

Dan pulled up an entry in the agency directory and turned the screen toward Craig so he could see. "That's who I thought you were talking about. I recognize him—can't stand that guy. He's been acting like he owns the damn agency since he got here. He plays tennis with the chairman of the Ways and Means Committee every week in McLean. He's always name-dropping about who he knows in our meetings with the deputy secretary."

Craig leaned back more comfortably in the guest chair.

"Do you know that prick had the audacity to cut me off when I was making a pitch to expand the C wing of the building?" Dan went on. "The first time he was ever in a meeting with the dep sec, and that asshole cut me off."

"He shouldn't have done that," Craig said politely.

Dan rocked back. "You know what? Go to that meeting and tell them I said you can't give up the money. If that dick plays hardball, tell him our investigator will have to go to the press, give them his name, and tell them that he's cutting our funding because he doesn't care if people die."

Craig winced. He didn't want to commit career suicide just yet.

Dan's expression changed. "Well, don't be that direct. But yes, you have my support."

Craig smiled. "Will do." He started walking to the door.

"I hope it feels like a punch in the nuts to that arrogant shit and knocks him down a notch. I don't care if he's dry-humping the Speaker of the House, that'll teach him to cut me off in meetings." Dan looked at Craig and smiled. "But don't mention that's why I'm backing your request."

"Understood," Craig said. He was glad for the support, even if it was more about revenge than about saving his office. Craig grabbed the door handle.

"Craig," Dan said, more seriously. Craig took his hand off the handle. "Honestly, I don't know how long we can hold off this guy. I can buy you some time, but despite what I just said, these politicos with connections always win in the end. You know that. See if your guy can finish, and we'll regroup late next week to see how to wind this thing down."

Craig nodded. He knew the connected always won in Washington. It was just a matter of time. But at least he had more time. He didn't have to terminate Jon this week. He would tell Jon to continue but come into the office late the next week to chat. That was enough for now.

▲ ▲ ▲

Jon kept running through the events of the day on the way to the hotel. Overall, it had been a good day, but strange. Going to the press had seemed to help. He'd had a good interview with the only living eyewitness. The operator had confirmed his theory: the accident happened because the level in the vessel got too high, and liquid ethylene got into the overhead line, which appeared to be made of the wrong type of steel—but the big question was, why? He would have to do more searches on the types of steel used in this application.

Then there was that odd conversation with Craig. He'd told Jon to continue the investigation but come into the office next week, and they would discuss the future of the investigation group. Not "this investigation" but "the group," which was just Jon.

It could be good news. Maybe they were going to hire more people, and even make Jon a supervisor. But if it was bad news—well, Jon didn't want to think about that.

Jon had told Craig how Leska had interfered with the interview. He'd still been able to get information, he told Craig, but it might be harder next time. If the engineer had something to do with the design of the unit, some of the blame might fall on him.

Craig had shared a trick he'd seen a lawyer use to silence an opposing attorney once, but Jon hoped he wouldn't have to resort to tricks. The company was cooperating now. Today was good, and tomorrow would be even better.

▲ ▲ ▲

Leska sat in his car, scouting the Hampton Inn parking lot from across the street. He watched Jon pull into the lot and then picked up the newspaper lying on the passenger seat.

62

Jon slept better that night, but he still had weird dreams. He was treading water, and strange men were clinging to huge PVC pipes floating by. Fog was everywhere, but he could make out one man clearly. The man was badly burned, with strips of skin falling off, and only meat underneath. With what was left of his mouth, he said something in a mechanical voice. It sounded like "I have no name." He kept saying it as the pipe sped up and floated away. Two of the pipes collided and clanked, jarring Jon from his dream.

The room was very cold, but the air conditioner was off. Jon looked at the digital clock. 6:17. There was no need to rush into the office. They'd told him before he left that the interview with the engineer would take place late in the day.

Jon turned on the TV. The handsome man with the perfect hair noted that it was early fall but would feel like winter the next couple of days. Jon thought about grabbing breakfast downstairs but opted for his favorite diner. On the walk, he mumbled his questions for the engineer to himself. He knew what had happened but not why.

As he stepped to the hostess stand at the diner, Flo was coming from the back. She refreshed someone's coffee at the counter. Jon smiled and waved, and a minute later she put down the glass coffeepot and walked to the stand.

Before he could say anything, she'd grabbed a menu. "This way. Your other party's already here."

Jon followed her, trying to catch her, since she had clearly made a mistake. He had been here so often—how could she mix him up with someone else? He was getting ready to speak when she stopped at a half-rounded booth. Someone sat in the middle, holding a newspaper in front of his face.

"He's here," she said, slapping the menu on the table.

One hand folded the corner of the paper down, and a bellowing voice greeted him. "Jonny boy, you're here. I found out you like this place, but I was beginning to think you weren't gonna show this morning. Have a seat." It was Andrew Leska.

Jon sat down, stunned. What was Leska doing here? Nobody knew his patterns. Or at least, that was what he had thought.

"I guess you're a little surprised to see me, but I like breakfast too. Besides, this will give us the chance to chat a bit outside of the plant. It's a bit stuffy there, don't you think?"

Still in shock, Jon said nothing.

"Honey, I need that cream!" Leska yelled across the room to Flo at the counter. "Coffee's getting cold!" He folded his paper in half. Still looking at it, he went on, "You know, Jonny boy, I like to get out to the heartland. These diners are a fixture in Americana. You meet interesting people, don't you? People you pity, but people just the same. Makes you thankful for what we have in DC, doesn't it?"

Jon just listened, though inside he felt like defending the people Leska pitied.

"Take old Flo, over there. She'd never make it at the Four Seasons in Georgetown, where I eat breakfast, but she's fine in a place like this."

Flo arrived with a small silver pot.

"Thank you, dear." Leska smiled. "These little packets of powdered cream just don't do it for me. I appreciate the accommodation," he said, mimicking a local accent.

He held the pot low over his cup as cream trickled out and then raised it slowly until his arm was almost fully extended, high above the cup. The cream fell in a steady stream, slowly forming clouds in his cup, the black turning brown, then mocha, then almost white. He tipped the small pot upright without spilling a drop.

"A tip I learned watching a guy pour Irish coffee in San Fran a few years ago." Leska wiped his mouth. "I order my coffee straight from Ethiopia. The place near my house in Bethesda's okay—not like this Sanka shit or whatever they serve here." He paused. "But I guess I can rough it while I'm here. We all make sacrifices for the job, don't we? Please, order, don't let me stop you. Conversations go better with food, right, Jonny boy?"

He turned to the waitress. "Hey, uh, Flo? Our friend Jonny boy here likes the Denver omelet, and uh, bring us both some orange juice and a coffee for him. I'll take chocolate chip pancakes."

Flo made a note on her pad and walked away, muttering under her breath.

Jon regularly ordered the Denver omelet. Apparently, Leska knew that.

"A Denver omelet in West Virginia. Funny. I hand it to you for making lemonade out of lemons, Jonny boy. You've had to make do before, haven't you?"

"What do you mean?" Jon asked, moving from shock to curiosity.

"Oh, I didn't mean anything bad, Jonny boy. It's just that some of us have had more bumps in the road than others. Sometimes things work out and you move on, and sometimes you don't. That's all. Take old Flo, over there. She probably wanted to move to Hollywood and be an actress. But she just wasn't cut out for it. Sometimes people need to find their place and just stay there, don't you think?"

Jon started to ask how Leska knew about the earlier conversation with Flo, but stopped. A different waitress brought the omelet and pancakes and then scurried away while Leska was sipping coffee.

Jon cleared his throat. "Mr. Leska," he started respectfully, "I kind of doubt you came here to talk about your coffee or Flo's dreams."

"You're a perceptive guy, Jonny boy. No wonder you wanted to be an investigator in the big city." Leska paused and took a bite of his pancakes. "But it's all related, isn't it? People have to find where they belong. And sometimes that means staying where they are." He pointed his fork downward to emphasize the point.

"Look," Jon said, a little more firmly. "All I'm trying to do is figure out what happened and try to keep it from happening again. I'd think you and the company would want that too."

"Of course we do. Thing is, we already figured that out. Like we said—bad maintenance. Why can't you just accept that and move on?"

"With all due respect, that theory doesn't make sense. There hadn't been any maintenance in that unit for a long time. You probably already know that."

Leska rocked back in the booth and dabbed his mouth with the napkin.

"And if it was poor maintenance," Jon continued, "what was the connection to high level in the vessel? It seems there was quite a concern about high level, so explain that." Feeling empowered, he leaned forward. "Tell me why the overhead line was made of the wrong steel. That's what I want to know."

Leska finished chewing. "You seen the news?"

"What?"

"It's interesting." Leska picked up his paper and held it up in front of him. It was not the local paper from Charleston; it was the paper from Cheyenne, Wyoming, dated one year before. Jon finally saw the headline that he'd hoped he would never see again: "Local Engineer Blamed for Death of Worker at the Refinery."

Leska flipped the paper over and started reading. "'An engineer at the plant, Jon Barrett, is blamed for ordering the wrong pump. The company said the wrong pump was installed, and that it malfunctioned on startup, damaging the casing and sending shrapnel outward like missiles.'" Leska folded the corner down and looked at Jon. "Like missiles—I love that part. 'The shrapnel hit the operator in the heart, and he was pronounced dead at the hospital. The company said the engineer is on administrative leave.' *Administrative leave.* I thought they only did that in the government. You were ahead of your time." Leska paused to take a sip. "Seems you got a bit of a past too there, Jonny boy."

Jon sat silent.

Leska put down the paper and fixed his gaze on Jon. "Now here's what's going to happen." Gone was his attempt at a local accent, replaced by angry arrogance. "You're going to interview the engineer this afternoon. We told the reporter we would do that, so we will. We've set it up for four o'clock. You're going to talk to him, and not probe. You are not going to ask about high level in the vessel or who said to do what during the design of the unit. That's old news and not relevant. You're going to tell your little reporter friend that the company has fully cooperated. Then you're going to go back to DC and tell the people there that we were right all along and it was bad maintenance. In return, we won't go to the press and tell them about you and how we had to ban you from the plant because you're a danger and we didn't know about your terrible past."

Jon swallowed hard. "They found out that it wasn't a problem with my design. It was a flaw from the manufacturer. That story wasn't true."

Leska laughed. Other patrons turned around at the outburst. Tears started rolling down his cheeks.

"Oh my God, now that is a good one. That's the whole issue here, boy, and you still don't see it." Leska leaned in. "See, Jonny, the truth doesn't matter. I would've thought even a few months in DC would've taught you that. It's what you can get people to believe that matters." Leska looked around as if he was telling a secret. "And who do you think they'll believe? An important company that employs thousands of people or a disgraced little engineer from Nebraska? Word is, not even the folks in your own agency are behind you.

"So, Jonny, here's the deal. You play ball with us, and we'll release a statement that you conducted a good investigation and we were glad to work with you. If you play this right, maybe we could even give you a reference—help you get a job, say, back in Nebraska or somewhere you'll fit in better."

Leska leaned back in the booth and looked away from Jon. "If you don't play ball—well, let's just assume it doesn't come to that." He picked up the check that Flo had laid on the edge of the table and started scooting out of the booth.

"Don't worry about this one, Jonny boy. It's on me." He paused just before he stood up. "And don't worry about the ethics rules. This is less than twenty-five bucks. Besides, this is just between us. I know the rules better than the lawyers in your agency." His attempt at a local accent was back.

Then he stood in front of Jon and leaned in, placing one hand on the back of the seat and one hand on the table, pinning Jon in place. Jon could smell his coffee breath.

"Enjoy the omelet, Jonny boy. And, uh, don't worry about getting to the plant before the interview. There's nothing for you to do until then."

The mix of customers in coveralls, jeans, and khakis watched the DC lawyer in the Armani suit walk up to the counter and slap down a hundred-dollar bill. Jon's mind was a fog. He couldn't hear what Leska said to the cashier, though he spoke loudly.

Leska waved as he walked out the door, not waiting for change.

Jon looked at his omelet. It was getting cold.

63

Walking back to the hotel, he almost stepped in front of a car. His mind was elsewhere. It was in Casper, Wyoming, a year ago.

There had been a loud crash, like the sound of a huge metal saw breaking. Reporters in the control room looked at each other, wondering if that was normal. Then confused panic over the radio. *Oh my God, Joe's been hit. Shut it down!* The PR liaison started escorting the media out, but the damage was done.

It was supposed to have been Jon's moment to shine.

Jon had been working as a mechanical engineer at the refinery when he was put in charge of adding some larger pumps. Putting in pumps didn't sound glamourous, but it was a good opportunity. He'd never led a project, and if he did well, it could lead to a promotion. He spent hours doing calculations to determine the exact pump size needed for the increased flow rates. He researched pump manufacturers and chose what seemed to be the best one for this application.

Refinery management had invited the local media to sit in the control room during the startup of the redesigned unit, looking to make public relations points. Operations personnel had worried that something could go wrong, but corporate PR said the positive press outweighed any negatives. It would be like embedding reporters with troops. The media would see the victory in real time. But that is not what happened.

Trying to get ahead of the story, the plant manager had jumped in front of the media caravan. "I hate it that this happened while you were here," he said. "But I assure you, we will get to the bottom of it. It looks like it may have been a bad pump design, and I promise you I'll hold whoever's responsible accountable." He stepped out of the way. "I knew I shouldn't have listened to them," he said as the last reporter left the control room.

After the accident, all fingers conveniently pointed at Jon. Newspapers ran stories. He was a pariah. Everyone knew someone who knew the man who died, and it was Jon's fault.

The investigation took months, but in the end, it was determined that there was a manufacturing flaw in that model of pump. The manufacturer issued a recall, but the damage to Jon had been done. The plant reluctantly offered Jon his job back, but refinery workforces are unforgiving, and everything he did after that would be suspect. His career was destroyed. What company would take a chance on him now? And as Leska would tell him a year later, the truth doesn't matter. Only what people believed mattered, and everyone believed he was guilty.

Karl, the head of the engineering department, felt sorry for Jon. He had understood that Jon had been a convenient target. Karl was good friends with Craig Higgins. When the job at Interior opened up, Karl told Craig he could take a chance on Jon. Craig was persuaded to hire Jon when they met. Broke, depressed, and unemployed, Jon accepted.

▲ ▲ ▲

The rest of the walk back to the hotel had been a blur. Jon lay on the bed in his hotel room, staring at the ceiling. The heater had just kicked on. The room was quiet. Everything around Jon was quiet, but nothing inside him was. He had spoken optimistically to Craig yesterday, but now he'd been given an ultimatum. He had one last fake interview. He would write a report saying the company was right all along and would finalize the investigation. Case closed.

The company clearly knew the explosion had not been a result of bad maintenance. If that had been the cause, they would have supported his investigation, or at least not been so hostile. Instead, they'd provided him with a joke of a drawing with all meaningful information stripped out. But who had given him a copy of the real drawing and real procedures? Someone else out there wanted the truth to come out. He was ready to give up, but he owed it to that person to continue.

He would interview the engineer. But he would do a real interview. If they put more pressure on him, he would go back to the media or Wanda Ripwhile and the environmental group. They would be happy to help him embarrass the company.

Leska was right. He didn't need to go to the plant early. He'd been sitting in that makeshift office as a prisoner long enough. He was not going to do it today. He would get there just before four. They'd been shamed into the interview by the media, and the engineer would be heavily coached. He had to be strategic.

He thought about walking by the river or going to his favorite coffee shop, but nothing felt right. He ran through the questions he would ask, thinking about how different answers might throw him off track. Finally, he closed his eyes, hoping he would not have that dream again.

64

Jon pulled into the Chemtrifuge parking lot around 3:30. He sat in his car with his hands on the wheel for a few seconds before getting out. As he strolled to the guard shack, he paused for a moment and looked at the sky. It was overcast, the clouds dark gray, as if it had either just stormed or was getting ready to. As he went through the sign-in process, he was surprised to see Leska, not Charlie, approaching the guard shack.

"I enjoyed our talk this morning, Jonny boy. Nothing like a good breakfast to start the day, huh?"

Jon didn't bother to reply.

They walked together to the admin building, Leska making small talk that Jon didn't listen to. He was in a fog. Stopping at the door to Jon's makeshift office, Leska smiled, appearing even more menacing when he did.

As soon as he entered, Jon noticed that his makeshift office had changed. There was a calendar on his desk and a large black mug with pens and pencils sprouting out the top. A nice navy-blue padded leather chair sat behind his desk. It actually looked like an office. Jon froze for a moment.

"We thought we'd make your time here a bit nicer," Leska said. "Besides, this is going to be over soon."

"Thanks," Jon said with a slight effort.

"I'll be back in about half an hour. Don't want to keep you waiting."

Leska must have convinced them that if they showed him respect, he'd take their deal, Jon thought. Moving a chair and supplies in was easy, but the company hadn't managed to do it before.

Eric, the engineer, was already in the conference room when Leska brought Jon in.

"How do you do, Eric?" Jon asked, not bothering to extend a hand.

"Fine," Eric replied coldly.

There was no need for small talk. Jon could feel the tension. He read the opening statement, pausing to ask if Eric consented to Leska's presence.

"Yes, that's fine," Eric said.

"Explain to me how poor maintenance could have resulted in the explosion that night," Jon said, jumping right in.

Eric seemed surprised at this directness, but Leska smiled.

"Well, if they don't replace a gasket in a line, or don't tighten the bolts correctly, it can cause a leak. Once flammable material is released and finds an ignition source, it ignites."

"And what could that ignition source be?"

"Those are all over a chemical plant. There's hot work, meaning welding and things like that. The surface of some equipment is hot. Sources are ubiquitous."

Jon nodded, making notes. "So if there's a release of flammable material like ethylene, safe to say it's just luck that keeps it from finding an ignition source and exploding?"

Leska stopped scribbling but did not look up.

"Okay, Eric. How long have you been with the company?"

"Twelve years."

"And do you hold any engineering certifications?"

"Yes, I am a PE in West Virginia and Maryland." Eric had started rocking back and forth.

"And just to clarify, PE stands for professional engineer, correct?"

"That's correct."

"Why do you have a Maryland license?"

"Sometimes I do design work for our plant in Baltimore. Even if I don't do the design calculations, I review and stamp drawings. They don't have a PE on staff there."

"You had to pass two tests, have experience, and provide references to become a PE, correct?"

"That's right," Eric replied. "It's not like in the old days, when you just had to apply. The tests I took were tough."

Leska cleared his throat. Jon assumed that meant that Eric was talking too much.

"And you have to practice by a code of ethics to stay licensed, correct?"

Eric hesitated a moment. "That's correct."

"The requirements to stay certified are the same in most states, no?"

"I think so. There are small differences in the continuing education hours, but the general requirements are the same."

Leska shifted in his seat.

"Thanks for that background. Now, do you think the explosion that night was caused because of bad maintenance?"

Eric rubbed his eyes. "I suppose there could have been a number of causes. Bad maintenance can cause explosions."

Jon nodded. "I agree with you, it can. But I am asking about this specific explosion. Do you think it was caused by bad maintenance?"

"Seems like you're asking him to speculate," Leska grumbled.

Jon turned to Leska. "He's a subject-matter expert. I can ask his opinion."

"It's just an opinion," Leska muttered, and started writing again.

Jon looked back at Eric. "Okay, Eric, what do you think?"

"I don't remember the question," Eric said unconvincingly.

Jon put down his mechanical pencil. "Do you believe that the explosion that night was caused by bad maintenance?"

"What do you mean by 'bad maintenance'?"

Jon was ready for this dodge. "You told me earlier that it would mean something like a gasket not being replaced in the pipe, or bolts not being tightened. Do you think that is what caused this explosion?"

Eric's eyes widened. "I can't be absolutely certain what caused the explosion."

"Let's state it differently. Do you think the most likely scenario for what caused the explosion was bad maintenance? I want your judgment as a professional engineer."

After hesitating several seconds, Eric spoke softly. "No."

"Could it be possible that the equipment being made of the wrong type of steel played a role in this explosion?"

Jon waited.

"That's possible," Eric replied with resignation.

Jon resumed writing. "Were you involved in the design of the unit?"

"Yes," Eric replied.

"Who did the drawings for vessel E-101?"

"I did. I did the drawings for that whole unit."

"How was the decision made regarding what materials to use in the vessel and the overhead line?"

Leska exhaled and pointed his pencil at Jon. "I've let this go on about long enough. These questions are way off base."

"Your subject-matter expert says it is possible that the wrong material of construction played a role in this explosion. I'm simply trying to learn more."

Leska looked at Eric. "You don't have to answer that. This is a voluntary interview, and you can walk out."

Jon looked at Eric. "You certainly can. But we have the power to subpoena you, and then you'll have to answer these questions under oath."

Leska looked away and scratched his temple. Then he looked back at Eric and nodded.

"Stainless steel is supposed to be used in processing plants with liquid ethylene," Eric replied, squirming.

"What about carbon steel?"

"That's a bad idea."

"Why?"

"Because it can get so cold that it becomes fragile, and any small stress can rupture it. It becomes like glass."

"And what was the piping in the overhead line made of?"

Leska jumped in. "I wouldn't answer that, Eric."

Jon decided to use the trick that Craig had suggested if Leska overstepped his bounds. "Mr. Leska," he said, "where are you licensed to practice law?"

"A number of states, including the District of Columbia. Why?"

Jon started making a note. "We just need to check and see what they say about impeding a federal investigation." He paused. "Now, Eric, I'll ask you again. What's the overhead line made of?"

"Carbon steel," Eric said, his voice breaking.

Jon was writing feverishly.

"And why is it made of carbon steel rather than stainless steel, as recommended for this service?"

"Carbon steel is cheaper. The project was over budget, so the decision was made to change the material of construction."

"Did you agree with that decision?"

"No."

"Who made that decision?"

Leska resumed his annoying nose exhaling.

"I'd rather not answer that," Eric said.

"What is ACQ?"

Eric and Leska looked at each other. Both shrugged.

"If I saw a comment on a drawing like this," Jon continued, "what would that mean?" Jon drew the flower symbol and inscription that he had seen on the drawing.

Eric nodded. "Oh."

"Did you write that on the drawing?"

"Yes."

"And does it indicate the source of the decision to change the construction material on the overhead line to the wrong material?"

"Yes," Eric said softly.

"So what is ACQ?"

Eric bowed his head. "That would be Mr. Quinn."

Jon was surprised. He'd expected to hear about a society of quality or something similar. "Who is Mr. Quinn?"

Leska slammed his hand down on the table, his rings and gold bracelet making a crash that reverberated throughout the room. "This interview is over!"

65

Alister Cain Quinn had always felt different. He'd never cared about being liked or fitting in. Even as a child, he'd never tried to please people. He had always done what he needed to do to get what he wanted. Thinking back on it now, it had been easy—he figured out other children's weaknesses and used those against them. When he wanted to copy other kids' homework, he didn't ask. He simply grabbed their backpacks. When they protested, he reminded them of something bad they'd done and how he would tell. The bad thing was usually something he had made them do—it was a good system.

His father left when Alister, as he was called then, was only seven. Alister didn't care. He didn't need his father, or even his mother. She was only useful in doing things for him he didn't want to do. She cooked and cleaned when she found time between her two jobs. Alister was an only child, and the epitome of a latchkey kid. He found his own way.

Later, other kids started teasing him about having the middle name Cain. They talked about how Cain was a murderer in the Bible and killed his brother. They said Alister Cain must be evil too. Far from being insulted, Cain was empowered. He liked being called Alister because he'd read about the evil Aleister Crowley. He enjoyed having something in common with the man some people had called "the wickedest man in the world," and he was disappointed that his name was spelled differently. He decided he would be known as Cain. He liked Cain. He studied Cain. It seems God didn't like Cain's sacrifice and liked his brother's, so Cain killed his brother. To Alister—now Cain—that seemed natural. You do whatever you must, to whomever you must, to get what you want. As the other Aleister had put it, "Do what thou wilt shall be the whole of the law."

But in high school, Cain's attitude changed. He no longer needed a reason to hurt other people. He wanted to hurt others simply because they *were* others.

He still saved the most torture for those who'd hurt him. Like the girl he sometimes dreamed about, who'd called him rude. Or the kid who'd lied and said he was out of cigarettes and didn't have one to lend. Cain had let the air out of that kid's tires and busted the windows in his car.

Cain had been at Chemtrifuge for a long time. He'd developed a reputation as someone who paired a shrewd understanding of economics with a technical prowess that was unique. He'd reached a level few ever reach in an organization, and was proud of that. Everyone knew not to cross him. It didn't trouble him that everyone hoped he did not come to their site—he liked the occasional rumors that came back to him. There were rumors that he had ties to organized crime and had threatened the company owner early on. There were also rumors that Cain had murdered a man for cutting in front of him at a bar for a drink, though no one knew if it was true. No one knew that it was *not* true.

Very few people knew much about his background or his family. Wheelan Drew was an exception, but Wheelan wasn't going to share anything.

Soon he'd be on his way to Charleston to take care of business, like he always did.

66

For over an hour, Jon had been sitting alone in the comfortable new chair in his office. He'd thought he would feel better after the interview with the engineer, but now he felt anything but comfortable.

"You shouldn't have done that!" were Leska's only words when he walked Jon to his office, before slamming the door behind him.

Maybe Jon had overplayed his hand. Maybe the company was well-intentioned, and they were just shocked by the accident. He'd seen that before. After the accident for which he was blamed, the refinery was in shock. No one had ever died there before. Maybe the way organizations deal with grief is no different from the way individuals do. When his mother was diagnosed with cancer, Jon initially blamed everyone and everything else. She'd told him one time that her family history meant she wouldn't live to see fifty. How dare she have him and cause him to love her, if she was going to leave him! How dare this damn world take his mother! Tears formed as he remembered.

He knew what to do. He'd give the company one more chance. He'd try to work with Charlie and Leska. He'd let them talk during the interviews and do the investigation like a party system, rather than acting on his own.

But what if he was wrong? What if they shut him down again? Well, his plan B was to go to the press and the environmental group. Yes, Wanda Ripwhile with SHEAN. She'd help him embarrass the company. That's what environmental groups do. Persuasion by shaming, that was their currency. He could work with them. He'd learned in media training that people gave the benefit of the doubt to environmental groups. They were given credit for their intentions. He, Wanda, and SHEAN could be the biggest pains in the ass the company ever had. That was plan B. Cooperation was plan A, he thought, rising from the comfortable chair.

He opened the door and stepped out of his office. It felt different, or maybe he felt different. He felt like John Travolta stepping out of his plastic enclosure in that movie about the boy in the bubble. Maybe this was what the company wanted. He could even share his experience with the earlier fatality. They already knew about it, after all. Leska had thrown it in his face. It wasn't that long ago that he'd been on their side—he would have been tight-lipped, too, had a man from the government shown up.

I have a plan B, but I won't need it, he thought.

Charlie's office was down the next wing. All Jon had to do was walk down the hall to the conference room and take a right. He'd been tough today, but he'd gotten what he wanted. Now he wanted to cooperate. He walked past the offices on the way to the conference room, trying to stay calm.

"It will be a good meeting," he told himself. But just a few feet from the conference room door, he hesitated. The door was partially open. He thought he heard his name, and he was pretty sure it was the union steward, Alphonse Scott, talking. They must have thought he would stay in his office. Then he heard a gaggle of voices, one after the other, saying things. Mean things.

He couldn't hear all the words, but he made out some. *Investigation. Shut it down. Get him.* He leaned toward the room to hear better. "Let's see what they think of him then," Leska was bellowing. "He won't be able to sell shit to geese." The others laughed. Then Jon recognized the voice of one of the guys he'd interviewed, the young guy with the older operator. "Hoo-wee," he said in an exaggerated country-boy voice, "I used to clean shit off my shoes in Knee-Brass-Kuh. Now I'm a big ol' investigator in DC."

His face went hot, and he took a step back from the door. He hadn't even been tough on that guy in the interview. Why was he mocking him? Then everybody joined in. *What kind of idiot family did he come from?* The voices seemed to oscillate between anger and ridicule, and it was all directed at him.

Jon turned to walk back to his office so they wouldn't see him. Then he froze. He couldn't believe what he heard next.

"He said the company had a theory that it was bad maintenance by contractors," a new voice was saying, "but that he didn't buy it. He said something else had happened, and he would keep digging. He mentioned my logs. I'm holding those out until we finish *our* negotiations. I told him some things, but not everything, you know, in case you guys reneged." They all laughed.

There was no denying that Jon had said these things. But only one person had heard them. And that person was in the conference room, betraying Jon, repeating his own words and colluding with Chemtrifuge management—Wanda Ripwhile of SHEAN.

67

Jon lay on his side in his hotel bed. After he walked away from the conference room, he had gone back to his office and then to the guard shack, trying to hold it together. His voice cracking, he told the guard that both Charlie and the lawyer were tied up.

The guard didn't question him. "Yes, let's not bother the very important lawyer," she said. From the mix of sarcasm and disdain in her voice, Jon guessed that Leska had made her feel worthless, like he did everyone else.

He also held it together on the walk to his car. Just a few more feet, he thought. He started the car, shifted into drive, and pushed the gas. He made it out of the parking lot. Then, as if from a shower head, the tears came uncontrollably. He heard himself scream. Then, he was numb. It felt as if he was someone else watching this pathetic man in his forties break down.

Before this investigation started, Jon could only remember crying two times as an adult—the day his mother died, and the day he and

Tammy finalized their divorce. In both those cases, he could rationalize that the outcomes were for the best: his mother would not suffer anymore, and he and Tammy could move on to better relationships. This was different. This was about him and his failure. He bowed his head at a red light, sobbing, until a car horn blew behind him.

He walked through the hotel lobby, avoiding all eye contact, and fumbled for the key card to his room. Someone passed and said, "Hi." He didn't look at them. He just mumbled something back. He was outside himself, saying and thinking things but not controlling them. He fell into bed like a bag of sand dropped from a building, still in his clothes and steel-toed boots, but without any dignity.

The company had won. They'd saved some money by using cheaper steel. They knew better, but they had done it anyway and left a ticking bomb in the process. They did what he'd been accused of doing before; only, what they did was worse. This company knew what to do, and they didn't do it; this was not an honest mistake. They'd saved some money but guaranteed a disaster.

Foggy thoughts floated through his mind. He thought about a class he'd taken years before about latent hazards in a chemical plant. Hazards could cause an accident, or fail to prevent one. In this case one problem, high level, guaranteed an accident. It was like designing a car so the tires fall off if it goes over fifty miles per hour. One day someone would drive that fast, the tires would fall off, and that someone would probably die.

But this whole scenario begged other questions. Jon rolled onto his back and draped his arm over his forehead. Why had they not just shut down the unit when things got out of control? Why had the automatic shutdown interlock on the drawing not worked? Had they overridden it? When they saw the level rising, and the guys outside couldn't open the valve to drain the vessel fast enough, they could have stopped the flow into the vessel. That was their last line of defense. It was that simple.

It seemed they tried to have Janet shut off the feed, but by that time it was too late. Why did they wait so long?

And why was the head of the environmental group on the company's side? That had been his plan B. The union was obviously in bed with the company, but shouldn't environmentalists support him, and the government? What "negotiations" would the company have with the environmental group?

Then one thought became clear. None of that mattered now. They had won, and he had lost. And "they" were not just the company. They were the company, the environmental group, the union, the fat politician and most—if not all—of the media.

He'd thought he was ensuring justice. People threw that word around, but what did it really mean? If someone intentionally did something wrong, shouldn't there be a consequence? If it was a company, how was that different? But again, none of that mattered now.

He wiped his cheek. They were right. He was just a stupid, naive little person from the heartland whose life didn't mean anything and who was wrong about justice. Not just wrong—laughable. Justice was not this old concept that right wins and wrong loses. Maybe justice meant that if you were powerful, you won. Who was he to challenge that?

The only thing that connected all these dots was that little people didn't matter. Some say they did, but they didn't. Buildings and bridges weren't named after little people. Even back in Nebraska, they were named after the wealthy and powerful. It was even worse in DC. Little people didn't matter. And he was a little person.

Three men had died. They were alive one minute, and then they were burned to death because of a decision someone more powerful made to save a few dollars. They were expendable. Jon was not naive— he knew that insurance companies and the government put values on lives, and that the value of little people's lives was simply less.

It was not just companies and the government. The media, the so-called watchdogs and guardians of the truth, didn't care either. The three men who died were little people, and they remained nameless. He couldn't even find their names in media reports. One powerful person, the Speaker of the House, sent some emails about sex, and the media immediately abandoned the accident to pursue that story. They left the identities of the men in the ashes of the plant where their lives and dreams ended.

But none of that mattered now. The company, the union, and the environmental group had made that clear in the conference room. This investigation was over. They'd even personalized it by mocking Jon. There was no plan B. Jon would go to the office tomorrow. He would give Craig the courtesy that Craig had never given him: he would tell him the news to his face. He liked his boss, but after hiring Jon, Craig had hung him out to dry. And what did Craig mean, they needed to discuss the future of the office? There was no future. This blip would look even worse on his résumé than if he'd never been part of this investigation. He had nothing to show for his work. The investigation, and the truth, also lay in the rubble of the plant.

What now? He couldn't go back to industry. He was a screwup engineer who'd become an incompetent hack for the government. Unemployment wouldn't last. Jon had drained his savings after the refinery accident. He thought about how embarrassing it would be for his father, having to explain what had happened. Jon couldn't do that to him. He might have destroyed his own life, but he wouldn't destroy the fantasy his dad had dreamed up that finally made him proud of his son.

Jon looked at the clock. 7:32. His feet hurt. As he sat up in the bed and took off his heavy steel-toed boots, he thought about the one person who might understand.

She picked up on the fourth ring.

"Tammy, is this a good time?"

"Jon, hi." She sounded cheerful. "I have to pick up my daughter from soccer, but I have a few minutes. What's up?"

"Tammy, I blew it. I failed. They're shutting down the investigation. I found out today that even people I thought were working with me are against me. I think they're even going to the media to dredge up that story about me and the pump."

"But that wasn't your fault."

"I know, but it doesn't matter. It's all about what you can convince people that the truth is. And I can't do that alone."

"What about your department? Your boss?"

"That's been one of the biggest disappointments. They pushed me out on a limb and helped the company saw it off." Jon could hear his voice start to crack.

"I'm sorry. What will you do now?"

"I don't know. I'll turn in my badge and phone tomorrow, and after that—I don't know. I'm one person, and I don't matter. I guess that's what hurts the most." He wiped his cheek with the pillowcase. "It's deeper than this investigation. I've failed as a person."

"Jon, did they do wrong?"

Jon sniffled, hoping she couldn't hear. "Yes. They did what I was accused of, but they did it deliberately."

"And did you do the right thing, trying to find out what they did?"

"I thought so. I thought I was serving some great cause for justice. I wanted to find out what happened, so I could help other plants be safer. I thought I had a purpose, but I was wrong."

Tammy hesitated for a moment. "Look, Jon, I know you. I know it looks bleak now, but you'll figure something out. Did you find out what caused the accident?"

Jon stood up and started pacing. "That's just it. I did. Even with all the obstacles, I figured out what happened. I still have a couple of questions, but I know what caused it."

"Well, maybe you can let people know. You could do it in the local paper, or maybe an engineering publication. There are ways to get the word out."

Tammy had always been optimistic, but he knew no one would listen to a disgraced former federal investigator. Even if some outlet published an editorial he wrote, he didn't have the energy to fight the blowback that would surely come from the company.

"Thanks, Tammy," he said anyway. "I'll think about doing that."

"Listen, I have to go, but call me later if you need to talk, okay?"

"Okay."

"And, Jon, remember what your grandfather used to say. Some things are meant to be, but we can still try to make other things work out. Keep your courage through this."

"Okay. You always see the good. Talk to you later."

Tammy had been encouraging, but Jon didn't feel any better. When he went to DC the next day, that would be the last time he would ever discuss this investigation. It had taken the last bit of dignity he had. It was over. He had lost.

▲　▲　▲

Jon walked out of the back door of the Hampton Inn into a large field. He could faintly make out a path between trees in the faint moonlight. He walked in a daze. Then thought he heard music. He looked in the distance and saw a tent lit up, supported by ropes with big spikes. It looked like a circus tent, about fifty feet high at its peak and half the size of a football field. As he got closer, he could hear that the music was actually hymns. This must be what he remembered as a tent revival.

Jon hadn't been to church in years. His family wasn't particularly religious, except for his uncle, who was a presiding bishop in the Lutheran Church. He started to turn around and walk back to the hotel, but decided to go inside for a few minutes. There was nowhere else to go. Besides, the music had a soothing effect.

A short, gray-haired man at the tent's entrance flap smiled and handed him a folded paper. Jon opened the bulletin and started reading. This revival, led by the Non-Denominational Prayer Disciples, was in town all week. The songs were listed, and there was a line for prayer time, followed by a line for the sermon with the Rev. Doug Gastone. The title of the sermon was "Find Your Courage."

Jon laughed out loud. How fitting for the shitty day he'd had. This guy was going to talk about how to go to God and magically get courage. It had taken courage to push the investigation this far, but that had only led to his downfall.

He pulled back the flap and looked inside the tent. At the front was a stage with a choir on one side, made up of Black and White parishioners in purple robes. In the middle, behind a portable podium, was a man in a peach suit with curly hair, dancing and clapping. The chairs had been set up in a semicircle, probably twenty rows. Jon didn't recognize the song, but it kept repeating something like "troubles and trials will soon be done."

The music stopped, and the clapping grew louder. The peach-suited preacher held up his hands until the clapping gradually stopped.

"Let us pray. Dear God, tonight we are going to talk about one of your servants, David, and how killing one giant wasn't enough. He had to keep fighting even when the odds were against him. Help us all to find the courage to name and fight the giants in our lives. In Jesus's name. Amen." A chorus of voices echoed "amen" in unison.

The usher who'd handed Jon the bulletin touched his arm. "There're a couple of seats in the front."

Jon would rather have stood in the back, but his feet still hurt, so he walked down the aisle between the rows of wooden folding chairs. He took a chair in the semicircular front row on the preacher's right side.

"Please be seated," the preacher said. "I'm only gonna read you one verse tonight. It comes from Second Samuel. You see, one of the best-known stories in the whole Bible is about how David fought a giant named Goliath against all odds and killed him. Everybody knows about that. I don't have to read that part." *That's right, preacher*, came voices from the crowd. *Amen.*

"What you may not know is how David had to keep that courage to fight other giants in his life. Second Samuel, twenty-one, verse twenty-two says, 'These four were born to the giant in Gath, and fell by the hand of David, and by the hand of his servants.' That's all I need for this sermon. You see, David had defeated Goliath early on, but he had to keep fighting giants even when he was older. I'm sure he wanted to just sit back and relax, but his life wasn't like that. Life isn't smooth. It's not tidy, and there're challenges all throughout."

The chorus of amens grew louder.

"Can you imagine if David had given up? But he kept courage. Now, folks, David wasn't perfect. You all know about some of the bad things he did. But he had courage. Oh, he was discouraged. When you read some of the psalms, they show that he wanted to give up many times. He felt like his enemies were waiting for him around every corner, and sometimes he even doubted God. But at the end of the day, he kept the faith. He knew what was right, and eventually he did it, even when it wasn't easy."

The preacher paused and walked away from the podium. Pulling his suit coat back, he flipped a switch on the black box on his belt to key the mobile mic and then stepped off the low stage and started walking around through the crowd.

"Brothers and sisters, what are the giants in your life? What are the things that seem so big and strong, you just can't believe you'll ever defeat them?" He paused for a moment, probably for effect, and then added, "But are there people in your life who can help you defeat them?"

Jon's mind wandered. It felt as if this sermon was directed at him. But David had God on his side. Jon didn't have anybody.

A woman seated directly across from him on the other side of the semicircular row seemed to be looking at him, but he was sure he didn't know her. He looked to his left and right to see if anyone seemed to be looking at her or waving, but everyone else was looking at the preacher.

After a few more minutes, the preacher wound up his sermon. Jon left to beat the crowd, taking one last curious look at the African American woman in the front row.

68

Jon opened his eyes and looked at the clock. The dim red light read 4:34. After lying in the bed for a few minutes, he got up.

Today, he knew, would be one of the worst days of his life. He dreaded the drive to DC and the talk with Craig. At least he could look presentable, though. His electric razor had died, and he had not shaved in two days. He only had a disposable razor and a small bag with shaving cream he got from the front desk. He had not used a blade in years. Zombie-like, he spread the small amount of cheap shaving cream thinly on his face, pulled the handle to stop up the sink, and started raking the blade across his face. The razor wasn't much of a match for two days' worth of stubble. He swished it around in the water and scraped harder. There wasn't much cream left.

He decided he'd done as much as he could with the cheap blade. He groggily cupped his hands together and in one swift motion scooped two handfuls of water against his face. There seemed to be a flash in the mirror, and in that instant, he saw his face transformed into a mangled, meaty mess. "Oh, God!" he cried, closing his eyes. He felt for the towel beside the sink and pressed it to his burning face.

He opened his eyes again, looked at the bloodstained towel, and then back at the mirror. His face looked sunburned and was cut in a couple places, but it was not the horrible meaty, mangled, and burned mess he'd seemed to see before. The combination of his fair skin (more fragile in cold weather), too little cream, a cheap razor, and his stupor state had caused him to scrape off the top layer of skin in places, and the splash of water, much hotter than he realized, had caused a rush of pain.

Jon watched a tiny trickle of blood flow down his face in the places he'd cut himself. He had felt a little pain, but his skin would heal. But that flash of meaty horror made him realize that he had tasted—only tasted—what the three men had gone through. Their experience was a billion times worse, and they would never recover. Their families would never see them again. People they were supposed to meet would never meet them. They would never pursue their dreams and succeed, or fail and get back up again. They would never have that chance because they'd been sent to their deaths.

Jon walked to his bed and sat on the corner, holding the towel against his face where it was bleeding the worst. Those men wouldn't even have identities anymore. The media preferred to chase some powerful person at the State House. Jon didn't know what justice was anymore, but he knew that this was wrong.

He looked at the red blotches on the towel and realized that it all hinged on him. If he gave up now, nothing would ever be right. The company, the union, the environmentalists, they would move on as if nothing had happened—as if those men had never existed. And Jon would live out his nonexistent life in some nonexistent place and always think about this failure. Somebody had to give the dead men a voice, and a name. Jon was that somebody. He had been humiliated and mocked, but they had been killed.

It would not be easy. The people at Chemtrifuge didn't care about the men who died, and they cared about him even less.

He knew he had to go on. No turning back. It might have been the tent revival, the sermon on courage, or the burns and cuts on his face. Maybe it was the call with Tammy and memories of his grandfather standing strong even when he stood alone.

This feeling was foreign to Jon. It felt like determination, anger, and fear mixed together, but the fear wasn't going to stop him anymore. The forces against him might beat him—he realized that—but they would not scare him away. He wouldn't make it easy for them. And he wouldn't go to DC today to hand in his badge and tell Craig it was over. He would go to the plant.

Somebody needed to see this investigation through, and he was that somebody. He would give the men who died a voice, even if his was silenced as a result.

69

Despite his newfound courage and determination, Jon didn't want to run into Leska just yet. He preferred to surprise him at the plant. He ate in the hotel rather than risk seeing him at the diner—the premade egg patties and hard biscuits made for much better company, anyway.

He grabbed a paper from the kiosk next to the coffee bar. It could not have come at a better time, or a worse time. It both encouraged and concerned him. It was running in the Wednesday paper, splashed on the front page.

Jon had no need to rush. No matter when he got to the plant, there would be a lot of waiting. He wolfed down his egg patties and biscuit and then moved to one of the striped upholstered chairs in the lobby. He took a deep breath and then set the paper on his lap.

IS CHEMTRIFUGE PLAYING NICE WITH THE FEDS OR NOT?

It has been weeks since a major accident in the ethylene unit at the Chemtrifuge Plant in Charleston claimed the lives of three workers. Soon thereafter, the federal government sent an investigator to the scene to determine what happened. The company called a press conference the day after the tragedy and, with local dignitaries on hand, initially indicated that it would cooperate. However, that cooperative attitude seems to have dissipated like the smoke from that fatal fire.

"They still have not made critical people and documents available," said Jon Barrett, the investigator from the federal government. Jon has been a constant presence at the plant, but he has spent much of his time waiting for the company to produce documents for him to review and people for him to interview. "I would think they would want to help me get to the bottom of this accident, but they seem to be in no hurry."

Jon stopped and looked up. He did not remember saying that, though it reflected how he felt. The reporter must have inferred it from his tone. He shrugged and kept reading.

Representatives from Chemtrifuge insist they have been cooperating and that accidents like this just take a long time to investigate. They indicated that the unit engineer and one of the critical witnesses were scheduled to talk to the federal investigator.

The Charleston plant has generally been viewed favorably by its neighbors and touts its work with local schools to have an annual tour-the-plant day. However, one of its neighbors is the president of a local environmental group, Save our Health through Environmental Action Now, or SHEAN. The president, Wanda Ripwhile, was contacted but had no comment about the investigation.

"I bet you don't," Jon murmured, "seeing as you're on their side for some strange reason." A white-haired man in plaid shorts and black socks to his knees was passing by and looked at him oddly.

Chemtrifuge employs over 350 people in the community and has five plants throughout the country. According to the company's website, the Baltimore plant is said to be a replica of the one in Charleston, based on the same technology and designed and built identically to the one here.

That was the article. It was short, but it hit the right notes: the company wasn't cooperating, Jon was trying to help, and the president of SHEAN had no comment. The reporter had gotten Jon's quote mostly right, though she'd dropped the part about him wanting to work with the company. He was sure the company would hate it and retaliate by bringing up the fatality he'd been blamed for.

As he walked to the elevator, got in, and pushed the button, he started thinking about what he needed to do. The company probably would not let him in the gate after they'd seen the article. He probably had only this day.

The bell dinged, and he walked toward his room, pulling out his wallet and fumbling for the plastic key among his receipts and bills. Once inside, he scanned the notes on his yellow pad and flipped to a new page. There were two things he needed to get at the plant today: first, proof that the line coming out of the vessel E-101 was carbon steel, and second, an understanding of who Mr. Quinn was and why he had made the decision that led to the accident. He needed proof that the pipe was made of the wrong kind of steel, or the company could claim that the notes on the drawing were inaccurate. Even if the pipe was scorched or covered in insulation, he had to get to the point where the explosion occurred and find markings on the pipe showing it was the wrong material. It would be great if he could get a sample, but he would take what he could get.

Getting into the plant would be challenging enough. Getting into the unit, taking pictures, and grabbing a piece of the pipe would be nearly impossible, but he had to find a way.

Jon rubbed his face and felt the freshly formed scabs there. He remembered the flash in the mirror. He thought about the tent revival. One way or the other, he would do this. He had to. There was no one else who could.

70

"What the hell did I just read?"

Cain Quinn was yelling through the speakerphone at Sam and Charlie in Sam's office. Leska got up to close the door. Sam wished he could choke Quinn but then stopped the thought immediately.

"Wheelan's secretary read me the whole thing—twice. You idiots totally lost control. Even the local press is against us!"

Sam rocked forward. "Mr. Quinn, we plan to contact the reporter and do a hit piece on Barrett. Leska's going to give them a full rundown of the accident he caused at that refinery."

"Yes, your plans have been working so well. What will you do when he shows up today?"

Leska laughed. "I don't think there's any way he'll show up today. If he does, we'll park him in that shitty office, put him on lockdown, and make him regret it."

Quinn didn't laugh. "That's not enough. I'll be there by this evening. If he is there when I get there, I'll finish what you little girls couldn't do."

Sam rocked back and rolled his eyes. "Mr. Quinn, I think we have it under control. The article was one-sided, but we'll correct that. We'll let them know we can't have someone like that on our site anymore. We'll tell them he is a liability and then launch a complaint with his employer, Interior."

Quinn snorted. "Oh, you're going to launch a complaint. What a brave piece of shit you are!"

Sam shook his head.

"I'll take care of him," Quinn continued. "It appears I'm the only one who can. I don't do complaints. If he comes in, put him in your so-called lockdown and leave it to me. I'll make sure he won't bother us anymore."

They heard the click as Quinn hung up.

After a minute, Charlie spoke. "I actually feel sorry for Jon if he comes back here."

"Me too," Sam and Leska said in unison.

71

Jon pulled into the plant parking lot just before five. Some sun was still hanging on in the sky. There had been no reason to get to the site earlier. Much of the business of the day would be over now, so it would be easier to have an uninterrupted conversation with management. Hopefully Leska had given up on him coming in and left, but no matter. He would talk to whoever was still there.

He would ask, then demand, to be taken to the scene of the accident. He knew he needed to borrow PPE, but he would demand that too. One way or the other, it would happen today. He had a pen, a folded sheet of yellow paper, and a phone with a camera to photograph equipment.

Men in faded coveralls and hard hats walked slowly through the turnstile beside the guard shack for the shift change. Jon took a deep breath and opened the car door. If someone spoke to him calmly, he would reply. If they yelled at him, he would ignore them.

As he walked past the men coming out of the gate and folded in with those coming in, the loud talk died down to a murmur. He no longer heard the shuffling of feet on pavement. They had stopped talking and were looking at him.

He walked up to the guard shack, ignoring them. "I need to see either Charlie or Leska."

The guard—her name was Ruby, Jon remembered—looked up, astonished. Without a word, she went to the back room. Jon stood at the desk, trying to stay composed. He sensed that he was being watched.

After a minute, Ruby reappeared. "Have a seat. One of them will be here."

"I prefer to stand." Whether they came to escort him in or tell him to leave, he would be standing.

Ruby shrugged. "Suit yourself."

The next minutes felt like hours. Hearing the shuffling of feet again, Jon looked out the guard-shack window at the turnstile. A beep sounded as one of the guys hovered his badge over the turnstile. In the many hours he'd spent waiting for Charlie, Jon had watched people going through the turnstile. Employees hovered their badges over the sensor. When the system clicked, people walked through the flywheel. If it beeped, they were randomly selected to have their personal effects searched.

The minutes wore on. Jon started worrying that they might make him wait a long time and then tell him to leave. Finally, he saw Charlie approaching the turnstile.

Charlie seemed more frustrated than angry. "I'm surprised to see you," he said.

"I'm working on the investigation."

"Follow me," Charlie said, his voice cracking a little. He wiped his forehead.

Jon crossed through the turnstile after Charlie. The first barrier had been crossed.

On the short walk, Charlie broke the tense silence. "You really shouldn't have come in today."

Jon looked straight ahead. "I still have a job to do."

"It would have been better for you if you'd stayed away," Charlie said without the usual bitterness.

Jon didn't respond. He wanted to talk to the whole management group—including this Mr. Quinn, whoever he was—and tell them he was expecting to tour the site today. Not a windshield tour from a golf cart. He wanted to go up the stairs of the platform, walk out on the catwalk, take pictures of the pipe, and identify sections to test.

"Where's Leska?" he asked.

"He left an hour ago to fly back to DC. We were convinced you wouldn't show up."

Charlie opened the back door. For the first time, he held it open for Jon. Jon stepped into his office. The old folding chair was back, and the executive chair was gone. It didn't matter. He didn't intend to sit down.

Jon cleared his throat. "Charlie, there's something I need to tell you and management, whoever's available."

Charlie looked at the desk and then back at Jon. "Just tell me. I'll convey the message."

Jon folded his arms and turned around, facing away from Charlie. He wanted to tell management himself, but he realized that the important thing was to get access, not who heard the request. He turned back around, put his hand on the doorknob, and moved in toward Charlie until their faces were a foot apart. He delivered his entire request at once.

"I know what happened, and I think you do too. To conclude the investigation, I need proof of the material of construction in the overhead pipe coming out of that vessel. I intend to get that proof today. I want access to the scene, and I want to take pictures of the pipe and take samples of it to test. I'll fill out any paperwork you need me to, and I'll share all photos with you. I'll also work with you on the testing protocols for the pipe samples."

"Jon, we're not going to do that. We know your past and consider you a danger to our site. We can't let you into our units. It's best if you leave—we're prepared to launch a formal protest with Interior if you don't."

Jon steeled his gaze. "I know what you mean about my past. That has been distorted. I was not responsible for that death. The question now is, who will be held responsible for the deaths of the men who died here? I'm investigating this, and I intend to get proof."

Charlie looked down as Jon continued.

"Charlie, I want to make sure that is the final decision of your management. It seems that many of you are guilty of interfering with a federal investigation."

Charlie looked up. "I'll verify, but that's our final decision. Wait here."

▲ ▲ ▲

Charlie closed the door to Jon's office behind him and took a deep breath. He knew the answer to Jon's request: No way. And it was for Jon's own good. They hoped to get him offsite before Quinn arrived.

As he turned the corner, he saw Cain Quinn go into Sam Page's corner office. Charlie quickly diverted into his own. Now that Quinn had arrived, everything had changed. Charlie had hoped to simply talk to Sam, have Sam say, "No way," and tell Jon to leave. But he knew Quinn would take a different approach. Quinn had a reputation of handling matters the same way the Mafia did, and Charlie didn't want to think about what he would do to Jon.

Charlie sat down at his desk. He wondered if he could make Quinn mad enough to just kick Jon off the site.

Then Charlie had another idea. Maybe he could keep Quinn out of it altogether. He'd tell Quinn and Sam that he was having Jon escorted out by security because he'd made such outrageous demands. Hopefully, Quinn would accept that. If he didn't—well, Charlie didn't want to consider that. Quinn was capable of anything.

▴　▴　▴

Jon was tapping his fingers on the desk. Charlie had been gone several minutes, and he'd started to worry. The best-case scenario was that Charlie had told management he wasn't backing down and they'd decided to give in. But Jon remembered what Charlie said. Their position wasn't going to change. Not only that, but they were going to complain about him to Interior, where he had no support. The company was not backing down. When Charlie returned, he would reiterate that and ask Jon to leave. This was it. Jon had only one choice to save this investigation. If there was another way, he would take it. But there was not.

72

Charlie took a deep breath and flung open the door to Sam's office. Cain Quinn was hunched over with his knuckles on Sam's desk, talking to Sam, who was gripping a glass of bourbon and looked like he had just been told he had one day to live. Both men turned toward Charlie, startled.

Charlie slammed the door behind him. "That stupid little shit! He showed up after all. But I'm gonna deal with him. He's bothered us long enough."

Sam rocked up in his chair. "What the hell you talking about? You mean the fed finally showed up today?"

"Yeah, can you believe it? Wants to tour and take pictures of the pipe and cut samples to test. That little bastard will never get back in here. I'll call security to kick him out right now."

"Where is he now?" Cain Quinn asked calmly.

"In the office by the back door of the building. I told him I'd discuss this with you guys first, but then I'll kick him out and make sure he doesn't bother us again."

Charlie wheeled around and was heading for the door when he heard Quinn's deep voice. "Uh, Charlie, hold up a minute."

Charlie closed his eyes and froze. His tirade hadn't worked. Quinn wasn't satisfied.

"Did you say he wanted to go on the deck where the explosion happened?"

Charlie turned around slowly. "Yes, that's what he is demanding."

"Then let's take him there."

Sam and Charlie looked at Quinn, surprised.

"It's perfect," Quinn said. "People slip and fall in chemical plants all the time. That's about six stories up—he'll never survive an 'accident.'" He air-quoted the last word. "We've already established that he's caused an earlier accident in a refinery. If he has another one here, not only will it end the investigation, but we can rail against the government for sending someone like that into our plant. We'll embarrass them so much they'll never think of sending anybody into any of our plants again."

Quinn had been looking into the distance as he spoke, but now he turned to face Charlie. "Let's take him to the scene, Charlie. Let's give him exactly what he wants. This is even better than what I had planned."

Sam took a sip of bourbon. "Do we really have to do it this way? We could just destroy him in the press. He'd have to stop his investigation then."

Quinn stood up and leaned over the desk toward Sam, breathing heavily. "We need to make the problem go away. I trusted you, and you didn't get it done. Now we're doing it my way."

Sam nodded weakly. "Okay. Charlie, help him out. Do you need me?"

Quinn shook his head.

"Is there anything else we can do? There has to be another way to handle this. You know—the press, his reputation."

Quinn didn't say a word, but the look he gave Charlie was answer enough.

Charlie bowed his head.

The radio in Sam's office came to life with a blast of static. It was kept on the emergency channel, so there was rarely any voice traffic.

"We picked something up on video." It was Turner, the unit supervisor. "I think we've got an unauthorized person in the ethylene unit."

Sam grabbed the radio and squeezed the handle on the side to key the mic. "Who is it, Turner?"

"I only got a brief glance, but I think it's that investigator from Washington."

"Where is he now?"

"Not sure. He seemed to be coming toward the control room, but we lost him. He went into the blind area where we have no camera."

Quinn grabbed the radio. "Keep an eye out for him. We'll take care of this," he huffed and then shoved the radio back to Sam, who fumbled with it momentarily.

Turner came back over the radio: "Should we have someone grab him if he goes into the processing area?"

Quinn looked at Sam and shook his head. Charlie knew what he was thinking—the fewer witnesses, the better.

Sam keyed the mic again. "No, just keep an eye on him. Charlie and Quinn will be there in a couple of minutes."

Ruby came on the line. "Do you need any help from security?"

"No, Ruby, we got this," Sam said. "Cease all communications on this matter now."

"We don't need security," Quinn said as soon as Ruby was off the line, "but we might need a coroner in a few minutes." He bellowed a rare laugh and then slapped Charlie's shoulder. "Come on, we got a problem to solve!"

"What if I don't?" Charlie finally mustered the courage to say, pushing himself off the credenza.

"Then you're next." Quinn held Charlie's eyes, his own narrowing. "By the way, how's your wife?"

73

It was now or never, Jon realized. Looking back over his shoulder, he walked swiftly toward the back door. He didn't see the janitor, who was crouched in the hallway doing something with a vacuum cleaner, until it was too late. Jon apologized as he disentangled himself from the vacuum but kept moving.

Outside, he zigzagged through the first processing unit, just outside the administration building, avoiding the dirt road used by golf carts. The towering vessels, pipes, and scaffolds were good cover, and the steam traps breathing in and out and humming pumps would mask any sound he made. He knew much of the unit was probably looped by cameras, so he moved randomly between equipment and pipe racks to throw the operators off. At one point, he saw someone silhouetted against the faint light of the early fall evening. Slowly, he moved behind a tall steel structure with cables and piping. No sudden movements, he told himself. But his time was limited. They would find his office empty, pick up his movements, and know exactly where he was heading.

He had no good exit strategy. There might not even be an exit for him, except in handcuffs or a body bag. But he planned to do one thing—email the pictures to Craig as soon as he took them. If he could find pieces of the pipe, getting them out the gate would be difficult. He would have to try to sneak them out, or hope his pictures were detailed enough to show that the material of construction was wrong.

Standing under the conduit rack holding the cables, with no other vessels in front of him, Jon realized he was at the end of the unit closest to the admin building. He could see the ethylene unit where the explosion had happened, about a football field away. Now it was time to run. It was an open, grassy field with no trees or equipment between the two units, so there was no option to hide. He ran like his life depended on it. He ran like the meaning of his life depended on it.

At the boundary of the ethylene unit, beside a small electrical substation in the shadow of the vessels, pumps, piping, and metal structures holding it all together, he stopped, bent over, and took deep breaths. His chest felt like it was on fire, and his legs were wobbly, but he knew he had to keep going. Then he heard the alarm, a rising *zuuuuh*, *zuuuuh* sound. He did not see fire, so the alarm must have been for him.

He had only seconds. The operators in the control room would be fanning out through the unit to find him. They'd expect him to go to the vessel that had exploded, so maybe he should hide where they didn't expect him to go. About one hundred feet to his left, he could see the back door to the control room. He'd basically be hiding in plain sight there—control rooms had a number of offices and other nooks and crannies where he could lay low until they assumed he was gone. He could sneak in the back while the operators were headed out the front.

As he made his way toward the back door, the alarm stopped. In the sudden silence, he thought he heard something shuffling behind him. A golf cart was bouncing along the dirt road about fifty yards away. Though it was hard to see in the dim light, he thought Charlie was in the passenger seat. Someone he didn't recognize was driving.

Cigarette butts littered the ground around the door, so there was a good chance it wasn't locked. Jon turned the handle and pulled it upward. The handle moved easily, but the door wouldn't open. Remembering that air flow sometimes creates a negative pressure in these buildings, he pulled as hard as he could and was able to force it open. He held the door steady as it closed, to keep it from slamming.

He found himself in the hallway that led to the control room straight ahead, with four doors off each side. People were talking in the control room, but he couldn't make out any words. Jon inched forward silently, trying to hear what they were saying while he looked for a place to hide.

The front door opened.

"Hey, Charlie," he heard someone say.

"Do you know where he is?"

"We think he must be somewhere around the base of the vessel." This voice was one that Jon thought he recognized from the interviews. "We have guys over there now. They know this unit in the dark, and he doesn't. If he's in there, we'll find him."

Jon could hear footsteps coming toward the hallway. He opened the door on his right, praying it wasn't an occupied office. It was a restroom.

"Come on, Charlie, I need to take a leak, and you do too," said a bellowing voice. Silhouetted against the light of the control room, a figure was approaching the hallway where Jon stood, holding his breath. He had no choice.

He stepped into the restroom, which was empty. Most of the operators must be in the unit, looking for him. Quietly, he closed the door behind him. Perhaps there were two restrooms down this hallway, and Charlie and the mysterious man would go to the other one. His heart sank as he heard the squeak of the doorknob turning. He jumped into the nearest stall and locked the door and then climbed onto the toilet seat, crouching so his head wouldn't show over the stall divider.

A voice he didn't recognize spoke first. "I didn't want to talk in front of the other guys. Here's the plan, Charlie. No matter where we find him, we drag him up to the catwalk, tear part of his shirt off and leave it lying there, and throw him off. We'll call the authorities, explain that he was trespassing in our unit and fell. We can say we had no idea he was such a careless individual and resurrect the story about that pump. The government will never investigate us again."

Jon fought to keep his breathing silent, though his heart seemed to be beating loudly enough to hear.

"Mr. Quinn," Charlie was saying, "isn't there another way we can do this? I mean, that seems extreme, and it won't bring anybody back."

Quinn didn't respond to the last part of Charlie's comment. "Extreme? Charlie, he is trespassing on our property. He is breaking the law and trying to destroy the lives of our employees. What would happen to the company if his findings ever got out? We could lose *everything*. Remember your wife."

Jon wondered why Quinn was talking about Charlie's wife. All he knew was that they planned to kill him. He heard two streams of water falling, not running like a faucet. They must both be at the urinals. Hopefully they'd leave soon.

Then it happened. His foot slipped.

He grabbed at the toilet paper roll to keep from falling, but the phone in his shirt pocket had worked its way out. It fell onto the tile floor with a sharp *clink*. Jon had been found.

The voices stopped. You could hear a feather float. Jon bowed his head.

74

Jon knew he was about to die, but his entire life did not flash before his eyes. He only saw his mother on her deathbed, the cancer having overtaken her entire body. She was using the last bit of her energy to have her final conversation with Jon. He was sitting by her bed in the hospital, holding her cold hand. He'd had a bad week, not in the same sense she was having one, but bad, nevertheless.

"Mom, I'm so sorry. I failed at work, and I failed at marriage. I know I disappointed you."

"Jonny, I've always been proud of you. I always will be. You were my special one, the one I hoped for. You've never let me down. You never could."

He'd held on to this moment through all of the pain in his life. At one point, someone had loved him and been proud of him.

Then his mind flashed forward to the present, to his earlier decision to leave his office and go to the unit. He had signed his own death warrant.

He heard two staggered flushes of the urinals, and then the door squeaked open and closed. They'd left the restroom and were waiting on the other side of the door to kill him. He stepped down off the toilet seat. There was no reason to be quiet now. In a few minutes, his body would be lying on the ground outside, or worse, impaled on a valve sticking up from a vessel on the platform. It depended on where they threw him. Jon had seen a display on impalement at a museum of torture, once. A fall to the ground from that height would kill him instantly. The impalement would be worse because he would suffer longer, but he'd still be dead by morning.

There was a shuffling sound overhead. They were coming to get him, and apparently they weren't taking any chances. They'd sealed off the exit through the only door to the restroom. If he went that way, they'd grab him.

The shuffling sound got louder. He looked up at the ceiling, faded beige square panels inside a painted steel grid. Jon's mind raced. Surely it would be easier to come through the door, but maybe they wanted to grab him from overhead, kill him, and discreetly move his body outside to minimize witnesses in the control room.

Jon had no illusions—none of the operators would intervene, even if they did see something. Quinn and Charlie would be doing them a favor.

He was trapped, like the cat in the box with poison. He remembered the story that his weird physics teacher, the one with the long hair and a bandanna, used to tell in high school. Hadn't it been Schrödinger who'd said that if a cat were trapped inside a box with a flask of poison and was going to die, there would come a point where the cat was both dead and alive? But if someone looked inside the box, they saw the cat as either alive or dead. Maybe Jon was both alive and dead, right now. His mind was swirling. Maybe he was already dead. Maybe there was poison coming in through the ceiling. No, that might hurt them. Now, he was thinking clearly. They would probably hit him on the head and knock him out and blame the injury on the fall. Could he fight back? No, they had him trapped. It would be better if it was a gun and he died instantly. He was both alive and dead, more dead now. No, wait—Schrödinger didn't agree. It was one or the other. Jon massaged his temples. He couldn't remember. Then clarity came back. They wanted to make sure he had no escape route—he didn't.

He looked up and saw the beige square panel being slowly removed. He closed his eyes. A few seconds passed, and nothing happened. He opened his eyes again, and saw a long, muscular brown arm with a tattoo, reaching down.

75

J on took another sip of sweet tea out of the glass with painted flowers. Ice clinked. He looked across the table at the four brown faces staring at him. The youngest was angelic. The older lady was smiling, tearing up. She looked like—no, wait, she *was*. She was the woman he'd seen at the tent revival. The third face looked firm and stoic. This face he knew too. It was the face of the man who'd looked down at him from the restroom ceiling, a face that had seemed faintly familiar even then.

Jon was still not clear-headed. He felt drunk. But the events of the last few hours would have made anyone question their sobriety.

"I know a way out," the man looking down at him from the ceiling had said. With a shock, Jon had recognized him as the janitor he'd spoken with about the investigation, the man he'd almost knocked down as he left the admin building earlier that night. Was this a trick? Was this man, like Wanda Ripwhile, a shill for the company?

Jon had looked into the janitor's eyes. They were firm but honest. He could trust this guy. And what other choice did he have? He knew what was waiting on the other side of the door. He definitely could not trust those men.

He had grabbed the strong brown hand and felt it pull him easily up through the space where the ceiling panel had been, into a steel HVAC tube. The janitor leaned down to move the panel back into place and then turned to Jon. "This way," he'd said. "When we get out, run like hell. Just follow me, and don't stop until I do."

The metal in the HVAC tube was cool but smooth. They'd wriggled through the rectangular tube on their stomachs, using their forearms to propel themselves. Twice they'd had to stop to heave themselves over the raised blades that separated sections of tubing. Once they had reached the edge of the building, the janitor held his finger to his lips. Slowly, he pulled a grille out of the wall that led to the outside.

The sounds of the plant had rushed in through the opening: the hum of pumps and the occasional hiss of steam through vents. The janitor had stuck his head out first, looking to the left and right. He'd slung his legs over the side, turned onto his stomach, and inched his way out. Then he'd disappeared from the opening. Jon had repeated his moves until his toes touched the fifty-five-gallon drum that the janitor was holding steady just below the opening. Once Jon was on the ground, they'd both pinned themselves against the outside wall of the control room.

"There's an old lean-to a few hundred feet away," the janitor whispered, just loud enough to be heard over the grind of the pumps and equipment in the unit. "Let's make it there fast as we can. Don't stop, even if you hear a gunshot. If we make it to the lean-to, there is a way out."

Jon nodded, and they'd started running. Jon's lungs felt like they were on fire by the time they passed by the electrical substation where he'd hid earlier, but he kept going. The janitor looked back to see Jon struggling to keep up, and for a few seconds he slowed down. But then the alarm sounded again, and Jon mustered the last bit of energy he had to run faster.

"Hey! Stop!" someone had shouted then; Jon's heart sank. They'd been seen.

Jon was about twenty steps behind when the janitor reached the lean-to behind the building. He was hunched over, fighting for breath, when Jon reached his side. "I was hoping we could stay here a minute," he said between gasps, "but they've spotted us."

A golf cart was approaching from the direction of the control room, its headlights bouncing on the rough dirt track. There were also two men with flashlights running toward them from a different direction.

The janitor put his hand on Jon's shoulder. "They already have the front of the plant and the main gate under lockdown, and they've got operators waiting at the other end, where the railroad cars come in." He pointed toward the side of the plant adjacent to the field between the operating units. "We need to go that way."

"But there's a fence there," Jon had said, distraught. He could hear someone shouting in the distance.

"The environmental group used to crawl under it to get samples, back before they started playing nice with the company. The gap should still be there. Count of three, okay?" He then held up his hand, barely visible in the fading light, and started counting down. They'd sprinted off.

The beam of a flashlight raked the tall grass only a few yards away as they ran. But beyond the lights of the plant, the near darkness allowed them to reach the fence unseen. "You look over there," the janitor had told Jon, pointing to his left. Jon started feeling frantically along the bottom of the fence, pushing on the taut wire between the tall silver poles. It didn't budge. Looking up, he could see a strand of razor wire at the top, menacing against the sky. The only option was to go under, but the fence was taut along the bottom and didn't give an inch. The voices were getting louder and the beams of light stronger.

"It's here, hurry," the janitor whispered, about ten feet away. "Be careful, the cut links at the bottom are sharp." Hunched over to stay low, Jon ran to where the janitor was holding up the bottom of the fence, just enough for him to crawl through on his stomach, the wire scraping painfully against his back. On the other side, he slid headfirst into a ditch filled with weeds. Cautiously, he'd risen to a crouch as the janitor slid into the ditch beside him. Just beyond the ditch was the narrow gravel shoulder of a paved road.

Glancing back through the fence, Jon could see the bouncing headlights of the golf cart and, inside it, make out the dark forms of Charlie and Quinn. The two operators with flashlights were close behind. The golf cart's motor whined as it struggled through the high weeds.

The janitor stood up. "Let's go," he'd said, but Jon had stayed rooted to the spot. "Come on!" The janitor slapped him on the shoulder, and he'd snapped out of his daze and started running. On the road, headlights were approaching.

"This way," the janitor said, cutting across the road toward the first row of houses. The clouds had shifted and the moonlight was brighter. Jon looked to his right, and recognized Wanda Ripwhile's house. That must be why the hole in the fence was there.

The janitor looked at him, huffing. "There's a cross street behind the next row of houses. We just have to make it there." They ran into a short fence and felt along it, eventually finding an opening. Past the last row of houses, an old red Chevy Impala was sitting by the road, its engine idling. Jon wasn't sure who was driving or how it had gotten there, but when the janitor opened the back door, he had fallen inside, exhausted.

Jon had lain on the back seat in a gray zone somewhere between waking and sleep. He didn't know where he was going and who was taking him there. As he'd stared at the dome light with the crack in it, voices had drifted in and out in disconnected bits and pieces. *Barely made it. Take the long way. Look for headlights . . . anybody following us. Darnell . . .*

He'd taken a deep breath into his sore lungs, and everything had gone blank.

76

"Let me get this straight." Jon took another sip of tea from the glass with the painted flowers. It felt like forever, but he now learned it had only been a few minutes since he'd passed out in the Impala and Darnell and another young Black man had helped him into the kitchen as he clumsily walked with his arms draped around their shoulders. A woman introduced herself as Kawana Coleman.

She told him she was the mother of James, who'd died in the explosion—and then offered him tea.

Now, Jon looked around the kitchen and ran his fingers over a chip on the edge of the table where he sat. He sat his glass on the art deco place mat and tried to pull himself together. "All the documents I found in my office—those came from you?"

"That's right. You see, after the explosion where James—" Darnell's voice cracked. He cleared his throat and shifted in his chair. "—where James died, I started hanging around more in the admin building. I especially hung around outside Mr. Page and Mr. Branch's offices. They talked about the explosion and didn't always close their doors. People talk in front of janitors. They think we're stupid and won't understand. They didn't know I was James's brother. To be honest, I don't even think they knew who James was. But I listened. I heard Mr. Branch say he was going to take care of the documents by putting them in the back of his credenza. One time, when he was gone, I pretended to clean in there. I loaded up the garbage can and put bags on top in case somebody saw me, and then I rolled the can down to your office and put them there. You and I had talked about the investigation, but I made sure nobody saw me talking to you—I didn't want anybody suspicious. At first, I thought they'd help you, but I could tell from what I overheard that they wouldn't. I need to know why my brother died."

Jon nodded. "Thanks. The investigation would have been dead in the water if you hadn't given me those documents. They gave me a doctored drawing that didn't help."

Darnell shook his head. "I knew those bastards were hiding something."

"Darnell, watch your mouth," said Kawana.

"Sorry, ma'am."

"I know what killed James and the other men." Jon drained the last of his tea. "That unit processes a material called ethylene."

"Is that like ethyl alcohol?" Darnell asked. Kawana shot him a dirty look. "What? I didn't say I was going to get some."

"Kind of like that, but without the alcohol," Jon said hastily. "Liquid ethylene is very cold, so the vessels holding it and the pipes it runs through have to be made of stainless steel to handle the temperature. When the company designed the unit, they used carbon steel in some equipment instead, because it's cheaper."

"Those bastards," Kawana mumbled. This time, Darnell shot her a dirty look. She looked back at Jon. "Uh, continue."

"Well, apparently, they had an upset in the process that night, and one of the vessels that held liquid ethylene got overfilled. The extra ethylene flowed out through the overhead piping, which was made of the wrong material. When carbon steel gets cold, it's kind of like glass that's been in a freezer. It gets very fragile. Just about anything can cause it to rupture. I remember hearing there was a storm that night. Even something like heavy rain hitting the piping could've been enough to cause the line to break. James and the other two guys were on the platform where the vessel was."

Kawana looked away, and Jon let her take a moment before he continued.

"There was a problem with the valve in the pipe at the bottom. It was supposed to open so the ethylene could drain out, but it malfunctioned, and they couldn't open it from the control room. They sent three men, one of them being James, out to the vessel to try and open the valve manually. While they were out there trying to find the right valve and force it open, the overhead line ruptured, ethylene came out, and the explosion happened."

There was silence at the table.

Finally, Darnell rocked back in his chair. "Why did they send James and the other guys? I believe all three had just started there. They probably didn't even know which valve it was, or how to open it."

Jon leaned forward. This part was hard. "Because they were contractors, which meant they were less valuable."

More silence. Jon cleared his throat. "I was able to piece this together from the documents you gave me, together with the interviews. You're responsible for me being able to figure this much out, and I thank you. But there are still three things I need to finish. One is absolute proof that the equipment was made of the wrong material. They haven't let me near the unit since the day it happened. I'm afraid if I go forward with my findings now, they'll just deny everything and say the material was stainless steel. They'll either say the engineer was wrong or get him to change his story. That's why I was going to the unit tonight, to get proof. But they'll never let me in now." Jon looked out the window and then looked back at Darnell. "You might be able to help me with the other two things I need."

"I'll help any way I can," Darnell said.

"I still don't know why they didn't shut down the feed to the unit earlier, as soon as the level started getting high. Why did they keep it running? Even if the guys got the valve on the bottom line open, I'm not sure it would have helped. By that point the vessel was probably full, or very close, and at the rate the ethylene was coming in, I don't think they could have drained enough to prevent the explosion."

Darnell nodded toward the young man with the cross earring who was slouched in the chair next to him, whom Jon suddenly recognized as the driver of the Impala. "Jackie was the security guard the night of the explosion. He called the proper authorities, and they canned him. But he might be able to help."

Jackie reached across the table and shook Jon's hand. "That night, they had problems with that vessel for a while. I was listening to them on the radio in the guard shack. They kept talking about how it was filling up, and somebody said, 'You know what can happen?' When they started getting frantic, I thought maybe we'd have an emergency, so I started recording it on my phone in case I had to notify somebody. On my other assignments, guards would make the emergency notifications. We'd be the ones to let ambulances in and direct them where to go."

Jon leaned in. "You recorded it?"

"Yes. I actually forgot I had done that for a while, but I saw the recording the other day."

"Do you have it with you?"

Jackie reached into his pocket and pulled out his cell. "It's a bit scratchy and hard to hear in places, but here it is." As he fumbled to locate the recording, he added, "It's only about twelve minutes long."

He started to hit play and then stopped and looked at Kawana. "Ma'am, you sure you wanna hear this?"

Kawana nodded. "Go ahead."

Jackie hit play. For the next twelve minutes, everyone was transfixed as the last minutes of James's life played out.

The recording started with a hiss of static and then, above that, a panicked voice. "We got to shut down. We've lost it—it's completely full." Another voice cut in sharply: "We need to call Mr. Quinn before we do that." Someone seemed to be talking in the background on a telephone, too distantly to make out the words. Then the first voice, nearer, with an edge of anxiety: "But he's the one who made us override the safety system." More chatter and then the second voice again: "Mr. Quinn said to keep it running and find another way. Price of ethylene's too high to shut down." Then a confusion of voices speaking over each other, with only a few phrases clear: "drain the vessel . . . contractors . . . risky . . . But why not . . . Now!" It was after that that the three men had been sent out to try to drain the vessel.

Jon had been right. They'd overrode the automatic shutdown, and then let the problem go on for so long that even if the guys had been able to open the valve, they couldn't have drained it fast enough—Quinn had sent three men to their deaths.

With an effort, Jon focused on the recording again. Another voice, even more staticky and distant, as if coming in over a radio: "I'm not sure if we have the right valve or not."

"Oh, my baby! James!" Kawana dropped her head into her hands.

Then, more clearly, the voices of two men in the control room: "It must have happened in that overhead pipe. That young engineer said it could, but—"

"Is your mic keyed?"

"Yes."

"Turn it off. Let's go in my office and talk."

That was it. Jackie put the phone back in his pocket.

Jon sighed. "Now we know why they didn't shut down sooner. The price of ethylene was high, so they sent three men to their deaths rather than risk losing money."

"Bastards," Kawana said.

Jon jerked his head up just then. "Oh my God, I just remembered—all the documents are in my room at the hotel. I have nothing with me!"

"I'll go get them for you," Darnell said. "They might be looking for you."

"No, baby—I'll get 'em," Kawana said. "They might recognize you from the cleaning crew and put two and two together. I don't intend to lose two boys to that company."

Jon nodded. "That's probably best." He gave her the hotel address, his room number, and plastic room key. "Good luck."

"You need me to go with you, Mama?" Emily asked.

"I think I do, child. I might need an extra set of hands to help me carry everything, the documents and Jon's clothes."

"Thank you," Jon said. "I forgot I had clothes and everything else there, too. Can you bring everything? I'll call in the morning and check out remotely."

"Leave it to me," Kawana said.

"I guess I need to get another hotel—they might be waiting for me there."

"Nonsense, baby," Kawana told him. "You stay here. You can sleep in James's room."

Jon smiled. "Thank you, ma'am."

"Call me Kawana."

"Okay, Kawana. There's one more thing. You could stop by the custard stand close to the hotel and pick up a peanut butter milkshake for the clerk. If it's the one who's usually there, it'll be a good bribe. If nobody can hear, you can tell her you're a friend of mine. I think if you bring her a shake, she'll let you take anything out, no questions asked. Might even tell you if anybody's been around, asking about me."

Kawana smiled. "I know just where that custard stand is."

Jon reached for his wallet, but Kawana held up her hand. "Put that away. This is a small price to pay to get the truth. This is for James."

Jon put his wallet back. "Thanks."

77

Jon slowly opened his eyes and looked around the unfamiliar room, trying to figure out where he was. A brown dresser with chipped paint sat under the window, and beside it was a small table with a large doily on top. Then he remembered: this was James's room. He looked at the digital clock on the nightstand. It was after six. He'd slept through the whole night.

Last night, for the first time since he started the investigation, he had found people he could rely on to help him. Kawana had gone to the hotel to get his documents and clothes while Darnell and Jackie retrieved his car from the company's parking lot. Jon had given Darnell his keys and told him where it was parked and what it looked like. Since the company had likely figured out which car was Jon's, the guards might be keeping an eye on it, but they had a plan. Darnell would lay low, open the door, get in, and drive it back to the house. Jackie would go to the guard shack to distract them while Darnell drove away, saying that he wanted to see how everyone was doing since he'd left. He would also try to pick up any information about the investigation or the company's plans.

Jon thought about last night. He'd taken a big chance and almost been killed, and now two things were clear. First, he would do anything to find the truth—he owed that to the families who'd lost loved ones in the explosion. Second, the company, led by Cain Quinn, would do anything to stop him.

Sunlight was streaming in through the venetian blinds, and Jon could hear pans clanging in the kitchen, an inviting sound. He got out of bed and looked in the mirror. He was always a scary sight in the morning, with the cowlicks in his brown hair going in different directions. He could see a gray hair here and there (more now than before), but the bags that had been under his eyes the last few weeks seemed to be hiding this morning. Then, something on the dresser caught his eye that he'd missed the night before. Folded on top was a pair of blue coveralls. Behind the coveralls was a white hard hat. This must have been James's extra set of work clothes.

The smell of bacon wafted into the room. A big breakfast would be great, Jon thought, pulling on his pants.

Kawana was at the stove with a spatula in her hand. "Oh, hello, baby," she greeted him. "Breakfast is almost ready."

Darnell, who was making coffee, motioned toward the table. Jon took a seat.

"How was last night?" he asked Kawana. "Did you find the documents and get them out of the hotel?"

"Every last one. The only thing left in that room was the soap and shampoo." She held her spatula at her side and turned to him. "I guessed you didn't need me to take that too."

Jon snickered. "No. Any trouble?"

"Not really, although there was a strange-looking man in the lobby. He was just sitting there in a chair, looking at something on his cell. He was wearing black clothes and cowboy boots. He had a rough face, not leathery rough like he got too much sun, but rough like he had seen a lot of trouble in his life, maybe caused some too. A lot of lines and scars. I said hi when I passed, but he just looked down at his cell. Nothing's so important you don't have time to smile." She turned back to the stovetop. "The milkshake worked like a charm. I gave it to the clerk, told her I heard that she liked those. She looked surprised, but she took it, and didn't ask how I knew."

Jon nodded. "She's not much of a talker, but that's probably good in this case."

"I did ask her about the strange man. I said, 'Do you know who that is, and what he's doing here?' She said she didn't, but that he got in around nine. She'd asked if she could help him, and he said he was waiting for somebody. I didn't take any chances. We took the car around to the back parking lot and brought your things out that way. Got your clothes in one trip, but it took a couple trips for the documents. Everything's in the living room."

Jon spooned sugar into the coffee Darnell had just set in front of him. "That's great—I can't thank you enough. It's good I didn't go. That stranger could have been from the plant."

Darnell set some cream on the table and sat down beside Jon. "I think it was. I only saw Mr. Quinn one time at the plant, but that kind of sounds like him. He's a rough-looking man, the kind you don't make eye contact with. Not that big, but rough. The kind that, if it was night and you saw him walking toward you, you'd cross to the other side of the road."

Jon must have looked at Darnell oddly, because Darnell laughed. "Hey, don't be surprised. We do that too. Some of you White folks scare the shit out of me, and not just the police!"

"Darnell!" Kawana stomped her foot. "Don't talk that way at the table."

"Sorry, ma'am." All three of them couldn't help but laugh.

There was a loud knock at the door. Startled, Jon jumped, almost spilling his coffee.

"Settle down—that's probably Jackie," Darnell said, getting up. "We asked him to join us for breakfast."

Darnell came back a few seconds later with Jackie, who took a seat across from Jon. "We got your car back," he said.

"Oh, great," Jon said. "I was so worried about the documents that I forgot about the car."

"I distracted Ruby while Darnell drove it here. If she noticed it was gone later, she might put two and two together and know that I'm involved. But I'm not worried about that now."

Kawana set plates on the table and then put a large bowl heaped with scrambled eggs in the middle, alongside a platter holding strips of bacon and another one of buttered toast. "Let our guest go first," she said as Darnell reached for the bacon.

Jon loaded his plate. This was much better than the frozen egg patties at the hotel.

"Here's some hot sauce for the eggs," she offered. "Some is so hot you can't taste the food, but this kind gives it more flavor than kick."

Jon poured some on his eggs and took another bite. "This is amazing, ma'am. I haven't had a meal like this in a long time."

Kawana smiled. "You're welcome, baby."

Everyone concentrated on their food for the next few minutes. "Jon," Jackie said finally, interrupting the sounds of chewing, "you need to be real careful. Sounds like Quinn's after you. I don't know much about him, but even the short time I was there, I've heard talk. Ruby was talking about him last night. There's a rumor—well, I don't know if it was a rumor or not—that he's killed people who got in his way. They say he knows special ways to hurt people. Everybody, even Mr. Page and Mr. Branch, seems to be scared of him—and not just scared for their jobs. He comes to the Charleston plant more than any of the others, not sure why, but he still spends most of his time in New York."

Jon put his fork down and swallowed. "I appreciate the warning. Last night, for sure, he intended to kill me—I heard him say so. But it seems like all roads in this investigation are leading to him. According to the notes on the drawing, he's the one who made the final call to use the wrong material for the pipe, just to save money. And on the recording you made, it's clear that he's the one who insisted they override the safety systems and keep the unit running, even though the level was getting too high. He knew what would happen, but he pushed forward anyway because the price of ethylene was high and he didn't want to disrupt production. He'd rather risk men's lives than lose a few bucks. And now I'm in his way, he's trying to get rid of me."

Heads were nodding around the table.

"I don't regret going into the plant last night. I knew it was risky. I only regret that Quinn got to me before I could get up on that platform. I still need proof that they used the wrong type of steel. If I don't have that, they can deny everything. But I'll never be able to get back in, so how can I get proof?"

Jackie finished his last bite and wiped his mouth with his napkin. "There's something else, Jon. Apparently the company got their side of the story into the paper today." He walked into the living room and came back with a newspaper, handing it to Jon. "Bombshell in Chemtrifuge Investigation: Company Claims the Investigator Is the Real Danger," blared the headline on the front page. Jon started reading aloud.

Officials from Chemtrifuge stated in a press release that, much to their surprise, the federal investigator sent to the plant had a history of actually causing accidents. "We are very troubled to learn of this," stated Andrew Leska, the attorney for the company. "We plan to launch a formal protest with his employer, the Department of Interior. Rather than help us understand the causes of the accident, which we had previously determined to be faulty maintenance by a contractor, his presence has impeded our investigation."

The article went on to give a brief history of the accident, summarizing the previous day's article.

"Boy, they're gonna love this in DC," Jon said. "I was accused of causing an accident at a refinery where I used to work, but it's not true—I was cleared. But no one's going to know that."

"We believe you, baby," Kawana reassured him. "They're just trying to rattle you."

"Yeah," Jackie chimed in. "They do that to everybody."

Jon's phone vibrated. He took it out and glanced at the screen—a call had just come in and gone straight to voicemail. It was Craig.

"It's my boss," he said. "Not sure I would have answered it anyway. I don't want him talking me out of my next move."

"What's that?" Jackie asked.

"I have no idea."

Jon listened to the voicemail and then put his phone in his pocket. "He said it's important that we talk this morning. I'll need to take a break and call him."

Jackie was reading the paper, oblivious to the discussion. "I'll be damned," he said.

Darnell looked at Kawana. "He's company," she said politely.

"Looks like A. C. Mounts is in real trouble," Jackie said. "There was another document dump yesterday. Paper says it shows there was a clear conflict of interest. He's gonna to do a press conference this afternoon."

Kawana rolled her eyes. "He's slick as snot," Darnell said. "I expect that guy to turn on the waterworks. He'll figure out a way to wiggle out of whatever he's done."

"Maybe not," said Jackie. "Says they're running a primary opponent against him. The head of the state Democratic Party says he's, quote, 'very troubled' by the information. Says Mounts tried to blame people who made the documents public, saying they're the ones to blame. But listen: 'However, one of Mounts's allies—who spoke anonymously—said the "blame the messenger, ignore content" approach won't work. He called the revelations "damning."'"

Darnell chuckled. "Slick Mounts will figure out how to get out of this. Trust me."

Jon exhaled. "I'm out of ideas. Darnell, Jackie, did you guys hear anything else that might help me figure out what to do next?"

Jackie shook his head. "Stay away from that Cain Quinn guy. That's my only advice."

Darnell rubbed his face. "You know, speaking of Quinn, I overhead someone saying the other day that he's going to the Baltimore plant on Thursday. I think he just came here to try to stop your investigation."

Jon looked into the distance, thinking. "The Baltimore plant. Maybe that's the answer. They'll be looking for me to try to get back into the plant here but not in Baltimore. I read on the website that the Baltimore plant is identical to this one. If they cut corners on the design here, I bet they did the same thing there." Jon slurped some coffee as the wheels started turning in his mind. "Nobody will be looking for me at the Baltimore plant. If I can get proof from there, that would be enough to show that the company uses flawed equipment."

Jackie put down the paper. "What if you run into Quinn there?"

"Then all this will finally come to a head."

Kawana shook her head. "We can't let you do that, baby. It's too dangerous."

"I know the risks, but I've come too far to stop. I owe it to the memory of those three men to prove what happened to them. And if they have the same equipment in Baltimore, somebody else could die."

One by one, everyone started nodding slowly. Kawana was the last.

"What do you need from us?" Darnell asked.

Jon paused. "Do you think they know you're helping me?"

Darnell didn't hesitate. "No way. I've covered my tracks. Even when I chased you through the unit last night, I knew where the cameras were and avoided them. Far as they know, I'm the dumb janitor."

Jon nodded. "You know, Darnell, one thing still puzzles me. It may not be directly related to the accident, but it's strange. Could you find out what the company is doing with the environmental group, and why they are so cozy with Wanda Ripwhile? She said something about negotiations in the conference room that night. Can you dig around and try to find out what she's talking about? If there's something inappropriate there, I might need to include that in the report."

"I go in at ten—I'll start digging immediately."

Kawana exhaled. "Let's pray."

Jon bowed his head while Kawana prayed for his safety.

"Do you need anything else?" Kawana asked when she had finished.

"Just one more thing," Jon said, getting up from the table. "Follow me."

78

Jon waved from behind the wheel at Kawana, Darnell, and Jackie, who were standing beside the foot-tall, boxed flower bed with remnants of pink blooms beside the wooden house with fading white paint. He glanced at the dashboard clock as he pulled away. 12:03, just about perfect. It was at least a six-hour drive to Baltimore, and he figured he'd roll in around dusk. He didn't want to get there with much light left.

He'd spent most of the morning listening to Kawana and Darnell's stories about James and looking at photo albums. Reliving James's life through their eyes had steeled his resolve to see this investigation through to the end. After that, he'd gone online to get the address for the Baltimore plant and study the plant layout on Google Earth.

He fiddled with the tuner as he drove up Interstate 79, finally giving up and settling on a song with a heavy synthesizer pop feel. He didn't know the song but thumped his thumbs on the steering wheel to the beat as he made the turn onto Interstate 68. He glanced at the phone lying on the passenger seat. He dreaded the call to Craig and had put it off from the morning, but he knew he needed to call. If Craig told him to stop the investigation, he would ignore that order. He was in too deep. No matter what Craig said, he would continue. This investigation was the only thing that mattered to him now.

At the next exit, he stopped for gas, bought a pack of trail mix, and then munched as he drove. It was now just before two. He thought about stopping to call, but he liked the symbolism of calling while he was on the move, like this investigation was now.

"Hello, Craig, this is Jon."

"Hi, Jon. I was beginning to wonder if you'd call."

"Well, there's a lot going on."

Craig cleared his throat. "Jon, I mentioned that you need to come to the office, and we need to chat."

Jon hesitated at his serious tone. "Yes, I think you said Friday. I'm planning to do that."

"Well, I wanted to give you the whole story. I'm going into a meeting in a few minutes, and we're going to talk about the budget again. You see, this other group wants to sweep the money from our office and use it for their own initiative. The other day, I got good news from my boss, Dan. He supports us keeping the money and continuing the investigation office, at least for now. But we need to do some contingency planning. That's why it's important for you to finish up what you're doing there and come in."

Craig's boss supported keeping the office "at least for now"? That sounded soft. A week ago this news would have devastated Jon. Not today. This was a new investigation, and he was a new man.

"Thanks for telling me, Craig. I expect to finish the investigation, hopefully today. I know what happened and why—I'm just working on a final bit of proof, in case anyone disputes my findings."

"That's great, Jon. I have to go to the meeting. I'll tell them to keep their hands off our budget." Craig faked a laugh. "But I wanted you to know. If I were you, I'd want to know. I'll text you how it goes."

"Thanks, Craig." Jon thought about the newspaper article. "Before you go, is anybody there discussing any news from here?" he asked cryptically.

"Oh, yeah. Everybody's talking about A. C. Mounts. He's even known here in DC. That came up in our staff meeting this morning. West Virginia politics—even more drama than here."

Jon exhaled. "Sure is."

"We heard about that, nothing else."

"Okay, thanks for leveling with me, Craig, and good luck at the meeting. One way or the other, we'll figure out how to move forward."

Jon was surprised how calm he felt after he'd hung up. The future of the office was the least of his concerns. He couldn't control what happened there. What he could *try to* control was his singular focus today: getting into the Baltimore plant and getting proof that the wrong material had been used for the equipment in the ethylene unit there. The company could still deny a photo, but the more evidence, the better. He would have a drawing, the testimony of the unit engineer, and hopefully a photo and even a sample of material, all showing that they'd used the wrong kind of steel. How many things could they deny?

Also, the news of the company's accusation against him had not yet made it to Washington. A. C. Mounts had apparently drowned out any other info coming out of West Virginia. It was ironic, Jon thought. He couldn't get any traction early on with the media, partially because Mounts stepped in to defend the company—not to mention the shenanigans of the state Speaker of the House. And now A. C. Mounts had resurfaced to absorb the news cycle again.

"Here's to A.C." Jon grinned as he held up his plastic water bottle in a symbolic toast. He hoped it wouldn't be the last time he smiled that day.

79

Jon arrived at the Baltimore plant around 6:45, but he wasn't ready to go in just yet. He drove slowly past the plant to survey the scene. Just as at Charleston, there was a large stucco building on the right and the guard shack and turnstile on the left. As the online map had shown, the rest of the plant was laid out just like Charleston's too. Behind the admin building were four square units. Two sat close to the admin building, side by side, with a dirt road between them. The other two were spaced similarly at the back of the plant. At the end farthest from the admin building was a railcar station where raw materials were brought in. Jon drove around the plant's perimeter, a big rectangle he guessed was about one mile long and a half-mile wide, to find entrances. Other than the entrance to the main admin building in front, there was only one more and it was at the back, at the railcar station.

After circling the plant, Jon went to a gas station close to the front of the plant to change clothes. He stowed his camera, a recorder, and a bag in his pockets in case he could find actual pieces of the pipe to use as samples for testing. He had no tool to cut into the pipe, but perhaps there would be pieces lying around from earlier maintenance work.

He bought an RC Cola, which he couldn't find most places anymore, and sat in the car sipping it and watching people go in and out of the gas station. He started thinking about his entry plan. An exit plan would have to come on the fly, since there were many things that could go wrong. He could try to get in through the back entrance, but that might raise more suspicions than going in the front. In his experience, only employees who worked in the back of the plant, like in the wastewater treatment facilities and railcar stations, used back entrances, and the guards there tended to know all of them.

He also contemplated where to leave his car. He could park it here, or by the back entrance. However, if the guards were watching and he just walked in without a car, seemingly off the street, that might look suspicious. Anyone going to work in the plant would park in the parking lot. The best strategy was to drive his car into the front lot, get out slowly, and walk at a normal pace to the turnstile. Getting out of the plant and retrieving his car were problems for later. Right now, he just needed to get on-site and raise the fewest flags possible.

Jon looked at the patch on the coveralls he had just changed into. "James," it read. Earlier in the day he'd asked Kawana if he could wear the coveralls to the Baltimore plant as camouflage. The operators there probably used the same coveralls, he'd explained, since companies bought them in bulk. It was a chance he'd have to take. He grabbed his duffel bag, dug under his shirts for the badge he'd swiped at the Charleston plant weeks before, and slipped it into the shirt pocket of James's coveralls. Then he started the car. "Never Surrender" by Cory Hart was playing. He laughed as he shifted into drive.

In the company parking lot, he found a space near the exit. Pulling out the badge, he attached it to a loose flap beside James's name patch. He touched the patch. "This is for you," he said.

He sat in the car a little longer, thinking about everything that had led to this moment in the last few months. Then he thought about the envelope he'd left on the dresser in James's room. That morning, between listening to stories about James, he'd found time to write a two-page summary of his investigation findings, referencing the evidence and adding that he'd left his notebook in the duffel bag in his car. Wherever that ended up, he'd thought, sealing the envelope. On the outside, he'd written, "Thanks for everything. If I don't return, please open."

Inside the envelope, he'd also left Craig's contact information. Even if he didn't make it out of the Baltimore plant alive, he wanted his findings to go to Craig. Maybe the investigation would continue, and his work would not be forgotten.

He put on James's hard hat and stepped out of the car. A couple of men were going through the turnstile. Plan A was to run the badge over the reader to open the turnstile. Hopefully, that would work. Plan B, if the badge was already deprogrammed, was to jump over the waist-high turnstile and run like hell into the closest unit and then zigzag through and eventually end up in the ethylene unit at the back.

Jon felt in his other shirt pocket to make sure the recorder was there, and then he felt his left pants pocket for the camera and his right pants pocket for the bag. *Check*. He also had one sheet of paper and a pencil. He walked calmly toward the gate, head down. The men in front of him wore coveralls like his. They would provide some cover tonight, in more ways than one. He walked by the guard shack, looking down and staying calm. No suspicious moves. He got to the turnstile, unhooked the badge from the flap on his coveralls, and hovered it over the reader. Nothing happened for a couple of seconds, and Jon heard himself let out a faint gasp; then he heard a click, and the light changed to green. He walked through the flywheel slowly, just like an employee.

"Hey," a voice behind him called.

He looked over his shoulder and saw the guard coming toward him. He thought about running but decided to play it cool.

"Are you here for those trials in the ethylene unit?"

"Yes," Jon said, thinking fast, "I'm here for the ethylene unit."

The guard nodded. "They said to expect a couple more this weekend. You need me to call an escort?"

"No, thanks."

"We can get you a ride in a golf cart. It's a long walk to the back."

"I'm fine—thanks anyway." Jon started walking away, as if the conversation annoyed him. The guard was being nice, but the last thing he needed was to have more people involved. He continued walking normally and after a few more steps glanced over his shoulder. Much to his relief, the guard had walked back to the shack and shut the door. He had passed the first hurdle. He was inside.

He headed for the first unit on the right. There'd be surveillance cameras, but he hoped that between his zigzag pattern and his plant coveralls, he wouldn't raise suspicions. Picking up his pace a little, he tried to stay behind vessels and underneath equipment as much as possible.

The hum of the pumps and hissing of stream traps merged to create a steady groan. He should have had earplugs in this area to protect him from the noise, but tonight he wanted to hear everything. Was that a shuffling sound behind him? As he looked back over his shoulder nervously, he collided with a short man in goggles who seemed to have materialized out of nowhere.

"What the fffff—" the man said, not finishing the expletive.

"I'm sorry," Jon said hastily. "I wasn't watching where I was going."

The man glared at him. "You need to be more careful."

"I know, I'm sorry."

"What are you doing back here anyway?"

This was already taking too much time. Jon needed to cut it off and get to the ethylene unit. He looked at the man's name tag.

"Herman—you're the outside operator in this area, right?"

"Yeah," the man said hesitantly.

"Yes, they told me I might run into you. I'm here for the trials in the ethylene unit."

Herman furrowed his brow and pointed. "But the ethylene unit is on down there."

Jon forced a laugh. "Yeah, I was just passing through. I was involved in some trials here a few years ago, and I was reminiscing. Sorry I bothered you—I'm going there now."

Herman's face was frozen in a suspicious look.

"Where's your safety glasses and earplugs?"

Jon was getting nervous. He pointed in the direction of the admin building with his thumb.

"I lost my glasses back there—I bumped into a pipe rack, and they fell off. Couldn't find 'em. I'll get a new pair in the control room." Jon hit his forehead with the ball of his hand. "Must have forget my earplugs. I'll get a pair of those too."

He'd started walking away when the man called out again. "Hey, you must have dropped this."

Jon turned around. The short man was holding the recorder up. "What's this for?"

"Thanks," Jon said, grabbing it and putting it in his pocket. "Must have fell out when we collided. It's just something for the trials—helps me keep a clear record. Thanks, Herman."

Jon walked toward the ethylene unit calmly. Jon assumed Herman was still watching or even following. Gone was the zigzag pattern. Jon was walking straight through the unit as if he worked there.

Beyond the first unit, there was a grassy area about as long as a football field, and the ethylene unit was on the other side. The online map was right—the layout here was just like the Charleston plant.

Jon looked behind him at the unit he was leaving. He couldn't see anyone there, but there were hundreds of places in the unit to hide and watch someone. He wished he had a Baltimore version of Darnell with him, but this was all Jon now. He'd walk through the field at a brisk pace but not run. A man running through the middle of a chemical plant would definitely draw attention.

The tall grass slapped the coveralls as he walked. This trip between units seemed to take forever. The moon was bright, and with no equipment or trees for cover, he felt exposed and vulnerable. He assumed he had only minutes to get what he needed. Despite his best efforts, someone might see him and realize he was not supposed to be here. He'd been careful tonight, but he was concerned.

His only asset was the element of surprise—they didn't expect him to be here. But once they started putting things together, they would figure out it was him. If Cain Quinn had been willing to kill Jon in Charleston, he'd have no hesitations about killing him in Baltimore. And apparently, he was here somewhere. Did his presence have something to do with the trials in the ethylene unit?

He heard the grass rustling near him and stopped. The rustling didn't. Jon wasn't sure what it was. All kinds of animals roamed the fields in chemical plants—snakes, coyotes, foxes, deer, rabbits—and they all loved nighttime. The rustling got louder. He froze, imagining that he could feel the winding of something at his feet. But already the rustling was growing fainter. He exhaled loudly and walked on again.

He was only feet from the edge of the ethylene unit, where the equipment and structures would give him some cover. Then the hard part would begin. One step at a time, he thought and then said under his breath, "One step at a time. You've come this far. One more task, and you're done." He'd reached a large structure holding mounds of conduit piping. Pulling off his hard hat, he wiped his forehead with his sleeve. It was a cool night, but he was sweating. Through the pipes and equipment, he could make out the control room to his left and the tower structure that held the ethylene vessels beyond that. This unit was also laid out exactly like the Charleston plant. At least he had a sense of where things were. He just had to find the right drum and overhead line, get his evidence, and get out.

"One step at a time," he told himself again.

▲ ▲ ▲

"Dammit, can't you bump that up any more?" Quinn was impatient and snapped at the board operator.

"Sir, I need to open the valve slowly," the operator replied politely. "I don't want to shock the system and cause a rupture."

"This system can take it. That's the whole reason I'm here. We've already made some changes to the unit so that we can get more through-put. Are you doubting me?"

"No, sir, we just need to take it slow."

The unit supervisor stepped to the console. "Mr. Quinn, we'll get there—we just need to phase this in. I've been here since we first started up. Even with the changes so far, we're stretching the limits of what this equipment can do. We need to be careful."

Quinn spun around. "Careful? Do you know the price of ethylene on the world market since those two units in Malaysia went down? Every second delayed means millions of dollars we're losing."

The supervisor nodded. "Well, sir, everybody wants to make money. We just don't want to get anybody hurt."

Quinn glared at the supervisor. "The equipment can take it. Your bonus is riding on this trial, so you better get serious!"

"Sir, we don't have all the changes made yet. We don't have that section of the overhead line replaced. Remember? We need a bigger line up top to handle the increased throughput."

Quinn waved his hand—he wasn't sure how much more he could stand from these morons. "We have to move forward now. Seconds mean dollars." He looked at the board operator. "What's the holdup?"

"We have the valve going into vessel E-101 open all the way, but it seems stuck. Even with that valve fully open, I'm not sure we can get enough flow to meet the targets you set. I think we need to wait for the rest of the unit upgrades before we push harder."

Quinn looked at the console display and focused on the feedline into vessel E-101 and thought about the problems they were having with the valves.

"Bullshit," Quinn snipped. "If that valve's not opening all the way, we'll open the valve on the bypass line to get more flow." He pointed to the valve on the bottom that could be manually opened.

"But somebody has to go up there and open it. It's too dangerous to have someone do that, unless we know how the equipment will react to a surge of material."

Quinn threw up his hands. "I've never seen such cowards!" He grabbed his hard hat. "Gimme a radio; I'll do it my damned self."

"Mr. Quinn, it's too dangerous. I can't let you—"

Quinn cut the supervisor off mid-sentence, putting his finger up. "I wasn't asking if I *could*. I'm telling you I *will*. It's my unit. Don't tell me what I can and can't do."

"Yes, sir." The board operator handed Quinn a radio. Quinn grabbed it and hurried toward the door. "We do this tonight, we do this now. Does everybody understand?"

"Yes, sir," the operators and supervisor said in unison as Quinn stormed out.

▲ ▲ ▲

Jon resumed his zigzag pattern through the ethylene unit, keeping his head bowed slightly so the overhead cameras couldn't focus on his face. Finally, he reached the back of the tower structure that held the vessels. It consisted of eight platforms, each about two hundred feet by one hundred feet, with vessels and multiple pieces of equipment on each one.

Jon stepped back as the lights flickered on with a buzzing sound. Metal stairs zigzagged up between the platforms. There was also a ladder at the back that went straight up all the way, with openings at each platform. The stairs would be the easiest to take, but were also the most heavily traveled. He'd climb the ladder, he decided. "One step at a time," he said, stepping on the first rung.

▲ ▲ ▲

Quinn keyed the mic from the tower's E-101 platform. "I'm at the line, but the valve's a little off the platform's edge. Can I open it by hand, or do I need a cheater bar to leverage the valve handle?"

"That valve hasn't been opened since I can remember," the board operator replied. "Better use the cheater bar. Be careful."

Quinn crawled over the rail, holding onto it with one hand, one foot on the platform edge and the other dangling in the air. With his other hand, he extended the cheater bar through the pinwheel handle on the valve and pressed down. He felt it give. He kept pressing, and slowly it opened more. Then it gave way completely, and he heard liquid surge through the pipe, as if a commode had just been flushed. There was a slight tremor in the pipe, and Quinn almost lost his balance. He grabbed the rail with both hands, dropping the cheater bar, which struck the platform's edge with a *clang* and then fell back onto the platform. He climbed back over.

Breathing heavily, he keyed the mic. "Valve's open. We're ready to crank open the main inlet valve now."

"Okay, we're on standby," said the board operator. "How much do you think we need to open the main inlet valve tonight, since the other equipment won't be in place till tomorrow?"

"All the way," Quinn barked.

"I thought you meant to get the unit ready for additional feed, not to go full throttle on production tonight," the board operator replied. "We still have to replace some pipes to be sure the equipment can handle the additional load."

"I told you, we're doing this tonight!"

"Okay, copy, Mr. Quinn. As soon as you get back, we'll go full throttle." Quinn heard a phone ring in the background through the radio. "Hold on," the board operator said. A few seconds later he came back on the radio. "Hey, I just got a call from the guard gate. Is the guy who came in for the trial up there with you? He didn't check in with us."

Quinn keyed his mic. "What guy are you talking about? The engineering rep is not coming until tomorrow."

"The guard said some guy came in tonight and said he was part of the trial. They got a call from the operator in the front unit, who said this guy bumped into him and seemed confused. They wanted to make sure he made it back here okay," the board operator explained.

Quinn had had enough. "I'm not expecting anyone."

"Well, there's someone climbing up the back of the tower," the board operator said. "I'm watching the surveillance monitor right now. Looks like he's getting off on the E-101 platform. I don't think he's one of our guys. Why would anyone sneak into the plant and go up to vessel E-101?"

Quinn scanned the equipment on the platform and inhaled deeply. Now it made sense. The government puke was braver than he thought. "I think I know who. Turn off the monitors. I'll take care of it."

"I'm sorry, sir. Did you say—turn *off* our monitors?"

"Yes, turn off all monitors with video feed."

"Yes, sir. Monitors off now."

"Good." Quinn unkeyed the mic and put the radio in his pocket.

He started slinking toward the ladder at the back of the tower. He'd get the unit to full capacity tonight, but he had one small problem to take care of first.

80

Jon went to three platforms before he found the right one. Fortunately, the vessels were labeled the same as the Charleston plant, so he knew to look for vessel E-101. The top of the vessel was almost even with his shoulders. He traced the pipe coming out the top—the overhead line, the source of the leak and explosion at Charleston. To his surprise, the insulation had been stripped off and the line was exposed. A large apparatus sat next to the vessel. He looked closer. It looked like a large crane neck with a big base. The base sat on the platform, and the pipe came up vertically a few feet and then curved and went horizontal at about the height of Jon's neck. It looked like piping that would connect directly to the vessel. There were also tools lying on the platform. This was replacement piping. What were they replacing?

Then it dawned on him. The insulation had been stripped off the existing pipe in the overhead, so they were going to replace that line. They must have learned from the explosion. Now they were replacing this line with the right material: stainless steel. He'd been wrong about the company. They didn't like the investigation, but they were finally doing the right thing.

Turning on the flashlight on his phone, he crouched to duck underneath the overhead line attached to the top of E-101. He ran the flashlight along the bottom until he found the label: *CS-101-847-14*. According to their nomenclature, the first two letters showed the material of construction. CS stood for carbon steel, and SS stood for stainless steel. The existing line was carbon steel. That was the problem at Charleston.

Jon smiled as he walked to the replacement pipe. This project would be expensive. This turn of events should be part of his report. Give credit where it's due. A company learned from its mistake and was proactively replacing its equipment at great expense. Maybe he would make it out of here tonight after all.

He held up his flashlight to the replacement pipe, moving along it until he found the pipe labeling. *CS-101-847-18-R*. His eyes widened as the truth hit him. This replacement pipe was also the cheaper carbon steel. It was bigger, was the only difference. They weren't replacing the overhead pipe to make it safer—they were replacing it to make it bigger, so they could process more material. They were debottlenecking the plant, so to speak. Companies Jon worked for had always tried to make the plant safer when they made upgrades, not just bigger.

Jon reached into his pocket and hit the button on his recorder. He would describe what he saw and record it for his report. But as he reached for his camera, he heard a gruff voice.

"Look who's here. You slipped away last night, but look where I find you now."

Jon whirled to see a man in light-blue coveralls standing a few feet away, one hand on vessel E-101, the other gripping a metal cheater bar. His face was shadowed by his hard hat, but then he raised his head, and

Jon saw the scars on his face and his icy eyes. Eyes so icy they could only belong to Cain Quinn.

"I have to give you credit," Quinn said. "You have more balls than I thought. You didn't scare off. Too bad it didn't work out."

Jon was startled, but he was also furious. "You must be Mr. Quinn. I've heard about you. I need to talk to you as part of the investigation."

Quinn flashed a sinister smile, like an evil child cheerfully watching a mouse caught on sticky paper, struggling. "Here I am. What did you want to talk about?"

"I understand you told them not to shut the unit down that night. You told them to keep pushing and override the safety controls, even though you knew the risks if the vessel filled up. Why did you do that?"

Quinn shook his head, as if the question annoyed him. "I pushed the unit because the price of ethylene was high. Every second we were down, we lost money, and lots of it." He patted the vessel. "We have to pump every pound out of this baby while we can. Which reminds me." He took his radio out and held up a finger to Jon. "I'm here at the overhead vessel," he said into the mic. "Get ready to crank open the main valve on the inlet line to the unit. All systems go."

"Copy," came a voice.

Quinn put the radio back in his pocket.

Jon's outrage was growing. "Is it all about money? Is that why you decided to make the overhead line out of cheap material—an accident waiting to happen?"

Quinn seemed unfazed. "You don't understand. You seem to think your purpose is to figure out this accident. Now, my purpose is to take care of this company. That's been my purpose for years. When our purposes conflict, my purpose wins. Regarding that line—yes, carbon steel is cheaper, and we needed to cut corners. A couple of things went wrong the night of the explosion, but shit happens. You're getting ready to find that out." He started slowly walking toward Jon.

Jon's eyes widened. "There's nothing wrong with making money. But you made a decision that created a hazard—one that everybody knew about. They could have shut down the plant, and you made them keep running." Jon's voice was getting louder. He put his hand on his chest and felt James's name patch. "But those men, they were in danger. They had dreams and people who loved them, but they lost their lives because of you. The problem is, your decisions have never cost you anything."

"You little shit," Quinn snapped, stopping. "I've lost more from that accident than you'll ever know." Jon thought he saw a flicker of some emotion in Quinn's eyes as he looked over the railing at the rest of the plant, a darkening, as if he'd felt a sudden pain. But the next instant they were hard and cold as ever. "My duty is to this company, to push as much product out these pipes as possible, no matter what."

He pulled the radio out of his pocket again and keyed the mic. "Open the valve all the way. Now! Don't wait for me to come down."

"Copy," the voice replied.

"And now my duty is to take care of you once and for all." Quinn raised the cheater bar over his head and charged at Jon, who dove behind the replacement pipe, landing hard on one knee on the platform's metal grating as the bar hit the pipe with a hollow *clank*.

Grimacing at the pain shooting from his knee, Jon tried to get up again, but his legs wouldn't comply. He could hear a sound in the background, like a jet plane approaching from a distance. Quinn raised the bar again, and Jon dropped and rolled out of the way just before the bar hit the grating with a force so hard that Quinn's hard hat came off. The background sound was growing louder. The bar was stuck in the grating, and Quinn was tugging, trying to free it.

Jon scooted toward the edge of the platform. With Quinn in the way, he couldn't make it to the ladder. His knee was still burning, and something wet was rolling down his shin. He had to do something, or just lie there and let Quinn kill him. Pushing himself up with both arms, he lunged at Quinn, who'd just freed the bar from the grating. They collided before Quinn could raise the bar again, the force knocking him back into vessel E-101. The back of Quinn's unprotected head hit the vessel with a thud, and he shook his head, dazed. Now it sounded as if the jet was directly overhead, and Jon felt the platform start to quiver.

Back on his feet now, Jon limped to the railing, leaning on it for support. Quinn yelled and began to charge at Jon, but just at that moment there was a loud *bang* behind him, and the platform shook. Jon ducked just as Quinn tripped on something, losing his balance. He stumbled past Jon toward the waist-high railing and grabbed it, but the momentum of his charge propelled him over the top. He clung to the railing with both hands, the rest of his body dangling off the platform's edge.

Slowly Quinn raised his left foot to the platform and began to pull himself up. There was an even louder bang, and the platform shook violently. Quinn's left foot slipped, and the thin metal railing came loose, separating from the frame. For a second, Quinn hung on, dangling several stories above the ground, but then the loose metal railing finally gave way, and he plummeted out of sight.

Jon hoisted himself up shakily and hobbled over to the platform's edge. He could just make out Quinn's body below. The man who lived life on the edge had finally fallen off. Cain Quinn was dead.

81

The platform was still shaking. The jet plane sound was so loud it hurt Jon's ears. He pulled out his camera and took a picture of the label on the overhead line, the label on the replacement line, and the railing where Quinn had fallen. Then he limped to the stairs. He thought about stopping and emailing the pictures to Craig in case he didn't make it out, but seconds counted. This might be the beginning of another explosion.

He was at the second level when he heard the fire alarm and started to feel a deluge pour out of the sprinklers. He hobbled to the ladder and jumped off the last six feet, hitting the ground with a piercing jolt, and then began half limping, half running toward the back entrance to the plant. But there was one last barrier he hadn't counted on.

The turnstile at this exit was not the same as the one in the front. In this one, he'd have to run the badge and step into a revolving-door cage, unnoticed—not an easy feat for a man who was limping, disheveled, and bleeding from one knee.

"Hold on." A guard with a beige outfit stepped toward him, holding up his hand. "Who are you? What are you doing here?"

"I'm here with Mr. Quinn. We were working on the trials at the ethylene unit. Something went wrong—I have to get a folder out of my car. We need to save the unit!"

The guard cocked his head, looking Jon up and down. "Where's your car?"

"Outside this gate. I parked down here in case I needed to get to it. I didn't bring all the boxes with my calculations in. I need out, quick!"

The guard reached for the mic draped over his shoulder. "I'll have to check on this."

"Go ahead and check. Tell 'em you're holding up Mr. Quinn's right-hand man. Tell 'em they may lose the unit because you want to play Mr. Bad-Ass Guard." Jon looked at the guard's name tag and stepped right up to him. "You tell them that, Clifton. I hope to hell you never want to work here or anywhere else around here again!"

Clifton let go of the mic and glanced uneasily toward the ethylene unit. "I guess it's okay. Looks like something bad's going on there." His voice was cracking.

Jon's final bluff had worked. He hovered his stolen badge over the reader and heard a click. It was a beautiful sound. He walked through the cage out to the road and the length of the fence to the front parking lot, his bum knee slowing him down. His lungs burned even worse than the night before. He sank gratefully into the driver's seat of his car, though it hurt to bend his knee.

The guards were just beginning to set up barriers at the plant entrance when he pulled out. They yelled and waved at him to stop, but he ignored them and drove on. In his rearview mirror he could see them getting smaller, setting the last barrier in place. They didn't bother to follow him. The signs for Patapsco Avenue shone in his headlights, and then he was threading his way out of the industrial park. He could hear music coming out of Paik's Bar and Grill as he exited the last junction and hit the main road leading to I-895.

Finally, finally, he was finished.

▲ ▲ ▲

Jon sat in James's coveralls on the edge of a hard motel bed. He dreaded the drive down to Virginia, so he'd decided to get a room in Baltimore. He looked down at Craig's text on his phone: *Held them off, all's good for now. See you next week.*

Jon took off the coveralls and crawled into bed. If the men float by in the river tonight, they will have voices, he thought as he drifted off. But if he dreamed at all that night, he didn't remember it.

82

Jon pushed the stage curtain aside a little and looked out. He'd been to functions in Interior's auditorium, but he'd never imagined he would be the subject of one. He was here to receive this year's Secretary's Award, the most prestigious in the department.

He could see Tammy and her daughter in the seats below. He smiled at how proud she looked. More than his ex-wife, she was his friend, who'd encouraged him at his darkest moments. Lisa and her cameraman, Kenny, were there too. They'd talked a little earlier. She'd decided to go into print journalism, she'd said. She'd also decided she liked Charleston after all. She planned to stay there and cover statewide politics, which had become more interesting as of late.

Jon's father was standing in front of his reserved seat in the first row, wearing the same gray suit he wore to Jon's mother's funeral—the only one he owned. He was talking to the secretary of the interior, Frances Murillo. Secretary Murillo was considered one of the most brilliant people in government. So many people lamented that, since she was not born in the States, she could not become the president. Jon's father was pointing at the program. "That's my son," he said, loud enough that Jon could hear him from the stage. "Did you hear what he did?"

Jon was embarrassed, but happy. He hadn't seen his dad smile since his mother got sick so many years ago.

Craig stepped to the podium first, as Jon took his seat. Craig recounted the investigation and talked about the courage Jon had shown. Then he called the secretary onstage, and she presented Jon with the award. Everyone gave him a standing ovation. He had planned to talk, but was afraid he would just choke up. "Thank you, Madam Secretary," was all he said. Then, in a nod to her native tongue, he added, "Gracias." She smiled.

When the attorneys at the Department of Interior heard Jon's recording of Quinn and saw the photos of the piping showing the code for its material of construction, they'd decided there was enough evidence to turn the case over to the Department of Justice. With Quinn gone, Chemtrifuge was surprisingly cooperative. Wheelan Drew and Sam Page were both charged, and each would spend a year in prison. The company had agreed to replace all the faulty equipment in all its plants, as well as spending $178 million on environmental projects around the state. Wanda Ripwhile's plan to sell her home to Chemtrifuge at an inflated price in exchange for backing off her criticism and shutting down the other members of the environmental group had been exposed. The group ostracized her, and she still lived in the same house. Alphonse lost the next union steward vote and was replaced by Janet.

The Speaker of the House of West Virginia, her lover and contractor, and A. C. Mounts were all indicted by the state attorney general for misappropriation of funds. The cocky deputy assistant secretary at

Interior interrupted the deputy secretary one too many times and was marginalized for the rest of his tenure. Much of his budget was transferred to Craig to expand his new investigation office, which had just brought much-needed positive publicity to the department.

▲ ▲ ▲

Jon's final report was comprehensive, right up to the accident in which Cain Quinn died. Forensic analysis showed that cheap carbon steel in the overhead line was not the only place where Chemtrifuge had cut corners. The railing that gave way when Quinn ran into it was of poor quality—too small and not welded appropriately. The decision to cut corners on the platform railing had also been made by Alister Cain Quinn. The platform shook because when the board operator opened the inlet line all the way, the surge of material hit equipment in the unit like a hammer. Jon reflected on the irony: the man who had put the lives of so many others at risk had been a victim of those same decisions.

Jon's report included an appendix. The three men who died would finally have names and voices. He included a picture of James and a couple of paragraphs about his life. Another victim, Mark Birch, had left behind a wife and young child. He had been active in his church and coached Little League baseball.

However, there was a gap. Jon had trouble finding information about the third victim. He decided not to ask Chemtrifuge about the victim. Although they were cooperating with the DOJ, he didn't want to push it. Lisa, the reporter, didn't remember either. All the media's resources at that time had shifted to the story about the Speaker of the House. Kawana recalled that the family of the third victim hadn't interacted with the other victims' families that night. The third victim was apparently closest to the explosion, she said, and so badly burned that he had not even been taken to the hospital—he was clearly already dead. She remembered hearing something about him being buried in Charleston Memorial Cemetery.

Jon decided to make one more trip to Charleston. He didn't even have a name, but he'd take a chance and drive out to the graveyard. Maybe someone working there might remember a young man's body being brought in around the time of the accident. Even if Jon couldn't get a photo of the victim and develop paragraphs about him, he could at least take a picture of the gravestone.

An old man was pushing a mower over the graveyard lawn when Jon pulled up. He rolled down his window, and the man put the mower in low gear.

"That's tough. Don't they give you a riding mower?" Jon asked, making conversation.

"Yeah, but I have to do some parts this way. Easier, with all the rocks and trees."

"I understand. Listen, I'm looking for a grave, but I'm not sure of the person's name."

"I know just about every grave here. Can you describe about how old they were, or when they came in?"

Jon nodded. "It was one of the men killed a few months ago in a big explosion at that large plant in south Charleston. Would have been a young guy, in his twenties, maybe."

The man took off his baseball hat and wiped his forehead with it.

"Yeah, I remember when that happened. I remember when they brought that body here. Real hush-hush, kind of weird." He leaned on his mower, pointing. "I believe it's that one on that hill just down off the road. You can park close to that tree and walk down. There's a recently dug one next to it, doesn't have any grass on it yet."

"Much obliged," Jon replied. He drove to the hill, parked under the tree the old man had pointed to, grabbed his backpack with his camera in it, and began walking down the hill slowly. He wished he had a story about this victim, but he would take what he could get. At least he'd have a picture of the gravestone in his report. It was time to close this investigation and move on. He had grown. In trying to give an identity to nameless victims, he had found his own.

Jon walked to the gravesite the old man had described. According to the dates on the stone, the third victim had been just shy of twenty-two. Then he looked at the name, and almost dropped his camera.

Some things made sense now, but there were blanks he would never be able to fill in. This young man, he guessed, probably wanted to prove himself to his father. Maybe he was someone who needed to learn the business and pay his dues. Maybe he wanted to make it on his own and that's why he didn't interact with the other operators. They didn't really know him or who he was.

And what about his father? Maybe he felt that throwing himself into his work was a way to move beyond his son's death, though that was assuming he actually felt pain, and Jon would never really know what he felt, if anything.

He looked from one name to the other, and back. Next to the recently dug grave of his father, Jon had found the grave of the third victim: Alister Cain Quinn the Second. Jon's arm shook as he raised the camera to his face.

ABOUT THE AUTHOR

 **STEPHEN J. WALLACE** says he is a writer trapped in an engineer's body, or vice versa. His first novel, *Hazardous Lies* (previously titled "Shelter in Place"), was a finalist in the Launch Pad Manuscript Competition. He has led several investigations at chemical plants, refineries, and laboratories. His short stories have appeared in the *Schuylkill Valley Journal*, the *Vita Poetica Journal*, and the *Mark Literary Review*. He has lived in the Washington, DC, area for several years but occasionally visits his home state of Kentucky. You can read more about Stephen and his work at stephenjwallace.com.